Praise for Anna Lee Huber's Verity Kent mysteries

"Readers looking for atmospheric mystery set in the period following the Great War will savor the intricate plotting and captivating details of the era."
—*Library Journal* (starred review)

"Action-filled . . . Huber offers a well-researched historical and a fascinating look at the lingering aftermath of war."
—*Publishers Weekly*

"A historical mystery to delight fans of Agatha Christie or Daphne du Maurier." —*BookPage*

"Huber's historical mysteries are always multilayered, complex stories, and *Penny* is an especially satisfying one as she interweaves social commentary and righteous feminist rage into the post-War period. With a perfect blend of murder, mystery, history, romance, and powerful heroines, Huber has yet to disappoint." —*Criminal Element*

"A thrilling mystery that supplies its gutsy heroine with plenty of angst-ridden romance." —*Kirkus Reviews*

Please turn the page for more praise.

"Masterful. . . . Just when you think the plot will zig, it zags. Regardless of how well-versed you may be in the genre, you'll be hard-pressed to predict this climax. . . . Deeply enjoyable . . . just the thing if you're looking for relatable heroines, meatier drama, and smart characters with rich inner lives."
—*Criminal Element*

"Huber is an excellent historical mystery writer, and Verity is her best heroine. Sidney and Verity are a formidable couple when they work together, but they are also very real. They don't leap straight back into life before the war but instead face many obstacles and struggles as they readjust to married life and post-war life. Nonetheless, the love between Sidney and Verity is real and true, and the way that Huber creates their re-blossoming love is genuine. Topped off with a gripping mystery, this will not disappoint."
—*Historical Novel Society*

"I loved *This Side of Murder*, a richly textured mystery filled with period detail and social mores, whose plot twists and character revelations kept me up way past my bedtime. Can't wait for the next Verity Kent adventure!"
—Shelley Noble, *New York Times* bestselling author of *The Beach at Painters' Cove* and *Ask Me No Questions*

"A smashing and engrossing tale of deceit, murder and betrayal set just after World War I. . . . Anna Lee Huber has crafted a truly captivating mystery here."
—*All About Romance*

"A captivating murder mystery told with flair and panache!"
—**Fresh Fiction**

A MOMENT'S SHADOW

Novels by Anna Lee Huber

Sisters of Fortune

The Verity Kent Mystery Series

This Side of Murder

Treacherous Is the Night

Penny for Your Secrets

A Pretty Deceit

Murder Most Fair

A Certain Darkness

The Cold Light of Day

A Moment's Shadow

A MOMENT'S SHADOW

ANNA LEE HUBER

KENSINGTON
PUBLISHING CORP.
kensingtonbooks.com

KENSINGTON BOOKS are published by
Kensington Publishing Corp.
900 Third Avenue
New York, NY 10022

All Kensington titles, imprints, and distributed lines are available at special quantity discounts for bulk purchases for sales promotion, premiums, fund-raising, educational, or institutional use.

This book is a work of fiction. Names, characters, businesses, organizations, places, events, and incidents either are the product of the author's imagination or are used fictitiously. Any resemblance to actual persons, living or dead, events, or locales is entirely coincidental.

To the extent that the image or images on the cover of this book depict a person or persons, such person or persons are merely models, and are not intended to portray any character or characters featured in the book.

Special book excerpts or customized printings can also be created to fit specific needs. For details, write or phone the office of the Kensington Sales Manager: Kensington Publishing Corp., 900 Third Avenue, New York, NY 10022. Attn. Sales Department. Phone: 1-800-221-2647.

Kensington and the K logo Reg. U.S. Pat. & TM Off.

ISBN: 978-1-4967-4010-6 (ebook)
ISBN: 978-1-4967-4009-0

First Kensington Trade Paperback Printing: September 2025

10 9 8 7 6 5 4 3 2 1

Printed in the United States of America

The authorized representative in the EU for product safety and compliance
is eucomply OU, Parnu mnt 139b-14, Apt 123
Tallinn, Berlin 11317, hello@eucompliancepartner.com

For my brothers-in-law:
Cameron, Shaun, Tristan, Neil, and Ian.
Steadfast, honorable, true.
Thank you for being you.

CHAPTER 1

Ar scáth a chéile a mhaireann na daoine.
In the shadow of each other, we live.
—Irish proverb

August 23, 1920
Dublin, Ireland

"Got no use for phosgene." The man's eyes narrowed suspiciously. "Least not unless the British use it first."

Despite the fact our friend had vouched for us, it was clear that Michael Lynch still didn't trust us. I supposed I couldn't blame him. My husband, Sidney, and I were, after all, British ourselves. We were also rather famous—or infamous, depending on how you looked at it—for exposing a nest of traitors and solving a number of highly publicized murders. It made sense that the man in charge of munitions for the Irish rebels would be reluctant to talk to us.

Though, it certainly didn't help when Sidney persisted in making snide remarks. "Why not? It would undoubtedly prove more effective than these homemade bombs your men keep using in their ambushes."

Alec and I joined Lynch in scowling at him. While it was true I'd read the same newspaper articles criticizing the Irish Republican Army's use of makeshift grenades and explosives in their ambushes of the Royal Irish Constabulary's barracks and patrols, I knew better than to rile the man. Not when we needed answers from him.

"Maybe so," Lynch retorted. "But the men aren't exactly trained in handlin' dangerous chemicals. I've already got men stickin' gelignite beneath their shirts next to their skin in order to thaw it out faster so it'll ignite, poisonin' themselves in the process. Not to mention a recent experiment with a lachrymatory gas, which exploded in one of my men's faces and blinded the lad for twenty minutes." He arched his thick dark eyebrows. "You were in the war, Mr. Kent."

This was common enough knowledge given Sidney's status as a war hero and his recently being decorated with the Victoria Cross.

"So tell me, how often did the poisonous gas that was released blow back in the men's faces when the wind shifted? How often did it fail to do anything whatsoever except to create panic?"

This was a point well-taken. As horrific and terrifying as poisonous gas was, more often than not its deployment had been less than successful.

Lynch shook his head. "Naw, Mr. Kent, phosgene would not be my choice. Not unless, like I said, ye *British* used it first." The way he said "British" was more of a curse word than a descriptor.

"As the leadership fears they might," I interjected, letting him know we were well informed of their concerns, as well as put some metaphorical distance between us and the Crown Forces and British government they were fighting against.

He grunted noncommittally, eyeing Alec as if he was the source of this information. But while Alec and the man he now worked for, Michael Collins, the director of intelligence for the IRA and minister of finance for Dáil Éireann—the Irish Republic's shadow government—had filled us in on a number of matters related to Mr. Lynch's work, they were not the sources for that particular tidbit. Rather we'd learned it from two of our contacts inside British Intelligence, which had intercepted a letter detailing the IRA's belief that since the British had used poisoned gas on the Germans during the war that they might use it versus the Irish rebels, and so they needed to be able to retaliate if necessary. However, I decided it was best not to share that detail with Mr. Lynch. Not when my and Alec's history with British Intelligence was complicated enough, and thus better kept concealed.

"Maybe so," Mr. Lynch conceded. "And rightly, if they do. But I'll still not be after advocatin' its use. Not unless we have to."

"Have you seen its effects?" I asked, curious how much of his aversion came from experience.

"Naw, but I've heard tell from returnin' nurses and some survivors." His sallow countenance tightened with strain. "I'm sure there are worse ways to die, but havin' your lungs burned by vapor and then drownin' in the resultin' fluid they release is a hell of a way to go."

Out of the corner of my eye, I saw Sidney stiffen even as I struggled to squelch my own reaction to this reminder of just how steep the stakes were if we failed. We were both acutely aware we were not talking in hypotheticals. The sole reason we remained in Dublin was to find a batch of phosgene cylinders that had been stolen during the height of the war. Cylinders we'd confirmed had been brought here to Ireland for some nefarious purpose.

We'd been chasing them and the man behind their theft for nearly a year, and yet the canisters' exact location and the proof to finally expose Lord Ardmore for the traitor he was remained elusive. We might have been drawn to Dublin in order to find Alec, who was both a friend and former fellow intelligence colleague, but we had stayed to stop Ardmore and prevent a catastrophe. Ardmore's arrival in Ireland seemed to indicate the start of some sort of endgame, but we were still no closer to finding the phosgene than we had been a fortnight earlier despite all of our concerted efforts.

It didn't help that with the implementation of the Restoration of Order in Ireland Act, the temperament of the war had escalated. The attacks on the Crown Forces by the IRA were growing fiercer and more widespread, and the retaliations and reprisals committed by the police swifter and more brutal. It seemed every day the newspapers reported another policeman had been ruthlessly killed and another village had been terrorized and vandalized in retribution. Barrack after barrack was raided, and creamery after creamery—the economic lifeblood of many rural communities—was burned. The barrage of tit-for-tat violence was unending, and it only threatened to get worse.

Even in Dublin, we couldn't escape it—be it Crossley tenders bristling with soldiers and guns racing through the streets, nightly raids on residences, or deadly ambushes in the narrow lanes. The British government was determined to characterize the conflict as a rebellion, but the fact was this was a war, and the people suffering the most were those caught in the middle. Those who might or might not have voted for Sinn Féin, the predominant Irish political party which had pledged to break the bonds of British rule and make Ireland a republic, setting up its own government, the Dáil Éireann, which the British government had promptly proscribed along with a dozen other Irish organizations.

But just because people supported Sinn Féin's aims did not mean they espoused the violent efforts of the IRA, or that they participated in them. However, the Crown Forces' reprisals didn't differentiate and they were steadily driving the moderates into the arms of the more radical republicans by lashing out at the most vulnerable instead of protecting them. The police blamed the IRA for their need to commit reprisals, but from the perspective of the average citizen it wasn't the republicans who were pillaging and burning their villages, destroying their livelihoods, and physically attacking and threatening them. It was the police. And the worst offenders seemed to be the demobilized British soldiers the government had brought in to shore up the dwindling numbers of the RIC. They'd been dubbed the Black and Tans because of their hodge-podge uniform—half regulation dark green RIC, half army khaki.

As we fell quiet, I could hear voices through the curtain that closed off this musty storage space from the bookshop proper. For a moment we all froze, intent on discovering if the owner, Máire, was speaking to a friend or foe. If the Crown Forces decided to raid the place, or British Intelligence had been tipped off to the clandestine activities that took place here, we could find ourselves in hot water. My eyes went to the rear door of the shop, which any self-respecting officer would have already ensured was covered. If the shop was raided, we would simply have to try to brazen our way out.

Fortunately, I had nothing incriminating on me. Though, with enough notice, papers were easily hidden in a bookshop by stuffing them between the pages of a random book. It was no wonder the rebels had taken Máire's offer to use this place as a drop point for urgent messages.

My gaze shifted to Sidney, wondering if he had a heftier problem. I'd urged him to leave his Luger pistol at the town house we rented, but he preferred to have it on him. A fact that, thus far, had not caused him complications, as his reputation preceded him among the British soldiers and police, so he was rarely searched. However, it only took one suspicious officer to create problems for us. Especially since no private citizens were supposed to be carrying weapons.

Then, Máire raised her voice just enough to be clearly heard before steering her customer away from the curtain toward where the book she was recommending was located. I breathed deep in relief, but recognized Lynch's deep scowl as an indication this interview would soon be over. Obviously, this bookshop on Dorset Street had been chosen as the meeting place for the sake of convenience for Lynch, and not its accommodations. Which meant the IRA's "munitions factory" that Lynch oversaw must not be far away. Though I didn't dare share this deduction with the others. I already knew too much, and I didn't need to give Collins a reason to regret letting me walk free, or Lynch a greater cause to regret talking to us.

"Where would phosgene most likely be stored?" I murmured before swiftly elaborating. "What type of facility? What type of conditions?"

Distrust still lurked in Lynch's eyes, even as he rubbed the dark stubble dusting his jaw. "How much?"

"As near as we can guess, several dozen cylinders." Our witnesses, the men who had loaded the phosgene onto the boats that would take it out to the *Zebrina* anchored off the coast of the Isle of Wight, thinking it was normal contraband, hadn't exactly been precise. "And a Livens Projector."

"Then an average-sized garage would do. Someplace the temperature can be kept relatively constant, but not too hot or too cold."

Sidney and Alec shared an aggrieved look, for they'd both believed the storage space would need to be larger.

"What about a cellar?" I continued, ignoring them.

Lynch tipped his head in consideration. "I suppose. If it were dry enough."

Which only made our search all the more difficult. After all, the warehouses throughout the Dublin area we'd been focused on up until now extended to a finite number. Even garages, while more plentiful, were easily located. However, it would be difficult to know which buildings contained cellars and which didn't, and altogether impossible to search many of them unobtrusively.

My frustration must have been evident, for Lynch seemed

to view this as an indication we were done. "If that's all then . . ." he murmured, moving toward the curtain.

"Just one more question," I interrupted before he could exit.

He glared at me impatiently.

"The phosgene. Does it degrade over time? While it's in storage," I added in clarification, lest he think I was asking about after it was dispersed.

"How old is it?"

"At least three years."

We'd discovered the phosgene had been loaded onto the *Zebrina* in October 1917, though we still didn't know how Ardmore's men had contrived to get their hands on it before transporting it to the Isle of Wight. The Royal Engineers had refused to cooperate when C, the chief of the Secret Intelligence Service, and my former superior, had requested information about the batch of phosgene that the three cylinders Sidney, Alec, and I had been able to recover had come from.

As C was in charge of the foreign division of British military intelligence, and the theft of any poisonous gas on British soil was a domestic problem, he couldn't force the issue. He might have asked Sir Basil Thomson, director of intelligence at the Home Office and ostensibly head of all British intelligence agencies, to intercede on his behalf, but such an effort would not only prove fruitless, as Thomson was good friends with Lord Ardmore, but it would also require C to openly concede that Thomson had some right to oversee his operations. I knew C preferred to function as if he answered to no one, not only for the safety of his agents and the sanctity of their missions, but also purely from a position of ego.

In any case, all we'd been able to uncover was that a batch of phosgene from a Royal Engineers depot in Wiltshire had been labeled destroyed in autumn 1917. We surmised that this was where the cylinders and Livens Projector had come from.

Lynch shook his head. "Don't know for certain how long it takes to degrade, but we're talkin' decades, not years."

I nodded, knowing it had been a forlorn hope to think the gas would no longer be viable.

His brow softened in a show of empathy before tightening again as he slapped his flat cap back on his head and strode through the curtain.

Alec waited until the fabric settled back into place before quipping in Irish brogue, "Well, we made a gaffe o' dat one."

Sidney glowered at him. "It's just us monkeys here. You can lose the accent."

"Maybe so, but Máire might hear."

I could appreciate Alec's desire to maintain the fiction of his origins with as many Dubliners as he could. After all, most people would not take kindly to the discovery that Alec had originally come here as a British intelligence agent tasked with infiltrating Michael Collins's inner circle. This, he had achieved, only to switch sides, taking on the alias of MacAlister. A fact known just by Collins himself and a few of his closest allies, as well as me and Sidney.

When Alec's reports had stopped reaching C and his handler had reported him missing, Sidney and I had been sent to Dublin to find out what had happened to him. The truth hadn't been easy to reconcile with, but by then our own doubts about the manner in which our country was conducting itself in Ireland had been roused. They'd compounded the disillusionment we already felt about certain revelations we'd recently uncovered about the British government's culpability in prolonging the war with Germany. Because of this, we'd made the uneasy decision to remain neutral and to not reveal Alec's duplicity. Rather, we'd reported that he'd probably been assassinated, either by Collins himself or his Squad of hitmen, sometimes referred to—in a tongue-in-cheek manner—as the Twelve Apostles.

Had I still officially been an agent of the SIS, this might have caused me greater moral qualms, but eighteen months ago I'd been demobilized along with most of the other women who'd worked for military intelligence. As such, all of the missions I'd undertaken for C since then, including our search for Alec, had been conducted in an unofficial capacity. Given this and the fact we stood the best chance of locating the stolen phosgene and finding the evidence to put away Lord Ardmore by working with both sides, our decision had been less fraught than it might have. Though that didn't make the thin line we were walking any less precarious. For now, Collins and the rebels were content to accept our pledges of neutrality and promises not to reveal what we knew about them, and the British still believed we were loyal subjects with no contact with the republicans. But if either of those states were to change, our entire world could come crashing down around our ears.

Still, it was evident from the mischievous glint in Alec's brown eyes that his reason for continuing to use an Irish accent was not solely fear of Máire overhearing. He also enjoyed irritating Sidney. Though, I had to admit I wasn't entirely sure which of Alec's flawless accents was his natural one. I'd seen him portray a German staff officer, a Belgian gentleman, an upper-crust Britisher, and now a middle-class Irishman. I'd recognized long ago what a true chameleon he was, shifting personas with what seemed the utmost of ease.

Ignoring that fact for the moment, and Alec's antagonization of Sidney, I redirected them to the point of this meeting. "So now that we know the phosgene could be stored in a garage or cellar, what are we going to do about it? We can't possibly search them all. Not without showing Ardmore our hand."

Alec sobered. "I'll see what I can uncover about any other aliases Ardmore might have used, or any companies he might have a secret partnership in." We'd already found a few. "It's likely the cylinders are being held some place he owns that we just don't know about yet."

"See what you can find out about any family and friends as well. Anyone with a connection to him we haven't yet looked into. Maybe he's using one of their properties." I crossed my arms. "I'll contact Kathleen and ask her to do the same." Kathleen Silvernickel was a trusted friend, a former colleague, and one of the last remaining women in the service. She still acted as C's private secretary. "There must be some link we're missing."

After all, we knew the phosgene was in Dublin. One of Lord Ardmore's henchmen had confirmed as much for us back in April as he lay dying, and Ardmore himself had broached the subject with Collins just a few weeks ago, in about as direct a manner as he ever did anything. Given that, the phosgene couldn't have just materialized. Someone must know something. Someone must have seen it, whether they realized it or not.

"And I'll touch base with Bennett and Ames," Sidney offered, his square jaw set as he lifted aside the edge of the curtain to peer through before letting it fall back into place. "It's doubtful they've uncovered anything. At least, none of their other anonymous tips have borne fruit in the past. But one lives in eternal hope they might prove useful."

I'd been furious with my husband when he struck up a friendship with the two British Intelligence officers, particularly Captain Bennett, who I was acquainted with from my time spent in Holland during the war. Because of his Dutch heritage, Bennett had been stationed with British Intelligence there. Meanwhile, I had frequently passed through the neutral Netherlands, either coming from or sneaking back over the electrified fence at the border with German-occupied Belgium. There I'd liaised with the various intelligence-gathering networks who were working for the British and undertook countless other assignments. It was during one of those missions that I'd first met Alec, who had been embedded with the German Army two years before the war even began, eventually rising to the rank of a staff officer stationed in Brussels. Few enough people knew what role I'd played for the Secret Service during the war. The fact that Bennett was one of them made him dangerous. Particularly as he was working under Colonel Ormonde de l'Épée Winter, otherwise known as O, the man tasked with running British Intelligence operations within Ireland. O and I didn't precisely get along. I thought he was a slimy little snake, and he was alternately dismissive and then suspicious of me. It depended on the day which of these opinions won out. However, I couldn't deny that thus far Sidney's friendships with Bennett and Ames had proved useful, and that they just might be the ones who helped us foil Ardmore in the end.

Alec seemed to agree, though he offered one piece of advice. "Just know that if Bennett starts tellin' ye stories about his father's duck decoy pond that he's on to ye."

I turned to him in surprise.

His voice was wry. "He's that obvious."

Bennett did have the rather annoying habit of trying to demonstrate how clever he was. In the process, usually indicating the opposite. I'd even gone so far as to warn my superior about this tendency, lest Bennett reveal more than he should to one of the German agents who were also crawling all over the neutral Netherlands. But perhaps in this instance Bennett's inclination was to our advantage rather than our detriment.

"I'll keep it in mind," Sidney muttered. His disinterest seemed to suggest he found the warning unnecessary.

I frowned, worried my husband still wasn't taking the matter seriously enough. He'd always possessed a bit of a reckless streak, one that the war had exacerbated. Not because he thought himself impervious, but because he knew he was not.

However, Alec merely shrugged it off, settling his own flat cap on his head.

"Has Ardmore tried to arrange any more meetings with Collins?" I asked, having hoped the Big Fellow might be able to convince Ardmore to at least share where he'd hidden the phosgene if not persuade him to hand it into the rebels' care. After all, he'd been the one to approach Collins about his possibly putting it to good use.

"No." Alec seemed pained to have to give me this answer. "But we've still got men tailin' Ardmore. Not that we expect him to lead us to the phosgene."

No, Ardmore was too cunning for that. He would be expecting to be followed, and so he wouldn't go anywhere near the stuff.

"We're still followin' Willoughby, as well." He grimaced. "That is, when he doesn't manage to give our lads the slip."

This also didn't surprise me. For Captain Willoughby was not only Ardmore's right-hand man, but also a former Naval Intelligence officer. He would have been trained in evasion techniques. Unfortunately, he was also the person most likely to be spearheading whatever Ardmore's objectives were for the gas. Not that he would venture near the phosgene often either.

"I'll contact ye as soon as I've somethin' to report," Alec told me, his tone conveying a confidence I lacked. Then with a nod to Sidney, he slipped through the curtain.

CHAPTER 2

I made no move to follow, knowing Sidney and I needed to wait an acceptable period of time before we emerged so that no one would connect us with Alec's departure. No one but Máire that is, who was still helping customers in the main room of the bookshop. This afforded me the opportunity to pin my husband with a stern glare. But before I could even speak, he cut me off with a glare of his own.

"I already know what you're going to say, Verity, and I don't need to hear it."

"Then you realize Alec's word of caution was perfectly valid," I retorted, ignoring his demand.

He flicked a peevish glance back at me from where he continued to peer through the edge of the curtain. "I'm already perfectly aware that Bennett doesn't have a subtle bone in his body. How he hasn't clicked it yet I'll never know."

Sadly, I feared it might only be a matter of time.

I blanched at the thought. After all, Collins's men knew who he was. They'd even been in contact with Bennett and Ames. And everyone knew the Squad focused on members of the police, the military, and the British government who sought to hinder the cause of the Irish republic.

They'd already crippled the Dublin Metropolitan Police by assassinating or injuring many of the officers on political duty with the G Division who had, in all but name, worked as intelligence agents for Dublin Castle. So much so, that the British government had essentially written off the DMP from being of any use in the fight against the rebels. Now that Intelligence had established its own branch within the Castle, the Squad's efforts would, by necessity, switch to the agents that O was recruiting, in order to neutralize them before they could threaten the rebels.

I understood how it worked, but that didn't make it any easier to know that some of my former colleagues might be killed in the line of duty. Just because I wasn't fond of some of them didn't mean I wished them dead. Yet, I also knew of the atrocities some of them were perpetuating against the other side. There were no angels in this conflict, only demons in various shades of gray.

"If Bennett gets suspicious we're playing both sides, I'm sure I'll know it," Sidney stated, continuing to stare through the gap in the brown curtain. "And I'll mitigate it."

"Maybe. Or maybe not," I challenged, drawing his gaze back to me. "Don't get cocky, Sidney. It's been the death knell of many a seasoned agent. If you get complacent and sloppy, it won't take a mastermind to catch you, just someone paying attention."

He looked as if he were about to argue this point, but then shook his head and turned away. "I think it's been long enough. The shop is clear."

I would have preferred to wait another minute or two, but it was obvious my husband was anxious to be away, so I slipped through the drapery into the bookshop proper. Dust motes danced in the light that spilled through one of windows placed high on the wall near the two-story ceiling, the sunlight bleaching the worn wooden floors of the central aisle blond. There were tables stacked high with books on either side while bookshelves spanned the perimeter of the space, each filled helter-skelter with more volumes.

I would have liked nothing more than to spend several blissful hours perusing the shop, but I knew by doing so I would risk drawing unwanted scrutiny to the premises if word got out. More than one store I'd patronized in London had received a boost in commerce when it was reported in the gossip rags that I preferred to buy my gloves or perfume or even lingerie there. Particularly when they managed to snap my photograph emerging from it. Sidney had once complained that—much like Lady Diana Cooper—those shops and designers should be paying *me* for the privilege of having me wear their garments, considering the number of customers I brought them. I'd reminded him Diana and Duff needed the money. We didn't.

I turned toward Máire where she stood behind the counter, catching her eye and nodding just once in silent communication before exiting the shop with Sidney now at my elbow. I looped my arm through his as we set off toward Frederick Street to catch a tram going south. The weather was mild and the sun shining, but my husband's shoulders were stiff as if warding off the cold.

I began to wonder if his petulance at Alec's remark was more to do with the specters Mr. Lynch had raised with his description of the effects of phosgene. After all, Sidney had survived three and a half years in the trenches, and while he'd never been gassed, like the other soldiers, he'd lived in constant dread of it. He'd known friends who were not so fortunate and witnessed the struggles of afflicted patients while visiting his injured men in the hospital. The lines of blinded, stumbling soldiers; the skin blistered with boils from mustard gas; the gargling, rasping breaths; the omnipresent, insidious fear of attack. They were not something one quickly forgot.

"You're not just annoyed with Alec, are you?" I murmured as we passed a pub, the scent of its yeasty interior spilling out into the street as a patron opened its door.

For a moment I thought Sidney might not answer me, but then he exhaled a long breath. One that told me he craved one of his specially blended Turkish cigarettes. Like most men, he'd returned from war with the dreadful habit of smoking dozens a day, to steady his nerves and make the foul stench of the trenches at least bearable. But at my urging, he'd steadily decreased the number he smoked to just a few per day, usually at more socially acceptable times. While escorting a lady down the street was not one of them.

"I thought we would have found it by now," he finally confessed, his voice tight with frustration. "After all, for the past fortnight, we've devoted ourselves almost exclusively to this task. And yet, we aren't any closer to finding it than we were before."

"That's not entirely true," I countered somewhat feebly. "We know more places it *isn't*."

Sidney huffed in exasperation. "Yes, but we don't need to know everywhere it *isn't*, just where it *is*. We're floundering in the shallows and meanwhile Ardmore is steaming forward with his plans, whatever they are!"

I was equally provoked by our failure to uncover the phosgene or even Ardmore's exact intentions for it, but was hesitant to admit it. My husband had made it clear on numerous occasions that he would prefer to have me out of harm's way, and while I didn't believe he would ever force the issue, I didn't care to test him. Nonetheless, I did prod to discover his level of discouragement.

"You're not regretting our decision to remain in Dublin, are you?"

We drew to a halt at a corner, waiting as a lorry carrying produce lumbered by, belching smoke. I lifted my hand, shielding my nose and mouth with my pale gray glove and the drape of my wide periwinkle sleeves, though the cross-hatched trim negated some of its effectiveness. Sidney seemed not to notice the officious fumes, standing broodily with his trilby hat pulled low over his eyes. He didn't try to speak, but I suspected that had more to do with the people who now clustered close around us than the distasteful exhaust.

Once the lorry had passed, we crossed the street, putting some distance between us and the pair of women behind us discussing the rising price of dairy—no doubt because the Crown Forces kept burning down the creameries. I pressed closer to Sidney to give a man approaching us more space, but he darted out into the street, lightly leaping up onto the outer step of an electric tram as it glided past, ringing its bell.

I turned my head to see beyond the tilted brim of my hat, thinking I might have to repeat my question, but I could tell from my husband's somber countenance that he knew I was still waiting for an answer.

"No," he conceded. "We agreed that we were the only people we could trust to see this through, and that hasn't changed. Bennett and Ames are still blind to Ardmore's true nature and susceptible to his influence. And while Collins might be aware of his underhandedness, I don't trust him not to turn a blind eye if Ardmore's plans are to his and the rebels' advantage, or for Xavier to be able to counter that sway."

I wanted to say something in Alec Xavier's defense, but there had been too many changes in my former colleague for me to trust I knew exactly who he was or what he would do anymore. One thing that *was* certain was that Collins had a strong influence on him. Alec had switched sides, after all, working against the orders of the government he'd always followed, risking life and limb before, during, and after the war. Though I understood his reasons and even empathized with them—struggling myself with the way our government was handling this situation—I couldn't help but question and instinctively mistrust his about-face. If it came down to it, I wanted to believe his conscience and his faith in me would win out. But Collins simply cast too large a shadow, and for the first time I saw Alec eclipsed in another's shade rather than standing fully in the sun.

Sidney frowned. "The fact is, we've got no choice in the matter. Not if we want to be able to live with ourselves. Neither you nor I will be able to forgive ourselves if we leave and the worst happens."

The worst being something we didn't know how to quantify as Ardmore's motives and intent were still hazy, though the possibilities were chilling.

His voice dipped so low I could barely hear him over the clamor of the midday traffic at the busy intersection we were approaching. "I've got enough regrets from the war. I don't need to add to them."

My heart squeezed as if a fist had been wrapped around it, for I knew some of those regrets, and I'd deduced quite a few more. In most of those cases, no blame could or should be laid at his feet, but that didn't stop him from feeling guilt and remorse all the same. Chief among them that he was alive when so many others were not.

Nor was I immune to the pang of regrets. I held a few of my own. They were like bruises, tender to the touch and slow to heal. But Sidney was right. I didn't wish to add to them either.

I gripped his arm more tightly in a show of empathy and solidarity.

One he promptly ruined as his brow puckered in agitation and he glanced down at me to remark, "Though I do wish *you* would return to London."

I'd known it was too much to hope he'd forgo any opportunity to voice this desire.

I arched a single eyebrow in vexation. "Not a chance."

He heaved a put-upon sigh but made no further complaint as we rounded the corner, hastening our steps to catch the tram idling nearby.

It being such a mild day, we elected to take seats on the top. There were less people and the air was fresher than the cramped lower level. The breeze was welcome against my flushed cheeks, but not so strong that I risked losing my wide-brimmed hat.

I tumbled into my seat in as dignified a manner as I could manage as the tram moved southward, approaching the Presbyterian church's tall spire and Rutland Square beyond. Sidney perched beside me, scrutinizing the long stretch of street before us.

I supposed I should be glad he'd put up no further argument to my staying in Dublin. Many men would have, insisting their wives do precisely what they told them to, and much of society would have agreed. But Sidney had never been like that, being wise enough to recognize that I would never stand for being ordered about. Especially not since the war, when I'd done far more dangerous things without his even being aware.

For the most part, he accepted my autonomy and respected my abilities. Though it certainly helped that we shared the same spirit of adventure, the same strong sense of justice. I knew the moments when he pressed me to leave were because of his care for me. Given that I also suffered from instances when I wished I could wrap him in cotton batting and lock him away safe, I could hardly remain angry at him for long. Not when love was to blame.

"Have you heard anything more from Bentnick?" Sidney murmured softly, even though it was doubtful anyone was close enough to hear us.

"No," I answered simply, knowing he would appreciate my discouragement without my having to say more.

George Bentnick was one of my dearest friends, but also a brilliant mathematician and cryptologist. In fact, he'd been one of Britain's foremost codebreakers during the war, working in OB40 for Naval Intelligence. He'd taught me everything I knew on the subject. So when I'd been unable to decode a journal owned by one of Ardmore's primary hench-men which had fallen into our hands, I'd given it to George to work out. Unfortunately, he'd since discovered that it was likely a book cipher, and without knowing precisely which book had been used, it was doubtful we'd ever decrypt it.

I'd had high hopes the journal might lead us to the location of the phosgene, or at least reveal Lord Ardmore's plans for it, so I had friends back in London trying to uncover what they could about Lieutenant James Smith—the journal's now deceased owner. Regrettably, Ardmore seemed to have antici-pated this as well, for Smith's file was missing from the War Office and his effects had long been cleared away. It was yet another example of Ardmore's exasperating ability to always be two steps ahead of us. I feared we might never catch up.

Sidney's hand stole into mine, as if sensing my distress.

Or perhaps it was the sight of the soldiers posted outside the Rotunda, presumably to prevent another attack by the IRA. The General Post Office having been burned during the Easter Rebellion in 1916, the post office sorting facility had been temporarily moved to the Rotunda, where a month ear-lier, the republicans had successfully raided the facility, steal-ing the mail bags bound for Dublin Castle—the seat of the British government in Ireland. It had been an embarrassing debacle for the British. One that had been lampooned in the press.

From the looks of the clusters of soldiers spaced at strate-gic positions around the building with their rifles slung over their shoulders, bayonets affixed, the British were determined this not happen again. As if to reinforce this, a lorry bristling with Black and Tans came roaring up Sackville Street with a Crossley tender close behind, sending pedestrians scattering to get out of their way. The Tan manning the machine gun swung it left and right at the fleeing Dubliners, as if at any moment he might open fire. The men lining both sides of the lorry, their guns pointed outward like deadly spikes, hollered greetings to their cohorts at the corner, drawing grins to their faces.

These sights were always discomforting to me, for instinctively I wanted to cheer on our Tommies, and yet the Crown Forces' behavior reminded me painfully of the Germans lording over the Belgians when they'd occupied their country during the war. Though, to be fair to the Germans, they'd rarely sped about the streets of Brussels purely for the purpose of terrifying its civilians. But then again, by the time I'd arrived, they hadn't needed to, having cemented their power in August and September 1914. Later they couldn't afford to waste guns and bullets on threatening noncombatants when they were needed at the front. Regardless, the comparison was not complimentary for the British.

Having gathered intelligence to help the British oust the German occupiers, I struggled mightily with the recognition of what was happening here in Dublin, within our own British Empire. The similarities were impossible to ignore and growing each day, and I was not the only one to have noted them. Newspaper reporters and even some government officials had also drawn the correlation. Though that did not thaw the cold lump of disillusion and disaffection growing inside my breast, or soothe the anxiety and resentment continually cramping my gut.

I wanted desperately to close my eyes, to pretend it wasn't happening, to claim ignorance in order to resolve the excruciating dissonance within me. But if my experiences during the war and its aftermath had taught me anything, it was that such a choice was cowardly and ultimately fatal to us all. Perhaps not to our own lives, but to our humanity. For willful blindness to the pain and suffering of others chipped away little by little at who we were as individuals and as a people.

So, I took it all in with wide eyes, ringing ears, and an aching heart. I squeezed Sidney's hand so hard I wondered why he didn't protest, but then he was holding himself just as rigid.

I turned to look at him, knowing this was no easier for him. Not when he'd gone to war for his country, killing countless numbers of men and losing even more by sending them over the top into battle to halt the aggressions of a bully. Now, what was he supposed to do when the bully seemed to be us?

Sidney didn't meet my gaze. I suspected he wouldn't . . . *couldn't*. Not here, not now.

Understanding this instinctually, I turned away, keeping my hand within his, but relaxing my grip. Maintaining our connection, but not adding to his grief. Holding on.

CHAPTER 3

"They haven't run you off, I see," I teased as Mark Sturgis bussed my cheek in greeting.

He grinned broadly beneath his mustache. "Not a chance. Though they *have* ordered us inside the Castle. Ghastly, drafty old thing."

I'd heard the government had instructed all seconded English civil servants to move from their lodgings at the Royal Marine Hotel in Kingstown into Dublin Castle for their own protection. This had included Sturgis, who had recently been appointed to the administration, acting as a sort of joint assistant undersecretary. It had not been a popular command, but given the number of assassinations the rebels had already committed and the increased unrest that had been expected after the Restoration of Order in Ireland Act went into effect, it was a necessary one.

"But didn't you say the National Gallery had lent you some of their pictures?" Helen Wyndham-Quin remarked, her dark hair a soft cloud about her features. "That ought to spruce up the place a bit."

"Yes, they let me poke about in their attics," Sturgis replied as he shook Sidney's hand. "The pieces I chose were delivered just today, though I haven't yet had a chance to hang them."

The fact that he'd been allowed to borrow paintings from the National Gallery of Ireland didn't surprise me. The rules had always been different for the aristocracy, and while Sturgis didn't have a title of his own to boast of, his father-in-law was the Earl of Wharncliffe. However, I did spare a moment to ponder our casual acceptance of this disparity in expectations.

"Did Lady Rachel return with you?" I asked, knowing over the past week he'd traveled to London and back.

"No, my wife stayed behind with the children. But I believe she intends to join me soon. She's anxious to see what all the fuss is about."

Sturgis plainly meant this in jest, but I struggled to return the brightness of his smile. "Fuss," indeed. As if this revolution was no more than a child's tantrum.

"She's anxious to see you, as well," he added, lowering his head almost conspiratorially so that I could see the severe line of the part of his hair down the center of his head. The deep brown strands were slick with brilliantine. "Could hardly believe it when I told her Verity Kent was in Dublin, of all places."

Then she hadn't been reading the society pages very closely, for Sidney and I had featured prominently in several of them since our arrival in Ireland three months' past. But of course, I didn't share this thought. Not when it would have sounded as if I was bragging, when the truth was, I wished it was the other way around. In our line of work, having our names and photographs plastered across the newspapers wasn't just annoying, but potentially dangerous.

"Well, tell her I look forward to catching up," I said politely instead, turning to survey the drawing room of the Private Secretary's Lodge.

As master of the horse and military secretary to the lord lieutenant, Richard Wyndham-Quin—or Dicky, as we called him—had been granted use of this house nestled inside the larger Viceregal demesne located within Phoenix Park at the western edge of the city. The lord lieutenant himself, Lord

French, resided nearby in the much larger and somewhat grander Viceregal Lodge, while the chief secretary, Lord Greenwood, made use of the Chief Secretary's Lodge, also part of the demesne.

This was the first time Sidney and I had been invited to the Private Secretary's Lodge, as in the past most of the dinner parties we'd attended had been held at the Lord Lieutenant's residence. However, it being the August holiday season, many people were away, including French and Greenwood. Even the British prime minister was said to be on holiday, enjoying a respite in Switzerland.

But while the cat was away, the mice would play. The old adage seemed somehow appropriate, and not entirely undeserved. I'd seen how the Quins were beholden to the lord lieutenant's whims, and I understood how mercurial he could be. After all, Sidney and I had nearly fallen from Lord French's graces simply because he hadn't liked the results of an inquiry he'd asked us to undertake on his behalf. Fortunately, he seemed to have forgiven us for not agreeing with his perceptions of the matter. Though I was rather glad he was absent for a time so that we needn't immediately put that to the test.

The exterior of the Little Lodge—as the private secretary's residence was often referred to—was no more impressive in appearance than the Viceregal Lodge. Long, squat, and rather austere, it took up a large amount of area but boasted few architectural details. However, either Helen, or a predecessor, had done their best to make the interiors more inviting. The drawing room walls were papered in a lustrous pale blue silk patterned with soft brown birds within golden cages. The gold was then picked up in the drapes and the upholstery of the handsome oak furnishings. The fireplace was faced in sculpted Italian marble with jasper inlays, forming a geometric pattern that was echoed in the rug at the center of the floor.

A phonograph sat in the corner, softly playing ragtime

tunes, while adjacent a long sideboard yawned with bottles, carafes, and decanters filled with various liquors. Dicky turned as we entered, approaching us with two glasses. One appeared to be filled with an amber-hued whiskey for Sidney while the other brimmed with ice and was topped with a lemon garnish.

I gasped in delight. "Is that a gin rickey?"

"It is. And a proper one," he promised me. With his equally dark hair and mustache, Dicky might have passed for Sturgis's brother if not for the differences in their bone structure. "I remembered how much you'd despaired of finding quality gin here in Dublin, so I made sure to have a few bottles sent over from London."

"Dicky, you are an absolute darb," I exclaimed, accepting the drink from him and taking an experimental sip. I closed my eyes, humming with pleasure at the refreshing tingle on my tongue.

The others laughed.

"Careful, Kent. If word gets out that the way to Verity's heart is a good bottle of gin, she'll be more assailed by admirers than she already is."

I turned to look into Rufus Beresford's twinkling eyes as his remark was met with general amusement. I hadn't known that he was acquainted with the Quins, but then he was the cousin of the Marquess of Waterford, and the aristocracy did tend to be familiar with those of their kind.

"Then, you and Mr. Beresford have been introduced?" Helen asked, her tall, graceful figure nearly drowning in lavender-gray taffeta. Not for the first time, I wished I could have a word with her modiste or whoever it was who helped with her clothing choices. She turned to include a dainty woman with blond curls in the circle of guests. "Have you been introduced to his sister, as well?"

"Yes, I've had the pleasure of meeting Doris and her husband, Hal," I replied, stepping forward to lightly buss the air beside Doris's cheek. "How lovely to see you again."

"Likewise," she murmured. As always, her voice sounded a little breathy. I suspected it was an affectation. One that was supposed to make her seem coy and endearing. She wasn't the first woman to employ such a technique.

It certainly seemed to work on her husband, who appeared to hop to his young bride's every request. Sidney and I had both been privately amused by his almost slavish devotion and her doting response, but then they were still newlyweds, married less than six months. I'd asked myself if Sidney and I had ever been so saccharine together, but of course, it had been a different world six years ago. We'd married in haste, enjoying just a few days together before he was shipped off to the front. In the years that followed, we'd rarely had longer than a week at one time together during his sporadic leaves, and we'd simply been so desperate to hold each other as long as we could, that any sweetness there might have been was tainted with anxiety and fear.

I wasn't certain what Hal Fitzgibbon had done during the war, but he had the soft, unblemished countenance and blithe mannerisms of someone who'd never seen the trenches. His brother-in-law, on the other hand, had undoubtedly served somewhere. That, or Rufus Beresford had developed his jaundiced air and acerbic wit through some other hardship. He had been speaking to Sybil, Lady Powerscourt, when we arrived. The viscountess rounded out our party, her husband apparently being unable to attend.

Greetings having been exchanged, we all settled around the hearth with our cocktails. Beresford remarked about the recent horse show at Ballsbridge, and the men—most of whom were horse-mad—were quickly absorbed in the discussion, along with Helen, who was a keen horsewoman herself. I suspected Sidney would have preferred instead to talk about the motor show that had taken place in Dublin the same week, but he was an avid enough rider and polo player to take part without any difficulty.

Sybil cast me a long-suffering look and I smiled, leaning closer to compliment her sage-green gown. Though nearly two decades older than me, the viscountess's flawless skin made her appear no more than five and thirty. The deep yet tasteful neckline of her pale green gown showed off her long neck and smooth shoulders to perfection. It was a design I had no choice but to eschew due to the scar on my shoulder from a gunshot wound. In any case, the ruffled panels of my skirt were far more daring and in accordance with my style than Sybil's sleeker fashion. Though the pale blush-pink shade of my gown was an unusual choice for me. With my auburn Castle-bobbed tresses, I usually avoided pinks altogether, but this hue had surprisingly suited me.

"How long does the lord lieutenant intend to be away?" Doris asked, evidently having decided the horse talk had gone on long enough.

"Perhaps a month," Dicky replied.

"I heard a rumor he's not returning," Beresford supplied, watching us all avidly through the haze of his cigarette as he took a long drag.

Dicky and Helen exchanged a brief but somewhat telling glance. "We haven't been told anything to suggest as much," he said. But they were concerned about it, nonetheless.

What was more, Sturgis hesitated to speak up, meaning he'd likely heard something similar.

There was no denying that Lord French wasn't particularly popular at the moment. He might have been a great favorite with the troops at the front when he'd served as field marshal during the first year of the war, but the Irish republicans had already attempted to assassinate him multiple times, and what powers he'd had over government policy in Ireland had mostly been stripped away in the past few months, making his role as viceroy primarily ceremonial.

"The lord lieutenant always takes a holiday in August," Sturgis finally stated diplomatically. "And no doubt, he deserves the respite this year. He'll need to gather his strength and his stomach for what's to come."

This assertion was somewhat jarring, even calmly spoken as it was, and it took considerable willpower for me not to look at Sidney to see how he'd taken it.

"Yes, His Lordship has made it clear enough he doesn't believe in compromise," Hal contributed in almost an offhand way, his attention more drawn to his wife, who was twirling a strand of her golden hair.

Beresford leaned on the arm of the sofa, swirling the dregs of his drink idly in its glass. "That seems to be the approach favored by most men in the British government."

This wasn't strictly true. There were plenty of officials who favored compromise. Many of them were part of the administration at Dublin Castle with Sturgis. But then Beresford was not privy to the debates occurring behind the closed doors of cabinet meetings like we were. Our friend Max, the Earl of Ryde, had been using his connections within the government to pass along such select information.

Dicky frowned. "You disagree?"

Beresford shifted his cool gaze from his whiskey to our host. "It's not my place to agree or disagree. I'm merely making an observation." He lifted his glass to swallow the rest of the liquid before gesturing with it. "Take for instance these hunger strikers." He scoffed. "They're not going to let them out. They can't."

Just a few short weeks ago, Terence MacSwiney, the lord mayor of Cork, had been arrested for possession of seditious documents and a cipher key utilized by the RIC. He'd been promptly tried by court martial under the new Restoration of Order in Ireland Act, rather than being given the usual jury trial, and sentenced to two years in prison. In response, he and ten other prisoners had gone on hunger strike, a form of nonviolent protest which had worked successfully for the rebels in the past. Most notably four months earlier when more than one hundred men who had gone on hunger strike were released from Mountjoy Prison. This, and a subsequent administrative mistake which caused the release of even more revolutionary prisoners, had been a severe blow to the morale of the police.

"He's right," Sidney conceded. "If they're going to release the republicans every time they threaten to hunger strike, they may as well offer terms to Sinn Féin."

"The RIC would collapse entirely under such a degradation," Dicky agreed.

Beresford stood to cross to the sideboard. "Or decide it's better to kill all the rebels outright rather than make an arrest and risk their pulling such antics."

I scowled at the dark hair on the back of his head, rattled by his urbane tone. It made the words he was spouting all the more chilling. Particularly given there was more than a grain of truth to them. That was obvious in the growing number of reprisals and murders.

"Couldn't they simply force feed them?" Doris asked, her head tilted to the side in what appeared to be genuine puzzlement. "Is that not what it's called?"

"Not after what happened to Thomas Ashe, dear," her husband replied, patting her on the knee.

Ashe, who had taken part in the Easter rebellion, had been forcibly fed after going on hunger strike in Mountjoy Prison three years prior. He'd died from the brutal treatment and been made a martyr to the cause. Since then, the British had been hesitant to attempt such methods.

"Rest assured," Sturgis consoled Doris, who was visibly distressed. "Despite the *Freeman's* claims"—his brow creased at his mention of the newspaper—"everything possible, save capitulation, is being done to keep the hunger strikers alive."

I'd seen the *Freeman's Journal*'s accusations that the British were simply going to let the hunger strikers die, but that wasn't what caught my interest. Scrutinizing Sturgis's face, I had to wonder what he meant by "everything." I'd heard rumors of tricks that were allegedly employed to keep hunger strikers alive, such as slipping albumen into the prisoners' water. If so, the rebels would be outraged if they found out, for the Irish character seemed to have a marked inclination toward martyrdom, believing that each sacrifice, each selfless act of devotion to their homeland, carried the torch forward for the next generation.

"I heard the rebels are secretly sneaking them food. Just enough to keep them alive," Sybil murmured. "Even Mac-Swiney in Brixton."

The lord mayor had been transferred to the London prison soon after the hunger strike began, in hopes his absence would break the will of the other strikers still held in Cork and also to prevent the republicans from attempting one of their infamous prison breaks.

"I've heard that as well," Sturgis admitted, crossing one leg over his knee. "And if so, all the better, though that makes them hypocrites."

"Someone should make sure the press hears that," Helen huffed, rising to her feet and offering to refill anyone else's glass.

I was quite certain someone had already informed the papers. After all, the hunger strikers were getting a tremendous amount of press internationally, making headlines around the globe and arousing sympathy for the republicans' cause. It was tantamount to a propaganda coup, particularly in democracies like the United States. Men imprisoned by military tribunal, without due process, willing to die for their cause in a nonviolent manner. The British were portrayed as cruel, unfair tyrants and the Irish republicans as victims of oppression.

Though I knew nothing was so straightforward, my stomach twisted with unease, nearly souring my taste for the good gin Dicky had gone out of his way to procure for me. For all that these people were our friends, it was difficult to hear them voice such unsympathetic and sometimes prejudicial views. I knew some of them were more moderate than others, but they were all firmly loyal to the Crown and certain of the superiority of the British. In my heart of hearts, I could no longer claim to be either.

And yet, Sidney and I had to pretend to be. To be charming and entertaining, and thoroughly trustworthy in order to continue to garner invitations from this set so that we could gather intelligence. Mark Sturgis, in particular, was a friendship we needed to cultivate, given his useful connection to the Dublin Castle administration. In truth, an acquaintance with him was relatively easy, for he was witty, amiable, and mostly good-hearted, but I was also attuned to his faults: his snobbishness and condescension—a hallmark of the British aristocracy, really—and his failure to truly grasp the republicans' mindset.

The butler appeared to announce that dinner was ready, and we all moved toward the door leading to the dining room.

"What does Winter think of all this?" Dicky asked Sturgis, and I was hard-pressed not to react to the mention of O, the director of intelligence at the Castle. My gaze shifted to Sidney, who had also heard the remark.

"That when MacSwiney dies there's going to be bloodshed in Dublin and Cork," Sturgis murmured in response, perhaps not wanting the entire party to hear him. "He claims the rebels are buying medical supplies and have three hundred thousand pounds' worth of German rifles on their way to Ireland, though the Navy will never let them get through."

I could almost see the thought forming in Sidney's mind as it formed in mine. Could this be the event Ardmore intended the phosgene for? He'd been biding his time, waiting for the right moment. With the temperament of the rebellion already running high and the people of the world watching, he might decide the timing was finally ideal.

"Well, if the clash is to come, better it be soon," Dicky muttered. "With all the labor threats in England, word is they may need to transfer ten battalions from Ireland to curb the strikes and unrest. Which would mean abandoning entire areas of the country to the shinners."

"Shinners" was a derogatory term often used to refer to those who supported Sinn Féin, which was pronounced "shin fayn." Though it was the IRA—the military branch of the rebellion—they feared taking control of greater swathes of the country, not the dominant Irish nationalist political party, which had formed a shadow government and declared themselves representatives of the Irish Republic.

Sturgis's expression was grim, obviously already cognizant of the issue. "Greenwood and Churchill"—the chief secretary of Ireland and secretary of war, respectively—"are suggesting we draft Ulster Volunteers to curb unrest if that should occur. But Anderson and General Macready"—the joint undersecretary of Ireland and the commander-in-chief of British military forces within Ireland—"say that would mean civil war."

They were right. The thought that some of the most powerful men in the British government were even entertaining the notion was appalling. They couldn't be unaware of the violent sectarian clashes occurring even now in northern Ireland in the counties of Ulster closest to Belfast. The Protestant unionists, all but supported by the British government—if not outright, then by their silent complicity and failure to interfere—had dispelled thousands of Catholic workers from their jobs and homes. More and more refugees were daily pouring into the Catholic-majority counties south of Ulster, which by and large also supported the republicans.

Dicky shook his head. "Better to have it out without the Ulster men."

Sturgis sighed. "If only. But I fear the rebels are too clever to be drawn into open combat."

This comment proved that Sturgis was shrewder than he seemed. For Collins and the leaders of the IRA understood they had no chance against the might of the British empire if they faced them across a battlefield. Their best chance was stealth. In ambushes, raids, and assassinations. In preying on the enemy's frame of mind so that they were never certain when or where an attack would come.

The British called this unsporting, but then again, *we* had been the ones to set the rules in the first place. Rules which had worked to our advantage for hundreds of years. The Irish were simply no longer willing to play that game.

I drifted toward Sidney's side, curious what his impressions were. As I did so, I noted that we weren't the only ones who had hung back to eavesdrop on Dicky and Sturgis. Rufus Beresford was also listening carefully. Though the flat sheen in his eyes made me wary of letting him know that I'd noticed.

CHAPTER 4

"Did you hear the jewel thief struck again?" Beresford seemed far too keen as he dropped this question into the lull in the conversation around the dinner table, but then again it was obvious by now that he was the very definition of a provocateur—eager to shock and elicit reactions from others and stir up trouble wherever he could.

I doubted this was the change of topic Helen had been hoping for when she ordered that there be no more talk of hunger strikers or rebellion, but she surprised me by responding eagerly. "At the Chathams? Yes, Laurel told me about it. He stole her grandmother's diamond and emerald brooch. It was worth a *fortune*. It was insured, of course. But its sentimental value is irreplaceable."

"Ohhh," Doris cooed sympathetically. "How terrible."

Her husband nodded in agreement.

"What's this about a jewel thief?" Sybil asked, lowering her fork.

I was relieved to hear I wasn't the only one confused by Beresford's remark.

"That's right. You've been down at Powerscourt these past few weeks, so it's unlikely you would have heard." Helen's eyes widened. "There's a jewel thief—a cat burglar, if you like—who's been targeting wealthy homes throughout Dublin and the surrounding environs."

Sybil pressed her hand to her collar where a stunning peridot and gold necklace shimmered in the light of the crystal chandelier overhead, as if to be certain it was still there. Her brow furrowed. "But I haven't read anything about it in the papers."

"That's because it's been kept out of them so far," Dicky replied before spearing a bite of halibut. "The victims haven't wanted the publicity."

It was quite a tall order to keep reporters from catching wind of such a juicy morsel, especially if the police were involved.

"How many victims are we talking about?" Sidney asked, having lifted his glass of sauvignon blanc but hesitated to drink as he puzzled over the question.

"Four," Beresford said at the same time Dicky said, "three." Both men eyed each other uncertainly, and Helen chimed in to answer.

"The Harringtons, the Daltons, the Maudes and, as we just said, the Chathams. But the Daltons were robbed at the Harringtons' home, so three incidents and four victims." Helen turned to Sybil and then me. "Oh, it's simply dreadful. As you may know, Lily Harrington recently became engaged to Robby Dalton, and the Harringtons hosted an engagement party for the couple."

I'd been aware of this much. Sidney and I had received an invitation, though we were barely acquainted with the families. As such, we weren't sad to decline when we had other plans.

Helen nodded absently to her butler when he appeared to bring out the next course. "Well, the thief struck *during* the party! Emptied Claudia Harrington's jewelry case as well as Lily's. He also got away with Roberta Dalton's twenty-carat diamond necklace. She was going to wear it to the party, but at the last minute decided it might be too gaudy and outshine the bride-to-be. So she left it in the bedside table in the guest chamber she was staying in."

Helen paused as our plates were swept away and the next course brought forth, leaving time for Sybil to commiserate. "That *is* dreadful."

Helen took a sip of her newly poured bordeaux, before turning to select a lamb cutlet from the serving dish a footman offered her. "Now the Daltons are accusing the Harringtons of associating with low company and the Harringtons are blaming Robby's friends, who apparently became sotted and caused quite a disturbance. The engagement is hanging by a thread."

The others mumbled their commiserations as we served ourselves from the new round of dishes, but I found my gaze drawn to the tall windows where outside the sun was just beginning to set on this August evening, painting amber and pink streaks across the sky. The chartreuse drapes had yet to be closed, so the deep blue walls served merely as a backdrop to the light spilling through the room and glinting off the gold frames and mirrors, as well as the silver utensils and crystal glassware. However, I was less interested in the décor than something Helen has said.

"Why are the Daltons accusing the Harringtons of associating with low company?" I finally asked though the conversation had shifted to debate what spices had been used on the roasted vegetables. Everyone turned to look at me, but I pressed on. "What could their associations have to do with it? Unless . . ."

"Unless they think the thief was someone on the guest list or that he somehow blended in with them?" Sidney supplied, following my line of thought. His midnight-blue eyes glinted in approval at me over the display of dahlias at the center of the table.

This evidently hadn't occurred to the others, who frowned and fidgeted.

"I'd assumed someone had broken in," Dicky supplied, his mustache twitching. "Or that perhaps a member of the staff was involved. They might be considered low company."

My eyes darted toward the members of Dicky's staff positioned along the walls, who couldn't help but overhear. Had he forgotten they were listening, or did he not care?

"But I suppose that makes less sense given the other burglaries that have occurred," he continued. "It strains credulity to believe the thief has such connections in every household."

"Unless they're rebels," Beresford chimed in to say, gesturing for his glass of bordeaux to be refilled.

I was about to ask what he meant when Sturgis confessed, "I wondered the same thing. Given their other . . . *proclivities* . . ." By this it was clear he was referring to their assassination of policemen and other officials. "The theft of jewelry seems rather minor in comparison, and they need to fund their revolution somehow." He arched his eyebrows. "Word is they're perpetually short on funds."

That wasn't the rumblings I'd heard. From what I understood, the Dáil Loan that Michael Collins, as finance minister, had appealed to the Irish people to help fund, was doing well, and the people of the United States were being more than generous in their donations to the cause, as well. Especially since the president of the Dáil Éireann, Éamon de Valera, was currently touring that country to raise further support. I eyed Sturgis closely, unsure whether he knew something I didn't or if he was playing coy.

"I certainly wouldn't put it past them," Hal proclaimed, and some of the others voiced their agreement. However, his wife seemed less convinced, or perhaps it was something else that had caused Doris's brow to wrinkle in concern as she picked at her food.

Sidney covered his silence by taking a long drink, but I could tell he was equally hesitant to accept such a theory. I supposed there was nothing to say it couldn't be the republicans, but it didn't seem congruent with their normal tactics. As terrible as the murders they'd committed were, they were to a very specific purpose—cutting off the British government's flow of intelligence, by taking out the men who supplied information about the rebels to the Crown before they were jailed or killed themselves. After all, for centuries and even as recent as the Easter rebellion in 1916, it had been the police who informed on their fellow Irishmen and enabled the British to arrest and foil their plots. Given this, the recent assassinations had been seen as an act of necessity to the revolution—kill or be killed.

Perhaps these jewel thefts could also be seen as an act of necessity, but I doubted the republican leaders would see it that way. Not when they were already funding their revolution in a more honorable manner with loans and donations.

It was Helen's turn to press her hand to her neck over her pendant. "To think that one's gems might be stolen to fund a rebellion. How vile!" She visibly shuddered, though I was suspicious she actually found the notion rather exciting.

"And I thought we need only worry about being raided for arms," Dicky retorted derisively, as a number of the homes of the gentry as well as police and army officers—both retired and still active—had been broken into by the IRA to confiscate their weapons. He turned to the other men. "The army is encouraging even the owners of legally held weapons to surrender them into their care, lest they find their way into the hands of the rebels."

Though I knew Sidney possessed a Luger pistol, his face revealed nothing of its existence or any of the other weapons he might have stashed away. I, on the other hand, had learned to navigate through German-occupied Belgium and northeastern France without one. The enemy's searches had been too frequent and erratic, and the penalty too steep for being caught with a weapon to even risk it. So I chose not to carry one now. In my experience, guns more often escalated violence than deterred it.

"Mrs. Fitzgibbon, I can see that you are rattled," Helen murmured sympathetically, having noticed the other woman's distraction as I had and attributed it to distress.

Doris startled, dropping her fork with a clatter. "Oh . . . yes," she stammered, seeming to search for her words. "These thefts, they're just so . . . vile," she parroted.

"Someone should really put a stop to it," Beresford declared, before adding in a mocking tone, "I'm not sure the police are up to the task."

Doris turned to scowl at him, but no one else seemed to take offense on the Crown Forces' behalf.

"Perhaps Sidney and Verity should take a crack at it," Dicky jested.

"Yes," Sybil exclaimed as a number of the others chuckled in agreement. "After your previous exploits, solving these jewel thefts would be practically tame."

Doris, meanwhile, was gazing at us wide-eyed.

Helen leaned around Sidney to explain, "They're quite the amateur sleuths."

I bristled internally to hear us referred to in such a way but had long ago accepted that the truth of who I was and what I'd done during the war and after would never be known. Not even my family knew how I'd actually done my bit during the conflict; as per the Official Secrets Act I was forbidden from telling them. Sidney had only found out because of the flapping gums of a male colleague. The men within military intelligence liked to belittle all of us women who'd served, bemoaning our alleged feminine incapability of being discreet, but the fact was we knew well how to keep our mouths shut. If not, the world would be better aware of just how many hundreds of us had worked in the various divisions during the war, and how many hundreds more had gathered intelligence behind enemy lines.

"We'll have to see if we can fit it into our busy social schedule," Sidney bantered, eliciting some amusement in return.

I was simply glad he'd spared me from coming up with a response. "Speaking of which, are we still on for polo Saturday?" he asked Sturgis and Dicky.

We spent the remainder of the evening discussing more pleasant topics while playing cards and listening to the gramophone. Doris, it turned out, was a voracious reader and she and I spent some time discussing our favorite books. However, the jewel thefts were still on my mind as we motored away from the Private Secretary's Lodge in Sidney's prized carmine-red Pierce-Arrow roadster.

It was only a little after eleven—early by our previous standards—but Dublin's curfew began at midnight. The lord lieutenant had procured us curfew passes to aid us during our previous investigation, though we preferred not to use them. The streets were a headache to navigate with all the barricades that were set up. Ones that were all but impossible to avoid in a motorcar. Perhaps most pertinent, the Crown Forces were also more unpredictable at night. Darkness had a way of amplifying dangers, whether real or imagined. And with nerves already strained from living among a hostile populace, it didn't take much for bravado to override reason. Given all this, it was best to be tucked up at home before the lorries and tenders issued forth from Dublin Castle and the various barracks scattered about the city.

It was a beautiful night, the sky being clear and the moon nearly full, illuminating the landscape of fields as we navigated over the River Liffey and along the South Circular Road which circumnavigated Dublin. Though Kilmainham Jail was undoubtedly a blot on the terrain. Sidney was quiet as we sped across the silver-hued countryside. I couldn't tell if this was because he was rehashing the evening's conversations like I was or if he was simply enjoying the power of his Pierce-Arrow's engine and the thrill of the wind through his hair. He'd long since tossed his hat in the rear seat to let his dark curls spring free.

I started to speak, but then subsided back against the leather seat, deciding I was too tired to hold a conversation at a volume that could be heard over the rushing wind. Instead, I allowed my gaze to trace the shadowed hills and the course of the Grand Canal as it encircled the city to the south. As we entered the streets of the city, Sidney slowed, alert to the pedestrians hurrying home, the clang and clatter of late trams, and the stench of coal from the fireplaces of those who could afford to light them given the current shortage. By the time we reached the mews behind Upper Fitzwilliam Street, the streetlamps were already being dowsed for the night—a countermeasure taken by of the city's administrative organization, the Dublin Corporation, in retaliation for the British government imposing a curfew.

Sidney parked the Pierce-Arrow in the former carriage house at the back of the garden and we hurried through the deepening chill toward the town house we'd rented from old acquaintances of our friend Max—the Courtneys—who had fled Dublin six months earlier. When we entered through the door on the landing between the ground floor and the servants' quarters, Nimble was waiting for us.

Having served as Sidney's batman during the war and now his valet, Nimble was our most trusted and loyal retainer. Though his name was somewhat of a misnomer. Nimble, he was not, but he rather lumbered about with clumpy steps, speaking sparingly in a rather thick tongue. He'd been injured during the latter months of the war by a shell explosion which had taken part of his left ear and blistered his skin near the hairline.

"Anything to report?" Sidney asked him as if they were still at the front and we'd just returned from a sortie. Which, in a sense, I supposed was the truth, despite the battlefield not being a shell-marked landscape strewn with twisted barbed wire and decomposing corpses and our home not a filthy, lice-ridden trench. And thank God for that!

"All quiet," Nimble reported as he took Sidney's hat so that my husband could remove my georgette silk wrap from my shoulders. "But Mrs. Kent did receive two letters."

We both perked up in interest.

"One from a courier with the bank," he added before I could ask, already reaching into the inner pocket of his coat to extract them. "And the other from London."

I accepted the two missives. "Did the courier expect a response?"

"He didn't wait for one."

I nodded. "Thank you, Nimble." Scrutinizing the envelopes, I turned to climb the stairs while Sidney took a moment longer to confer with his valet. With an absent glance into the parlor, I moved on to the second floor and the private sitting room attached to our bedchamber. It contained a writing desk, and all my implements should I need to immediately pen a response. I pulled a letter opener from one of its drawers and slit open both letters before crossing toward the Sheraton sofa. Switching on the floor lamp, I settled down to read the missive delivered by the courier first.

When we'd traveled to Ireland in late May, we'd been directed to make contact with Tobias Finnegan at the Bank of Ireland. He was to serve as our handler, the same as he'd operated for Alec before he'd gone missing. At the time, I'd harbored suspicions that he might be the reason Alec had vanished. That Alec might have deliberately done so because he didn't trust Finnegan.

I'd been partially right.

Finnegan *had* been one of the reasons Alec had "disappeared," but not because he didn't trust him, but rather because he *did*. For Finnegan was loyal to Collins and the republicans rather than British Intelligence. He was a double agent. One I found it far more difficult not to expose than Alec, given Finnegan's frequent trips to London and direct contact with C. However, I'd given my word, and the man had proved useful. So until at the very least we'd located the phosgene, I'd resolved to bite my tongue.

The previous day when I'd paid a visit to the Bank of Ireland, located in the old Parliament House on College Green, I'd found that Finnegan was away, but expected to return the following day. Having been assured that since I was now aware of his true allegiance it would be safe to leave a message with one of his secretaries, Miss Clancy, I'd done so. The missive from the courier merely confirmed his receipt of it and in the vaguest terms made his assurances that he would do as requested—contact C and Miss Silvernickel and ask them to delve deeper into Ardmore's possible aliases, holdings, and business allies.

Sidney entered the room as I was setting the note aside in favor of the second more interesting one. "What have I missed?"

I lifted the courier slip and passed it to him, keeping my eyes trained on the other letter. I recognized the handwriting as Etta Lorraine's. She'd addressed the missive to Nimble, as directed, to help deflect suspicion from its contents. After all, the postal service was not only being monitored by the British, but also susceptible to interception by the IRA.

Of course, if the Secret Intelligence Service hadn't had the audacity to open and censor my private correspondence when it was originally delivered through Finnegan, I wouldn't have needed to resort to such extremes in order to gain the full picture of the events that were unfolding. Events that directly affected and endangered my and Sidney's lives, not to mention our staff. Nimble had already been falsely arrested once, and I worried for our maid, Ginny, an Irish girl who lived out. Even our cook, Mrs. Boyle, who resided belowstairs, faced some risk.

In any case, as things now stood with Sidney and I precariously walking the line of neutrality, we would have needed to establish a different method of communication with our sources back in England anyway. Sidney scanned Finnegan's message before discarding it and dropping down onto the sofa beside me. "What does she have to say?" he asked, aware of who the second letter was from. Rather than answer, I tilted the letter so that he could read over my shoulder.

Etta Lorraine was the best jazz singer this side of the Atlantic—and that was no exaggeration. She performed at Grafton Galleries, a London nightclub I'd frequented during the war and after. Initially, I'd cultivated her acquaintance because I'd recognized she'd make an invaluable source for information, as men tended to fawn over her. Drunk men with loose lips. However, we'd quickly become friends, helping each other out of any number of scrapes.

I'd not shared Etta's role as an informer with C and the SIS. Namely, because I'd known they would discount the intelligence she shared with me if they were aware of the source. It had always bothered me that she would never be given her due, such as it was within the very closed circle of the intelligence community. But *now* that secrecy had worked to my advantage.

Etta wrote in her usual chatty style sprinkled with wit and the French turns of phrase she'd never discarded from her childhood in Martinique. It almost made me feel as if she was seated in the room with us. She shared a few insights she'd gleaned from patrons at Grafton's, and I filed them away in case they might prove illuminating later. Then she got to the crux of her missive.

I've included Ryde's latest letter. But I must tell you, your bel ami *is frazzled. Something has agitated him. Not even a shot of single malt could calm him. Perhaps he's simply concerned for your safety,* ma

petite, *as I admit am I. Come home soon,* bébé. *And
bring that darling man with you. I'm sure you've heard
it said, "you never see the bullet with your name on
it." Considering the number of bullets that are flying
about Dublin these days, it's worth remembering.*

These last lines made the hairs on the back of my neck
stand on end. I knew Etta meant well, but the last thing I
needed was to be reminded of the danger we faced. If anything, I was already too conscious of it, and having her evoke
such an ominous expression felt rather like having a cat walk
over my grave.

Sidney stiffened as he came to Etta's closing, but I chose
not to remark on it. What was there to say? Instead, I quickly
flipped to Max's enclosed missive. Had he uncovered something unsettling from his contacts within the government and
the War Office? Or did his agitation have more to do with
Ardmore, whom he had more reason to loathe than even Sidney and I did?

Max began with a brief overview of Cowes Week, for
which he'd been absent from London. As the Earl of Ryde, his
estate was located on the Isle of Wight, and so he often played
a prominent role in the regatta that took place there every
year at the start of August. When he'd returned to London,
he reported there were continued rumbles about the Restoration of Order in Ireland Act—or the "coercion bill" as many
of the Irish had taken to calling it—throughout parliament
and society. There was divided opinion as to how effective
the policy would actually prove, and how much damage it
might do to future peace efforts.

None of this surprised me. Neither did the rumors he'd
heard that British Army officers in Ireland were soon to be
advised to send their wives and families back to England for
their own safety. Though I did wonder if this might be part

of the source of his anxiety. It certainly didn't comfort me to hear how much our government was privately conceding that the situation was deteriorating and yet publicly claiming they had everything under control.

Then Max returned to Cowes Week and the time he'd spent at home. When he explained that he'd revisited the remains of the Roman villa at Brading, the site where we'd found the first clue Max's father had left for him, allegedly leading him to the place where his father had concealed the evidence of his treacherous dealings with Ardmore during the war, I grasped the true source of his agitation. Ardmore had manipulated his father, the late Earl Ryde, into betraying his country and then had him killed when he grew a conscience. He'd had their partner, Lord Rockham, killed as well.

Not that we could prove any of it. At least, not enough to counteract the hold Ardmore had on the government through his powerful connections, who protected him as surely as a machine gun turret.

Max understandably struggled with this. Just as he struggled with the fact that even though we'd followed the late earl's clues to the end, the evidence that he'd claimed to have left for his son was still missing. Though that hadn't dampened Max's determination to find it. Which I supposed explained why he'd returned to Brading to speak with the curator who had known his Roman-enthusiast father well. A visit that may have been fruitful.

I explained to Mr. Oglander about the key Father left me. Of course, I didn't tell him where we'd really found it.

Buried in an old golf ball tin on the grounds of Burgh Castle, another Roman site, this one a former Saxon shore fort in Norfolk.

> *Only that it seemed to have something to do*
> *with Father's interest in Roman antiquities, but I'd*
> *yet to figure out what it opened. He made a rather*
> *remarkable suggestion. While I was aware that Father*
> *had donated a number of his acquisitions over the*
> *years to the British Museum, I hadn't realized that*
> *he had also been granted storage space there. Mr.*
> *Oglander suggested it might unlock some sort of box*
> *or locker within the museum. I am off to investigate*
> *this tomorrow as soon as the museum opens and will*
> *report what I find.*

I could sense Max's excitement that *this* might prove the answer to our conundrum and finally spur the downfall of Ardmore. I sensed it because I felt it, too. But that expectancy was also tempered with wariness. We'd believed we'd discovered the solution before, only to be disappointed when we were proven wrong.

I also had to admit that, while the phosgene was still missing, I feared Ardmore's downfall as much as I desired it. For there was nothing quite so dangerous as a man who believes he has nothing to lose.

A similar thought seemed to weigh on Sidney. "We *have* to find those cylinders," he murmured as he finished reading.

I turned to look into his midnight-blue eyes, letting him know I was in complete agreement. "Did Bennett and Ames have anything helpful to share?" I asked, knowing that he'd met the British Intelligence officers for drinks earlier that day.

His expression was glum. "Nothing worth repeating." Then his gaze dipped briefly to my abdomen before he arched his eyebrows. "Though Bennett did ask how you're faring."

I grimaced, regretting now my decision to let him believe I was expecting. It had seemed clever at the time, as it deflected suspicion from me, leading Bennett and his superiors to think that I couldn't be undertaking any dangerous work if I was with child. That my delicate condition would naturally inhibit me.

Had I known we would still be in Dublin all this time later, I would never have perpetuated such a ruse, for it couldn't continue much longer. Not without a greater level of subterfuge than I was willing to undertake. Of course, ending it would also require a deception I was equally uncomfortable with, especially as I was already intimate with the emotional pain of a miscarriage, having suffered one during the war.

"Sooner or later, he's going to figure out we lied."

"We didn't *lie*," I argued. "We just . . . didn't correct his assumption."

Sidney's glare was cynical. "Bennett won't see the distinction."

I sighed. "I know." I lifted my hand to my forehead where a headache had begun to build behind my eyes. "But I'm afraid a solution isn't going to present itself tonight."

His voice softened with sympathy. "Tired?"

I nodded.

He gathered up the letters and then reached for my hand, pulling me to my feet. After extinguishing the lamp, he towed me toward the door to our bedchamber and urged me to climb the steps to the tall four-poster bed. Then he knelt to remove my shoes.

I smiled softly down at him. My husband was an attractive man. One who was highly capable of making my heart race and my body sing with pleasure. But it was during tender moments like this, when the dark curls he normally kept so ruthlessly tamed waved about his face, softening his square jaw and sharp cheekbones, that he made my entire being warm with my love for him.

He looked up then, finding me watching him, and tilted his head in query.

I just shook my head and drew him up so that his face was level with mine and allowed my lips to do the talking.

CHAPTER 5

"There they are," Sidney declared several days later as we strolled along the edge of the polo grounds at Phoenix Park. The match had already begun, the riders in brilliant white thundering up and down the field on their steeds. The grandstand was more than half filled with spectators as well as the surrounding lawn, but Sidney was still able to locate Mark Sturgis—nattily dressed in gray tweed trousers and coat and a loose ecru jumper waistcoat—and his companion, Joint Undersecretary Anderson.

I'd met Sir John Anderson a number of times before and developed a favorable opinion of his intelligence and abilities. Truth be told, if he had been left to manage matters as he saw fit, I suspected everything would have run more smoothly at the Castle. But alas, he was forced to work at the behest of less reasonable men who had little understanding of the situation on the ground and egos too great to admit it. It was true, the Scotsman was rather dour and humorless, but he'd also recently lost his wife, so I attributed much of his demeanor to that.

Sturgis caught sight of our approach and flashed a broad grin, waving us over. I was relieved to see they had secured seats within an open-walled tent, for the day was a warm one and I'd known it would be rude to keep my parasol open and obstruct the views of those behind me. I closed it now, glad for the broad brim of my hat to shield my eyes from the bright sun.

Both men greeted us warmly as we joined them, and then redirected their attention to the match as an exciting play had just occurred. However, even after they'd subsided, neither appeared in any hurry to share the reason Sturgis had asked us to meet them here, seeming content to exchange pleasantries or commentary with Sidney about the players and horses. Had their party included women or Sidney alone been invited, then I wouldn't be so certain there was an ulterior motive to the request. Though I was hard-pressed to guess what it was.

Of course, I'd entertained fears that our association with some of the rebels and even Collins himself had been discovered, but then I'd dismissed the possibility. If we were found out, Sturgis and Anderson were not the people we would be called before to answer questions. Nor would the venue be a sunny polo match, but more likely one of the dank interrogation rooms in the Castle I'd heard mention of. So it must be something else.

I decided if they were in no rush, then neither would I be, and settled back to enjoy the match. Undoubtedly, they would make matters plain during one of the intervals between chukkas or at halftime. Though, I had to admit I would be sorry to miss the divot-stamping that spectators were allowed to take part in, restoring the mounds of earth the horses' hooves had torn up from the field during the first half of the match. It was oddly satisfying to stamp the divots back into place.

Observing the men as much as the polo-riders, I soon realized Sturgis and my husband were far more invested in the match than the undersecretary. His interest was more polite than genuine, as were his periodic courteous remarks to me. However, I didn't attempt to engage him in lengthy conversation. Not when it was evident that this match was to serve as a respite from his other duties, which I was certain were numerous and strenuous, as much of the administration's ability to function fell to him.

The man nominally in charge, the chief secretary, was more often in London than Dublin, and he was currently in Switzerland on holiday with the prime minister. Anderson may only have been named joint undersecretary, but everyone knew that the man he shared the post with, James Mac-Mahon, had remained in his position solely because he was Catholic, as the government had felt they must be seen to have at least one among their senior civil service ranks since such a large majority of the Irish population were Catholics. As such, rightly or wrongly—for I had no way to ascertain the genuine level of MacMahon's competency—the bulk of the work fell to Anderson.

At one point, a junior staff member of some sort appeared with a pot of tea, and I set about pouring. A gentle breeze rife with the scents of grass and earth rustled the flaps of the tent as I passed cups to the men and then settled back in the canvas chair with mine. I wasn't wrong in suspecting this was a signal to get down to business, for Sturgis took one long drink of his tea before turning away from the field.

"Right, then. We appreciate you joining us here today. Though I'm afraid this wasn't purely a social invitation." Sturgis looked from Sidney to me, as we gazed back at him unruffled. "But you knew that already, didn't you?" he added self-deprecatingly.

"We're rather accustomed to searching for the hidden meaning in such requests," I confessed, trying to ease any pang of conscience.

Sturgis's dark eyes sharpened, and Anderson turned to look at me with interest. Perhaps I shouldn't have admitted as much, but if it would get him to his point faster, then so be it.

"Do you recall the jewelry thefts we discussed over dinner at the Little Lodge?" Sturgis asked.

"Of course," Sidney murmured, still attempting to watch the polo match.

"We'd like your help in putting a stop to them."

This succeeded in capturing his full attention as he first turned to look at Sturgis and Anderson, and then me. But I could offer him little direction, for I was just as surprised as he was. Of the many motives I'd considered for this meeting, the jewel thefts were not one of them.

"We're aware of your reputation, as well as the assistance you rendered His Excellency." Sturgis nodded at his colleague. "Anderson has even been in contact with Verity's former superior."

My stomach dipped as I turned to meet the undersecretary's gaze. I wondered if his long, beak-like nose was what made his stare seem so starkly probing, like he could see straight through my polished veneer to the truth.

"Smith-Cumming had rather high praise for you," Anderson stated in a tempered Scottish brogue, making it clear that it was C he'd spoken to. "Something that I understand is not easily given."

There was fortunately no need to respond to this. The Official Secrets Act forbade me from doing so even had I wanted to confirm this. In any case, my mind was still too absorbed with panic, wondering what exactly C had revealed to them. It would undoubtedly not have been much, as the chief reveled in secrecy. But the very fact that these men had discovered my connection to the Secret Intelligence Service and C had confirmed it made me want to utter several foul curse words.

Anderson turned to Sidney, who was now frowning. "And your war record speaks for itself. After all, you received the Victoria Cross."

Sidney ignored this gambit, instead focusing on the request itself. "I would think these jewel thefts would be a matter for the police."

"Aye," Anderson conceded, finishing his tea and setting it aside. "It should be. But I'm afraid the victims have proven rather uncooperative."

My husband and I shared a speaking look. This again! Our investigation on behalf of the lord lieutenant had been hampered by the same problem.

"Why?" Sidney queried. "Don't they trust the police?"

"I don't think it's so much that," Sturgis hedged, meaning that was exactly it. Or at least, *part* of the victims' motivation. "But rather that their insurance companies have convinced them not to."

I stiffened in confusion, my tea arrested before my mouth. "Why on earth would they do such a thing?"

"Because the insurers would rather hire a middleman to retrieve the jewelry by negotiating a cheaper price with either the thief directly or, more likely, the fence the thief sold the jewels to, than the value of the policy they would have to pay out to the owner," Anderson explained.

"So, if the policy is worth fifty thousand pounds, but the middleman can convince a fence to part with the jewelry for twenty-five thousand pounds, it saves the insurer twenty-five thousand pounds in the long run, if the police are unable to recover the jewels," Sidney clarified.

"Precisely." Anderson set his tea aside and sat back, lacing his long fingers together. "And let's be realistic. There are many cases in which the police never recover the jewels even if they do catch the thieves. So if a middleman can recover the jewelry, many insurers argue it's the soundest solution, for it returns stolen—sometimes sentimental—property to their customers and saves them money in the process." He spreads his hands. "It's unscrupulous, to be sure, and could be considered obstruction of justice, but it's a common practice all the same."

"Which is where you come in," Sturgis interjected, ignoring the polite applause that accompanied the end of the chukka. "We believe the victims will be more open and direct with you." Because we were one of them. That is, part of the upper classes. And we were not the police. "For certain their insurers will have no objection. Though the private investigators they hire as middlemen might." He paused, smoothing his fingers over his dark mustache. "Best to be circumspect."

As if we wouldn't be.

I bit back the thought, noting that he was speaking as if we'd already agreed. However, after the last inquiry we'd undertaken on behalf of a government official, I was not so easily swayed and decided to be blunt. "Why is this a concern for Dublin Castle?" When neither man answered, but rather returned my stare somewhat reluctantly, I pressed my point. "I mean, yes, burglary is terrible and illegal, but the theft of such expensive jewelry from people who are wealthy enough to afford it is hardly a life-or-death situation. And there are already enough of those to contend with in Ireland as it is. So why is the government concerned?"

I had a notion of the impetus behind their sudden interest, as I suspected did Sidney, but I wanted to hear it directly from their mouths.

Sturgis looked to Anderson, who nodded for him to continue. He cleared his throat, lowering his voice. "You may recall our discussion at dinner about certain . . . unscrupulous individuals who might be using the proceeds from such thefts to fund their activities."

He was, of course, speaking of the suggestion that the republicans were behind the thefts, having stumbled upon a scheme to help fund their rogue government.

A deep furrow formed between Sidney's eyes. "You honestly believe that's a possibility?"

Sturgis looked to his superior again, who answered for them. "I don't rightly know how probable this theory is, but given the stakes, I'm afraid it can't be overlooked."

It was as good an answer as we were likely to receive. At

least, it seemed Anderson was being frank with us. There *was* a possibility the rebels were behind the theft, and so it would be foolish to ignore it.

But that didn't mean we wanted to get involved. I could tell from Sidney's tight lips that he felt much the same.

"May we have a few days to consider?" I asked.

Sturgis's eyes widened in evident surprise, but Anderson accepted my answer more measuredly, even, dare I say, respecting my refusal not to be pressured into anything too hastily. "Of course," the undersecretary replied.

"And perhaps you might be willing to share the name of the police inspector in charge of the investigation so that we might confer with him before we make a decision?" If nothing else, it was the courteous thing to do.

"Detective Inspector Burrows," Anderson replied.

My gaze collided with Sidney's.

"I could write you a letter of introduction."

"Thank you," I demurred. "But we're already acquainted with DI Burrows."

"Then you needn't his direction."

I turned back to Anderson, suddenly quite certain he'd already known of our past association with Burrows. "No."

He nodded, at least not insulting my intelligence by pretending he wasn't aware that I'd realized the truth.

The matter concluded—for the moment at least—we allowed our attention to waver back toward the polo match. However, our earlier easiness had dissipated, so at the end of the next chukka, Sidney and I excused ourselves. He took my arm, guiding me across the lawn as I held my pale blue parasol aloft with the other.

"Burrows is going to be livid," I remarked.

Sidney's voice was grim. "And one can hardly blame him."

We'd met DI Burrows when we conferred with him on the inquiry Lord French had asked us to investigate. He was assigned to the G Division of the Dublin Metropolitan Police at

Great Brunswick Street. Most divisions of the DMP oversaw certain areas of the city, but G Division was considered their investigative division, much like the CID at Scotland Yard. Officers were assigned to one of three roles—criminal, political, or traffic control. It was those tasked with political duty who had run afoul of Collins and his Squad because of the intelligence work they'd done for the British. However, Burrows was assigned to the criminal investigation sector.

In that previous inquiry, he had been investigating an assault, but the family and witnesses had proven uncooperative, making it impossible for him to do his job properly. Now, it seemed, he was dealing with uncooperative victims of theft, which had to be equally frustrating. I couldn't help but think of the complaints I'd heard several times about the ineffectiveness of the DMP, and how they were all but in the pockets of the republicans. I wondered how much of that alleged ineffectiveness was actually the fault of the police and how much the fault of the citizens themselves?

"I suppose we'd better seek him out on Monday," I said with a sigh, unenthused by the idea of becoming embroiled with another investigation for Dublin Castle. But it was important to at least appear as if we were collaborating with the British government. I also couldn't deny that it would give us contact with certain officials that later might prove important if we ever did manage to compile enough evidence against Lord Ardmore.

Sidney seemed lost in quiet contemplation, but then surprised me. "Do you think it's actually possible the rebels are behind the thefts?"

"I don't know," I conceded. "Though I would have to say I find it doubtful." I frowned. "To tell you the truth, I'm rather surprised Sturgis gives it such credence."

"I suspect I know why."

I turned to him in question, finding his expression troubled.

"He told me this morning during our ride that there was a bit of an incident at the Castle yesterday evening."

I stopped walking, but Sidney urged me along.

"Nothing serious. But it clearly rattled him."

"What happened?"

"Apparently some of them were up late playing cards when the electricity gave out. Soon after, they heard three gunshots in the distance, and when the officer of the guard attempted to get on the telephone he couldn't. They feared that the lines had been cut and that the Castle was under attack, but it proved to be nothing but faulty equipment."

"And the gunshots?" I asked in concern.

"They never found out."

I turned forward, considering the matter as we navigated a narrow ditch. "Well, I suppose I would have been rattled, too."

"And it's not the first time it's happened," Sidney asserted. "About a fortnight ago, they heard shouting in Dame Street and then gunshots fired from the vicinity of Castle Gate. The troops took up positions with their rifles, thinking the Castle was under attack, but it eventually proved to be nothing as well."

I frowned in consideration as Sidney opened the door of his Pierce-Arrow for me and I slid inside. I waited until he'd rounded the roadster and joined me before I remarked, "Incidents like that would indeed prey on one's nerves."

He made no move to use the electric starter, instead sitting tensely with his hands on the driving wheel, staring out through the windscreen. From this vantage, we could see the far end of the polo field as the riders turned and spurred their steeds off in the opposite direction, but somehow, I knew that what he was seeing in his mind's eye was far different. He often got the same look upon his features when he was thinking back on the trenches and the hellscape of the war. It was an ever-shifting mixture of forlorn, angry, uneasy, and haunted. Though I knew he held good memories, too, mostly of friends and comradery, even though many of those friends were now gone.

"After my time at the front, I comprehend the type of strain the Crown Forces are under. Never knowing exactly when or where or how or even *if* the enemy will strike. You feel you have to stay vigilant, and yet remaining in a state of such prolonged alertness eventually shreds your nerves. Men get jumpy, their judgment suffers, and tempers fray." He released the driving wheel and turned to look at me. "Which is why maintaining discipline is so important."

"Yet, here, the officers aren't keeping it."

It was the complaint we heard most often, and the excuse the government touted out time and time again for why their forces were running amuck, lashing out in drunken sprees of violence.

Sidney's gaze dipped to his lap. "By letting discipline falter, they're not only failing the Irish populace but also our own men. For one day—sooner or later—those men will awaken to what they've done, what they've been allowed to do, and it will either poison them or make it even more difficult to live with themselves."

He started the engine, effectively ending the conversation, but his last remark had reminded me that many of the Crown Forces—the Black and Tans and now the arriving Auxiliaries—were veterans of the war. That many of them were already forced to live with the burdens of their time at the fronts, with the things they'd seen and heard and done. How much more were we blackening their souls by not holding them accountable, by allowing them, or even spurring them, to perpetuate the same horrors here that their enemy, the Huns, had committed in Belgium and France and elsewhere?

It was a sobering thought.

CHAPTER 6

"Why am I not surprised to hear from ye?" Detective Inspector Burrows had proclaimed with a sigh when I'd rung up the Great Brunswick Street Police Station on Monday morning. "Aye, I can meet ye. The usual place."

By this, I deduced he was worried someone might be listening in, and so he wished to rendezvous at Burgh Quay overlooking O'Connell Bridge.

The day was yet another warm one with thick clouds scuttling across the sky. It hadn't rained in over a week, and parts of the gutters had begun to reek with stagnant unmentionables. The River Liffey also had a stronger stench. One that, while not unpleasant, wasn't precisely agreeable either. However, its water sparkled and eddied, buoying the rowboats moored along the opposite quay as it flowed eastward toward the sea.

DI Burrows stood gazing out over the river, leaning his elbows against the cement embankment which divided the quay from the Liffey itself. He was a short man of about the age of sixty with a waxed mustache and a certain sartorial taste when it came to his three-piece suits. Today's selection was a herringbone pattern of burnt umber bordering almost on orange. I noted he seemed a trifle more haggard than the last time I'd seen him, and I could only surmise it was due to stress.

He turned to greet us affably enough, but with a reserve and watchfulness I'd come to realize was habitual for him. Or at least, it had become so during these difficult years. Sidney, for his part, was far more genial than the last time the pair had met, though Burrows seemed undecided whether this was a good thing or not.

"I don't imagine you want us to beat around the bush," I murmured as we turned to face the river. "So I shall come straight to the point. Dublin Castle has asked us to investigate the rash of recent jewel thefts. They said the victims have been uncooperative with the police but might be more receptive to us."

I'd expected Burrows to react with irritation if not outrage, but if anything, his expression seemed resigned. "Can't say I wasn't expectin' somethin' like this when ye telephoned. Though I'm surprised the request came from the Castle." He darted a look at us. "I'd heard ye riled a few people there with your last inquiry." A smile briefly quirked his lips, letting me know he'd enjoyed learning this.

"Yes, well, apparently, we've been forgiven for not toeing the line." I frowned. "Though I'm not certain how long that will last if once again our findings do not align with what they want to hear."

I looked up to find the inspector scrutinizing me more closely. "What would ye be needin' from me? The details of the investigation so far? There's not many."

"We understand the insurers are to blame for the victims being unwilling to assist the police," Sidney ventured. His trilby hat was pulled low over his forehead, to shield his eyes from the sun.

"That and the fact they don't trust us not to sell their information to the press," Burrows muttered dryly. "There is a certain class of citizen that believes we're all amenable to bribery." It was obvious this bothered him, though he tried to shrug it off.

"Seems to me like a practice that needs to be stopped," Sidney remarked with furrowed brow. "Don't they understand that at least some of these middlemen are probably in on it? That rather than deterring these thieves, they're merely encouraging them to continue."

"Aye, but the practice 'tisn't goin' to be changed here and now. Not unless it affects the Castle's ability to fight the rebels."

Like if the money the insurers paid the middlemen was going straight into the pockets of the republicans? Though Burrows didn't know it, a challenge might already be mounting, whether the IRA was proven to be behind the thefts or not.

"Based on what you *have* been able to glean from the victims and witnesses, how do you think this jewel thief is operating?" I asked as we watched a double-decker tram cross over O'Connell Bridge, which had the distinction of being wider than it was long. The last time I'd stood here with Burrows there had been a police barricade holding up traffic so that vehicles and pedestrians could be searched, but everything was running smoothly today.

"Whoever he is, he's clever and collected." Burrows gestured with his hand. "Take the Harringtons' soiree, for instance. He wandered upstairs while a hundred or more guests were milling about the rooms and garden below and, as cool as ye please, helped himself to what jewelry he could find."

"Including Mrs. Dalton's twenty-carat diamond necklace."

"Aye."

"Then, you don't think the thief climbed in through a window or gained access another way?" Sidney questioned.

"Why would he go to such trouble and risk, when, with the right set of clothes, he could merely blend in with the other guests?"

It was an intriguing prospect.

"After all, if ye were at such a party and saw a man lookin' respectable in his black evening kit, descendin' the stairs or comin' from a more private part of the house, what would ye think?" Burrow pressed.

"I would probably think he was just returning from the lavatory," I admitted.

"That, or a private tête-à-tête," Sidney added.

I turned to him in pursed-lip amusement.

"Precisely," Burrows continued, either oblivious to Sidney's scandalous implication or, more likely, choosing to ignore it. "He is just another guest. Why would he be up to no good?" I had to agree the theory had merit. Though I was also willing to go one step farther. "Perhaps he even *was* a guest."

Burrows's sense of wariness returned as he replied in his gentle Irish brogue, "I confess, the possibility did occur to me." He tapped the palm of his hand on the cement barrier. "I think . . . I think he—or *she*—was, as the Americans say, casin' the place. Inspectin' the jewels on display on every neck and wrist and finger, and selectin' who he should rob next. But then he heard Mrs. Dalton mention how she'd intended to wear her twenty-carat diamond necklace that evenin' but at the last minute had changed her mind. So he decided to take advantage of the opportunity presented to him, nipped upstairs, and pocketed the necklace and a few more trinkets."

"It's fiendish," I murmured, reluctantly impressed by the thief.

"Aye, but your lot doesn't always understand what ripe partridges for the pluckin' ye present to the criminal element," Burrows cautioned, almost in disapproval. "After all, a cursory glance at the society pages of any newspaper and its photographs will tell them who's who, and what they own, and where they'll be."

He was right. How often had Sidney and I appeared in those society pages with accounts of our comings and goings, and detailed descriptions of everything we were wearing, jewelry and all? This was not always by choice. More often than not the photographers took our pictures without asking permission. But other people sought out the celebrity of these mentions.

"What of the employees of all the homes burglarized, as well as any additional staff that might have been employed for the Harrisons' soiree?" Sidney queried, pulling his battered silver cigarette case from his pocket, a gift from me before he left for the war. "I take it you already ruled them out as there was no crossover."

"Aye." Burrows accepted the fag Sidney offered him. "They each might have had the opportunity for one of the thefts, but not the others." He spoke around the cigarette in his mouth as he lit it with a match pulled from a book in his pocket. "So, they'd have to be workin' as a larger team, and that seems unlikely." He exhaled a long stream of smoke. "Though one of 'em might have seen somethin' suspicious. I didn't have long to question 'em before I was ushered out the door."

"Were there any fingerprints?" I asked.

"Only from the owners and their staff. Which leads me to believe the thief wore gloves."

He'd said the thief was clever.

"Did Mrs. Harrington have a guest list for the party?"

"Wasn't given that either." His eyebrows were arched almost in scolding at the naivete of the question, and I recognized he had a point. If the Harringtons weren't cooperating fully with the police, then they certainly weren't going to hand over their guest list to cause further embarrassment to themselves.

I nodded in acknowledgment, considering the problem if we were to take on the investigation. After all, there was no guarantee Mrs. Harrington would share the guest list with us either.

The traffic behind us on Burgh Quay was as brisk as ever, with bicycles and carts and lorries whisking by along with bustling pedestrians, but none of them seemed to pay us any mind. Immediately opposite us, the buildings destroyed or damaged during the rebellion four years prior were still undergoing reconstruction and repairs, though little seemed to have changed since our arrival in Dublin three months prior. And so life, as it was, still carried on around their shell-battered façades and empty lots.

In many ways, this encapsulated the experience in Ireland. The revolution and reprisals raged on while the people of the isle persisted—shifting, adapting, and surviving as best they could. But then, even a cursory study of their long history revealed, even during the direst of times, that's what they'd always done. Find a way.

"I thought it was common for jewel thieves to break up their hauls as quickly as possible?" Sidney remarked, proving he knew more about the business than I did.

"The savvy ones do," Burrows replied. "They know hangin' on to the loot is the surest way to be caught. Better to remove the gems and sell 'em separately, even scatter 'em among a few trusted fences, who are usually jewelers or wholesalers who don't mind lookin' the other way. Then they either bust down the gold or pitch it in the river cause they know 'tis the part most likely to incriminate 'em. Which is why 'tis so difficult to catch 'em."

Sidney narrowed his eyes into the bright sun. "But wouldn't the middlemen need to recover the jewelry in one piece for their clients?"

"Sometimes the recovery of the gems is enough, for 'tis the most valuable part. But aye, that's supposed to be what they do." The men exchanged a speaking look.

"Which means . . ." Sidney didn't bother finishing his sentence, knowing Burrows was already aware.

"Aye. These middlemen are most likely in on the scheme somehow. 'Least if they're recoverin' intact pieces often enough."

Sidney's eyes briefly flitted to mine, telling me he was thinking the same thing I was. If these middlemen were involved, and if the thieves were, in fact, republicans funding their shadow government and revolution, then the middle-men were also.

Burrows put a crimp in this theory as he exhaled one final stream of smoke before pitching his cigarette into the river. "But as far as I know, none of the jewelry from this recent rash of thefts has been recovered."

"So we could be looking at an experienced thief," I supplied. "Or at least, someone who's done his research."

He straightened his coat, as if preparing to leave, but then offered one last parting comment. "If the thief was able to mingle undetected among a crowd of high society, then he might risk leavin' Dublin with his spoils, thinkin' no one will question his havin' it in the event he's searched."

"And take it where? London? Belfast?"

He shrugged. "'Tis merely an observation. After all, there would be less scrutiny elsewhere."

Especially in a place like Belfast, which had been in upheaval since June, with sporadic outbursts of violence. Word was it had been a veritable battleground the past few days, with the Catholic minority bearing the brunt of it. In fact, if someone appeared trying to sell the jewelry there, the fence was far more likely to attribute it to looting during the riots and burning of Catholic homes rather than a burglary in Dublin.

With this last remark, Burrows tipped his hat to us and then strode off in the direction of the Corn Exchange, dodging the swerving path of one bicyclist who hollered back his apologies. The inspector merely shook his head and carried onward.

"Are we taking the assignment, then?" Sidney asked, turning to face me with one elbow resting on the embankment. From his expression, I could tell he wasn't thrilled with the prospect.

I frowned downstream at the dome of the Custom House

revealed beyond the metal girders of the railroad bridge and the smaller Butt swing bridge. "To be honest," I murmured, "I'm not sure we should." My gaze shifted to meet his. "But what choice do we have?"

"We could simply say no."

I fastened him with an exasperated look. "Yes, I'm sure that will go over well, refusing the undersecretary and his assistant. Particularly given what they know about me."

This seemed to give Sidney pause. "You think Anderson will complain to C."

"He could."

I wasn't entirely certain what Anderson would do, or how C would react if Anderson did complain. All I knew was that we didn't need C taking a closer look at our activities here or questioning our loyalty. We were here to locate the phosgene and any proof of Lord Ardmore's guilt, true enough, but I knew our methods and rebel contacts would bear condemnation, especially as we hadn't reported them. Some might have even deemed the failure treasonous, specifically my failure to report Alec's defection.

I might be able to successfully argue that diverting our attention and resources from our main objective was risky; as experienced intelligence agents knew, the swiftest way to be caught was to have a hand in too many ventures. It made you sloppy and exposed you to too many risks. Focusing on one central objective was the safest way to remain undetected. But I strongly suspected that C or any other intelligence official would argue the same rules didn't apply. Not when we were the occupiers.

Sidney's hand clenched into a fist where it rested on the cement barrier and then released. "You're not officially an agent. They demobbed you at the end of the war," he reminded me in a measured voice, as everything I'd done on C's behalf since then had not been formally sanctioned. "You can walk away," he insisted.

"Can I?" I murmured wearily, for it didn't seem like it.

His resolve wavered, and I could tell that, as loath as he might be to admit it, he was no more certain of that than I was.

I smiled apologetically and then looped my arm through his, turning him away from the Liffey. "Come on. Let's stop in to see Finnegan. Perhaps there's been word from London."

There wasn't.

Though that didn't mean I'd given up hope that someone might turn up something that would lead us to the phosgene and we could confiscate it and leave the country before we had to give Anderson and Sturgis an answer. As it was, I was growing impatient and restless. If I'd thought bearding the lion or his cub in their den might yield any worthwhile intelligence, I would have screwed up my courage and gone straight to see Ardmore or Willoughby, but I feared at this point I risked giving up more than I gained.

Thus far, the rioting O had predicted had not occurred, but then, MacSwiney and the other hunger strikers were still alive. But it was anyone's guess how long they could survive without food, or whether either side would yield first.

CHAPTER 7

Though it had been more than three years since I'd had a lady's maid, I'd decided to take an interest in the maid-of-all-work we'd hired in Dublin and train her up in how to dress and style a lady. A prospect Ginny had agreed to eagerly. After all, lady's maids earned higher wages than housemaids and possessed a more elevated position among the staff.

This was how, late the following afternoon, I found myself standing before my wardrobe with Ginny, coaching her as she selected a gown for me to wear to dinner that evening. Helen Wyndham-Quin had sent a note earlier that day, begging us to come to dine at the Little Lodge again this evening. I gathered she was slightly intimidated by one of the other guests and wished for some friendly faces. At least, that was what her words conveyed. However, I also wondered if those guests were to include Sturgis and Anderson and if they intended to pressure us about our undertaking an investigation into the jewelry thefts. Regardless, Sidney and I accepted the invitation, refusing to hide.

I waited patiently as Ginny carefully scrutinized my gowns, a small furrow forming between her brows. She was a petite young woman with fair hair and features and a determined personality. "This one," she proclaimed in her musical Irish brogue, pulling a jade-green gown with a beaded bodice and drop waist from the wardrobe.

"I admit, this is one of my favorites," I told her. "But for a dinner party with a guest list that almost certainly will include a number of senior civil servants or other government officials, it might prove a bit too daring, even for my reputation." I smiled to soften the blow of my correction as I turned the gown to show her how deep the vee in the back extended.

Ginny's eyes widened before she swiftly made her second choice—a marigold-yellow crepe in a summery gauze. "How about this one?"

"Excellent," I said in approval. The color complimented my auburn hair, and the cut was flattering but more conventional than some of my other gowns.

I allowed her to hang it on the exterior of the wardrobe, while I crossed to the jewelry box on my dressing table. Opening it with a small key, I began rifling through the contents. "With that neckline, I don't think it needs a necklace. Just a flashy bracelet and a ring." I pulled the topaz-encrusted cuff I was looking for and its matching ring from the case.

"Not your rope of pearls?" Ginny questioned, appearing beside me before I'd realized she'd crossed the carpet.

A long rope of near flawless pearls was one of the most coveted pieces of jewelry a woman could own, and I happened to possess one. But after all the talk of a jewelry thief, I'd decided that perhaps it might be best not to be seen flaunting my best pieces. So I'd had Sidney place them in the small wall safe hidden behind a painting in the sitting room.

"Not tonight," I said simply.

Ginny accepted this without further comment, but I could tell she was curious, so I offered her a different explanation. One that would hopefully prove useful once she was ready to take the position of lady's maid in the future. "The role of jewelry is to accentuate the clothing and, even more importantly, the wearer. If it detracts or diverts or outshines the person wearing it, then its purpose is no longer to beautify but to adorn. And once you stray into adornment, it becomes far too easy for such things to become gaudy and gauche. That might serve for those American millionaires," I said with a grin. "But never among British or, I gather, Irish society." Ginny nodded, digesting this with interest as she scrutinized my features. "Then perhaps just a pair o' simple gold chandelier earrings." "Yes. That's the idea." "And for the shoes." She turned to look back at the wardrobe. "Somethin' flatter in case ye might tower over some of those topty-lofties from the Castle." "Well, I'm not so sure I'd go that far. After all, *I'm* not a diplomat's wife. If they want to take offense that I'm taller than they are, they can take it up with the fresh Yorkshire air."

Ginny smiled softly in amusement before asking a more personal question as I relocked the jewelry box. "Is . . . is that where ye grew up?"

"Yorkshire? Yes. It's in the north of England. Quite rural."

She hesitated a moment before venturing, "Me mam was born in County Tipperary."

"That's in the middle of the country, isn't it?" I asked, hoping to keep her talking. I knew she lived with her mother and perhaps some of her siblings, and that when I'd offered to add board to her wages so she could live here, she'd declined, saying, "Mam needs me at home." This had led me to speculate that perhaps her mother was ill, but there'd never been an opening for me to find out more.

In general, Ginny was very private about her life away from Upper Fitzwilliam Street. When she'd first begun working for us, I'd known this was because we were British and outsiders, and so she and Mrs. Boyle had been understandably guarded and mistrustful. I'd also suspected that at least one of them might be informing on us to the rebels, and so we'd had to take particular care to conceal our movements and our reasons for being there. But ever since I'd stormed the Castle, so to speak, to demand Nimble's release after he'd been arrested by a group of Black and Tan louts he'd been defending Ginny from, there had been a thawing in their relations with us. It may have also helped that I'd warned the inspector general of the RIC, in no uncertain terms, to keep his men away from my staff.

"Yeah," Ginny replied. "She didn't move to Dublin 'til she met me da." She reached up to fidget with her collar. It was a gesture I was familiar with, and I wondered if perhaps she had a crucifix hidden under her dress. Neither Sidney nor I took any issue with her Catholicism, but I knew there were many Anglo-Protestant families within Ireland who did. They would hire her but expect her to keep her Papish beliefs to herself.

"Now that Da is gone"—she surprised me by continuing—"she's talked about movin' back. 'Specially now the miracles 've happened in Templemore."

I'd read the accounts in the newspapers of these "miracles." Allegedly, soon after British soldiers attacked Templemore in reprisal for the IRA volunteers killing an RIC officer, a young farm laborer outside the village was visited by the Virgin Mary, who said she was troubled by the conflict in Ireland. After she departed, he claimed three statues in his home began to bleed. These statues were taken into Templemore, where a man who had been crippled for life was seen dancing in the streets after seeing them. Thereafter the town was inundated with pilgrims. One paper suggested as many as ten- or fifteen-thousand people per day were descending on the village seeking their own miracles. Others were more skeptical of the situation.

Sidney and I had overheard two men inside the Bank of Ireland lobby mocking the yokels for being naïve and uneducated enough to believe that the bleeding statues were real and not rigged and that they were a sign of divine intervention. They saw it as proof the Irish weren't fit to govern themselves.

"Though it has all had one positive effect," one of the men

had remarked. "The volunteers there haven't attacked any members of the RIC since."

"Someone needs to write Macready. If all it takes is a bleeding statue of the Virgin Mary to get them to lay down their arms, then pass them around to all the parishes," the other man jested. "We can squelch the shinners without another shot."

I was more inclined to believe the statues were a fabrication than an authentic miracle, but I also understood why some of the Irish wanted to believe in them. They were caught in a desperate place, besieged in many ways by both sides, with little control over their circumstances. How tempting, then, to believe that Providence was on their side. That if they but persevered, spiritual power would triumph over the enemy's worldly advantages.

The wretchedness of their situation did nothing but rouse my compassion, and so I said nothing of my opinions on the matter to Ginny. "Would you go with your mother?" I asked instead.

Ginny's gaze dipped to where her hands were clasped before her waist. "I . . . don't know. Dublin's the only home I've ever known."

I nodded. "It's a lot to think about." I wished I could pry further, to ask after her mother's health and whether there was anyone else she called family, but I could tell that Ginny was already on guard. If I pressed too hard, she might withdraw again.

Though I did feel a pulse of anxiety on Nimble's behalf. I knew he was sweet on the maid. It was true, I didn't know that anything resembling a romance had blossomed between them. I didn't know how one *could* when Nimble was bound to return to London with me and Sidney, but I resolved not to worry about it until it became necessary. But if Ginny moved to County Tipperary with her mother, that concern might arise sooner than I'd expected.

*   *   *

Helen was the first to greet us upon our arrival at the Little Lodge that evening. As the butler took Sidney's hat and my wrap, she came bustling out of the drawing room in a gown of orchid-pink silk trimmed with silver. "I'm so glad you could come," she exclaimed softly, as she reached for my hand. "I know it was such a last-minute request and you and Sidney must normally be inundated with invitations."

This was true enough in London, though less so in Dublin, and Sidney and I had become quite select in what invitations we accepted. Our focus was almost exclusively directed toward foiling Ardmore. As such, there were times when the soiree we would have most liked to attend was turned down in favor of one that might gain us an important contact or garner pertinent intelligence. Even tonight's last-minute decision to alter our plans had not been altogether altruistic. Not that I would ever admit as much.

"We're happy to be here," I replied instead, dancing around Helen's implied question.

Helen smiled gratefully, causing me a twinge of guilt at my duplicity. "Come," she said, lacing her arm through mine as she urged us toward the drawing room. "You know Dicky and Mark, of course. And I believe you're acquainted with Colonel Winter."

My gaze lifted to lock eyes with the man in question, barely restraining the curse that sprang to my lips at discovering his unwelcome presence.

Colonel Ormonde de l'Épée Winter had been appointed director of intelligence in Ireland and deputy advisor to the police by Basil Thomson, and Winter was very much a man in Thomson's mold. Kathleen Silvernickel had even warned me about Winter before we'd departed England, for he was a snake, plain and simple. He even slightly resembled one, with his pale skin, high forehead, receding hairline, sharp nose, and unctuous presence. Small and dapperly dressed, he'd adopted the affectation of using a monocle in one eye, an unsuccessful attempt to court C's favor, no doubt, for C also used a monocle. Just as Winter's adoption of "O" as his code name emulated C again.

O and I had already clashed once, and I had been avoiding him and our seemingly inevitable second clash ever since. I was hard-pressed to keep my aversion of him from showing. An aversion I extended to the man beside him as Helen made the introductions.

"But allow me to introduce you to a colleague of the colonel's, Mr. Frank Caulfield."

I extended my hand to the lanky fellow. "Delighted, I'm sure," I murmured, offering him a calculated smile as I tried to assess just how crucial a role he played to O. If he was here, then he must be important to his intelligence operations.

Caulfield's hand shook ever so slightly as he pressed my fingers with his long spindly digits. "Likewise."

His voice betrayed him as English, but not from Britain itself, but one of the colonies. I would have to hear more to take a stab at which one. Just as it would require more scrutiny to understand why his hand had been unsteady. Was it a medical condition or did something about the situation disconcert him? I cranked up the charm, twinkling at him as he shook Sidney's hand, attempting to gauge his reaction.

Unfortunately, O seemed determined to rankle me, his eyes glinting with a cold contempt that belied his false smile. "Ah, Mrs. Kent. How kind of you to save dear Mrs. Quin from the tedium of our dry masculine discourse. Now, the pair of you can happily indulge in your feminine chatter, trading the latest on-dits and comparing fashions."

Helen gave a strained, yet polite laugh, while I was trying to decide whether it was too early in the evening to skewer the man. In the end, I chose the better part of valor by allowing myself to be distracted by the gin rickey Dicky had prepared for me.

"Thank you, darling," I told him genuinely as we bussed each other's cheeks. From the humor lurking in the depths of his eyes, I could tell he'd been aware of my reaction to O's patronizing remark. "Keep 'em coming," I murmured so that only he could hear.

His shoulders shook with silent laughter.

"Now, now," Sturgis protested somewhat belatedly as he turned from greeting Sidney. "*I* want to hear all the latest on-dits. You know I practically *live* for a good piece of gossip," he emphasized, ever the peacemaker.

"Well, what of the hunger strikers?" Dicky proposed, after passing his wife a cocktail—something with a cherry floating on top. "I heard the lord chancellor of Ireland is scheming to get MacSwiney to stand trial again, this time before a committee of English judges, if he'll agree to go off strike. Though it's doubtful he'll agree. Probably because he knows the ruling will be the same if not harsher than his sentence from the court martial."

"He won't," Sturgis agreed. "Especially not now that the Church has announced that if the hunger strikers die, their deaths will be deemed sacrificial rather than suicidal. Damn them!" he muttered as an afterthought before tossing back the rest of his drink.

I eyed his rigid back as he stalked over to the sideboard to refill his glass. Obviously, the issue of the hunger strikers weighed on him more than he wished to let on. How could it not when there were dire predictions of violence erupting if the strikers died in custody, and equally dire predictions of outrage and unrest from the Crown Forces if they were released? It seemed Dublin Castle's only hope was that the republicans would realize their bluff had been called and order the strikers to eat. But given the Irish reverence for martyrs, this seemed unlikely.

"He won't die," O pronounced as he lit a cigarette and settled into one of the armchairs, crossing one leg over the other. "How can you be so certain?" Helen asked, taking the bait he'd laid with the quiet confidence of his statement. He exhaled, allowing smoke to emanate through his nostrils. "Because I have it on good authority that MacSwiney is being secretly fed." He flicked a bit of ash into the pewter dish at his elbow, before casting a coy glance over the assemblage. "Though perhaps not with the Dial's consent."

He pronounced it "dial" rather than "dayl," though it was clear that he meant the Dáil Éireann—the republican shadow government's parliament.

"At their meeting today, Griffith"—the acting president while de Valera was in America fundraising—"said he wouldn't be able to hold in the extremists within the party if MacSwiney dies. So clearly, he's unaware."

This statement was obviously meant to impress us. Not with its content, but rather with the fact that he already knew what had been said in today's meeting of the Dáil, which was forced to meet in secret because they'd been proscribed by the British government. This immediately raised my skepticism. Not because I wanted to believe O was incompetent. I knew perfectly well that he was capable. But rather because his own man seemed mildly surprised by this information. It was true that Mr. Caulfield might not be privy to every bit of intelligence that O was, but I still found the wary side-eye with which he observed O to be as indicative of deception as the calculation of O's statement itself.

Regardless, I was determined not to show my interest, instead meandering over to the landscape hung on the wall over the sideboard to pretend to study it as I sipped my gin rickey. That this would irritate O, I could only hope. Perhaps it would even provoke him to speak out of turn.

"What of your plans to photograph the entire population of Ireland?" Sturgis asked him.

"Oh, we're already seeing results," O declared. "And it's certainly put the wind up the shinners." He chuckled.

For good reason. I knew that many of them gave false names when they were arrested so that their past records wouldn't be attached to them. This enabled some of the most dangerous rebels to slip through British fingers on minor charges. That would be far more difficult to pull off if there were photographs to identify them.

I had to admit it was a sound plan. As long as it was carried off well.

"I hear reports that Collins is enraged," O continued, making my ears perk up. "Word is he's furious at the shinners' milk-and-water policy. Wants to set the gunmen loose." I heard the purse of his lips against the paper of his cigarette as he took in a long drag, and I could imagine the smoke seeping from his orifices as he continued to pontificate like a self-important old dragon. "I think it's because he knows it's only a matter of time before they're all caught. Their finances are running out and we're on to them. He's even grown a beard to try to throw us all off. It won't work."

I felt my brow crease in confusion but swiftly smoothed it, chary of anyone catching sight of my reflection in one of the surfaces in the room and realizing I was more invested in O's disclosures than it seemed. Truth be told, I wasn't certain how much of it to give credence to. From the intelligence I'd gathered, the Dáil Éireann's finances weren't in trouble. Yes, local governments, such as the Dublin Corporation, were struggling since they'd pledged their allegiance to the Dáil and the British had withdrawn their funding. In fact, there was some concern that Lord Ardmore was attempting to capitalize on this by stepping in with his own banks to fund and potentially control them. But for now the Dáil itself seemed secure.

As to the rest, I hadn't seen Collins in weeks, so I couldn't attest to his growing a beard or not, or his views on Sinn

Féin's policies. However, O's speech had the particular stench of so much hot air. Though, to be fair, his natural speech was also arrogant and boastful.

Footsteps alerted me to someone's approach, so I wandered toward the next painting. "Anderson told Boyd," Sturgis informed us as he paused near the sideboard, speaking of General Boyd, the commander of the Dublin District Special Branch, "that under no circumstances were they to lay a hand on Griffith and his lot." He cast me an almost apologetic smile though he couldn't quite hide his curiosity as to what I was doing over here. "But that they were to do all that they could to apprehend Collins."

"Because everyone knows Griffith and his ilk are the moderates within the party," Sidney chimed in to say rather indolently, I supposed taking his cue from me. I could almost hear the yawn in his voice as if he was bored with this conversation and lifted my glass to my lips to hide my amusement.

"Well, I don't know what Boyd has been doing," O derided, displaying his disdain for the head of army intelligence who his service was supposed to be cooperating with. "But *we're* already on Collins's track."

Sturgis's brown-eyed gaze met mine again as he finished pouring himself another glass of brandy. That he was also hearing the bluster in this claim was evident in the arch of his brows. "Really?"

"I daresay we'll have him sewed up in, oh, what do you say, Caulfield? A week?"

"That should do it, sir," Mr. Caulfield replied evenly.

CHAPTER 8

This was too much to feign to ignore and so I returned with Sturgis to the chairs and sofas where the others were clustered.

"And how, pray tell, have you finally managed that?" Dicky asked in astonishment, as if the feat had already been done.

"Sadly, in far too predictable a manner. A woman." O's gaze shifted to me as he said it, as if directing all his scorn at this female on me, and for a moment I feared that I was the actual woman to whom he was referring. But then reason asserted itself. I couldn't be. He was merely making his contempt for me known.

"Sturgis, you'll appreciate this," O continued. "For I intended to send a report to the undersecretary, one he would undoubtedly have showed you, about how we'd discovered that Collins is staying with a particular girl once a week regularly, but I simply couldn't bring myself to dictate such a thing to the chaste miss who takes shorthand for me." He shook his head in amusement as he stubbed out his cigarette. "I had to tell Anderson in person."

The men all chuckled. All save Sidney, bless him. But I felt my temper rile.

"The implication being he's bedding her?" I found myself asking in a perfectly reasonable voice.

Their mirth slowly died as they turned to look at me.

"Or do you merely know he *stays* there?" I continued with as much sangfroid as I could muster. "For I've heard he has many such places where he sleeps. That he never stays anywhere for longer than one or two nights." To avoid being apprehended.

O scoffed, turning to the others as if to coax them to laugh at me. "Do you not think Collins is capable of taking advantage of a pretty girl?"

"It's not Collins I'm worried about. I'm sure he can take care of himself. But this woman"—I shrugged one shoulder, downplaying my reaction, for I could feel Sidney's eyes on me, cautioning me to watch what I said—"well, it seems unfair to tarnish her as a whore if she's simply providing a bed."

"Collins is a fugitive, Verity," Sturgis reminded me, as if I'd forgotten.

"Oh, I'm aware. And I know you'll argue she should refuse him or turn him in, but does she really have a choice? Seems to me that if the Irish genuinely trusted us to protect them from retaliation, that there would be far more informants, and this war would already be over."

Though uttered in an offhanded tone as I took a drink, I'd used the word "war" quite deliberately, refusing to shy away from it. I might not be able to tell O and the other men off in the manner I wished, but I was damned if I was going to placate them with the delicate language they'd chosen to adopt to salve their consciences from the brutalness of reality. And I'd be damned if I stood by and said nothing after watching the women in Belgium who'd been forced to quarter and cater to the occupying Germans during the war later be classified by us and our allies as horizontal collaborators. Heartlessly tarred, tried, and condemned without an ounce of compassion for the impossibility of their situation. In this instance, the situation was slightly different, for the woman had undoubtedly willingly allowed Collins to stay at her residence, but the principle remained the same.

So Sidney could glare at me all he liked. On this, I would not be silent. Not when O and his ilk believed a female agent's greatest and only asset was the pillow talk she gathered after sleeping with a target. Something I had *never* done.

"She has a fair point," Dicky remarked with a glance at his wife, who appeared to at least be in partial agreement. Sturgis and Caulfield seemed interested as well—the latter, perhaps uncomfortably so. But I knew it was too much to hope that O would see merit in my assertions.

"Yes, but these Irish don't ascribe to the same sense of morality as we British do. 'Tis why they propagate like rabbits. Why, just look at the rampant amount of venereal disease amongst their population."

But I'd read the articles by Dr. Kathleen Lynn, Sinn Féin's joint director of public health, and I'd seen the pamphlets put out by the Committee for the Protection of Ireland from Venereal Disease formed my Cumann na mBan, the women's auxiliary to the IRA. They had been asking for urgent action since 1918 when demobilized soldiers started returning from the war, cautioning that they would bring a plague of syphilis and other venereal diseases with them. That it was the moral failing of the British, for whom the Irish men had gone to fight, that had infected those men, who were then returning home to infect their wives. It was viewed by many as a particularly odious and shameful demonstration of the Irish's continued subjugation to the British Empire.

"No, Mrs. Kent," O continued with a patronizing smirk. "I don't think you need to be concerned with this woman's virtue, or lack thereof. Not when they're not even concerned with it themselves."

Though tempted to snap a retort, I felt Sidney's hand glide across the small of my back as he made his way past me toward the sideboard, reminding me of the role I was meant to play. Turning toward him, I shook the ice in my glass.

"Another?" he murmured, his gaze quietly assessing me.

"Please," I replied demurely, letting him know I would behave myself despite the fury still burning in my veins.

"In any case, it's about to become much easier for citizens to inform on their neighbors without risk of exposure or retaliation," Mr. Caulfield chimed in to say cheerfully—his smile seeming at odds with his hooded eyes.

"Yes, yes," O interjected before anyone else could speak up, eyeing his cohort with disfavor, perhaps at having his thunder stolen. "You'll see the announcements in the newspapers soon enough asking citizens to send information by letter to the Scotland Yard."

The others seemed enthusiastic about this plan, but I wondered how many people would actually risk sending a letter to such an incriminating address all the way in London. The Irish knew how vulnerable the mail was to periodic raids by the IRA.

Dinner passed relatively peacefully, especially as Helen had broken protocol and seated me next to her, enabling us at times to ignore the men's discussion. Since Sidney was there, I needn't fear missing something important, so I allowed Helen to distract me with far more pleasant conversation.

After dinner, Helen suggested cards, but before a game could be decided, O began to show off the card tricks he knew, much to Sturgis's and Helen's delight. I had a brother who was fond of such sleights of hand, so I was less interested. Mr. Caulfield seemed equally unimpressed, perhaps having seen them all before. He stood near the French doors which were open to the garden, smoking a cigarette as he gazed out at the twilight-tinted hedges and flower beds.

It was a lovely evening with just a hint of a chill in the air. As I approached the doors, I could smell the night-blooming jasmine growing in planters along the terrace. Its perfume lent a lighter note to the musk of the Turkish tobacco in Caulfield's fags. He looked over at me as I paused on the opposite side of the doorway and then reached inside his coat to offer me his cigarette case. With a shake of my head, I politely declined, but did not speak. With O otherwise occupied, I was curious what Mr. Caulfield might reveal and if he would feel compelled to fill the silence between us.

For a time, we companionably stood listening to the gasps and laughter of the others and the sound of grasshoppers and crickets in the grasses. The sunlight hadn't yet entirely faded, and I could see beyond the hedges to the edge of the drive where it met the gate pillars. A pair of guards had paused there to confer for a moment during their usual rounds. It was a reminder that the civil servants and government officials with which we were fraternizing were constantly under threat.

"I hear that you and Mr. Kent are looking into the matter of this jewel thief," Mr. Caulfield drawled before inhaling another drag from his cigarette. His eyes cut sideways toward me, narrowing against the smoke.

"We're considering it," I replied noncommittally, unwilling to pledge myself to something before I was ready.

He nodded. "Your reticence is probably wise." His gaze dipped to my still flat abdomen, his eyes narrowing further. "Especially in your condition."

I suppressed the urge to blush, having wondered if and when O would refer to my alleged pregnancy. For him to do so earlier in front of everyone would have been an unforgiveable breach of etiquette, but having his cohort do so during a private discussion was a different matter.

Ignoring his pointed remark and all too obvious suspicions, I crossed my arms to conserve heat as a cool breeze brushed over my arms, raising goose bumps. "Then you know something of it?"

"I know that the thefts are almost certainly being perpetuated by the Volunteers, and these rebels are not a lot you want to tangle with." Witnessing his icy demeanor now, I

wondered if it had been nerves causing his earlier hand trem-
ors or a craving for a smoke.

"Why do *you* think it's the republicans?" I asked, wondering whether he had more solid evidence than merely the claim
they needed more funding.

"Who else?"

When I didn't respond, but continued to stare out at the
deepening shadows in the garden, he began gesturing with
his cigarette.

"I assure you, Mrs. Kent, revolutions are expensive to conduct. They must be in constant want of financing. And we
know they're capable of breaking and entering. Why, just a
few days ago they stole a number of papers from a safe at the
Flying Corps." He scoffed begrudgingly. "Even left a note behind taking credit. 'Many thanks, will call again.'" He shook
his head. "Cheeky bastards."

"They broke into the safe?" I asked, for that was no small
feat. Hopefully the papers inside hadn't contained anything
particularly sensitive, but if they were being kept in a safe in
the first place, they must have been important.

"Well, the safe was left unlocked," he said, backtracking.
"But the office was secured, and they still managed to jimmy
their way inside."

Though I thought I'd given no visible reaction, apparently
Mr. Caulfield saw something, for he hastened to continue his
argument. "The point is, they are more than capable." He
took one last drag from his cigarette before pitching it into
the darkness and looking at me pointedly. "And considering
all the funds they've recently lost, they're definitely in need
of more."

I watched as he strode over to join the group, wishing I
knew exactly what he'd meant by that last statement. We'd
discovered that O had been trying to get his hands on the
rebel Irish government's funds, which seemed to be deposited

among various banks under various different account holders' names, the better to conceal it and prevent it from being seized. Had O uncovered a stash of it and taken it?

Or did he only want me to think that was the case? What if *he* was somehow behind the jewel thefts?

Perhaps it was a bit of a stretch to entertain such a notion. But considering what we'd learned recently about soldiers and police officers in the Crown Forces falsely filing malicious injury claims—claims which were knowingly endorsed or overlooked by their officers because they were paid by the Irish people—it was an idea worth considering.

And one I raised with Sidney later that evening.

"I don't know, Ver," he hedged as I removed my earrings. "Just because the chap is an amoral bounder doesn't mean he's guilty of every crime that catches our notice."

I swiveled on the bench before the dressing table to glower at him.

"He got under your skin tonight, and you didn't do a good job of hiding it," he scolded.

"You cannot tell me you don't find that man and his opinions to be the most revolting pile of rubbish!"

"I've already admitted he's a right bastard." His eyebrows arched. "But you cannot give in to his goading, no matter how he tries you. If you start doing that, the game will be up, and we'll be lucky to escape with our lives."

I heaved an exasperated breath, turning back toward the table. "I know!"

"Not to mention the fact that if you start losing your temper with O, how do you expect to keep it with Ardmore?"

"I already said 'I know,' Sidney. There's no need to continue to pile on." I sat fuming, though the truth was, I was angrier at myself than Sidney. I'd known that I'd let O get under my skin. That I should have ignored his insufferable remarks about women. I didn't need Sidney to remind me of my error. I'd behaved more like a raw recruit than a seasoned agent.

"It's understandable," Sidney murmured, clearly trying to placate me. He propped his hip on the edge of the dressing table. "Why, I wanted to plant a fist squarely in his jaw several times, too."

"Yes, but you didn't." I yanked the cuff bracelet from my wrist and the matching ring from my finger, slapping them down on the wood.

"Verity, look at me." He grasped my shoulders. "Look at me."

I reluctantly lifted my gaze to meet his.

"So you made a mistake." A dark lock of his hair fell over his brow as he shrugged. "I've also made my share of them. Now, you've got to let it go and move on."

"That's easy enough to say but, in this sort of work, all it takes is one mistake, and it could cost us our lives," I argued, now irritated that he wasn't as furious at me as I was.

He shook his head. "You're not perfect, Ver."

"Obviously," I muttered dryly.

"Then why do you expect yourself to be?"

I looked up to find his eyebrows arched in challenge, conceding he had a point.

He lifted his hands from my shoulders. "Do me a favor? At least extend yourself the grace you would me, or Xavier, if one of us made an error."

I frowned at my hands where they rested against the oak table. They appeared as fragile and delicate as any gentlewoman's were supposed to be, but if I looked closely, I could see the scars hidden there. One from a piece of barbed wire that had nicked me while crossing the border between the Netherlands and Belgium. Another from a prickly bush along a roadside near Charleroi where I'd dived for cover to avoid an approaching patrol. And a third from the slip of a knife as I'd forced open a locked door at a hôtel de ville. Each scar was evidence of a mistake, a miscalculation, as were the others writ across my body. Knowing this, it was hard to forgive myself, especially knowing there were lives other than my own at stake.

"Besides, you and I, we're supposed to be a team," Sidney cajoled, leaning down to catch my eye. "Isn't that what you said? Stronger together. When necessary, making up for the other's lack." He spread his hands. "So tonight was my turn to do so."

He was right. We were supposed to be a team. And there had been times when I'd been forced to cover for his gaffes. It only made sense that he should return the favor.

I sighed, feeling my shoulders release some of their tension, and then nodded.

"Incidentally, O asked me about your condition."

I stiffened, realizing he meant my feigned pregnancy. "Candidly?" Or at least more candidly than Mr. Caulfield had queried me about it.

"Obliquely." Sidney's voice dipped with wryness. "Snidely."

Then O had also noticed I wasn't showing.

Sidney's mouth flattened. "I told him it was best not to mention it to you. That it's a . . . touchy subject."

I realized immediately what he'd meant to imply, and while it still made me uncomfortable to feign such a thing, I recognized it was the simplest solution to my predicament. Truthfully, we'd been fortunate my lie hadn't spread beyond the intelligence service and become a major liability.

"I see," I murmured. "Well, then . . . I suppose that's that."

Presumably O would share what Sidney had told him with the others who'd been told, and hopefully that would be the end of it.

I pushed to my feet, assuming that was the end of the discussion, but when Sidney didn't follow, I realized he had more to say.

Reaching for my hand, he drew me toward him, so that I stood between his legs. "And . . . my insinuation . . . may have inadvertently provided an excuse for your behavior."

I frowned in confusion.

He eyed me warily. "At least to O."

Irritation spiked within me. "I see. Evidence of the emotional, irrational female."

The brush that men had forever been tarring all the women within the intelligence service with, despite ample evidence to the contrary.

But there was no use in taking it out on my husband. Not when he was merely the messenger.

I draped my arms loosely around Sidney's broad shoulders. "I suppose I deserve it."

"No," he asserted, resting his hands around my waist. "O is still a bounder. But leave him to his ignorance if it works to our advantage."

I melted into him in agreement, resting my head against the warmth of his shoulder. I could feel the bristles of his facial hair along my temple as he tipped his head to press his lips to my hairline. If not for the sudden knock on the door, we might have stood that way for some time, drawing comfort from each other. But there was only one person who would rap on our bedchamber door at this hour, and Nimble wouldn't disturb us unless it was necessary.

I stepped away and Sidney straightened, calling out for his valet to enter.

"Apologies," Nimble said. "But I forgot this came for Mrs. Kent while ye were out."

I crossed the room to accept the paper he was holding out, fully expecting it to be another message from Mr. Finnegan. However, before I'd even touched it, I could tell it wasn't printed on the fine stationery he normally used. A glance at Nimble told me he'd noted the same thing.

"How was it delivered?" I asked, feeling the crude foolscap.

"Slipped into the letter slot."

Definitely not delivered by a courier with the Bank of Ireland then. "Thank you, Nimble," I told him in dismissal.

He bowed his head stiffly and then retreated, closing the door behind him.

I didn't waste time speculating about who it was from, for I already had an inkling.

The honor of your presence is requested tomorrow evening. Same time, same place. —M/X

"What is it?" Sidney asked, obviously responding to my annoyed frown. I passed him the missive, which took him all of a moment to peruse. His gaze returned to mine in query. "Xavier?"

"I presume the M stands for MacAlister." Alec's code name.

"And same time, same place?"

I crossed my arms over my chest, suddenly feeling uncertain and a trifle vulnerable. "More code. Though this one is less clear." After all, I'd met with Alec a number of times since my discovery that he was alive and well, and that he'd switched sides, despite how hard he'd tried to conceal all of that from me. However, only one of those meetings had taken place in the evening. The first. "But I suspect he means Devlin's." A pub off Rutland Square which was owned by a man who'd moved to Dublin from Scotland, of all places. He also happened to be a supporter of Michael Collins and the republicans and allowed them to use the place as needed.

Sidney stilled, apparently pondering the same thing I was. "Does that mean Collins will be there as well?"

"I don't know," I replied, realizing that was what most troubled me. After all, it was one thing to pledge neutrality and quite another to meet with the British government's enemy number one and not report it.

Alec was a different story. Despite his recent change of allegiance, I knew his years of faithfulness and fidelity to the British Crown were still ingrained in him, and so I trusted him not to go too far. I also trusted him not to unduly test me or Sidney. He knew that while we shared his disaffection with our government, at least in part, that if push came to shove, we were likely to side with the British.

But there could be no deceiving ourselves when it came to Collins. His duty and commitment were to the establishment of an Irish republic, and he had ordered the killing and maiming of soldiers, policemen, and officials to achieve those ends. We might empathize with his aims, might even accept the necessity of his methods—from a purely strategic standpoint—but we could not condone them. And so by the rule of law, we should have aided in his capture, even knowing it would likely cripple the Irish cause that we sympathized with.

If Collins intended to be present tomorrow evening, then it would prove to be both a strain to our consciences and also a test of our loyalties. Something I was quite sure the Big Fellow was aware of. Undoubtedly, he was also testing us. Alec had warned me Collins intended to recruit me and was not one to give up easily. There was no chance of that happening, but that wouldn't stop Collins from pressuring me and assessing my principles.

Sidney's jaw hardened as he muttered some rather choice words to describe Alec. I couldn't disagree, knowing my former colleague must be fully aware of the agitation this request would cause. My husband gestured toward the hearth with the paper, and I nodded, for it was always best to obliterate all evidence of such correspondence. After all, no hiding place was ever foolproof, no wording vague enough, no code unbreakable. The very possession of such correspondence was often enough to condemn not only yourself but others, as many of my fellow intelligence agents had found out to their detriment during the war.

I joined Sidney where he stood watching the paper char and curl, disintegrating before our eyes as the fire consumed it.

"I suppose we have to go," he said.

"Yes."

For Alec might have information about the phosgene. If so, it would prove a salve to our scruples. If we could find the cylinders, if we could stop Ardmore, we could return home, classifying our interaction with Collins as naught but a means to an end.

Unfortunately, war rarely laid itself out in such neat rows or allowed you to believe in such tidy fictions for long.

CHAPTER 9

Devlin's pub was as bustling the next evening as the last time I'd visited the establishment. Much like everywhere else in Dublin, citizens here were eager to squeeze in a few hours' pleasure after their shops and businesses had closed for the day and the first shift at factories had ended, before heading home to beat the midnight curfew imposed by the British.

The building was a rather nondescript four-story brick structure along Great Britain Street near the junction with Moore Lane, save for the two large glass windows and the sign which read "Devlin's". Inside, it appeared much like any other pub, with a long bar worn smooth from use, shiny brass fittings, and cozy wooden snugs. The air smelled of hops and malt, with underlying notes of fried onions and wood polish. As usual, Liam Devlin stood behind the bar, laughing and joking with his patrons in his deep, bluff voice.

Sidney and I had dressed with care, not wanting to draw attention to ourselves, but also uncertain we should don actual disguises, so we'd chosen a middle ground. My blouse and skirt weren't entirely uncharacteristic of Dearbhla Bell, the persona I'd adopted in order to blend in with the population as we'd searched for Alec, but they also weren't so worn and outdated as to be unsuitable to Verity Kent either. Meanwhile, Sidney had opted for one of his least fashionable suits and a flat cap rather than his traditional trilby.

Nerves fluttered in my stomach, but I ruthlessly suppressed them, knowing perfectly well that this was one instance where I could not show weakness or reticence. Not when we could be walking into a veritable lion's den.

If Devlin was aware of my real identity and that I'd previously played him for a fool, he gave no indication of it when our eyes met. However, he was obviously cognizant of my reason for being there. His head bobbed minutely in the direction of the door which led to a back room, and then he nodded upward, I supposed indicating we should take the stairs. I'd expected to find Collins and Alec in one of the snugs like the last time I'd seen them here, but apparently a bit more privacy was in order.

I didn't know if this was a good or bad thing, but one glimpse over my shoulder toward the snugs as we passed through the room revealed that several of Collins's IRA intelligence cohorts were peering over the partitions watching us. They made no move to follow, but I was still highly conscious of their presence and the possibility of an ambush.

When Mrs. Devlin met us at the top of the stairs with a warm smile, I felt some of my tension ease. Surely Collins wouldn't have wanted her there if he had nefarious plans for us, and I doubted she would have received us with such convincing delight if she'd been given any reason to think ill of us.

"Right through here," she coaxed in her lilting accent. "Can I take yer coats?"

I hesitated, not having anticipated the offer and uncertain whether I wished to give it up in case we needed to make a quick escape. Fortunately, it was chill enough that my polite refusal could be mistaken for nothing more than a desire to keep warm.

Though no more than a decade older than I was, she eyed me as a mother might her child, even being so bold as to lift her hand and press the back of it to my cheek. "You'll forgive me for sayin', but ye look a wee bit wan, dear. I suspect yer no' eatin' enough," she declared with a nod, confident in her diagnosis. "Not if Mick has ye runnin' to and fro like all the others. I'll fix ye somethin' to eat once yer finished." She eyed Sidney, including him in this offer. "There'll be a bed made up for ye as well, should ye need it."

Before we could decline either offer, she turned to lead us down a short corridor. After just a few steps, I stumbled to a stop upon peering into the open doorway to our right. The room was in absolute shambles. The curtain rod hung by one hook; the drapes looped over it trailing across the floor. The furniture more resembled kindling than tables and chairs, and a pile of Delph pottery had undoubtedly once been an ewer or basin.

I turned wide eyes to Mrs. Devlin, silently asking what had happened. If they'd been raided by the Crown Forces, I'd seen no indication of it below.

Her features softened into another maternal smile. "It eases his mind."

When she said nothing further, I realized she was referring to Collins. The Big Fellow had done this?

With that discovery, any sense of reassurance I'd derived from Mrs. Devlin's warm reception evaporated. For if Collins could demolish a room like this and the Devlins be so accepting of it, what *would* they object to?

I'd not heard of Collins himself physically using violence on others. Rather he gave the orders to the men under his command to threaten or kill a target. However, that didn't mean he wasn't capable of it. A man in his situation had to be prepared for such an eventuality at any moment.

As such, Sidney and I, in turn, had to be ready for anything when we walked through the door Mrs. Devlin indicated at the back of the building. Or as ready as it was possible to be. Near as I could tell, there would be no other exit but this one. Though from what I could sense of the layout of the building there should be a window which looked out on the alley where I'd confronted Alec and Collins some six weeks prior. If necessary, we might be able to jump out the window without incurring too great an injury and run for cover in the stables nearby or disappear within the warren of adjoining streets.

I exchanged a look with Sidney, each of us acknowledging we only had each other on whom we could rely. There was no guarantee Alec would intervene against Collins or his men. If things went awry, we had only each other to turn to, so we had to work together.

With this in mind, I took a bracing breath and lifted my hand to rap on the door. It was opened almost immediately by Alec, whose expression was maddeningly unreadable. He offered us neither a warning nor encouragement, but instead stepped aside, allowing us to enter.

The chamber wasn't large, but it boasted a sofa, a table, and two chairs, one of which was missing part of its back. Michael Collins sat on the sofa positioned against the window, his posture at ease. Tall and broad-shouldered, he possessed a dynamic presence. One that bristled and crackled in the air around him and might have turned intimidating or over-awing at times.

"Ah, Mrs. Kent," he declared, rising to his feet politely. "Good of ye to join us." He had such an emphatic way of moving that his thick brown hair jostled atop his head. Though unlike O's claim, he sported no beard, which strengthened my suspicions that everything the spymaster had alleged to have learned about his rival was so much hogwash. "And Mr. Kent," Collins added, offering Sidney his hand.

Both men were sizing the other up, for it was the first time they had met face-to-face. In terms of physicality, they were probably equally matched. Sidney was taller and possessed great strength and dexterity, but Collins boasted the sturdy frame and musculature of a brawler. I also didn't doubt he had somehow discovered the locations of Sidney's war injuries and would use that knowledge to his advantage. If an altercation broke out, it would no doubt come down to which side Alec favored, for while I could defend myself and I was certain I was more than a match for their wits, there was little hope of my prevailing over them in any physical confrontation.

Fortunately, this didn't appear to be Collins's intention. Not when he flashed Sidney a merry grin and gestured for us to have a seat before sinking back down on the horsehair sofa. I chose the opposite end while Sidney opted for the ladderback chair that still possessed a back, though the legs seemed a trifle wobbly.

"I know you've kept yer word, Mrs. Kent," Collins remarked in his musical Cork accent as he crossed one leg over the other and adjusted the coat of his brown tweed three-piece suit. "And I appreciate that."

I arched a single eyebrow at his choice of phrasing. This had hardly been done as a favor, after all. He'd given me no choice. His threats against Sidney had proven quite effective, as had my fear of what might happen to Alec if his treachery was exposed.

"Now," Collins continued. "MacAlister has some information he's after sharin' with ye that I'm sure you'll want to hear."

My gaze snapped to Alec, deciding he must be referring to the phosgene.

"But *first*," Collins stressed before flashing me a broad grin, "I've a request to make of ye."

A request? My second eyebrow joined the first in disbelief.

"Sure, I know," he said, both acknowledging and dismissing the audacity of his making a "request." "But 'tis one you've already received, so should be no hardship."

I turned to Sidney to discover he was frowning in confusion like I was.

"We want ye to find out who's behind the jewel thefts plaguing Dublin," Collins explained.

"It isn't you?" I countered as much in surprise as exasperation with the man.

"I know there are those at the Castle who have accused us of as much, includin' the Holy Terror." Which was what Collins and his men called O. "But no one in the IRA is behind it." His gaze hardened. "And before ye question me . . ."

As I had opened my mouth to do.

"Yeah, I would know about it."

This seemed to belie what he'd claimed when I'd told him he needed to order his men to stop assaulting and forcibly cutting the hair of women who were fraternizing with the enemy. He'd asserted then that he had less power over the IRA brigades than I believed; that he gave no orders directly to those men. I'd not believed he was accurately depicting his sway over the men then, and now I felt vindicated. However, I said nothing, knowing full well that it was best not to rile the man.

But that didn't stop me from questioning his motive.

"If that's true," I replied, earning a sharp warning glare from Alec, "why do you want us to investigate?" I looked at each of the men in turn as I strove to make my point. "I mean, you can't truly care what Dublin Castle is claiming about you." And I'd heard far more ridiculous things than this allegation that jewels were being stolen to finance the rebellion. "So why not just leave it at a denial of culpability? Why ask us to actually pursue the issue?"

Judging from the crease between his eyebrows, I could tell that Collins wasn't pleased I was probing the matter. He turned to Alec almost in accusation.

Alec shrugged. "I warned ye she wouldn't take the matter at face value."

Rather than argue, Collins's expression turned speculative. I fought the urge to squirm under his stare, surmising that he was contemplating again his determination to recruit me to his side.

Sidney seemed to sense something similar, for he spoke into the silence that had descended, redirecting Collins's attention. "You must think there's something to be gained from uncovering the truth."

Collins was slow to release my gaze. "For one, some of our allies have proved to be the thief's targets."

I was surprised by this revelation, for I'd not suspected any of the victims of being republican supporters but all rather staunch unionists.

"And second, it would be of benefit to the Castle to see us blamed. Not only are they losin' face over this issue with MacSwiney and the other hunger strikers, but they've not had much luck seizin' what finances we *do* have." He clearly relished this fact. "They'll be after anythin' that might give 'em greater leverage to raid a bank's records and accounts."

I was already aware of O's efforts to do just that, so I couldn't argue with this logic.

The commotion of what sounded like a loud cheer suddenly rose from the pub below before the voices faded again.

"Then, you think the government is behind these thefts?" I queried somewhat absently, half my focus being on listening for any more noises coming from the pub below. In particular, noises that might indicate the building was being raided by Crown Forces.

Collins shifted to peer through the window down at the alley below while Alec opened the door a crack to listen. After a moment, both of them seemed to be satisfied there was no cause for concern, returning to the conversation.

"Not necessarily. But we're familiar with Colonel Winter's propensity for more colorful schemes. Disguises and letter campaigns and such." Collins and Alec shared smirks. "And becomin' adept at findin' ways to counteract them."

I supposed he must be speaking of O's advertisements that

informants loyal to the Crown should write to Scotland Yard anonymously since contacting Dublin Castle was too conspicuous.

"I do believe the lads are enjoyin' this chance to inform on their loyalist neighbors," Alec said. "Not that they're likely to raid Macready or Hoppy or Captain King on some anonymous chap's word. But some of the letters might cause 'em to chase their tails for a time."

That was the plan, then. To flood Scotland Yard with false claims. I could only imagine Basil Thomson's reaction, particularly if the letters were naming such figures as General Macready, the commander of British military forces within Ireland. I wasn't familiar with either Hoppy or King, but made note of their names, for they were undoubtedly important if Alec was singling them out. Perhaps they were intelligence officers within Dublin Castle. Ones I'd yet to meet.

"So I wouldn't be discountin' the notion that Winter has added theft to his repertoire," Collins concluded, bringing us back around to the point.

I couldn't either. After all, I'd mentioned the possibility just the evening before to Sidney. Though, I had to concede, it still seemed improbable.

"At the least, their motive is as good as any they might attribute to us," Alec argued, evidently sensing Sidney's reticence.

"If what you say is true," Sidney began, eyeing both men closely, "if you're not involved, then what precisely do you need us for? Surely, with your contacts, you're more aware of the players that might be involved than we are. After all, this is your city."

This last statement sounded vaguely like a challenge. One that I wasn't certain Collins would take kindly to. Nor would he appreciate the possible insinuation that he should be familiar with any criminals that might have a hand in the matter. Collins met Sidney's defiant stare with one of his own, forcing me to turn to Alec with an imploring look, lest this devolve further.

"Of course, we've done our own sniffin' around," Alec retorted impatiently. "If it was as simple as locatin' the fence or second-story man, we wouldn't be askin' ye."

"Then you have some idea who the fences for such a job might be?" I asked, ignoring the self-satisfied glint in my husband's eye, who seemed to view this as confirmation of his veiled accusation.

"Sure," Alec admitted, speaking pointedly at Sidney even as he answered my question. "All ye need do is ask the reputable jewelers. They know which of their competitors aren't entirely on the up and up. And none of the fences admitted to handlin' the jewels from the robberies."

Hearing laughter from below, I shifted forward on my perch. "How can you be certain they're telling the truth?"

Alec turned to Collins.

"Let's just say, we're certain," the republican responded after a moment's careful consideration.

I wanted to press the matter, but seeing the gleam in Collins's eye—which was part menacing and part amused—I decided to take him at his word. "So where are the jewels?"

"Maybe the thief is after hangin' on to them. Maybe they were sent out of the country. Or maybe they're draped round the throats o' yer intelligence officers' mistresses. At this point, yer guess is as good as mine." Collins reached for the pack of cigarettes resting on the table at his elbow. "Which is why I want ye to find out." He placed a fag between his lips, speaking around it as he lit it. "Unless ye don't think yer up to the task." This taunting remark was made with a fleeting look toward Sidney, whose expression remained unchanged. Collins blew a stream of smoke into the air. "I'm sure I can find someone else who's more up to the mark."

I nearly rolled my eyes, for I was aware that one of Collins's greatest flaws was his insistence on baiting people, even

friends and allies. Alec had noted it in one of his reports before he'd gone silent and switched sides.

"No, you can't," I snapped, unwilling to play his game.
"For you need someone with connections within the Castle.
Someone who the victims will talk to. Which is why you
risked calling us here even though you know perfectly well
that we could be playing *you* for the fool."

This was perhaps too frank. But honestly, the man de-
served a taste of his own medicine.

"If you expect us to resolve this matter," I continued, ignoring his cold-eyed stare, "then I expect *you* to share anything
you learn about it that might have even a whiff of pertinence.
No halvers or prevarications," I warned before turning to
Alec, tired of this discussion when a more important matter
had already been hinted at. "Now, what's this information
we'll be interested to learn?"

Before Alec could respond, Collins muttered the Lord's
name in vain, an expression of emphasis I'd noticed many
Irishmen favored. ". . . Almighty! No wonder the pair of ye
are in love with her."

I scowled into his admiring gaze, fighting a blush. The
laughter in his eyes told me once again he was baiting. Or
rather setting the cat among the pigeons, for my history with
both men was complicated. Not only had I worked with Alec
periodically during the war when we were both stationed
behind enemy lines in Belgium, but I'd slept with him after helping him escape into the neutral Netherlands when his
position within the German Army was compromised. It had
happened just once, and it had occurred during the fifteen
months when I'd believed Sidney to be dead. A gambit he'd
taken in order to uncover a group of traitors. However, knowing and accepting the extenuating circumstances behind each
other's actions didn't make the emotions surrounding them
any easier to navigate, nor the awkwardness disappear.

Neither Alec nor Sidney commented on Collins's assertion, though they both frowned at him.

"I've uncovered two more locations where the phosgene may be kept," Alec told us as we straightened with interest. "I thought ye might wish to go with me to take a look."

"Now?" Sidney queried.

"'Tis as good a time as any," Alec confirmed.

But rather than push to my feet to join them, I turned to Collins, deciding to take advantage of his presence while I could. "You're still in contact with Lord Ardmore?"

He took another leisurely drag of his cigarette before answering. "Sure."

"But you don't trust him," I suggested, more in hopes that this was true than certainty of it. Alec had assured me that Collins was no simpleton. That he was aware that Ardmore was dangerous and almost certainly playing both sides.

In response, he stubbed out his cigarette before holding up his hand. "I only trust about the same number of people as I have fingers, Mrs. Kent." He paused, making me wait for him to continue. "And Ardmore isn't one of them."

I nodded, aware of the unspoken truth that went along with this. That Sidney and I weren't among them either.

"But ye should be aware," he added, halting me as I rose to my feet and began to turn to go. "He knows we're in contact."

A pulse of alarm moved through me.

"Believes we're in contact more often than we are, in fact, though I've neither confirmed nor denied." His gaze shifted to Alec. "Though I don't believe he's aware of MacAlister's true identity."

I supposed that was a small blessing. I narrowed my eyes. But if Ardmore was unaware of who Alec was, then I had to wonder how much Ardmore truly knew about my and Sidney's connection to Collins, since it came through Alec.

The Big Fellow nodded, as if reading my unspoken thought. "Ardmore is nothing if not a man of calculated risks. He makes calibrated guesses in hopes of convincin' people he knows more than he does. 'Tis a clever ploy and it often yields results, but not because he's omniscient, but rather because others are gullible."

I felt this was a rather keen insight, and corroborated many of my own observations of Ardmore, though I may have given him more credit than Collins did for the knowledge he did possess.

"He'll realize soon enough 'tis far harder to pull the wool over my eyes." He looked like he relished that prospect. "Dáil Éireann and the Dublin Corporation, as well." He pushed to his feet, taking a pocket watch from his waistcoat to check the time. "In the meantime, he has his uses."

CHAPTER 10

Devlin's pub was even busier as we passed through it to depart. People stood at and around the tables and bar, forcing us to inch our way through the crush. I caught sight of Tom Cullen, Liam Tobin, and several other of Collins's men still seated in one of the snugs with the door ajar. Tom raised his glass to me as our eyes met, and I noted that like last time its contents appeared to be lemonade. Despite the stereotype of Irishmen as drunkards and the rumors to the contrary, it seemed Collins was determined his intelligence unit keep their wits about them.

I elected not to respond to his greeting and was glad of it when I noticed a man in my peripheral vision watching me. Smartly dressed in a pin-striped suit, he made no effort to avoid my gaze, even being so bold as to smirk. The tan had long faded from his skin and the sun-bleached blond of his hair had darkened to almost a light brown. I refused to acknowledge him as well, not willing to give him the satisfaction of a reaction even though my stomach had dropped to the vicinity of my knees.

But once we were outside, I grasped hold of Sidney's arm to halt him. "Did you see Willoughby?"

"Where?" Sidney demanded as Alec turned to hear.

"Inside. At a table near the corner."

Sidney looked at Alec, whose jaw had hardened.

"Give me a moment."

We waited on the pavement, watching the door to be sure Willoughby didn't sneak past us.

When Alec rejoined us, his expression was grim. "Devlin's on it," was all he said before turning his steps to the east, leaving us to scramble to keep up.

"I thought you had someone following him?" I wanted to know.

"I did. Apparently, he gave him the slip. *Again*." A fact he was none too happy with. "Devlin'll warn the others and set another tail on him."

Hopefully this one would do a better job.

"Where are we going?" Sidney asked, darting a look behind us, presumably to see if *we* were being followed. We'd left his Pierce-Arrow at the town house, for it was much too conspicuous, and taken a tram to Devlin's. We were nearing the intersection of Great Britain and Sackville Streets where we might have hopped aboard another, but Alec veered away from the lines.

"The first place is near Amiens Street Station."

Which was quite a distance away on foot, especially considering full darkness had now fallen and we had about two hours until curfew and a second building to inspect. However, it appeared Alec had a different mode of transportation in mind.

Just outside of Dawson and Co. booksellers and stationers, a pair of lads stood with three bicycles at the ready. Understanding the advantages they provided in navigating a city like Dublin, I grasped hold of the smallest one's handlebars without delay. Soon we were pedaling across the width of Sackville Street and coasting past pedestrians, trams, and horse-drawn carts as we continued east. At Marlborough Street, Alec veered right, riding by the pubs, restaurants, and theaters bustling with business.

We were approaching the cathedral when suddenly Alec

slammed on his brakes, nearly causing me to crash into him, and Sidney into me. "What the devil, Xavier," he exclaimed, but then fell silent as he caught sight of the same thing we had under the dim glare of the streetlamps.

Up ahead near Talbot Street, a convoy of RIC tenders and lorries had drawn up and Black and Tans were clambering out, deploying up and down the street. We could hear the shouts of their officers and the clatter of equipment. Citizens had begun retreating back toward us, eager to escape before they were boxed in and subjected to whatever treatment the Crown Forces had in mind.

"I guess they were eager to begin their raids early tonight," Alec quipped through gritted teeth before darting a glance to the left. "This way," he ordered, navigating through the stream of pedestrians toward a narrow alley between buildings. "Stay close," he called over his shoulder once we were able to mount our bicycles again.

My eyesight could barely pierce the gloom that permeated the dank, close mews Alec led us through, but all I had to do was keep my gaze trained on the back tire of his bicycle. He called out a warning of any obstructions and did his best to veer around the fetid puddles. Even so, I was well aware that my garments were being splattered with unmentionable things.

We had just reached the crossroads with a larger thoroughfare, and I was about to suggest we rejoin it when a gunshot rang out somewhere in the distance to our right and behind us. Whether it was a warning shot meant to frighten or one fired with deadly intent, I didn't know, but I swallowed my appeal and followed Alec across the street and into another narrow lane.

We weren't the only ones navigating these close alleys, and our passage was met by a number of protests and curses, though most said nothing. It was the way of the world in this part of Dublin at present, I supposed. Everyone was trying to avoid the notice of the Black and Tans, to survive in a place where affordable housing was scarce, sanitation was abominable, and a stray bullet could end your life at any moment.

At some point we passed between the trestles elevating the railway Loop Line and veered right. Then about two hundred yards further on, Alec stopped.

"There." He pointed toward a squat building a short distance away. I would have still considered it a warehouse, but a far smaller one than the type we'd recently been searching. It boasted one rolling type door through which cargo could be unloaded, a narrower door for humans, and a few dingy windows near the roofline. Everything appeared shut tight, but that wouldn't stop us.

"Bolt cutter or lockpick?" I asked him, curious what supplies he had stored in the bag passed to him by the lads who'd brought us the bicycles.

"Let's try the lockpicks first. Best to leave as little trace of our presence as possible." He turned toward me as if I might argue, but I merely nodded, conceding to his logic.

"Have you a torch?" Sidney queried, his head lifting to indicate the lone streetlamp more than fifty feet from the warehouse door.

Alec rummaged in the bag slung over his shoulder for a moment and then passed a bulky electric torch to him. "Let's leave the bicycles at the side of the building out of sight from anyone passing along the street."

Doing as he directed, we stashed the bicycles and crept carefully around the corner of the building to the smaller door. By unspoken agreement, Sidney left the torch off until Alec pulled his set of lockpicks from his pocket.

"Shall I do the honors?" he murmured to me.

"If you can be quick about it," I replied shortly, conscious of our exposed position to anyone passing by with headlamps. The vicinity was all but deserted, but I could hear traffic passing along Talbot Street nearby, and who knew what route the Tans took while on patrol. I certainly hadn't made a study of the area.

Alec set to work on the lock while Sidney steadied the beam of the torch. Meanwhile, I stepped away so that my back was to them, the better to maintain my night vision as I kept watch. Other than the distant sounds of traffic and a far-off train whistle, I was surprised by how still the night was. Nothing moved through the shadows except a scrap of newspaper, tumbling and scuttling across the pavement, and the silhouette of a cat or some other small animal running along the edge of the circle of light cast by the streetlamp.

Though it had probably been less than two minutes, it seemed like over a quarter of an hour had passed before I heard the snick of the lock opening. I turned as Sidney stepped back and Alec replaced his picks in his pocket.

"Let's see what we have," he whispered, pulling the door open gingerly. No matter, it still groaned on its hinges like a beleaguered ghost, shattering the night's silence.

I flinched. "So much for stealth."

If anyone was inside, they knew we were coming. Fortunately, there didn't appear to be anyone around. Unfortunately, that was because the warehouse contained nothing but a bit of rubbish and a few metal rods. We searched the space for any places of concealment, but it rapidly became apparent that this was not the place Ardmore had stashed the phosgene cylinders.

"On to building number two," Alec muttered as we filed out the door.

He reset the lock and we set off on our bicycles again. This time headed south toward the river. We skirted the imposing edifice of the Custom House in the shadow of the elevated Loop Line as we made our way toward Butt Bridge. So far, we hadn't seen any soldiers or Black and Tans this far south, but we knew that the Crown Forces often targeted Dublin's bridges, halting the flow of traffic north and south over the Liffey.

Pedaling quickly, we reached the swing bridge, relieved to see that it was still open to street traffic and not closed so that a barge could pass along the river or barricaded by troops. However, a troop caravan could swoop in at any moment from Beggars Bush or Portobello or any of the dozen other barracks positioned around the edge of the city and we could find ourselves trapped in the middle of the bridge's expanse with a rather incriminating bag of tools. As such, we zipped along its length as speedily as we dared, our eyes trained on the quay at the opposite end.

Reaching the shore, I exhaled in relief, my legs burning from the effort. Alec turned left, coasting along the cobblestoned quays which lined the south side of the river.

"Another warehouse?" Sidney queried as the traffic grew sparser and we were able to ride three across.

"This one's more of a garage," Alec replied. "Not far from the Sailors Home and the Grand Canal Docks."

Struck by the tone of his voice, I turned to look at him, curious if he'd read anything into this fact. After all, the war had left many sailors injured and unable to work in their normal capacity. Could Ardmore have enlisted the aid of some of them, be it wittingly or not?

The area around the canal docks was mostly industrial, with large cranes, and great soaring smokestacks belching smoke and noxious odors into the sky. However, at this hour, it was even more deserted than the streets surrounding the warehouse north of the river. Regardless, none of us let our guard down, circling the block where the garage was located twice before approaching.

The trouble was that it directly abutted the road and the buildings next to it, and a streetlamp stood just a few feet from its door, leaving no way to conceal ourselves. So we elected to leave our bicycles inside the mouth of a dark alley half a block away before advancing on foot. Once there, we took up the same positions as before, though Sidney's torch was less needed.

Either Alec's skills had improved, or this lock was easier to pick, for we were inside within thirty seconds. A fact my nerves were grateful for, even if the effort once again proved to be fruitless. The garage housed a lorry and the tools of a mechanic, but no cylinders of phosgene or anything that might conceal them.

"Blast!" Sidney exclaimed as he replaced the tarp draped over the contents in the back of the lorry, speaking for us all.

I'd been puzzling over the necessity for so many small animal cages, when Alec leaned over to suggest, "Must be a vermin exterminator."

"You mean. . . ?"

"A rat catcher."

I struggled not to react, not being particularly fond of the nasty little rodents. I knew Sidney wasn't either, for they'd had to contend with them in the trenches. Not that he'd told me, but I'd heard the horror stories from others. How some of them were as big as cats from gorging on the remains in No Man's Land.

Sidney didn't even bother to hide his disgust. Or perhaps it was directed at our failure to find the phosgene. "Let's go," he stated, retreating toward the door.

But once outside, I spotted movement down the street to the right while Alec reset the lock. I pressed a hand to both men's arms, silently alerting them, and then nodded in the direction of concern when they turned to look at me.

"You both go," Alec said in a low voice. "I'll follow."

I understood what he meant. Sidney and I were supposed to put on a show, to act normal. Perhaps like a young couple out for a stroll. Accordingly, I threaded my arm through his, leaning toward him dotingly as we set off down the block. A few moments later I heard Alec follow.

As we neared the mouth of the alley, I risked a glimpse over my shoulder but could see no one pursuing us through the gloom. Though that didn't mean they weren't there. Or maybe I was jumping at shadows, contemplations of giant rats making me paranoid. Regardless, we grabbed our bicycles and pedaled furiously in the opposite direction, circling back around toward the south and the busier thoroughfares near Westland Row Station.

After passing beneath the massive arch over Cumberland Street upholding the railway tracks leaving the station, we stopped outside the rear entrance to St. Andrew's Church. The buildings lining this avenue were somewhat shabby and run-down, the address being undesirable for a number of reasons, particularly the noise and stench of the trains. It was not the sort of place I would want to linger long, but for the moment it was deserted, and it served our purposes.

"I'll see what other potential locations I can scrounge up," Alec said, panting lightly from our exertions. His countenance was tight with a frustration I echoed. "Though I'm running out of ideas. I take it C and the lovely Miss Silvernickel haven't passed along any other possibilities."

"I'm afraid not." I frowned. "But I'm past due for a report. Perhaps tomorrow." In intelligence work, much of the time it seemed one was living in a state of perpetual hope. Hope of uncovering the information you sought. Hope that you would pass undetected. Hope that you would make it home unscathed.

He nodded, narrowing his eyes in the direction we'd come. I could tell there was more he wished to say, but he seemed reluctant to do so. "Maybe . . . maybe we need to look into whether Rockham or Ryde have properties in Dublin. Or rather, used to."

I now understood his reticence. The late lords Rockham and Ryde had been allies in Lord Ardmore's plans, albeit ones that appeared to have been kept in the dark as to the specifics of his schemes. The fact that they were both dead—killed by the machinations of Ardmore—made it difficult to know exactly how much they'd been cognizant of and how much they'd been duped. For the sake of Max, we pretended that his father was more guilty of naivete and foolishness in trusting Ardmore than willful treachery. But neither precluded the possibility that the late Lord Ryde or Rockham had, either wittingly or not, given Ardmore access to their property here. In fact, it would be entirely in keeping with Ardmore's normal mode of operation, always thinking three steps ahead to obscure his culpability.

"Yes," I agreed. "You're right. We should."

His face registered surprise at my easy agreement, but there was no more time for false resistance or lying to ourselves. Not if we were to foil Ardmore before it was too late.

"I'll write to Max." I only hoped he would see the matter the same way. "And I'll send a letter to Rockham's heir and his ex-wife as well. Perhaps Calliope knows something."

Rockham's first wife, an American heiress whom he'd divorced in order to wed his mistress, had recently remarried. But Calliope had spent twenty years wed to Rockham and probably knew more of her late husband's secrets than anyone. I also presumed her business-savvy millionaire father had insisted upon a full investigation into his future son-in-law's holdings and assets before he allowed his daughter to marry him and handed over her dowry. Any reports generated from such an inspection would come in handy, especially if the properties her son inherited differed from those the late Lord Rockham had entered their marriage with.

"Really we should have thought of this sooner," Sidney remarked. His voice was taut with impatience as he glared down at the handlebars of his bicycle. An impatience I could empathize with.

"The important thing is we've thought of it now," I stated firmly. "And we need to think along similar lines in the future."

Sidney seemed irritated by this observation. I supposed it was an obvious one. But before he could issue a snappy retort, we were distracted by a loud noise coming from the end of the street.

At first, I thought it might be a train, but then I realized it was instead a military convoy. Engines revving, vehicle after vehicle sped past—lorries and tenders bristling with Crown Forces, searchlights, and even an armored car fitted with a turret gun—all bound westward along Great Brunswick Street, deeper into the city.

Standing as we were in the shadow of the arch, they wouldn't have been able to see us, but I felt myself shrinking deeper into myself, anxious not to be spotted. Where, during the war, the sight of our boys speeding through the Belgian or French countryside would have roused elation and relief within me, now I only felt dread. Even dressed in my glad rags and out on the town as Verity Kent, social darling, a sense of wariness sat heavy in my chest. For this was Dublin, not a shelled countryside overrun by Germans. The people they were policing with such battle gear were not foreign combatants, but British citizens. And for all that most of these soldiers were good-hearted souls, weary of the work, all it took was one bad apple to spoil the bushel.

"It must be nearly curfew," I murmured, lest someone overhear us in the dark. We were still blocks away from our town house, though that was through the relatively safer streets of the southeastern part of the city, and Sidney and I, at least, had our curfew passes should we be stopped. Alec did not, and he had the far more fraught route back into the heart of the city and across the River Liffey.

I had not planned on ever inviting any of the rebels, including Alec, into our home. That seemed a step too far and too precarious to our determined neutrality. But knowing the gauntlet Alec must now run to reach shelter, I found myself torn.

"Where will you go?" I asked. "Surely the river is blocked by now."

As if realizing what I was on the verge of offering, Sidney straightened and turned to me, clearly trying to catch my eye, but I avoided it.

However, Alec was not blind nor oblivious. "Have no fear, Kent," he told Sidney before addressing my question. "There's always somewhere nearby. I don't just sleep at Devlin's, you know. In fact, tonight might not be the best night to stay there if Willoughby's been sniffin' about."

I remembered then that Alec had no real home. Like Collins, he moved from place to place, ever wary of the authorities, attempting to evade capture. I knew how exhausting this must be. After all, I'd rarely slept in the same place more than two nights in a row when I was inside German-occupied Belgium, always hiding and trying to remain undetected by the enemy. It wore down the soul. But it was far more dangerous to be predictable and easily found.

Recalling O's comments about Collins's routine and one of the women he regularly stayed with, I found myself issuing Alec a soft-spoken warning. "You'd be well served to vary your schedule for a time."

How much he comprehended of what I was saying, he didn't indicate, but I could tell from his quiet scrutiny and the simple bob of his head that he would take my advice. Just as I could tell from Sidney's own bristling silence that he didn't entirely approve of my issuing this warning.

I turned to mount my bicycle, but then paused, realizing this was not my property. I looked to Alec for direction.

"Leave 'em behind the apothecary shop on Lower Baggot," he said.

In my mind, this raised more questions than it answered, but I knew better than to voice them.

"Come along, Ver," Sidney urged, and I obeyed, conscious of the time slipping away. Knowing we'd set out on foot in our pseudo-disguises, Nimble would no doubt be pacing the floor by now, and I didn't want him to worry. Alec could take care of himself. Or so I hoped.

CHAPTER 11

"Well, that was an utter waste of time," I grumbled as Sidney slammed the door of his Pierce-Arrow. Pasting on a fake smile, I lifted my hand in farewell to Mrs. Maude who had come out to Belgarde Castle's courtyard to see us off, her small dog clutched under her arm. As soon as the motorcar pulled through the gates, I dropped all pretense with a grunt. My husband cast me a sidelong look as he maneuvered down the drive. "Come now. You didn't actually expect the Maudes to be forthcoming."

"I knew they certainly weren't the allies Collins mentioned." For Anthony Maude was a rather staunch Tory and a unionist. We'd had to sit through a number of his rants against the rebel republicans during their house party a few weeks past. What's more, he was good friends with Lord Ardmore—a rather black mark against him. "However, I thought when we mentioned Dublin Castle had asked us to investigate, they might prove more cooperative about their stolen jewels."

"Apparently, they have more trust in their insurance company," Sidney muttered dryly.

"Or Anthony Maude does. For a moment, I thought Mrs. Maude was going to give me the guest list from her dinner party two evenings prior to the theft." I turned to look out the window. "Housekeeper misplaced it, my foot. She forgets

I've met the woman. She knows every square inch of that castle down to the smallest cubbyhole. Had we been able to speak with her, I bet we would have discovered she'd already interviewed the rest of the staff and could concisely share with us any pertinent details she'd gleaned from them."

I heaved an aggravated sigh, rubbing my temples between my thumb and forefinger. As exasperating as it was, there was nothing we could do short of lying in wait for the house-keeper to leave Belgarde, or sending a note via another staff member and hoping she would disregard her loyalty to her employer and meet us. Both seemed too much like skulldug-gery and far beneath our dignity, especially when there was no guarantee she had anything useful to impart.

"On to the Harringtons, then?" Sidney asked, pointing the motorcar back toward Dublin.

"Yes," I responded, aware that they were the jewel theft victims he had wanted to begin our interviews with in the first place. I had been the one to insist we question them in order of the burglaries, so I had no one to blame but myself for wasting our time by driving out to Belgarde.

We hurtled silently through the rain-soaked countryside with nothing but the revving of the engine and the flick of the windscreen wipers to accompany us. There were about half a dozen pressing issues occupying our thoughts that we might have discussed, but like me, Sidney seemed cognizant there was really nothing to say. Not until we'd gathered more information.

There'd been no word from Alec since we'd parted ways the previous night, but then I'd not truly expected there to be. If he'd been detained, we'd no doubt hear about it from Col-lins soon enough. Otherwise, we should assume he was well.

As for the queries about Lord Rockham's and Lord Ryde's holdings, I'd written the missives before retiring, and Nimble had taken the letters for Max and Calliope to the post office this morning, as well as my latest report for C to be dropped off for Finnegan at the closest branch of the Bank of Ireland. He'd returned with a letter from Etta.

Eager to find out if Max had located his father's proof against Ardmore hidden away at the British Museum as he hoped, I'd skipped over Etta's note to read Max's enclosed page. It was brief and to the point.

No luck.

They were but two simple words, but I knew they contained a world of disappointment, frustration, agony, and grief. I knew it because I felt those emotions in miniature, as well as a healthy dose of fury at Max's father for putting him in this position. For falling in with Lord Ardmore and his treasonous schemes in the first place, and then for leaving such a mess for his son to clean up. I knew, of course, that the late Lord Ryde hadn't chosen to die, but I was still angry at his passing anyway. At the manner in which he'd left things and the obscurity of his clues. What good was his concealing the proof from Ardmore if the people who needed it to expose him couldn't find it either?

We needed to find that evidence and we needed to stop Ardmore as much for Max's sake as any other reason. It weighed too heavily upon him and I feared my dear friend might never sufficiently recover.

Etta's note only substantiated this when she warned that Max had the blue devils, and she'd feared it might drive him to drink. I'd only seen Max corked once. In Etta's dressing room at Grafton Galleries, in fact, after she'd rescued him from the clutches of a scheming debutante eager to land herself an earl. Then, as now, his father had been the reason for his drinking.

Being so far away, I felt a sense of futility at not being there in London to help him. Particularly when we couldn't even find the blasted phosgene cylinders. I knew Etta would do what she could, but she couldn't be there always. I would have to write to his sister. Max wouldn't thank me for it, but I would rather suffer his ire than mourn if some sort of calamity befell him.

After resisting the need to investigate these jewel thefts for almost a week, I'd expected Sidney to insist on more of a discussion over the matter, but he'd been the one to emerge from the bath this morning to suggest we speak with each of the victims. I supposed he'd also recognized we really had no choice since everyone seemed to think we'd already agreed to it. I'd conceded it was as good a use of our time as anything, given we were left waiting yet again, hoping one of our cohorts would write to us or that we might happen to ask the right person the right question that would enable us to stumble upon the information we needed.

However, I found myself feeling rather ambivalent about the jewel thefts, in general. After all, no one had been hurt, and the people who had been burglarized had insurance to cover their losses. Even Dublin Castle's desire to see the republicans blamed and Collins's suspicion that it might be a ploy by O and British Intelligence seemed predictable. Truth be told, the entire affair seemed rather like a nonstarter.

Or maybe that was just my lack of sleep talking. It had been some weeks since I'd had a proper rest. I often lay awake staring up at the bed canopy or listening to the sounds in the street below, anxious not to hear anything that might resemble a military convoy or hint of an impending raid. When I did manage to drift off, I was often awakened by the tiniest of noises, be it rain drops on the window or the distant shriek of a ship whistle.

My sleep deprivation was beginning to show in other ways as well. Such as the mild headache I'd been fighting for days, which had now worsened to a throbbing behind my eyes. I considered telling Sidney to forget the Harringtons and take me home, but when I looked up, I realized we were just a few blocks from their home in Rathmines at the southern edge of Dublin. Determined to ignore the pain, I sat taller in my seat and straightened my appearance.

When we were swiftly shown into the drawing room, I felt rather more encouraged than I had at the Maudes', especially when Mrs. Harrington rose to her feet with a smile.

"Helen told me you would be calling," she said with a graceful gesture toward her butler, no doubt signaling for tea.

"Did she?" I replied, stifling a pulse of annoyance that Helen Wyndham-Quin had presumed as much, though I knew such a feeling was worthless when I should be grateful she'd paved the way for our reception.

"Yes, and I know it's at the behest of the Castle." Mrs. Harrington's gaze seemed more penetrating than necessary, and I found myself wondering if this was because she knew our inquiry was at the behest of Michael Collins as well. Were the Harringtons the allies he'd spoken of? Without knowing for certain, we would have to tread cautiously.

"Does that mean you'll cooperate?" Sidney asked playfully, pouring on the charm.

Color crested Mrs. Harrington's cheeks as she gave a soft laugh. "I shall try."

As we were seated, I took a moment to observe our hostess and our surroundings. Claudia Harrington was tall and slim, and her dress and mannerisms were like many of the wealthy Anglo-Protestant class, with one key difference. She seemed to have an affinity for avant-garde art and design. There were just touches of it evident in some of the paintings, the wallpaper in the entry, her choice in earrings. Not enough to upset the stodgy, classicist society in which she lived, but it gave her a sense of style and modernism that many others lacked. If this had been purely a social call, I would have asked her about it, specifically the Metzinger painting hanging in the corner near the bookcase. But it wasn't. A fact Mrs. Harrington reminded me of as she settled onto her crisp white settee—a bold choice.

"Helen said you believe the rebels might be behind these thefts?" She leaned forward to ask, her voice pitched so that it didn't entirely hide the scandalous excitement this caused her.

I exchanged a look with Sidney. "We think it's too early to make such a determination. But we do wonder if, whatever their motives, the thief somehow contrived to blend in with the guests at your daughter's engagement party."

I'd opted to phrase this suspicion with care, not mentioning that we wondered if the thief had actually been *invited* to the soiree, lest she balk at providing us further information.

Mrs. Harrington pressed a shocked hand to her chest, displaying a rather ostentatious flower ring—one the thief evidently didn't make off with. "Truly? How dreadful."

"Did you greet your guests as they arrived?" Sidney asked. "Did you know everyone?"

"Yes, for a time. But there were, naturally, late arrivals, as there always are." She blinked rapidly. "Oh, but we didn't know everyone. Some of the guests were invited at the behest of the Daltons. Friends of their family, some of Robby's army chums, people like that. Though, none of the people I met *seemed* untrustworthy to me."

"It's doubtful the thief would have seemed out of place," I told her. "Not if he—or she—was as experienced as we suspect. And you weren't *looking* for someone who might have nefarious intent. It does make a difference."

DI Burrows was right. It was the perfect setup for such an opportunistic thief. Since none of the hosts knew everyone who'd been invited, the thief could safely presume he might pass unnoticed, assumed to be a guest of the other family. As long as he arrived late and didn't draw undue attention to himself, he could mingle among the crowd, eyeing the jewelry on display and gathering information as he waited for an opportunity to slip away. Even better if he actually *was* on the guest list.

"Oh, and *that woman* implied that it was our fault. That *we'd* drawn in the rabble," Mrs. Harrington fumed. I assumed by "that woman" she meant Mrs. Dalton, whose twenty-carat diamond necklace had been stolen. "Well, it could just as easily have been *them.*"

"Very true," I conceded, uninterested in being drawn into their squabble. "Then, we've already established that you didn't see anyone who seemed out of place, but did you notice anyone behaving oddly or perhaps coming from a room where he or she shouldn't be?"

She appeared to search her memory and then shook her head. "No. Nothing like that."

"Might we be allowed to ask your staff the same questions?" Sidney coaxed. "Perhaps one of them noted something. After all, their job was to pay attention to the guests and anticipate any of their needs."

"Yes, of course. Though . . ." She frowned. "I would have hoped they would have already spoken up if they'd noticed anything questionable."

"Perhaps they didn't realize it was questionable," I interjected. "After all, if the thief appeared like any other guest, they might not have recognized the situation was off. Not if they were expecting the thief to be dressed all in black and wearing a mask."

"True," she said after consideration, and then she nodded. "Yes, you may question them."

"And the other guests?" I prodded gently. "One of them might have seen something as well. A person coming down the stairs at a peculiar time or acting strangely. Would you be willing to share the guest list?"

"If you think it's necessary," she hedged.

"We do," Sidney assured her. "We'll be discreet."

My husband's masculine confidence seemed to do the trick, for when her butler returned with tea, she directed him to have her social secretary make us a copy. This was completed with an efficiency I couldn't help but admire, as was the roundup of the staff. About a dozen maids, footmen, and groundsmen lined up in the black-and-white tiled entrance hall. Everyone but the kitchen staff, who had never left the servants' domain during the party and presumably would have already reported someone out of place there. Truth be told, I would have preferred to question the staff without their mistress looking on, but we could hardly object now.

Sidney succinctly explained our intent, but no one seemed able to recall anything out of the ordinary about the evening. No one but an upstairs maid, that is, who'd been enlisted to act as a server.

"There was one gent," she disclosed hesitantly in a lilting Irish accent. "He was comin' up the stairs when I was goin' down. Mrs. Dalton had sent me to fetch her shawl," she told the housekeeper. "He said he was lookin' for the closet." A polite euphemism for the lavatory. "So I directed him back down the stairs to it, and that's the last I saw of 'im." She glanced anxiously back and forth between the housekeeper, Mrs. Harrington, and me and Sidney. "I didn't think anything of it. He was dressed to the nines, he was, and spoke just like Mr. Harrington. Thanked me and everything. For sure he didn't look nothin' like no thief!"

"You've done nothing wrong," I reassured her. "For all we know, he might have been exactly as he appeared. But for the sake of thoroughness, can you give us any details about his appearance? The color of his hair, for instance. His height."

Her brow furrowed in concentration. "He had dark hair, and he was tall, but not over much."

"Was he handsome?"

She shrugged her shoulders. "Sure." Which I took to mean in an average way. This wasn't much to go on.

"Anything else you remember about him?" I pressed, but she shook her head. "Would you recognize him if you saw him again?"

Her head tilted to the side. "Probably."

I turned to see if Sidney felt he could get more out of her. When he didn't speak up, I thanked her and all the Harringtons' staff, and they were dismissed.

It wasn't until they were filing away that I noticed the young woman gazing down at us from the staircase above. This must be Lily, the bride-to-be. Or perhaps no longer, depending on the Daltons' control over their son.

She hurried down the steps toward her mother. "Are they truly going to find the thief?"

"We're certainly going to try," I affirmed in response to Mrs. Harrington's entreating look.

"Oh, thank goodness," Lily exclaimed tearfully. Her hands fisted at her sides. "They can't get away with it. They just can't!"

I suspected she was speaking more of the damage they'd done to her engagement than the actual theft of the jewels, and I couldn't help but empathize with her. Though I had no desire to have yet another young woman relying on me. Not after the last time. Not the way it turned out.

I smiled wanly as I told her we would do all we could, before departing. But although I'd thought I'd done well to mask my reaction, I caught Sidney watching me out of the corner of his eye.

"Is there something you wished to say?" I challenged as we strode across the damp gravel toward his Pierce-Arrow. The rain had temporarily ceased but the skies remained leaden.

"Just that you can't fault Miss Harrington for her sentiments."

"Who said I did?" I deliberately kept my voice light.

"It's just, I can imagine you speaking in the same impassioned tone." His lips lifted at the corners. "I suspect you said something remarkably similar to what Miss Harrington just did in order to convince your father to allow you to marry me before I left for France."

I felt my shoulders bow. "That seems like a long time ago."

"Not so long. Just six years." He sighed wearily as if feeling the weight of those war-torn years and their aftermath as well. "But yes, it does feel like a long time ago."

Lily was probably eighteen, the same age I'd been—just barely—when I'd wed Sidney. Yet a lifetime seemed to have passed since then. One which made it easier for me to identify with women like Mrs. Harrington than a girl just six years my junior.

"I sometimes wonder," I began as we reached the motorcar. Sidney paused with his hand on the door handle, waiting for me to finish as I stared into the middle distance at the line of trees which marked the edge of the Harringtons' property. "If I'm the same person," I finally confessed in a voice that was barely a whisper.

"You are," he replied with quiet certainty after a moment, drawing my gaze. "And you aren't." His mouth creased into a humorless smile, recognizing this sentiment was less than helpful. He reached for my hand. "What I mean is . . . my soul, my heart . . . whatever it is within me that connects to you, has never not known who you are. Not after months of separation . . ." His expression turned haggard. "After slogging through hellish circumstances. After recognizing now that you must have faced similar hellscapes and difficulties. I still knew you."

My chest grew tight at the look in his eyes, and I suddenly struggled to swallow.

"Knew you and wanted you. Even now." His mouth softened into the semblance of a grin. "I suspect I always will."

I gasped a laugh that was perilously close to tears and swatted his shoulder. "You'd better. For it seems I can't stop loving you, even when you do abominable things like march off to war and fake your own death." I sniffed, arching my chin. "You shall never be rid of me. I vow, even in death, if I go before you, I shall haunt you."

At this, Sidney grasped hold of my waist tightly, pulling me to him. "Don't say such things," he ordered harshly. "Don't even invoke it." His voice was hushed, almost as if he feared who was listening.

The words had been meant in jest, an endeavor to suppress my urge to weep, but I had to admit a sense of uneasiness now stirred inside of me, creeping its fingers along the back of my neck. I didn't like it, or the alarm still written across my husband's features.

"Sidney, you've never been superstitious," I contested in the same hushed voice he'd used.

He loosened his grip on me. "No, but that doesn't mean I want to put it to the test."

I could concede the reasoning behind this, even if I didn't like it. I allowed him to open the door and help me inside the motorcar, but chose to focus my attention on the copy of the guest list Mrs. Harrington had given me as he rounded the bonnet to join me.

I recognized a number of the names, but this wasn't surprising. After all, Dublin society was relatively small, particularly since many had fled the city due to the rebellion. Lord and Lady Powerscourt, the Wyndham-Quins, Mr. Sturgis, and several more representatives of the Castle administration, as well as Mr. and Mrs. Fitzgibbon, Rufus Beresford, and some of the members of the lord lieutenant's privy council, whom we'd associated with previously, were all included, among others. However, two names caught my interest.

The first was Frank Caulfield, the chap we'd met at the Quin's most recent dinner party who worked with O in some capacity for British Intelligence. I'd been unsure of his exact social standing, but obviously he boasted enough rank or connections to garner an invitation to such a soiree. Given my hazy suspicions about O's potential involvement with the thefts, I found Caulfield's presence to be curious, to say the least.

The second was the Chathams. As the third victims of the jewel thief, it was somewhat suggestive that they'd attended the engagement party. Had the burglar marked them out as his next target after seeing the gems Mrs. Chatham was wearing that evening? It would be interesting to discover what she'd worn.

I told Sidney as much, but when he asked if we should pay them a call next, I realized I didn't know their address. We might have returned to Mrs. Harrington to ask, but by that point my headache was worse than ever.

I closed my eyes against the pain. "No, I'll simply have to ring up Helen and ask. In any case, the Chathams will likely be at that charity gala tomorrow evening. We can speak with them then."

"As well as a number of the other people on that list, I imagine," he replied.

I allowed my silence to be my agreement.

"Then, you weren't thinking of driving to Dundalk to see the Daltons?" Sidney ventured a few moments later.

"No." I grimaced before admitting, "Truth be told, I just want to lie in a dark, quiet room."

I heard the shift of his clothes as he turned to look at me. "Migraine? I suspected you might be suffering from an aching head. Why didn't you say something sooner?"

"Because I thought I could manage it."

He didn't argue. Perhaps because he was just as bad about denying injuries. Instead, I heard the engine rev and felt the car accelerate.

"We'll be home in a jiffy," he promised. And I believed him.

CHAPTER 12

The ballroom at the Shelbourne Hotel was decked out in splendor the following evening. Its Georgian interiors were made festive with flowers and garland, and a grand orchestra had been hired to serenade us. I would have preferred a jazz or ragtime band, but the establishment was having none of that. Though they did adapt some more modern favorites, as well as music from Joplin, Harney, Lamb and others.

I'd directed Ginny to pull my black satin gown with an overlay of net from the back of the wardrobe. It was decorated in seed pearls with a scrolling acanthus leaf pattern on the bodice and skirt and sheer turquoise fabric draped over each sleeve. However, I elected once again to leave my long necklace of perfectly matched ivory pearls at home to avoid tempting the jewel thief in case he might be in attendance tonight. That is, if we were correct and the thief was at least able to blend in with the other guests in order to choose his next targets.

The gala was meant to be a benefit for some of the local hospitals, those that relied solely on public funds rather than the institutions set up by a religious order, which were deeply in debt. Tonight was but one of a number of planned fundraisers to help the cause. Lord and Lady Powerscourt had taken a great interest in the initiative, and through them, Sidney and I had become involved. Though I would be lying

if I said the worthy cause was the only reason for our attendance. Even before we'd realized a number of the guests from
the Harringtons' party would also be attending, we'd anticipated that at least a smattering of members of the Castle administration would be there, as well as a number of military
officers. Any of whom might possess useful information.

We'd also wondered if Lord Ardmore might make an appearance. After all, he was on friendly terms with Lord Powerscourt. But as I waltzed with Mr. Sturgis, I saw no sign of
him among the assembly.

In fact, I was so preoccupied with my search at first that
I didn't notice Sturgis was being much quieter than usual.
Once I did, I also couldn't help but note that the cast of his
features even appeared a trifle sullen.

"I understand a number of your colleagues are away at the
moment," I said, attempting to broach the topic delicately.
"I'm sure that must be trying."

"Yes, I saw Anderson off to the boat before I came," he
replied dully. "And with several of the others gone, I suppose
you could say, we're rather short-handed at the moment. But I
can't complain. Many of them have been here far longer than
I have, and without leave."

I nodded. "I've heard what they say. Too much work isn't
good for a gentleman's constitution. Or his wit."

It was perhaps a lackluster attempt to jolly him out of his
sulk, but he seemed to take the hint. "Apologies, Verity. I'm
afraid I've been sunk in a fit of gloom today. One I don't seem
to be able to triumph over."

"About?"

"Everything." He turned to watch the other dancers twirl
by. "This peculiar country. Why everything has to be such a
great secret." He huffed. "We're told that all of Ireland longs
for settlement but is too terrorized between the gun-toting
shinners and the Orange Order to even speak in whispers.
These Irish desiring peace send emissaries to us but won't do

anything concrete to bring that peace about. They expect us civil servants to do it all."

I could only wonder what "emissaries" he'd been meeting with, and on what authority they spoke for the majority of the population. Their assertions that most of Ireland wanted peace but were too intimidated by both sides to say so might very well be true, but it just as likely could be false, depending on the source and their motives. But of course, I said none of this to Sturgis. If he didn't already know, he soon would.

"I'm sure all this news about the hunger strikes isn't helping," I said instead, attempting to empathize with him. After all, he hadn't chosen the policies he was forced to uphold.

"They are an hourly worry," he confessed with what could only be candor. "But what can be done? If we release them, it would entirely demoralize the police. We can't crumble on this, or we might as well capitulate completely." And yet their deaths could mean even more trouble from the rebels, if reports were to be believed. It was a sticky wicket, to be sure, and not one of his making.

"Have you heard from Lady Rachel? How are the children?" I asked, hoping talk of his family might cheer him.

"They are well. I'm to meet them at Wortley on the twelfth," he reported.

I listened to him rattle off his plans for his visit to England, joining his family in Yorkshire at his father-in-law's estate. It couldn't be easy being separated from them, but such was the life of civil service at times. Before the waltz ended, I found time to ask him about the Harringtons' party, but he confessed he'd been detained in London longer than he'd expected and been unable to attend. Though he was pleased to discover that Sidney and I were now investigating the jewel thefts in earnest. That Anderson would be glad to hear of it as well, for he'd inquired about it before he departed for Scotland.

I feigned gratification as the waltz ended and he led me

from the dance floor. But my taut smile grew even more strained at the sight of the man standing before us, a smirk playing across his lips.

"Willoughby!" Mr. Sturgis exclaimed. "Good to see you. I wasn't sure you could make it."

"Yes, well, my business in Belfast was postponed."

I could tell by the look in his eyes that he was aware I was listening. And because he was aware, and operated as essentially Lord Ardmore's right-hand man, I didn't know what to make of this information about Belfast. Was it meant as a ruse to make us think Belfast somehow factored into Ardmore's plans? Or had he expected us to reckon it was a bluff and so boldly mentioned it, expecting us to dismiss it? Whatever the case, the very fact that he knew I was at that moment frantically calculating the odds of the value of such information was maddening!

"Mrs. Kent, you look lovely," he murmured, his eyes dancing with devious delight.

"Don't sound so shocked, Captain?" I taunted lightly.

"It's only that the last time I saw you, you were looking rather drowned and worse for wear."

He was speaking of our meeting in a rainy wood outside Baarle-Hertog, Belgium, where he shot and killed his colleague for defying their master's orders. Where he would have shot Sidney had I not outwitted him.

"You're forgetting when I bumped into you outside Kennedy and McSharry." The encounter that had first alerted me to his presence in Dublin.

Too late, I realized our most recent interaction had been just three nights ago inside Devlin's pub. Something Willoughby was perfectly conscious of, judging from the gleam in his eyes. Just as he was aware that I would not welcome his mentioning this in front of Mr. Sturgis.

"You're already acquainted, then?" Sturgis asked us.

"Verity knows what a bounder I am," Willoughby jested, making Sturgis laugh.

I'd not given him leave to use my given name, and Sturgis clearly had no idea how close to the truth he'd spoken, but there was nothing I could say that wouldn't draw undesired interest.

"So she won't be surprised when I insist on stealing her away for the next dance," he continued in challenge.

Still laughing, Sturgis gestured for him to proceed. "By all means."

I resented the notion that I was some sort of property to be passed off, but refusing would cause a scene.

As Willoughby took my arm, I turned to look about me as unobtrusively as possible for Sidney, to be sure he was aware of the potential snare I'd gotten myself into. Just as Willoughby pivoted me into his embrace as the strains of a foxtrot began, I caught sight of him dancing nearby with Sybil, Lady Powerscourt. He nodded once to indicate he'd seen me and then I did my best to ignore him and focus on my dance partner.

The song being a livelier number, this wasn't hard, as I had to concentrate on my steps and where Willoughby was leading me. Fortunately, he proved to be a more than competent dancer, masterfully spinning me around the floor. In fact, I might have enjoyed myself had I not been so keenly aware that I had to mind not only my tongue and my facial expression, but also any tension in my body that might be communicated to him.

When he didn't speak for the first half of the song, I was careful not to be lulled into a false sense of complacency, for I knew better. Willoughby hadn't sought me out because he simply wished to dance with me. There was a reason he'd cornered me into accepting.

"As always, Mrs. Kent, I'm surprised by how you *do* get around," he finally murmured.

Conscious of the implied insult and the leading nature of the remark, I countered lightly. "I could say the same about you." I paused a beat before adding, "And your boss."

"That may be," he continued in a conversational manner. "But I think you're aware that His Lordship has rather more influence in certain circles than you do. His words are liable to carry much more weight, and his accusations to be taken much more seriously. He should hate for certain . . . *associations* of yours to come to light."

"You mean, he should hate to have to accuse me of them?" I charged, determined to call a spade a spade, even as my heartbeat pounded in my ears, vying with the rhythm of the music.

Willoughby tilted his head in an approximation of a shrug as he maintained his dancer's posture. "I'm merely the messenger."

I arched a single disdainful eyebrow. "You're much more than that. You're a bully, a torpedo, and a swindler. And you know it. So quit trying to sell me that line."

He guided us through a turn with more intricate footwork, gripping me more tightly before releasing me. "It doesn't matter what you think. The truth is that Ardmore isn't going to let you interfere with his plans."

"Which are?" I interjected.

Willoughby shook his head, his grin ill-humored. "I know you've only seen the gentlemanly side of His Lordship."

I scoffed, for I wouldn't say that. Not when the number of murders I could ascribe to him was close to a dozen.

"But he can be ruthless when he is crossed." He glanced in the direction of Sidney dancing with Sybil a few feet away. "He tolerates your husband because he enjoys sparring with you. But should you get in his way, he won't hesitate to remove him. Or to remove *you* if you prove too great a threat."

Fear clutched at my chest, but I refused to be cowed. "And what of you?" I challenged. "Do you honestly think that as

long as you do as he bids, he'll protect you? If I know anything about Ardmore, it's that his loyalty is only to himself."
A furrow formed between his brows. "This isn't about
me."

"Yes, it is," I countered sharply, drawing the interest of
a couple we moved past. "Because if anyone possesses the
knowledge to bring him down, I suspect it's you," I hissed.
His stony gaze shifted over my shoulder, refusing to meet
mine. I couldn't tell if he was being willfully ignorant, frightened, or if his allegiance to Ardmore was simply too great
to be overcome. Was it because Ardmore was a nobleman? I
knew that as the impoverished orphaned great-grandson of a
duke, Willoughby had been raised by a dowager aunt within
spitting range of the aristocracy but made to understand that
he would never be a part of it. As such, he undoubtedly had
a rather unhealthy view of, and perhaps even an obsession
with it. But I'd read a summary of his stellar war record, and
most of what he'd achieved had been through his own steely
resolve and merit. He had no need of Ardmore.

"Why are you building the scaffold on which he's going to
hang you?" I pleaded, thinking if I could just turn him to our
side, we might have a chance. "You know that's what's going
to happen."

"No, I don't," he snapped. He audibly inhaled through his
nostrils, clearly agitated I'd been able provoke him into such
a reaction. "Not if there's never any reason to," he continued
in a more level voice, his eyes narrowing.

We glided to the edge of the dance floor as the final flour-
ish of the song was played, halting abruptly. "Think on what
I said," he leaned down to utter darkly, before striding away.

I turned to watch him go, wondering if by being candid,
by pushing too hard, I'd made a mistake. Sidney touched my
elbow lightly as he and Sybil joined me. There was concern
in his eyes, and I allowed the flicker of a smile to form across
my lips to reassure him.

"Who was that gentleman?" Sybil asked as Willoughby was lost in the crush of the crowd.

"Captain Lucas Willoughby, of the Royal Navy." Or perhaps *formerly*; I had never been entirely clear on that point given his connection with Ardmore.

She nodded, curiosity pursing her lips, but before she could say more, Sidney spoke up. "Her Ladyship didn't see anything of note at the Harringtons' party, but she suggested we question the members of the band they'd hired."

"Yes, I noticed a number of them lingering near one of the rear entrances smoking during their set break and I thought, perhaps, if the thief used that door they might remember him."

I supposed it was a possibility. If the thief had not been a guest but an opportunist, they might have felt safer slipping out through a less conspicuous entrance. I thanked her, mentally making a note I would need to telephone Mrs. Harrington to ask for the band's direction.

"Of course," Sybil replied, but when I would have turned away, she grasped my arm. "And I do hope you'll join me for lunch one day this week. I've been meaning to invite you and suddenly asked myself the other day why on earth I haven't." Her eyes twinkled with gentle humor.

One I couldn't help but respond to. "I'd like that."

"Good." She released my arm. "I'll ring you tomorrow and we'll set a date." With that, she allowed herself to be beckoned over by a portly gentleman in a too-tight waistcoat.

Sidney draped his arm loosely around my waist. "I saw the Chathams in a cluster near the tables of items up for silent auction," he explained, correctly deducing my next objective.

"Lead the way," I urged him before someone else asked me to dance.

Keeping me close to his side as we navigated through the crush of bodies, he turned his head to speak into my hair. "What did Willoughby have to say?"

"Threats. Of the 'give up your meddling or you'll regret it' variety." I waved my hand as if to say it was all negligible, but Sidney knew better.

"Should we be worried?"

I didn't like the notion. I didn't like the idea of giving Ardmore the satisfaction of ruffling me, but I also couldn't pretend I wasn't concerned. "We should be careful," I corrected, deciding that was a fair balance.

Sidney, once again, knew better, but he let me maintain my delusion. "Right."

The crowds parted, and I suddenly spied the Chathams, who appeared to be debating a piece of art with a number of others. Or rather Mr. Chatham was debating a piece of art with Mr. Fitzgibbon, of all people, and another chap while their wives were discussing another woman's recently completed rope of matching pearls and Mr. Beresford looked on in boredom.

"Thank God," he gasped in blasphemy as we approached. "Mr. and Mrs. Kent, save us from this drivel."

Mr. Fitzgibbon and Mr. Chatham scowled while the third fellow appeared sheepish, but it was Doris Fitzgibbon who was surprisingly the one who scolded her brother. "No one forced you to stay here and listen to us, Rufus. You could have taken yourself off somewhere else at any time."

"And here I thought you'd miss me," he drawled nastily. Like a five-year-old, Doris actually stuck her tongue out at him before turning away.

Ignoring this, I smiled at all of them in turn. "Just the people we've been looking for." I hesitated when I came to the mystery gentleman. "Well, I don't yet know you, but I'm sure I would have been looking for you too if I had."

"Of course," Mrs. Chatham, a petite brunette, stepped in to exclaim. "Mrs. Kent, allow me to introduce Dr. Archie McCarthy."

I extended my hand as Mrs. Chatham finished the introductions, noting that the man had a rather nice smile. Dr. McCarthy was about my husband's age or perhaps a few years older, with medium brown hair and an average build. He was an attractive enough fellow, but I suspected I would never have noticed him before now if we'd passed in the street.

"Lovely to meet ye," he told me and Sidney, exhibiting a gentle Irish accent.

"Likewise. And I apologize in advance, for we may be about to bore you."

They all swiveled to face us, appearing—quite contradictory to my claims—intrigued.

I stifled a laugh. "We would like to ask you about the Harringtons' party and your own run-in"—I nodded to the Chathams—"with this jewel thief."

"Oh, well, then, Dr. McCarthy won't be out of place at all," Doris interjected, her hands flapping in excitement like two birds. "He was also at the Harringtons' party."

"Oh, excellent," I replied, now able to place why his name had sounded so familiar. I must have read it on the guest list.

Dr. McCarthy rocked on his heels, seemingly pleased to be included. "What did ye wish to know?"

"We wanted to know if any of you noticed anyone or anything peculiar that evening. Were there any guests acting oddly? Did you see anyone in a place they shouldn't have been? Were there any commotions? A dropped tray, for instance." This last thought had just occurred to me, for it might have given the thief a chance to move up the stairs or around a corner unobserved.

They all conferred with each other with their eyes, and I watched to see if any of them seemed uncomfortable or evasive. Not that this would necessarily signal guilt in the jewel theft. They might just as easily have been attempting to conceal something else. But it could be indicative.

Doris's gaze dipped almost immediately, her fingers worrying the buttons on her glove. Her brother noticed this and frowned, making me wonder if he was aware of the reason behind her anxiety.

"I ... I don't believe I recall anything," Dr. McCarthy hedged, being the first to answer. "I'm sorry. I'm afraid that's not terribly helpful, is it?"

"That's all right," I assured him. "If everyone had seen something, then it wouldn't be so difficult to catch the thief, now, would it?"

"I suppose not."

"What of the rest of you?"

The Chathams shook their heads while Beresford merely shrugged.

"I ... I may have seen something," Mr. Fitzgibbon stammered. "But then again, I just as easily might not have."

His brother-in-law snarled at him. "Well, that's useful, Hal. If those are the qualifications, then I may have seen something, too."

Fitzgibbon turned to scowl at Beresford, missing his wife's wide-eyed look.

"Go on," I coaxed, keeping one eye on Doris.

"Well, you mentioned people in places they shouldn't be."

"Yes?"

"At one point, I saw a gentleman emerge from the servant stair."

I glanced at Sidney, who asked, "When was this?"

Hal tipped his head in consideration. "Hmmm, closer to the latter half of the evening than the beginning, but I'm afraid I can't tell you more than that. And it may mean nothing," he hastened to add. "The Harringtons' house is large, and the fellow may have just decided to nip down that staircase for convenience."

This was true, but there was also the possibility he had been the thief.

"Can you describe him?" Sidney queried as he shifted aside to let someone pass. "Would you recognize the man again if you saw him?"

"I think so," Fitzgibbon began hesitantly and then with more confidence. "Yes. Yes, I would. He was rather tall and spindly, so I suspect I would."

I couldn't help but note that this could describe O's man Frank Caulfield, who had been on the guest list, but it also might have described at least half a dozen other men. I wished Mr. Caulfield was present so that I could point him out to Fitzgibbon.

"What of you, Mrs. Fitzgibbon?" She startled as I addressed her directly. "Did you notice anything out of place?"

"I . . . No. Sorry." She gave a nervous laugh. "I'm afraid I'm not overly observant."

I nodded as if this answer was reasonable, and Doris tucked herself in close to her husband's side, seemingly relieved to have passed my test. However, Beresford seemed aware that my interest had only been heightened. He eyed me in displeasure, and while I could appreciate his desire to protect his sister, that was not going to stop me from making further discreet queries.

"Mr. and Mrs. Chatham, what about your burglary? I understand it happened while you were out."

"Yes, we'd gone to the Pillar Picture House to catch a matinee," Mr. Chatham answered reservedly, perhaps thinking of the instructions from his insurance company.

"And no one noticed anything?"

Laurel Chatham's voice was soft, as if recalling the shock of the discovery. "It was our footman's day off and our maid was out running errands."

Giving the thief an opening to slip in unobserved and undisturbed. I wondered if this was luck or if he—or she—had been watching the Chathams' household for several days before striking. The latter seemed more likely.

Sidney seemed to agree. "Did you notice anyone hanging about on the street outside or in the mews behind, during the days before?"

"Well . . . no," Mr. Chatham said, his surprise making it evident this question had yet to be considered. He turned to his wife, who shook her head.

The opening chords of a Joplin number were being played, drawing our attention, and Mrs. Chatham seemed eager to join the couples flocking to the dance floor. However, I still had one more question. "Mrs. Chatham, do you recall what jewelry you were wearing at the Harringtons' party? Were they some of the items stolen?"

"Why, yes. My grandmother's diamond and emerald brooch, my opal ring, and my malachite drop earrings." She clutched the pendant dangling from her neck—an item either missed by the burglar or newly purchased. "What does that mean?"

"Only that the thief may have noticed your jewelry at the Harringtons' soiree and decided then to rob you."

"Oh my!" Mrs. Chatham turned to Doris, who appeared to share her horror at this disclosure.

I didn't caution them about wearing their flashiest pieces. I suspected the message had already been imparted.

As the Chathams and Fitzgibbons drifted away, Dr. McCarthy stepped closer, his brow furrowed. "How many of these thefts have occurred?"

I'd not forgotten that the matter thus far had been kept out of the papers, though I wouldn't wager on that fact lasting much longer. It had always been bound to get out. "Three incidents, that I'm aware of." My gaze slid to Beresford, who lingered.

"So far," he added somewhat ominously.

Sidney turned to him in interest. "You think there'll be more?"

"You don't?"

Sidney tipped his head, acknowledging this was a fair point.

I turned to study the crowd, many of whom were Castle-walking across the dance floor, the glittering gems draped around their necks and wrists and nestled in their lapels sparkling in the chandeliers' light. Even now, the thief might be choosing their next marks, noting which people were adorned with the greatest fortune. Only time would tell.

CHAPTER 13

Two days later, I strode into Jammet's on St. Andrew's Street across from the grand old church for which the street was named. The French restaurant was among the finest in Dublin, so I hadn't been surprised when Sybil had telephoned and asked me to meet her there. I'd just come from the Bank of Ireland around the corner, where Mr. Finnegan had passed me a letter from Kathleen. A brief perusal had revealed that she'd uncovered a number of Ardmore's potential connections as well as addresses where he might have had access to store the phosgene cylinders. I knew Sidney was lunching with Bennett and Ames, and there was every chance they might have pertinent information to share with him as well.

Because of this, there was a hopeful spring in my step as I was led past the tables with crisp white tablecloths and gleaming table services. The patrons quietly conversed over the click of their cutlery or smoked postprandial cigarettes. Though the two gentlemen seated at one table had their heads buried in newspapers, all but ignoring each other.

I'd read the headlines that morning. The hunger strikers were still alive and eating up print space, but there was also word of more reprisals. Apparently in County Roscommon some days earlier the Crown Forces had burned part of a village and dragged the body of an IRA man they'd killed through its streets in retaliation for the shooting deaths of two RIC constables. Then in County Cork just the day before, another IRA Volunteer was killed after approaching a British Army lorry that appeared to be broken down but contained soldiers waiting in ambush inside. The brother of two members of the local RIC was killed in the same manner with a shot to the head a few hours later, undoubtedly by the local IRA. And so the tit-for-tat violence continued.

I hastened to keep up with the maître d' as he showed me to the table where Sybil was already seated. However, the lightness in my step turned to lead when I discovered she was not alone. Mark Sturgis sat across from her and to her right hovered Lord Ardmore.

It had been some weeks since I'd seen the man whose machinations occupied too many hours of my day and night, and I felt my heart quicken with impotent rage at the sight of him now. Just shy of fifty years of age, his pale blond hair was streaked with gray and exhibited a small mole above his left ear at the hairline. He remained tall and trim and distinguished in appearance, with a perpetual aura of cool indifference that I knew from experience rarely slipped.

My hands involuntarily clenched, and I had but a moment to gather myself before he turned his head and saw me. I knew I'd been successful in erasing all evidence of my shock, though Ardmore's mocking green gaze tried to suggest otherwise. Ignoring him, I first greeted Sybil, leaning over to buss her cheek.

"Verity, there you are," she said, returning my greeting. "Lord Ardmore and Mr. Sturgis were just arriving when I was, and they absolutely *insisted* we join them. I hope you don't mind." Her expression as she relayed this suggested that *she* did, but had been unable to politely extricate herself. Knowing this, I couldn't add to her irritation.

"Of course."

Her smile softened into something more genuine as the maître d' helped me into my chair. "His Lordship said you know each other from London."

"Yes," I replied simply, but it seemed Ardmore wasn't content with that.

"We met over the Marquess of Rockham's dead body. Oh, not literally," he continued in response to Sybil and Sturgis's shock. "But the evening of his murder in any case. Mrs. Kent and I were both quite misled in the character of his widow. His second wife, you know." His eyes gleamed innocently across the table at me as an aperitif was poured. "Though that didn't stop Mrs. Kent from assisting Scotland Yard to see her prosecuted."

I was quite honestly stunned by this recitation and suspicious of its purpose. For one, it seemed a bit hypocritical to call Ada Rockham's character into question when he had been her lover. He'd also been the one to convince her to kill her husband, though I'd not been able to uncover enough evidence to prove it. Ada had gone to her grave still refusing to denounce him or reveal the source of his hold over her.

His last statement was also a bit jarring, for while it was true that I'd provoked Ada into confessing and provided the testimony needed to put her away, I'd not done so out of spite. In fact, at first, I'd done everything I could to prove it *wasn't* her. It was later that I'd realized the truth, and that justice had to be done. However, Sturgis and Sybil didn't know this, and my launching into such a lengthy explanation would only further emphasize the matter.

"Then it seems we were right to approach you and your husband about investigating the jewel thefts," Sturgis declared after taking a drink. He seemed almost self-satisfied about this fact. He was definitely in a better mood than the last time I'd seen him.

"Is that so?" Ardmore murmured in a patronizing tone. *Among other things.*

I bit back the retort before I could utter it, knowing that he was baiting me. Something it was never wise to succumb to, but after Willoughby's warning, it could be downright dangerous. In any case, I needed to tread carefully not to tip him off to anything we knew. Especially not before we'd had a chance to investigate the locations Kathleen had listed in the letter currently burning a hole in my clutch, which I kept tucked in my lap.

"Yes," I answered simply after a drink of the aperitif. It was crisp and rather refreshing.

The men looked at me as if expecting me to elaborate, but I decided I wasn't going to humor them. Truth be told, I'd hoped to ask Sybil about Doris Fitzgibbon's nervous behavior the other night, but I wasn't about to do that now.

"How is your daughter?" I asked Sybil instead. "I heard there was a riding accident."

"Merely a sprained ankle. She has my father's temperament, unfortunately." This was said with a smile to remove any of the sting. "Tell her not to do something and she's bound and determined she will."

"I suspect Sidney would say the same about me," I jested, making her and Mr. Sturgis laugh.

"That's interesting," Lord Ardmore drawled, ruining the lightheartedness of the moment. "Mrs. Kent, I'd always pegged you as a far more calculated person, prone to considering all of your options prudently before choosing your course."

"Just because a person is willful doesn't mean they don't prudently consider their options beforehand," I countered in a measured tone. "I prudently considered the question of whether to return to Yorkshire with my parents after my new husband left for the Western Front or remain in London, where he could more easily reach me when on leave and where I could be of use to the war effort. But that didn't stop my parents from accusing me of being willful."

"Excellent example," Sturgis proclaimed, picking up his menu. "Just as I am prudently considering my options at this fine dining establishment and choosing the grouse when I should probably select the consommé." He patted his stomach before flashing a grin. "My wife would no doubt call that willful."

We all laughed, taking that as a cue we should select our own meals. I opted for the sole meunière with lemon and herbs. The conversation drifted to more inconsequential things until our dishes were set before us. Then Ardmore suddenly turned serious, apparently bent on ruining at least my appetite.

"Colonel Winter tells me you've proved to be quite an able administrator," Ardmore informed Sturgis as he sliced a piece of meat from the grouse he'd also selected. "That he's been keeping you well-informed."

"Yes, we've had a number of enlightening discussions," Sturgis confessed with a pointed look at Sybil and me, as if to ask Ardmore if this was really an appropriate discussion to conduct in front of us.

Ardmore brushed this unspoken query aside with a simple statement. "Lady Powerscourt and Mrs. Kent are patriotic women."

While he didn't look at me, I felt the barb of his words, struggling to swallow my bite of sole. I covered this by taking a drink.

"But I suppose we should be wary nonetheless," Ardmore added after some consideration. He discreetly surveyed the other patrons within the restaurant, none of whom were close enough to overhear. "Collins has informants everywhere, after all. Even in this restaurant, I'm sure."

While Sturgis and Sybil shifted their gaze to the tables closest to us, I felt Ardmore's land squarely on me. It was brief, but long enough for me to arch one of my eyebrows to convey that I wasn't intimidated by his veiled insinuation. So he knew I'd had contact with Collins. He must be aware that I knew he also had. His implication was rather like the pot calling the kettle black.

"How do you know this?" Sturgis asked.

"Come now." Ardmore almost tsked. "Winter has shared enough with you that you must realize by now that we're currently being beat at our own game. Both in intelligence gathering and propaganda." He grimaced as he reached for his glass. "Though it's difficult to make diamonds from the muck of all this foolish shooting and burning."

"Now, much of that is fabrication," Sturgis countered. "It's been a strain to get real, solid evidence of these reprisals rather than a bunch of distorted and inconsistent reports."

"Are you simply handing out the party line or are you truly that feckless?" Ardmore retorted, coming as close to losing his temper as I'd ever witnessed. "Of course, there is evidence," he continued more urbanely. "Or the authorities *can* get it, if they choose to. It simply behooves the police and army administrators to remain in the dark. Or pretend to." He dabbed his mouth with his napkin. "But these newspapermen are catching on, and mark me, sooner rather than later there's going to be proof splashed all over the international press that can no longer be denied. Macready and Tudor would be better served to get ahead of it before it's too late."

I was struggling to withhold my surprise at this monologue, and the unsettling sensation of being in agreement with Ardmore about something. But then, that was what made Ardmore such a master manipulator. He would find the point on which you agreed and then exploit it, gradually coaxing you into doing and supporting things you would never have previously dreamed of.

Is that what he was trying to do now? But who was his mark? Me or Sturgis?

"I've warned them as much," Sturgis replied with a shake of his head, evidently having already moved past any insult he might have taken at being called "feckless" in order to try to earn Ardmore's approval by convincing him that this was far from the truth. It was classic manipulation, and it left a sour taste in my mouth.

I set down my fork and picked up my wine, hoping to wash away the residue. I turned to Sybil, curious what her reaction was to this conversation. Her brow was lightly furrowed, but otherwise her expression remained placid. Though I noticed she wasn't eating much either.

"And you know the rebels won't take this sitting down." Ardmore absently swirled the contents of his glass. "Yes, these ambushes and raids are one thing, but thus far the more moderate members of Sinn Féin have been restraining the more radical element, making the most of the propaganda it affords them. However, Collins and these IRA brigade commanders are only going to be restrained for so long." He arched his eyebrows. "Word is they're planning something big."

My sense of disbelief only deepened as I waited to see if he would actually mention the phosgene in front of me and Sybil. The discussion, as it was, had gone far beyond polite discourse. But a mention of poisonous gas would be beyond the pale.

Sturgis leaned toward him to ask, "Does Winter know about this?"

"Of course," Ardmore replied after finally taking a drink. "We've been in discussions about what could be their ultimate target."

"The Castle?" Sybil guessed, reminding Sturgis of our presence. Ardmore, naturally, was aware that I was listening, or he would have timed this conversation differently.

Dublin Castle would be the natural first assumption, for it acted as the British government's seat of power, housing all of its most important officials and civil servants, as well as the offices of many of its Crown Forces. But it was also heavily fortified and stood in the middle of the city. Machine guns were positioned on the roof of the Record Tower monitoring the gates, and even the subterranean accesses were watched, with wire entanglements positioned across the points where the culvert for the River Poddle ran beneath the castle, and a Royal Engineer stationed in the cellars with a listening set to detect any attempts to tunnel through the surrounding soil. A successful attack seemed all but impossible, even if the IRA got their hands on the phosgene and Livens Projector.

But Ardmore didn't disabuse her of this notion. "Have no fear, my lady. We are on to them."

I scrutinized the charming smile he flashed Sybil. Was that his plan then? To engineer a way for the rebels to be caught red-handed with the phosgene? In the grand scheme of things, I supposed that was better than a plot which involved the gas actually being deployed. But it could prove disastrous for the republicans, not only in terms of arrests, but also propaganda. Though I struggled to understand how his bids to privately bankroll parts of the rebellion by extending loans to city and county councils who had pledged allegiance to the Dáil would benefit him if the republicans failed entirely in their aims.

We would have to tread lightly in our search. For if *we* were caught red-handed breaking into a garage stockpiled with phosgene, Ardmore might find a way to turn that against us.

All of this weighed heavily on my mind—as Ardmore no doubt intended—later, when Sybil and I strode from the restaurant arm in arm, parting ways with the gentlemen. The bells of St. Andrew's Church chimed the hour, covering the sound of Sybil's voice as she leaned toward me.

"Well, I've certainly had pleasanter luncheons. Had I known what they intended to discuss, I would have tried harder to extricate us. Though I will give points to His Lordship for exerting his charm to soften an otherwise unsettling topic." Her mouth flattened into a thin line as she pondered this. "But one does get the sense that it was all to a purpose. That he *intended* to unsettle us."

I studied her out of the corner of my eye, realizing Lord Ardmore, and even I, had underestimated her. It was a happy discovery, but I still spoke carefully. "If I know anything about Lord Ardmore, it's that his words and actions are always quite deliberate."

She hummed in displeasure at the back of her throat, glancing right and then left with me as we crossed a narrow intersection and continued our stroll.

"Was there something particular you wished to discuss when you invited me to lunch?" I asked, deciding it was best to be direct rather than waiting for her to get around to it.

Her response was delayed as she visibly pulled herself away from wherever her thoughts had gone, back into the present. "No. I just wanted the chance to get to know you better." Her lips pursed. "Which was rather spoiled by our unexpected guests."

"Then we'll simply have to reschedule."

"Yes, let's," she agreed. "Though it will have to wait until I return from Powerscourt."

I recalled she'd said she was returning to her husband's estate south of Dublin the following day.

As we crossed the junction with Wicklow Street into South William Street, I turned to look down its length toward the Wicklow Hotel. I wondered how surprised the hotelier Peter would be if I dropped in to see him, dressed as Verity rather than the reticent Irish lass, Dearbhla Bell, I'd pretended to be when I'd been gathering information to find Alec. He might already know we were one and the same. After all, I now strongly suspected that he was an informant for Collins. But on the chance he was not, I decided it would be best to avoid revealing myself unless I had to. Particularly since he'd been so kind to me. I hated lying to good people. It was one of the hardest things about intelligence work.

"There was one thing I thought I should mention," Sybil broached. "Though I'd hoped to remember more before I brought it up."

I turned to her in interest.

"The man you were dancing with at the gala. Captain Willoughby?" Her brow furrowed. "I could swear I've seen him before."

"About Dublin?" I asked, not quite following.

"Maybe?" She sighed. "I just can't remember. But . . . when I saw him the other night, I had this vague sense of . . . apprehension." She shook her head. "No, that's not quite right. It was more that there was just something off about it?"

I assumed she was questioning herself rather than me.

"Oh, I wish I could recall!" she announced in frustration.

"Well, if you do, I hope you'll tell me," I said, trying not to sound more than vaguely interested, even though I was intensely curious.

Where could she have seen Willoughby that made her feel something was not quite right about his presence at the Shelbourne Hotel? The most obvious presumption was that it had to do with rank and wealth. That wherever she'd seen him before had led her to believe he would be out of place at such a fundraiser. This wasn't altogether telling, for, as a naval intelligence agent, he might often don less than fashionable attire and venture into unsavory company. But given the trouble the men Alec had detailed to follow Willoughby had in staying with him when he didn't wish to be tailed, it would behoove us to uncover what we could. Though my intrigue was tempered by the fact that it was unlikely Lady Powerscourt had seen him in much of an out-of-the-way spot, even if it was through the safety of her motorcar window.

As if to emphasize this, I spied the grand Georgian edifice of Powerscourt House ahead of us across the street. It was hard to miss, its Palladian gray stone exterior overshadowing everything else on the narrow street. However, it was no longer the Dublin residence of Viscount Powerscourt, having been sold a century earlier. It was now owned by Ferrier and Pollock, a haberdashery wholesaler.

As we approached, I couldn't help asking, "Do you ever wish your husband still owned a town house here in Dublin?"

Recognizing why I was asking, she turned to look at it. "Heavens, no. The upkeep would be tremendous. Besides, the estate is no more than an hour away by motorcar. And the Shelbourne does nicely for me when I must come to town for more than a day."

I nodded, for this made sense and helped me recall something I'd wanted to discuss with her. "How well do you know Doris Fitzgibbon?"

A speculative gleam lit her eye. "Well enough, I suppose. Why?"

"She was behaving peculiarly the other night when I questioned her about the Harringtons' party. Now, I'm not suggesting she has anything to do with the jewel thefts . . ."

"I'm not sure she has the brains for it," she quipped dryly, perhaps revealing more about herself than Doris.

"But something definitely made her nervous, and I wondered if you might know what it is."

She tilted her head in contemplation. "She doesn't invite me into her confidence, so I'm afraid I can only speculate. But I can't say that I've ever considered her to be possessed of an anxious sort of temperament. She has no need to be anxious, when her husband and brother manage everything for her. And I haven't heard any particularly titillating gossip surrounding her." She frowned. "Nervous, truly?"

"Yes."

"Hmmm. Then perhaps she was nervous on someone else's behalf."

That was an interesting notion. Especially since she had two people for whom to worry if there was something to hide. If that was the case, I found Beresford to be the far more likely candidate. Hal Fitzgibbon seemed too blithe and trusting. But appearances could be deceiving. I knew this well.

It seemed I needed to have another conversation with Doris. This one, preferably in private.

CHAPTER 14

Sidney was seated outside in the garden when I returned home, and I could tell immediately that he had as much a need to speak with me as I did him. So, conscious of the listening ears of our Irish staff, even if we now mainly trusted them, I invited him to stroll through our small plot. We perambulated slowly down the narrow path, scarlet pimpernels and violets brushing my powder-blue serge skirt in the afternoon sun.

"How was Jammet's?" Sidney prompted once we were far enough from the house.

"Delicious. Though the food was nearly spoiled by the company."

Sidney's gaze met mine in surprise.

"Ardmore."

He cursed.

"Yes. Quite. He and Sturgis essentially forced me and Sybil into joining them."

He scowled. "I wouldn't have expected that of Sturgis."

"Oh, I suspect that was all Ardmore's doing and Mr. Sturgis merely thought they were being cordial."

"Still," he grumbled.

"It was the most extraordinary conversation." I relayed everything that Ardmore had said, uninterrupted but for the periodic blasphemy muttered under Sidney's breath. When I finished, we both fell silent, pausing next to the fence which bordered the vacant home next door as we pretended to examine the trailing vines growing over the side.

"Are you going to inform Xavier?"

I knew he was speaking about the possibility that Ardmore intended to double-cross Collins and arrange for his men to be caught with the phosgene.

"I suppose I should. Though, I don't know if it will do any good. I've already warned them that Ardmore isn't to be trusted."

He paced a few steps away, clutching the back of his neck, before pivoting to face me. "I don't like it, Ver. I don't like it one bit."

I could tell something more was bothering him than just Ardmore toying with me and potentially revealing his intentions.

He exhaled a long breath, dropping his arm. "I also arrived to lunch to discover an unwanted guest."

My mind scrambled to decide who could have insinuated themselves into his meeting with Bennett and Ames. My first guess was O, for he'd been in contact with Sidney before, attempting to recruit him. But I was wrong.

"Willoughby."

It was my turn to curse. They were turning the tables on us faster than we were them.

Sidney's midnight-blue eyes were jaded and weary. "Bennett invited him because he had some brilliant notions on the location of the phosgene."

"Of course, he did," I growled, my fists clenched at my side. I was so angry I wanted to hit something. But one look at Sidney's face made me temper my own feelings. "What did you do?"

"What *could* I do but play along? We have no proof, Ver. Not of Ardmore or Willoughby's complicity. And now Ardmore is meeting with O, telling him God knows what." He turned away, scraping a hand down his face, as he grappled with this. "It's not good, Ver."

I wrapped my arms around my middle, feeling his distress amplify my own.

We felt backed into a corner, and whenever that happened, the instinct was to kick out. But that was exactly what Ardmore would be expecting. We couldn't lose our cool. We couldn't panic.

I inhaled a deep breath, forcing myself to take a step back and assess the situation. "All right, so Ardmore is attempting to infiltrate all of our information sources and turn them to his will. He wants us to feel like we're out of options. But we're not." I lifted my gaze to his. "Not by a long shot."

"Ver . . ." Sidney began to argue, until I pulled the letter from my pocket. "What's that?"

"A letter from Kathleen, and she's uncovered some things."

He moved to stand beside me as I opened it and then passed it to him, perusing it again as he did for the first time. "We need to search these sites." I pointed to the list of locations provided and then the list of potential contacts. "And we need to ask Alec what he can uncover about these men."

His brow furrowed. "And when these don't turn up anything? When we find ourselves starting over yet again? What then?"

Surprised by this outburst, I attempted to jest. "When did you become so pessimistic?"

"Since I realized Ardmore might expose us and have my wife incarcerated or *worse*."

I shook my head. "That's not going to happen."

"You can't know—"

"I can!" I snapped, unwilling to entertain anything else. Not when giving in to our fears meant giving up. Which meant Ardmore won, and whatever horrible plans he had for that phosgene would go unchecked.

Sidney grasped my upper arms. "Verity—"

"No. Listen to me," I pleaded, gripping his coat. "This isn't about us. Don't you see? If Ardmore is going to this much trouble to interfere, then that's proof that he has intentions for the phosgene that are not good, and that he's worried we'll spoil them. Otherwise, he would never bother. Not to this extent. You *know* this."

His clasp on my arms loosened, and I could sense the turmoil inside him.

"We *can't* just walk away from this. Not knowing what could happen. Not knowing that hundreds of people could die if they deployed those canisters in the right conditions at the right place. Women and children even, depending on the circumstances."

Sidney's head hung low as he wrestled with himself.

"You know I'm right," I rasped.

He lifted his gaze to mine as he spoke in a broken voice. "And if he destroys us in the process?"

I felt a quaver run through me, knowing that he also spoke the truth. Ardmore could and very possibly would take his revenge swiftly and savagely. If we succeeded, it was still likely our lives would never be the same. We might even have to flee Britain altogether. This was no small thing, particularly when nearly all of our friends and family lived there. When the title and estates Sidney would one day inherit from his uncle were there. When we had both already given so much for the preservation of it.

And yet, there was no other possible choice we could make. Not without destroying ourselves with guilt and regret.

"We just have to be prepared," I said with as much confidence as I could muster, though my words still trembled at the end.

His lips creased into a mournful smile. "Then I suppose it's a good thing that I asked Finnegan to begin discreetly transferring some of our assets to a bank in America."

I blinked at him in shock. "You did?"

I'd known he was troubled by the precarious line of neu-trality we'd been forced to walk as we investigated, but I hadn't comprehended how much. Hearing that he'd taken such steps to protect us made tears burn the back of my eyes. Tears that spilled over as he pulled me into his embrace.

We clung to each other for a few moments, buoys to the other in the face of this potential storm. When my legs and breath had steadied enough for me to pull away, Sidney passed me his handkerchief. I dabbed at my eyes while I tried to refocus on what needed to be done next.

"We should contact Xavier." Sidney lifted the letter he'd refolded. "About this and the rest." He glanced toward the house. "I can have Nimble deliver a note to the Capel Street library." Where they would relay it to Alec.

I sniffed. "I have a message I need him to deliver, too."

He looked at me in question as I straightened my shoulders.

"We need to know what Ardmore and O are discussing. And fortunately, I know someone who might be able to tell us."

I'd met Nancy O'Brien by chance when I'd gone toe-to-toe with O, demanding Nimble's release after he was arrested by a couple of Black and Tans for verbally defending our maid Ginny's honor. The initial extension of friendship had been a contrivance on my part, for I'd needed information, but we'd quickly become friends in truth. At least, the affection was genuine on my part, even though I'd since begun to sus-pect she was one of Collins's informants. Whatever the truth, Nancy worked within Dublin Castle, and she had access to sensitive information in her role there. I didn't know precisely what that role was, but that it sometimes brought her into contact with O.

"Do you think that's wise?" Sidney asked.

"Maybe not, but I don't think we have a choice. And given what I suspect about her, we know there's little risk of her reporting to O about us."

This agreed upon, we separated to pen our missives, sending them off with Nimble. Alec's response was swifter than I'd anticipated, arriving barely an hour after the valet returned to our town house. Nancy's was dropped into our letter slot just before we were departing to meet Alec that evening. She'd agreed to join me at the Pillar Picture House for a matinee the next day. It was just the sort of concealment we needed.

The cinema was stuffy when I arrived, making it quite natural for me to remove my coat. Sliding into the back row, I slung the garment over the seat in front of me, discouraging anyone from sitting there. This earned me a dirty look from the woman seated a few seats away, but I ignored her, not about to risk the privacy I needed to speak with Nancy. Especially now that it was more imperative than ever that we learn just what Ardmore and O were discussing, and who else was party to it.

Our search of the buildings on Kathleen's list the evening before had been fruitless yet again. Or three of them had. The fourth had proved to be a busy warehouse still in use. Which did not preclude the possibility that the phosgene was being stored there, but it would have to be searched a different way. Even now, Sidney and Alec were arranging that, but I held little hope that they would find the cylinders there.

Alec had also taken the list of names Kathleen had supplied, promising to contact us as soon as he learned anything that might be pertinent. In addition, I'd decided to send a copy of the list to my journalist friend Michael Wickham, asking him to meet me. I'd thus far avoided telling Wick everything about the reason Sidney and I were in Dublin, but it seemed now might be the time to come clean. He had contacts at all levels, and he was sympathetic to the republicans. He might prove critically helpful, though I knew it would come at a cost. But if I was already willing to risk my life and my freedom to stop Ardmore, what were a few pieces of possibly sensitive information?

Nancy slipped into the theater just before the Pathé newsreels began showing. She plopped down into the seat next to mine with an exhalation of relief. "Sure, but don't ye know, they've got barricades up over O'Connell again."

"They must have just put them up," I replied, for I'd passed over the bridge with no trouble.

"I was on the first tram goin' through, or I'd never have made it in time."

"Well, you're here now," I said with a smile.

She grinned broadly as she removed her hat, her wavy dark hair settling around her head like a cloud. I elected to leave my short-brimmed cloche-style on my head.

"I imagine they're keeping you busy at the Castle. I was afraid you wouldn't be able to get away," I admitted. At least, not for a few days.

"'Tis my day off," she confessed in her lyrical Irish accent. "So your letter arrived at the perfect time."

The theater darkened as the newsreels began to spool and the pianist played the opening chords. We sat silently for a few moments before I shifted closer so that I could speak softly with my eyes still facing forward. Nancy did likewise.

"Though I have to confess, I also had an ulterior motive for wanting to see you."

"I suspected so," she admitted lightly, easing the guilt I felt at making the request I was about to. The fact that Nancy had no illusions as to our friendship being purely fraternal was a relief.

"Are you acquainted with a man named Lord Ardmore? I understand he's been meeting with Colonel Winter."

"I know who ye mean. He's been meetin' with Tudor and some others as well."

This wasn't surprising given Major-General Tudor was acting nominally as an advisor to the Royal Irish Constabulary, though in reality he was in charge. He was responsible for the Black and Tans, as well as the new Auxiliary Division made up of former British Army officers who had begun arriving in Ireland. O served in conjunction with him.

"I don't know precisely what your duties are at the Castle, and I'm not asking you to tell me," I murmured, choosing my words with care. "But is it possible for you to find out what is being discussed during those meetings? I wouldn't ask, but . . . it could prove vitally important."

I turned my head to meet her gaze, letting her know how earnest I was being.

Her dark eyebrows had settled into concerned slashes, and guilt stirred in me anew. "I think I've a way," she finally said before turning back to the reel. "I do be there about an hour or more before the rest of 'em, so I can have a nose around." She broke off before cautioning, "They'll not have taken many notes."

I suspected not. They wouldn't want a paper trail.

"But one of the adjutes who works for O is sweet on me, *and* he's prone to braggin'. I'll see what he knows."

Feeling a stirring of alarm within me, I reached over to grip her arm, surprising her. "Be careful," I whispered, as her eyes found mine again in the flicker of the lights from the screen. "Ardmore recently stated that they know Collins has informants everywhere. And if you're caught, you might be mistaken for one," I fumbled to add in an effort to maintain the farce of my not knowing what she really was.

However, I could tell that she knew that I knew, and she could tell that I'd seen this recognition. Her lip curled upward at one corner as she answered with a simple, "Sure."

Seeing this rekindled my anger that Collins had not taken more care to protect her. The information she'd provided me during our last investigation had been important, but she'd risked much in getting it to me, and the very act of her doing so had tipped me off to her likely association with IRA

Intelligence. If I had figured it out so quickly, I worried others would not be far behind.

But I said none of this, instead squeezing her arm and then letting go. Gazing up at the film projected across the screen, I was acutely aware of the pinch in my abdomen, the acknowledgment that I was being somewhat hypocritical. For here I was asking Nancy to take risks on my behalf as well. A request that I had no right to make. For while it was fair for me to risk my own life and freedom to stop Ardmore—after all, it was *my* life—was it fair to risk Nancy's? And how would I feel if she paid the ultimate price because of me?

The only thing that kept me from telling her I'd changed my mind was the fact that Nancy was already aware of the dangers. She willingly ran them every day for Collins, and she, no doubt, saw prisoners brought into the Castle and heard what happened to them during interrogation. She was conscious of how much was at stake. Still, the ache beneath my breastbone did not abate. I suspected it wouldn't until Ardmore's plan was foiled, and he was finally exposed.

Over the next few days, while our investigations stalled, Ireland continued to seethe with pockets of violence. A gun battle on a crowded platform at the Galway rail station, resulting in the deaths of an RIC driver and an IRA volunteer, led to another rash of burnings and shootings throughout Galway City by Crown Forces. Republican-leaning newspapers were reporting that the nightly terror was ongoing, while unionist papers and even Dublin Castle denied any RIC reprisals had occurred at all.

In County Roscommon, an old farmer was shot by a passing lorry filled with Crown Forces, while at the Kilkenny Post Office yard a driver was beaten by men with blackened faces and eleven post office bags stolen. This last incident would have seemed to be perpetrated by the IRA but for the blackened faces, for in the past they had not resorted to such measures, calling the allegiance of the offenders somewhat into question. A carter who was hard of hearing was shot in Belfast when he failed to heed an order from a military patrol to stop. Elsewhere, four more RIC constables had died, though one had been accidentally shot in his barracks and another had committed suicide.

Meanwhile, in Dublin, a Great Northern Railway driver from Belfast was accosted outside a pub and tied to a pole in Talbot Street with a sign stating, "SCAB. This is Robert Bruce who continued to drive munitions trains on the GNR while his comrades are being DISMISSED." The railroad and dockyard strikes were still in full swing, as many of the workers refused to load, unload, or transport munitions or military personnel. Just as the hunger strikers still garnered significant print space in the press and engaged strong public opinion at home and abroad. Masses and protests by pockets of the country continued, including a massive one by four thousand Guinness workers who held a special mass for Mac-Swiney and the other strikers. Dublin Corporation adjourned for a week in protest, and even a meeting of the magistrates of Dublin city and county passed a motion requesting the lord mayor of Cork's immediate release as the conviction had been legally unsound.

The British Army had also issued orders that all guns—even those with permits—were to be collected from civilians. Alec had jested that the rebels were happy to help them with that. Sidney viewed this as confirmation he'd been right not to register his Luger pistol, for after the busy warehouse had proved not to store the phosgene cylinders, he was even more determined to remain armed. While I'd often argued against this, I had to concede that recent events had made me begin to question my belief that protection from such a weapon was unnecessary.

CHAPTER 15

I was standing before the wardrobe, selecting my clothes for the evening, when Sidney suddenly burst through the door after only the most perfunctory of raps.

"There's been another jewel theft," he informed me.

"Where?"

"The Shelbourne. Not an hour ago."

I blinked in astonishment. "You're jesting?"

He scooped up the Prussian-blue jacket from my walking ensemble that I'd discarded on the bed, holding it out for me. "Burrows sent a constable requesting our presence."

Ginny goggled at us as I slid my arms into the sleeves.

"My mauve roll-brimmed hat, please," I prompted her.

She nodded, fumbling it when she pulled it from the shelf.

I offered her a reassuring smile. "It doesn't appear we'll be going dancing after all," I informed her before allowing Sidney to hurry me out the door.

Though the hotel was only three or four blocks away, at the corner of St. Stephen's Green, time being of the essence, Sidney insisted on taking the Pierce-Arrow. At first, a constable standing along the pavement before the hotel objected to him parking there, but another officer explained the situation to him and we were waved on. As we were hustled through the opulent lobby, I spotted a number of reporters, which told me this string of jewel heists was not going to remain out of print much longer.

We rode the elevator to the floor where I knew from our stay here in late May some of the most opulent suites were located. The door to one of the parlors stood open, and we entered to find DI Burrows and a sergeant speaking with a couple, while their maid perched awkwardly on one of the chairs. At our entrance, she began to rise, but I waved her back down with much the same reassuring smile I'd given Ginny not ten minutes earlier.

Burrows was the first to speak. "Mr. and Mrs. Kent, thank ye for comin' so swiftly."

"Your missive was, of course, brief," Sidney replied, appearing cool and collected, and every bit the affluent gentleman and former military officer, despite our haste in getting there. "Did I understand you correctly? There's been another jewel theft?"

"Information it would've been helpful to know *before* now," the man seated on the settee in a smart Saville Row three-piece suit grumbled.

The woman whom he had his arm around, presumably his wife, pressed a restraining hand to his chest.

Burrows ignored them, rising to his feet to address me and Sidney. "Near as we can tell, the thief entered either through this door"—he pointed toward the entrance to the parlor—"or the one in the adjoinin' bedchamber." At this, he led us through to the next room, where a pair of men were dusting for fingerprints. Of course, if the thief had worn gloves, like he had at the other crime scenes, they wouldn't find any from the burglar.

"Either way, it appears he had a key, for there's no evidence of a lock bein' picked." Burrows scowled. "And neither Mrs. Thatch nor her maid heard anythin'."

"They were here?" I gasped in astonishment.

He nodded toward the door leading to the next room. "In the bath chatting, and yet the thief crept in here, bold as brass, and rifled through the drawers. He didn't make a quick go of it either." He led us closer so that we could look into the top open drawer of the bureau. We could see several pieces of jewelry still nestled inside, in particular two ropes of pearls. "He took the real pearls and left the fakes."

It wasn't actually all that difficult to tell real pearls from fakes. The real ones felt different. They were heavier and cool to the touch, and they were slightly gritty when you rubbed them against your teeth. But not everyone knew these things or had handled enough of them to recognize the difference. It was telling that the thief had.

"This chap must have some pluck not to turn windy when he discovered the suite was occupied," Sidney remarked, leaning closer to examine the jewelry that had been left. "I can't imagine how he meant to explain his presence, rifling through the bedchamber drawers, if they came in and caught him."

"Not even a member of the hotel staff would have such permission," I agreed. Not when the guest had a maid of her own, and certainly not without first knocking.

"A member of the staff was my first suspicion as well," Burrows said, leading us back toward the parlor. "Or someone pretendin' to be." It couldn't be that difficult to get your hands on a uniform. "But all of the Shelbourne's employees deny knowin' anythin'."

I paused at the threshold, looking back at the men still at work. "I presume you'll wish to fingerprint them all."

"Aye."

"Then have one of your men start the rumor that you've found the key and there are fingerprints on it."

Burrows eyed me consideringly. Perhaps not having expected me to be capable of such wiliness.

"That's how you think the thief gained entrance, isn't it? That a member of the staff gave him—or her—the key."

"He—or she—might just as easily have returned it," Sidney pointed out.

I shrugged. "Then they'll know we're lying. But if the key wasn't returned . . ."

"They might decide to confess so they can tell their side of the story while they still can."

Burrows beckoned his sergeant over and briefly explained. The sergeant nodded, a gleam in his eyes. "I've just the man."

As he departed, we returned to where Mr. and Mrs. Thatch and their maid waited. If they thought it odd that we'd been invited to consult on the theft, they didn't let on. I suspected our reputation preceded us.

I properly introduced myself before sitting down in the second chair, upholstered in plush cream fabric, so that I was at the women's level. "I understand the theft occurred while you were both in the adjoining bathing chamber," I said to Mrs. Thatch and the maid. "And that you didn't hear a thing."

"Not a sound," Mrs. Thatch asserted with wide eyes as her maid mutely shook her head.

"How were you so certain the theft occurred at that time then?"

"Because we'd just discussed what jewelry I intended to wear tonight."

"While Mrs. Thatch was finishin', I went to lay out her clothes," the maid murmured, speaking for the first time. "I noticed the jewelry drawer was open and thought we'd left it that way. But when I went to close it, I realized some of the pieces were missin'."

Then that explained how the theft had been noticed so quickly. It also suggested that the maid might have almost walked in on the thief. My gaze lifted to Sidney and DI Burrows, noting they'd recognized the same thing. Given that fact, it was unlikely the burglar would have taken the time to return the key. They would have been intent on slipping away unnoticed before the alarm was raised.

"Have any other rooms been burglarized?" I asked Burrows.

"Not that we know of." His answer and his expression were both circumspect, but I could surmise that the hotel had not wished an uproar among the other guests, so the possibility remained that there had been other thefts which had simply not yet been noticed.

"Did you happen to attend a party at the Harringtons' residence out in Rathmines?" I asked the couple, who exchanged a glance and then shook their heads.

"We're not acquainted," Mrs. Thatch replied.

"What of the charity fete held here a few nights' past?"

Mrs. Thatch's eyes widened, giving me my answer before she spoke. "Why, yes. 'Tis one of the reasons we came to town."

"Were there thefts at the ball?" Mr. Thatch demanded to know. "If so, this is the first time I'm hearin' of 'em."

"No, I merely have a hunch that the thief might have been taking note of the jewels guests were wearing. Or perhaps he read the society columns that reported on the event," I explained, reminding myself we had to keep that in mind.

"Oh, there was that article in the *Telegraph*." From the manner in which Mrs. Thatch blushed, I suspected before now she'd been pleased to be mentioned.

Her husband's brow lowered thunderously. "I would like to return to the issue of the other jewel thefts and *why* the public was not informed so we could take better precautions to protect ourselves."

DI Burrows looked as if he'd like to smack the contemptuous sneer off the fellow's face, but he answered in a respectful tone of voice. "It is not the Dublin Metropolitan Police's policy to report on crimes to the press, *especially* when the victims have requested that we not do so."

Mr. Thatch opened his mouth to retort, but Burrows had already turned to me and Sidney.

"Any further questions for the Thatches and Miss Waters?"

Sidney stood with his hand on the back of my chair. "I suppose you've already asked if they noticed anyone hanging about, observing them."

"I have, and the answer was negative."

I eyed Miss Waters, the maid, closely as Burrows reported this, for sometimes servants were hesitant to speak in front of their employers, but she did not exhibit any signs that she was keeping anything from us.

Burrows's gaze shifted toward the doorway where his sergeant had reappeared. "If there's nothin' else, then I'll leave ye to finish providin' an inventory of all that was stolen to Sergeant O'Neil."

At his prompting, Sidney and I followed the inspector from the parlor back to the bedroom where the fingerprint men were finishing up. "Hopefully, 'twon't be long 'til we discover whether yer ploy is successful," he informed us.

"I don't think you'll be able to keep this one out of the press," I told him after a few beats of silence, wondering if he knew that even now reporters were gathered outside the hotel.

"And all for the better." He tugged down sharply on the coat of his three-piece suit, this one gray with black pin-stripes, his neatly waxed mustache twitching.

I supposed I couldn't blame him for his indignation, not when all the secrecy had prohibited him from doing his job properly. Yet he would be held at fault for not catching the thief. In any case, the insurance companies' middlemen had been given long enough to recover the jewels for their clients. The fact that they hadn't suggested they wouldn't, and indicated a great deal about how the thief was operating. Namely that they were breaking the jewelry down into its components and had no desire to risk exposing themselves to a middleman.

"Ye think the thief decided to target Mrs. Thatch after seein' her pearls at that charity fete?" Burrows asked us.

"I think it's likely," I confessed. "I didn't see Mrs. Thatch there myself, but I heard others talking about a rope of pearls a woman had recently completed." Some women spent years collecting pearls of the right shape, shade, and size. I shrugged and sighed. "But the thief could have learned of them elsewhere."

He nodded, his brow furrowed in consideration. There was a knock on the door, and he bade whoever it was to enter.

A spry constable of about five and twenty entered with a slightly older man dressed in the Shelbourne's uniform, his shoulders drooping. "This fellow has somethin' to tell ye, sir." With this, he nudged the man forward.

"What's your name?" Burrows asked him, even as the employee scrutinized me and Sidney.

He startled. "Bates, sir."

"And what have ye to tell me?"

"The key the thief used." His prominent Adam's apple bobbed up and down as he swallowed. "It might've been mine."

"It *might* have?" Burrows repeated, to which Bates nodded. The constable's expression was cynical. "And just what leads ye to believe that?"

"Because I . . . I can't find mine."

"You lost it then?"

He hesitated, before agreeing. "Aye, sir."

"Rather careless of ye, don't ye think, to lose a key like that?"

"Aye, sir." Bates drew himself ever taller and straighter as Burrows continued to question him.

"And what exactly did this key of yours open?"

"All the rooms on this floor."

Burrows paced to Bates's other side. "And when did ye say ye noticed it was gone?"

"A-after your constable questioned us the first time," he stammered.

"I see." Burrows paced around him again. "And we're simply to take ye at your word on this, are we?"

"Aye?" It emerged sounding more like a question than a statement.

"'Specially when there's only one set of fingerprints on the key."

"But that's because—" Bates broke off, meeting each of our gazes in turn with his panicked one.

"Because what?" Burrows prompted.

When Bates didn't speak up quickly enough, the constable answered for him. "Because the other chap was wearin' gloves."

"I never said—" Bates rounded on him to declare, before making a sound as if he wished he'd swallowed his tongue.

The constable grinned.

Burrows arched an eyebrow at him before dismissing him, though this did nothing to dampen the constable's spirits. "What did the man wearin' gloves look like?" the inspector asked the footman.

Bates's hands clenched into fists at his sides, as if he intended to argue, but then he abruptly deflated. "Like every other swell what walks in here." He scowled. "Had dark hair and a smug smile."

"Did you notice anything more distinctive?" I asked.

"Didn't pay that close attention."

"Yet you gave him your key."

His brow furrowed into deep lines.

"And he was wearing gloves." Sidney's deep voice communicated his disdain. "Didn't that raise any red flags?"

"They was drivin' gloves," Bates griped as if this explained it.

Burrows stood scrutinizing him with his hands in his trouser pockets. "Did this swell tell ye why he wanted the keys, or were ye just content with the blunt he slipped ye?"

His eyes narrowed. "He said he was havin' an affair with the lady in this room, and he was after somethin' incriminatin' he'd dropped. That he wanted to spare the woman the shame and perhaps her marriage if 'twas found by her husband."

"And ye believed him?" Burrows didn't bother to hide his skepticism.

"Yes." Bates spread his hands wide, suddenly dropping all trace of his earlier defiance as he pleaded. "I certainly didn't know he was after stealin' jewelry! I'd never have lent him my key if I'd thought that. But he was the picture of the perfect British gentleman. How was I to know?"

I couldn't tell if Burrows believed him, but I suspected Bates was telling the truth. His description of the thief corroborated what we already knew or had begun to suspect, and the fact that none of this had been made known publicly only strengthened its credibility. Unfortunately, the attributes of the culprit weren't distinctive enough to suggest anyone in particular. Though maybe Burrows would be able to get more out of him later.

Regardless, as Sidney and I made our way back to his Pierce-Arrow, I found myself searching the throng in the hotel lobby and along the pavement for anyone who might fit Bates's description as the reporters called our names and photographers snapped pictures. I'd heard that sometimes criminals would return to the scene of their crime to indulge their curiosity, and I wondered if the dark-haired thief would also.

Sadly, there were just too many who matched the parameters. I spied Mr. Chatham and Rufus Beresford, as well as

Robby Dalton and even Dr. McCarthy, who we'd met in the Shelbourne ballroom just days before. O's minion, Frank Caulfield, was also there, his hooded eyes taking everything in. As we reached the motorcar, I even thought I caught sight of Alec, his sharp gaze observing us from beneath the brim of the flat cap covering his dark hair, but the man disappeared into the crowd before I could be certain.

However, a message delivered for me a few days later made me suspect he had, indeed, been there. For Alec teased me about our failure to apprehend the Irish Raffles.

True to our suspicions, the press had had a field day with the discovery that there was a jewel thief at work in Dublin. After months of depressing articles related to the ongoing rebellion and the government's response to it, they all seemed eager for the lighter fare provided by the dramatic antics of such a suave criminal. The press had even already dubbed him the Irish Raffles, after the gentleman thief portrayed in the popular adventure stories by author Ernest William Hornung. Raffles was an urbane and polished gentleman of leisure, a cricket star by day and an amateur cracksman by night. But of course, this Irish Raffles was even more fascinating because not only was he real, but he'd stolen a string of flawless pearls worth more than eighty-two-thousand pounds during daylight.

Not that the press had stopped reporting on the revolution altogether. Overall, the hunger strikers still took up more page space. It was also announced that the United States had decided to send a committee to Ireland to investigate conditions. Whether this would make much of a difference either way remained to be seen, but it was a victory for the Dáil and an embarrassment to the British.

Alec promised me news of an even greater embarrassment if I attended a meeting the next day, at a location on Great Brunswick Street he disclosed, ordering me to keep it secret. Given that inducement, I decided I couldn't refuse.

CHAPTER 16

When I arrived at the offices of the newspaper *Young Ireland* in Great Brunswick Street the next day, I discovered that, as a woman, I was in the decided minority. All but one of the individuals crammed into the small inner office scattered with desks were men of the more respectable variety dressed in suits, albeit with ink-stained hands clutching notepads. Having neither, I tried to appear as inconspicuous as possible as I stood near the back, looking for Alec. Instead I found Wick.

Michael Wickham was a reporter for the *Irish Independent*. We'd met in a field hospital outside Amiens where he was recovering from shrapnel wounds that he'd received while reporting on the Germans' 1918 spring offensive. I was there because I'd nearly lost my life in a shell explosion while delivering a message from HQ about a suspected traitor among a brigades' intelligence staff. I'd been posing as a French refugee fleeing the chaos of the Germans' advance but had given away the fact that I was actually English—though thankfully not my role with British Intelligence—while I was out of my head from the shelling.

Wick being as observant as he was, of course, had suspected I was lying when I'd claimed I'd been near the chaos of the front searching for French cousins fleeing the Germans' rapid advance, but he'd never attempted to expose me. In fact, his friendship and irreverent Irish humor had gone a long way to helping me regain my faculties and my footing. Something I would never forget.

He presented himself as a dashing, absent-minded journalist, complete with windblown overgrown hair and ink-stained cuffs, but those who knew him or had been the subject of one of his stories knew that he was as sharp as they came. As easygoing as he appeared, I knew what steely determination he hid underneath. I liked to think it was hinted at in his square-cut jawline, but that was merely fanciful thinking—something I was rarely prone to. What *was* true was that he'd proved invaluable in providing information on a number of critical matters since our arrival in Dublin, and seeing him, I hoped today might be no different. Though, I also understood that meant I would have to give up something in return.

He hadn't seen me yet, so I sidled closer to him before leaning in to murmur, "Not ignoring me, are you?"

He turned to me in surprise and then recovered quickly, smiling. "Aye, and sure. You've run me ragged." He leaned in to buss my cheek. "Good to see ye, love. I've only just received your message. I've been away on assignment."

"Is that so?" I teased.

But he gave nothing away, instead searching the room behind me, presumably for Sidney. "I'm surprised to see ye here of all places."

There was a question in his eyes. One I wasn't going to answer. "I was told I wouldn't regret it," I said with a little shrug.

As for Sidney, though he hadn't been happy about it, it had been necessary to split up. While I'd obeyed Alec's summons, Sidney had gone to meet with the band from the Harringtons' party as we'd previously planned. Claudia Harrington's social secretary had been able to give me their direction, and they'd agreed to speak with us, but seemed likely to balk if we asked to reschedule or didn't show. Their apprehension made me hopeful they *had* witnessed something pertinent, so we'd had no choice but to pursue our separate tasks.

A glance around the room showed me there was still no sign of Alec, yet the appointed hour was drawing nigh. It was true, Alec hadn't said he would be here, he'd simply indicated that *I* should be. But I'd assumed he would also make an appearance. However, looking around at all the reporters, I began to think perhaps that might not be a good thing. A number of them spoke with foreign accents, betraying them as French, or Spanish, or American, but there were several who were clearly Irishmen, and they might not all be friendly to the rebels.

Wick eyed me curiously, and I wondered if he knew any more than I did about what was about to happen. A press conference of some sort, it seemed. One undoubtedly called by someone with Sinn Féin or the IRA. But beyond Alec's mention of further embarrassment for the British government, I hadn't the slightest idea what was going to be said.

Before I could give in to the temptation to ask Wick what he knew, the door opened and in walked Arthur Griffith, the acting president of Dáil Éireann while Éamon de Valera was in the United States lobbying for funds and support. Griffith was considered a moderate among the leaders of the rebellion, and so I'd heard the Crown Forces had been ordered not to arrest him if he was found, for he was more useful exerting his influence over the more radical members of the movement than in prison. Even so, Griffith remained hidden much of the time, not advertising his whereabouts for fear that the British would change their minds. Though he still conducted regular press conferences at locations that remained undisclosed until the last minute.

Griffith's appearance had always struck me as that of a younger, perhaps more dignified brother to the former US president, Theodore Roosevelt. They both sported similar mustaches and pince-nez eyeglasses. However, Griffith's speaking style was very different.

However, Griffith wasn't alone. A fair man of approximately the same age accompanied him, peering around the room with interest. At the sight of him, the reporters each adopted relaxed positions, concealing their notepads as if given a signal. Wick's gaze darted from mine to the ladder-back chair next to me and I took the cue to sit down. Now I was beginning to grow annoyed with Alec, for this was clearly not a simple press conference.

"Gentlemen, and ladies," Griffith announced as his gaze swept around the room and paused briefly on me and another woman in brown. "This is the man I have been telling ye about, Frank Digby Hardy. He is here to offer his services to the cause."

Griffith gestured for Hardy to speak, and he stepped forward, almost preening. It was immediately apparent that he was English, and almost just as obvious that he was rotten. Hardy told us a little of his background and then elaborated on his decision to aid the republicans. That he believed he was speaking to a room filled with senior members of Sinn Féin or the IRA was obvious, for he certainly didn't suspect the truth. Otherwise, he would never have announced that he was sent to Dublin to work as an agent for the Secret Intelligence Service but had become disillusioned and was willing to become a double agent for Sinn Féin.

My chest constricted upon hearing this, but then realized it was unlikely he had the slightest clue of my own role with the SIS.

Hardy then proceeded to propose that he could arrange to have his handler, a Captain Thomson—a name that made my ears perk up—appear at an isolated section of Kingstown pier so that the IRA could either assassinate or capture him. But in order to do this, he insisted he needed to know a location where Michael Collins would be, so that he could supply this intelligence to promote his position within the Secret Service. He promised to suppress the information until the time had passed when Collins would be in danger, and then share it with British Intelligence so that his cover would be protected.

While some of the journalists masked as members of Sinn Féin peppered him with questions as if they were seriously considering his offer, I ruminated on his handler's name. There was only one Thomson I knew of within intelligence circles—Basil Thomson himself, the director of intelligence at the Home Office. But I struggled to imagine him acting as handler to such an incompetent man. Then again, he'd also recruited Byrnes—purportedly the best intelligence agent in the agency—and he'd been killed by Collins's Squad. Of course, Captain Thomson could be an alias, though a rather clumsy one, if that was the case.

After listening to Hardy propose to lead a unit of Auxiliaries into an ambush and promise to assist the IRA in finding British arms caches, Griffith had presumably heard enough malarkey.

"Thank ye, Mr. Hardy," he proclaimed, silencing the man. "I do believe you've given these men, all distinguished members of the press, sufficient evidence of your intentions and motives."

Hardy's eyes goggled as he looked around at those gathered, all of whom began to remove their notepads from their places of concealment and furiously jot down notes.

"However, just to make matters perfectly clear, I do have an extract from a newspaper article touting your distinguished thirty-four-year career as a criminal, as well as the details of your early release from prison by none other than Lord French, the lord lieutenant himself, so that the British might make use of your skills here in Ireland."

Hardy was noticeably agitated and distressed as this information was read out, detailing numerous stints in English prisons for forgery, misappropriation of ship's funds, bigamy, fraud, and other confidence scams.

When Griffith finished, he turned to glare at Hardy in disgust. "The way I see it, ye have two options. Leave Ireland and never return, or remain in Dublin and face the consequences." Whether he meant from the British or Collins's assassination Squad was unclear. "I strongly advise ye to be on the boat leavin' Kingstown at nine o' the clock this evenin'." With that, he turned and walked away. Hardy slinked away a few moments later as reporters hollered additional questions at him.

I remained where I was, frankly still stunned. An uncomfortable feeling had settled over me, for I'd begun to wonder if Alec had invited me to the press conference for a different reason than the one touted. Was this meant to be a warning? A threat to expose me and Sidney in just as horrifying a manner if we did not cooperate to Collins's liking?

This possibility did not sit well with me, and neither did Alec's absence. Which, if anything, only made the probability of this being a threat even higher in my mind.

Wick scoffed aloud, rising to his feet from where he'd propped himself at the corner of one of the desks while the other reporters began filing out. "While it's undeniably false that the British are grantin' release to every convicted felon who agrees to serve the Crown here in Ireland, as Sinn Féin's propaganda would have us believe, 'tis occurrences like this that make the public wonder." He waited for me to gain my feet, perhaps recognizing I was still struggling to grapple with everything we'd just heard. "I've got to get this written and to press, but I've time to stand ye a cup of tea if ye wish to discuss what ye wrote me about."

"I'd like that."

He held the door for me, calling out in farewell to the news editor from the *Freeman's Journal* still inside.

A tram trundled by as we set off down the pavement, the placard at its top advertising Bovril, a food my husband had confessed he hoped to never drink again after consuming interminable cups of it as part of his rations during the war. At the corner stood a pair of newsboys in their shabby street clothes—one with ragged shoes and one without—hawking rival papers. Wick tossed them each a penny without taking a paper, for which they cheered him. But he merely raised his hand and kept strolling down the cross street.

I knew better than to say anything. Men like Wick and Sidney didn't wish to be praised for such displays of kindness. It would only embarrass them. But I allowed the reminder of what type of man Michael Wickham was to hearten me about what must be done.

Having tucked his notepad away, Wick stuffed his hands in his pockets before casting me a sideways glance. "I'd ask ye how ye came to be at Griffith's press conference, but I don't think you'd answer me."

"Because it was suggested I do," I said before he'd even finished speaking, before I could second-guess myself. "Same as you."

Wick studied me for a long moment before replying. "Maybe, but I don't think my invite was as personal as yours."

I fought a flush as he reached out to open the café door, ushering me inside. What he'd meant by that, and whether he'd noted the potential for it to have been a warning directed at me, I didn't know, but it didn't help to soothe my frayed nerves.

We found a table near the back and ordered a blend of Assam and Ceylon teas before discussing anything of importance.

"Now then," Wick prompted gently, reminding me he had a deadline. "Why did ye need to see me so urgently, love?"

"I don't believe I used the word 'urgent,'" I countered as I draped a napkin over my lap, struggling to come to the point.

Wick ignored this. "Is it somethin' to do with this Irish Raffles?"

I wasn't surprised he'd heard of our involvement with the jewelry theft inquiry even if he'd been away on assignment. "I'll come to that. But no, it's something else." I inhaled a breath past the tightness in my lungs as he watched me patiently. "It's to do with that missing . . . shipment you asked me about at Croke Park."

I trusted he would recall the particulars. He'd asked what we knew about a shipment of phosgene falling into the republicans' hands, and we'd been able to honestly answer at the time that, while we knew about it, we didn't know who had it. We'd since discovered precisely whose hands it was in. Unless we and Alec were being played for fools and fallen for it—hook, line, and sinker. But I didn't think that was the case.

Wick's gaze sharpened. "I see."

I lowered my voice further. "We know that it's in the hands of Lord Ardmore."

His expression betrayed little, but I caught the minute tightening of his lips.

"Do you know him?"

"Aye."

I waited for him to elaborate, but for the moment, he held his peace.

"We can't prove it, of course. And we don't know exactly where he's storing it except somewhere in Dublin." I heaved a sigh. "Unless it's been moved." I shook my head, forbidding myself to go off on a tangent. I pressed my hands flat on the table. "What we do know is that he has something terrible planned for it. Perhaps at a demonstration in support of the hunger strikers or a riot if they die. I don't know." My voice had tightened with distress, and I had to force myself to speak calmly. "But we fear we're running out of time to stop him."

I sat back, waiting as Wick processed this information. Rightfully, he might have demanded to know how we could be certain of this, and I knew my answers wouldn't be convincing enough. I knew this intimately, for it was the reason we couldn't go to the wider British government for help. If C hadn't trusted my instincts and trusted his own impressions of Ardmore, we would never have gotten as far as we had. But as a journalist, Wick was different. He followed facts, not suppositions, wherever they might lead him. As such, he might very well tell me to buzz off.

But he didn't. He allowed the tea to finish steeping and then poured us each a cup of the fragrant brew. Then he urged me to tell him everything.

So I did, as succinctly as possible, beginning with Lord Rockham's murder when I'd first tangled with Ardmore. When I finished, my tea was nearly cold, but I drank it anyway, trying not to overanalyze the furrow that had carved itself deeper and deeper into Wick's brow.

He reached out to pour himself a second cup, splashing milk into it almost absently, and then gave a decisive nod. "Then what ye need most is to find the location of this phosgene."

"Yes." I gasped, relieved that his voice seemed to hold no doubt I was telling the truth. I smiled tightly at the pinch-faced matron who had turned to look at me, and then I continued in a more moderated voice. "But he seems to have hidden it at a property held in the name of some unknown pseudonym or associate."

He hummed to himself in thought. "Let me see what I can uncover. I've got a few resources I suspect even your SIS doesn't," he stated smugly.

"Thank you!" I clasped my hands in front of me, lest I try to reach out and grab his hand and shock the matron still periodically casting me disapproving looks.

"Aye, well . . ." He offered me a coy smile. "I do expect to be given first crack at all the details to be able to break this story when the time is right."

I gave a little laugh. "You will." But my amusement abruptly faded as I peered toward the front of the café, conscious that we might have been seen together. After all, Willoughby continued to appear at odd times, and who knew how many other men Ardmore might have in his employ, keeping tabs on us. "But be careful," I warned him. "You've just heard what he's capable of." I pressed a hand to my throat. "Don't make me regret telling you."

Wick's gaze met mine, firm with reassurance and perhaps a touch of fondness. "At least now I understand why you're still here. And why ye haven't given up all your skullduggery."

I shook my head. He knew I hated that word, whether it was true or not.

With a swift glance at his wristwatch, he topped off his tea once more. "Now, tell me about these jewel thefts. I hear they're right devilish."

CHAPTER 17

"It was an utter waste of time," Sidney groused under his breath as we made our way up the steps into the Abbey Theatre. It was the first chance he'd had to inform me how his meeting with the band who had played at the Harringtons' soiree had gone. Not well, apparently. Or not fruitful, in any case.

"I'm sorry, darling," I told him genuinely. "But at least now we know."

He shook his head. "I should have realized there would be too many people coming and going for them to keep track. Chauffeurs, and caterers, and footmen desirous of a smoke, and the like."

"It's still a worthwhile discovery."

The look he fastened on me told me he knew I was placating him, and he didn't appreciate it. I squeezed his arm. "Cheer up." I lowered my voice and leaned closer as I caught sight of the couple we were meeting. "Or Sturgis shall make it his mission to do so."

Sidney glowered at me and then fastened a smile on his face as he turned to greet Mark Sturgis and his wife. Lady Rachel had crossed with him on the ferry two evenings prior, and I was pleased to make her acquaintance again.

"Verity," she exclaimed as we bussed each other's cheeks.

"How lovely to see you." She turned to press her hand to her husband's shoulder. "When Mark told me you were in Dublin, I could hardly believe it. But I'm glad of it, if for no other reason than I've someone else who I know will look after him. Helen is a dear, but she's not precisely made of the sternest stuff."

"But of course," I replied, for what else *could* I say, and then swiftly changed the topic. "I trust the weather was good for your crossing."

"Oh, yes, indeed. There was a spot of rain, of course, but I slept right through it." Lady Rachel looked elegant, as always, in a gown of mauve crushed silk with her dark hair swept up on her head.

Mark bussed my cheek in greeting, and then pressed a hand to his wife's back, urging us toward the stairs to the balcony. I noted his gaze trailing over those assembled in the theater lobby and wondered if he was at all anxious about being there. Truth be told, he was probably safe enough as long as their motorcar picked them up right at the door. It was doubtful Collins's Squad or the IRA would try anything in such a crowded space where they couldn't make a getaway, but even the thought of having to be prepared for such a thing made me anxious on his account. Sturgis wasn't a bad man—in truth, I believed he was among the men urging the government to make peace—but he was in a bad spot, being so high up in the Castle administration.

At the top of the stairs, his hand was seized by a gentleman passing by us in the other direction. "Sturgis," the fellow exclaimed jovially. "I want to hear your thoughts on this Clark fellow when I return," he informed him with a wag of his finger as he descended.

I supposed he meant Sir Ernest Clark, who had recently been appointed assistant undersecretary for Ulster—the counties in northeast Ireland surrounding Belfast, which

boasted a large Protestant and unionist population. I heard
Sturgis explaining as much to Sidney as we were led to our
seats by the usher.

"I spent the day yesterday with him, and I can't say I'm
impressed," he murmured. "But I wouldn't have his job for
anything." He scoffed. "It's too absurd to mind not being offered a position which I should *loathe* to take."

From this, I deduced this was a question he'd been forced
to field from a number of people, and one he was tired of
answering. The situation in Belfast was volatile and complicated, and not an assignment, I should think, any civil servant would relish.

As we settled in our seats, opening our playbills to note the
cast of the play *Family Failing*, I spared a moment to think of
Mr. Hardy. I presumed he was waiting for the ferry Griffith
had suggested to him. I certainly hoped so, for his sake. Part
of me wanted to warn Sturgis about the disastrous story that
was about to appear in print the next day, but I realized that
I couldn't. Not without explaining how I knew.

At least some of the reporters would no doubt connect
Hardy's claims about SIS operations with General Macready's recent interview with a French newspaper, claiming
that they had the names of most of the leadership of Sinn
Féin and would make a clearance of them soon. A statement
which was, no doubt, in part a bluff, but a poorly timed one
now.

While Sidney and Lady Rachel quietly conversed about
one of the actresses, Sturgis took the opportunity to ask if we
had any updates on the jewel thief. "I heard about the theft
at the Shelbourne." He shook his head. "Shocking!"

"Yes, but at least now we have some sort of description of
the fellow, limited though it is. And with the public aware of
the thefts, perhaps others will come forward with information."

DI Burrows and the men in the G Division would be field-
ing those tips and not me and Sidney, but I trusted the inspector would share anything pertinent. And if the DMP were
able to apprehend the thief without our assistance, all the
better. Neither Sidney nor I were devoting ourselves solely
to investigation, and neither did we wish to. Not when the
phosgene was our primary objective. Perhaps if our attention had not been so divided, we might have been closer to
catching the thief, but we couldn't be held at fault for the
circumstances.

The lights began to lower and the murmur of voices in the
audience fell silent, but not before Lady Rachel invited us to
join them for a drive into the Wicklow Hills the following
afternoon. The suggestion at first struck me as rather rash. It
was well-known that there were members of the IRA hiding
out in the more isolated areas of the Wicklow Hills, either to
train or because they were known and wanted back home.
But Sturgis insisted it would be perfectly safe and that we
would have an escort.

I had to admit, I was curious to see another part of the
country and one I'd heard so much about. Not only because
of the IRA but because it was purported to be lovely. Plus,
it might afford us a different perspective on our current predicament. One look at Sidney told me he was thinking much
the same thing.

So we agreed, and the following day, after lunch, piled into
a couple of Crossleys with Mr. Wylie and his wife and our
escort, and set off into the Wicklow Hills. Wylie acted as a
legal advisor to Dublin Castle. I had met him once before
when he'd proved invaluable in helping me extricate Nimble
from O's clutches. His wife was equally as pleasant.

True to its reputation, the landscape was wild and glori-
ous, about as far from the crowded squalor of parts of Dublin
as one could get. The leaves of the ancient trees had begun to

change at certain elevations, their shades of gold and orange brushing against remnants of purple heather scattered across the hillsides. The water in the lakes and streams was clear and cold, reflecting back the magnificent landscapes.

We paused near a farm to enjoy tea with a pleasant farmer, who was soon chatting amiably with Sturgis about horses. To us, he presented himself as friendly and a great character, but I knew that didn't mean he wasn't privately a supporter of Sinn Féin or even a member of the IRA. The Irish were clever enough to know when it was best to hide their true thoughts.

This was something that some members of the British government seemed unable to understand. Because every Irishman they met was sociable and easygoing to their faces, they believed this must mean they were all amenable to British rule. They couldn't appreciate the distinction that one could be polite and otherwise amicable and still loathe your policies and overlordship.

Being part of the entourage, I was better able to see how the larger rural Irish population viewed the British, as well as the well-to-do and prosperous Protestant unionists and Castle Catholics, as they were called, who collaborated and socialized with them. They might be cordial and receptive, but beneath it lurked fear and misgiving—a sharp consciousness that we could turn on them. It was a look I'd seen stamped across the faces of the Belgians and French living under German occupation, and it made my gut churn to see it directed at me.

I could see that some of the others were aware of their wariness, as well, particularly the members of our military escort. Though there were some who undoubtedly reveled in the power they felt from inspiring such fear, I suspected the vast majority were as unnerved by it as I was. How difficult must it be to be confronted with it day in and day out? How much must it prey on them to know that the populace's guardedness was at least partially justified? I suddenly wondered if some of the German soldiers had felt the same.

Sidney was quiet as he unlocked the door to our town house upon our return, and I was curious if similar thoughts were weighing on him. I was considering what to say as I laid my handbag on the petticoat table in the foyer and began removing my gloves, when the patter of feet hurrying up the stairs from below captured my attention.

Ginny raced toward us before lurching to a stop a few feet away. She bobbed an awkward curtsy—something we were still working on—struggling to catch her breath as she spoke. "Sir. Ma'am . . ."

My first thought was for Nimble. The last time I was met at the door by an anxious Ginny, he'd just been hauled away by the Black and Tans. "Nimble?" I gasped.

"Oh!" She flushed, shaking her head. "Naw. He's grand. Just had to run to the PO. But he told me to give ye this *straightaway* if'n ye returned afore he did." She pulled an envelope from her pocket, holding it out for Sidney.

I exhaled in relief as Sidney unfolded the missive. "Very good. Thank you, Ginny," I told the girl, dismissing her.

She bobbed another awkward curtsy and returned the way she'd come, glancing back at us once or twice. Her interest was obvious, but she also recognized she shouldn't hang about hoping to hear what the note contained.

Sidney read it quickly before passing it to me with a grunt.

"Another?" I exclaimed as I skimmed the message from DI Burrows. The jewel thief had struck again. This time at a different hotel.

"Come on," Sidney urged, grabbing his hat.

Fleming's Hotel was located in Gardiner Place just a few blocks northeast of Rutland Square and not far from Mountjoy Square. It was an unremarkable address, and except for some lovely black wrought-iron balcony railings, the remainder of the five-story brick façade was altogether uninspiring. It was a respectable enough place to take accommodations, but far below the caliber of the Shelbourne, and not the sort of place I would have ever expected our jewel thief to target. In fact, if not for the crowds and the policemen standing out front, I would have believed we were in the wrong place.

We were directed upstairs to where Burrows and a man who turned out to be the hotel manager were being berated by the room's occupant while his wife reclined in a chair fanning herself. "What incompetence! I took a room here precisely to *avoid* this sort of thing from happenin'. What do ye have to say for yourselves?" The man continued to ramble, neither letting up nor allowing either the inspector or manager to answer.

Sidney and I waited in the doorway, surveying the room's contents, which were relatively minimal. A bed, clothespress, wardrobe, and two chairs with a table. The fingerprint men had already finished, for the victim was now demanding to know who would be cleaning up the dust they'd left behind. Deciding I'd been subjected to enough of the man's yelling, I stepped forward to squash it.

"Sir!"

He rounded on me in startlement, opening his mouth as if to spew further abuse—this time at me—but I spoke before he could.

"If you chose this place precisely because you believed it wouldn't be burglarized, why would you expect *they* would?"

His mouth opened and closed several times before he found his voice. "Now, see here . . ."

"Do you have a hotel safe?" I asked the manager, noticing the man's wife had perked up at my voice and now stared at me goggle-eyed.

"Uh . . . yes, ma'am. We do," the manager stammered.

"Then why didn't you use it?" I asked the room's occupant. Normally, I wouldn't blame the victim, but the fellow was being so unpleasant I felt not an iota of guilt turning the tables on him.

"Everyone knows you don't use the safe," he retorted as if I was an utter moron. "That's the first place a thief looks."

Rather than respond, I merely arched a single eyebrow, allowing him to figure out just how ridiculous he sounded and how faulty his logic was.

He spluttered. "This doesn't concern ye, madam."

"Harry," his wife hissed.

"So I suggest ye take your meddlin' elsewhere."

"Harry!"

"Sir," he addressed Sidney. "Kindly restrain your wife."

"Harry!" his wife was now practically shouting.

He rounded on her. "What?"

She pointed at us. "That's Mr. and Mrs. Kent."

"And what does that—?" He broke off, evidently making the connection, and turned toward us with a fuming frown.

"Where was the jewelry stored?" I asked Burrows, ignoring the man.

"The sock drawer," the inspector stated with clipped irony, because this was such a secure alternative.

"Anything else we should see?" I was eager to speak with Burrows further, but not where this gentleman or his wife could listen in.

"Follow me," he urged, leading me several doors away to a small parlor that the DMP had confiscated for their use.

"I take it there were no potential witnesses to this one conversing in the adjoining room?" Sidney quipped, for the rooms here were not suites, and were far too small for anyone to pass unnoticed.

Burrows cast him a wry smile. "They returned to find the room locked and everything in order, but the jewels gone."

I perched on the edge of one of the garish plaid chairs. "What did he get away with?"

"Allegedly a ring and a necklace."

My eyes widened at the sum he named that they were supposed to be worth.

"Allegedly?" Sidney countered, picking up on the same word I had. "You doubt their story?"

Burrows rubbed his thumb and forefinger over his mustache. "Let's just say I'm skeptical someone of such means would willingly choose to stay here, even if a jewel thief is at large in Dublin."

It was a fair point. Fleming's Hotel wasn't just a step down from the Shelbourne, it was several rungs below.

"Though they claim they attended that charity gala at the Shelbourne where ye believe the thief noticed Mrs. Thatch's jewels. But I still have a question for Mr. Cantwell." Burrows stuck his head out into the corridor, gesturing to someone. A few moments later, the manager appeared. "Did ye happen to see any of the jewelry that Mr. and Mrs. Jones described as being stolen?"

"I didn't," he replied. "But I can ask my staff if they did."

"Please."

While Mr. Cantwell scurried off to do so, Burrows beckoned to one of the constables standing in the corridor. "Keep an eye on him," he directed.

"Do you suspect him?" Sidney asked once the constable had departed.

"Not of the jewel theft, but we've another issue." The inspector's expression was grim. "A session of the Dáil was bein' held here when the Joneses raised the alarm."

Sidney and I glanced at each other in comprehension. "You mean, in secret?" he clarified.

"Aye."

The Dáil had been proscribed by the British government the year before, along with Sinn Féin, the IRA, and a number of other Irish nationalistic organizations. Consequently, they'd all been driven underground and forced to meet covertly in order to conduct the business of their shadow government.

It appeared Burrows was none too happy at the discovery they'd been meeting here, and I didn't think it was because he disapproved, but rather that he preferred to continue looking the other way and he'd been forced into a situation where he couldn't. It also raised some unsettling questions.

"Do you think that's a coincidence?"

His gaze met mine, telling me he was aware of the implications. "I don't know."

I had all but discarded the possibility that the IRA were involved in the jewel thefts, using them to fund their revolution, but I couldn't deny that a number of them had undoubtedly been in the building today. It was feasible one of them could have committed the theft, but incredibly risky, if so. Not only to themselves, but some of the most important men of the movement, including Collins and Griffith.

On the other hand, it was possible this theft had two motives. To steal jewels and also to expose or paint a target on the Dáil. Though if O or anyone else in the Crown Forces had been aware of the secret session, I couldn't imagine them preferring such an unreliable ploy to descending on the Dáil en masse and rounding up all the rebel leaders.

"The Joneses said their room was locked?" Sidney leaned back against the door trim with his arms crossed, his thoughts clearly focused on another point.

"Aye, and Sergeant O'Neil has been questionin' the staff to see if one of them abetted the thief like at the Shelbourne, but so far, all the keys are accounted for, and no one is admittin' to anythin'." Burrows turned to scowl into the dormant hearth. "'Tis a smaller hotel with fewer staff, so 'tis possible the thief simply slipped behind the desk at a moment it wasn't attended and took the key, returnin' it when he left."

As a well-dressed gentleman, even if he'd been caught doing so, it was unlikely any suspicion would have fallen on him other than being too impatient to wait for a clerk to return to the front desk.

"Then it seems you have matters well in hand," I confessed, not seeing that there was anything further we could do, unless he wanted help in interviewing the staff. But he waved us on, and I trusted he knew what he was about. Though I had to confess that for all my earlier disinterest, the thief was growing more fascinating by the day. I couldn't help but wonder just what sort of man he would turn out to be.

CHAPTER 18

The Phoenix Park Races were the next day, and as we'd already promised the Sturgises we would attend, we set out early in Sidney's Pierce-Arrow to meet them. The park had a festival atmosphere and was crowded with spectators, both for the races *and* the finely dressed ladies and gentlemen in the grandstand. Ginny had helped me choose a warm juniper-green woolen ensemble to combat the chill of the day and a magnificent broad-brimmed hat.

At one point, Sidney and I were hailed by a cluster of reporters and photographers, and we paused politely to pose, prepared to defer the questions we expected to be asked about the Irish Raffles. However, they must have caught wind of our involvement with the investigation into Miss Kavanagh's assault several months earlier, for instead they wanted to hear my thoughts on the attack on a woman named Eileen Baker. Miss Baker had given evidence in the military court of inquiry about recent events that had occurred in Galway City, and apparently the IRA had taken exception to her testimony, for they'd cut off her hair. Then in retaliation, Crown Forces had assaulted and cut off the hair of five women who were members of Cumann na mBan—the female auxiliary division of the IRA.

For obvious reasons, the issue was a touchy subject, and not one I could stand idly by and silently condone. "I think both sides need to find a more honorable form of warfare than terrorizing and shaming women," I responded tartly before flouncing away.

Sidney hurried to catch up with me, slowing my stride to a stroll.

I turned to look up at him, still agitated by the reporter's question. "Aren't you going to scold me for my failure to be circumspect?" I charged.

"I wouldn't dream of it," he replied evenly, nodding to an acquaintance we passed.

Some of the fight drained out of me upon realizing he wasn't going to contest it.

"Though, you do know they are all going to quote you in their papers."

Of course, he was right. I'd known it when I opened my mouth. And while I still didn't regret saying what I had, I did feel a pang of uncertainty whether it had been a good idea to draw that sort of attention to myself. An inquiry into jewel thefts was one thing, but members of the Crown Forces might take exception to my remarks about the hair-cutting— even truthful as they were. They might look unfavorably on us when we needed them to at least remain neutral.

So wrapped up was I in these contemplations that Sidney had to jostle me back to the present. "Ver, did you hear me? I'm going to place my bets."

I nodded, waving him away, continuing to stroll along toward the paddock to watch the thoroughbreds being paraded before they were taken to the racecourse. Though I would never say so in front of all the horse-mad men, I always felt rather sorry for the beasts. Who said they wanted to be haltered and forced to race hell-for-leather down a track, bumping and jostling each other? If I were a horse, I'd rather do my galloping through an open meadow when I jolly well wanted to. Then again, who was to say they didn't relish it?

Like schoolboys who delighted in periodically thrashing each other in the name of sport.

While absorbed in this useless speculation, I was joined at the rail by none other than Captain Lucas Willoughby, and found I was rather glad of the likely mark on which to vent my continued annoyance. "I was wondering when you'd turn up."

"Were you?" he drawled, charm practically oozing from his pores.

"Rather like a bad penny, you are," I ruminated. "Or blisters when one chooses a pair of shoes that are too tight."

"Don't take it out on me because you've failed to heed my advice," he drawled. "People are taking note of the questionable company you keep."

"Hmmm," I replied, refusing to be intimidated, especially by such a vague remark. "We must be getting close." I focused on the bay filly, whose jockey was trying to soothe the nerves evident in her juddering gait. "At least too close for comfort." I cast a sideways glance at Willoughby before returning my gaze to the filly. "Otherwise, Ardmore wouldn't be having you tail me about or pop up periodically to 'warn' me."

"Who says I'm here at Ardmore's bidding?"

I turned to look at him fully, arching my eyebrows in open skepticism.

"Perhaps I keep popping up, as you put it, because I don't want to see you hurt." His gaze turned troubled. "Because I don't want to be the one who's ordered to do so."

This remark seemed far too truthful, and it skimmed too close to the bone for the both of us, sending a chill down my spine.

"Then don't," I told him flatly. "Ardmore only has the control over you that you allow him to."

He sighed, shaking his head. "You may be plucky, Verity, but you're also naïve."

That was probably the first time someone had suggested such a thing about me since I was eighteen, watching my husband, brothers, cousins, and friends march off to war. I didn't believe it now any more than I'd believed it then.

"Think what you want," I told him in dismissal, turning back toward the paddock.

But he seemed determined to have the last word as he leaned closer to speak into my ear. "If Kent were suddenly locked up in an interrogation cell beneath the Castle, his life in danger of being stripped away from him, I suspect your definition of control would be quite different."

I turned to scowl at his back as he strode away, even as terror struck at my core. For he and Ardmore both knew my husband was my weakness. Frankly, I was terrified of what I might be willing to do if he was genuinely at risk.

I was about to turn away when just beyond him I spied a man and woman watching me. The chap I recognized immediately, for we'd interacted on several occasions. He was Tom Cullen, an IRA intelligence officer working for Collins. A less experienced agent—and a woman less infatuated with her husband—might have fallen for his boyish good looks and charm, but I'd remained firmly unmoved. The woman I judged to also be an operative of some kind. She might have been simply a girl he was stepping out with, but her gaze was too frank, too knowing. As such, when I approached and he introduced her, I disregarded the name, for it must certainly be false.

Sidney joined us shortly after, and I maneuvered matters so that I might have a few moments to speak with Tom alone while my husband chatted with the woman.

"You saw Captain Willoughby?" I murmured as we strolled. "Whom your men are supposed to be following."

Tom frowned. "He's a slippery one. Slipperier than most of you Brits."

I couldn't tell if the look he gave me meant to imply I was

slippery, too, and whether that was a compliment. Ignoring it, I pressed my point. "What have your men been able to discover about him?"

Tom straightened, correctly hearing the criticism in my voice. "Lots. Where he boxes, where he gambles, where he whores."

If this last remark was supposed to make me blush, he was in for a disappointment, for I merely gazed back at him in silent rebuke.

"We know he prefers beef to mutton, but most of your British toffs do. We also know he's taken rooms at multiple hotels."

Now, *this* was useful information. "Where?"

He rattled off several names, including the Shelbourne and the Gresham, and more surprisingly the Wicklow. I supposed this was so that he could obscure his movements more easily. Regardless, I decided it was time I paid a visit to my old friend Peter.

But not before I tended to the contents of the missive Tom stealthily passed me as we clasped hands to take leave of one another. I had to wait until I had a moment to slip away to the ladies' retiring room to read it. It was from Alec, asking—or rather ordering—us to meet him in St. Stephen's Green the next day.

Wadding up the paper, I dropped it in the pit. This time his summons had better mean he was meeting us in person, or I would find a way to make certain he felt my displeasure.

Alec was seated on a bench overlooking a path in the less populated southeastern quadrant of St. Stephen's Green. The trees overhead were tipped with autumn color, befitting the cooler weather that had settled over the city, encouraging me to place an order with my modiste for some warmer garments. He didn't rise to his feet as we approached, but rather waited for us to sit beside him. I might have taken offense at this, except for the fact that he was plainly trying to obscure from the pair of gentlemen strolling by in the opposite direction the fact that we were meeting. Once they'd disappeared beyond the trees, he finally spoke.

"I can tell you're vexed with me, Ver."

I clasped my hands before me, refusing to acknowledge this baiting remark.

"You've this way of puckerin' your mouth. Just the *slightest* crease to your lips. I suspect you've noticed it, too, Kent."

"Leave me out of it, Xavier. I don't need her vexed at me, too."

"True. Ye do have to live with her."

"Will the pair of you quit it," I snapped. "What does it matter if I'm vexed? Just say what you summoned us here to say, or issue another veiled threat and let us go on our way."

I'd not meant for it to slip out like that, but I'd succeeded in startling him. So much so that his gentle Dublin Irish accent slipped. "It wasn't meant as a threat, Ver," he vowed, at least having the grace not to pretend he didn't understand to what I referred. "Truly."

Looking into his solemn eyes, I wanted to believe him. I wanted to believe that this man I'd waltzed with amidst the enemy and faced down death with and invited once into my bed would never seek to intimidate me in such a hurtful way. But he was working for a different master now, one with which I wasn't as familiar, in whom I only held the thinnest thread of trust. "Perhaps not by you," I suggested softly.

To Alec's credit, he didn't flinch, and neither did he immediately dismiss the possibility. Instead, he lowered his gaze to his lap, giving the matter his careful consideration. Perhaps half a minute passed before he lifted his head, shaking it. "Not Mick either. Though I can understand why you might have thought so. I intended to be there." He gritted his teeth. "But there were complications." He turned to look at me. "And I knew Wick would look after ye."

I didn't question how he knew about my friendship with Wick. After all, it wasn't as if we'd taken great pains to conceal it.

I sat very still for a moment, ostensibly watching the flight of a pair of birds who appeared to be playing a game of tag, when in actuality I was still struggling to come to terms with what Alec had said and decide whether I believed him. Sidney's hand stole into mine, warm and reassuring, and I realized that in the end, perhaps it didn't matter. We still had a job to do, and Alec was our best ally, whether his commanding officer had threatened me or not.

"So why did you ask us here?"

Alec looked like he wasn't as content to move on from the revelation of my mistrust, but he seemed to realize that further pleas of innocence were not going to resolve the matter. "I wanted to let you know that Ardmore's attempt to control the Dublin Corporation through their bankroll has failed."

I turned to him in surprise. "What do you mean?"

"The Bank of Ireland has come to the rescue, agreein' to advance them a significant loan in addition to continuin' to cover their overdraft."

I found myself exhaling in relief, knowing Ardmore had been privately offering loans to the Dublin Corporation, which acted as the city council. It had been obvious this was a bid to gain control of the local government here, as a precursor to doing so elsewhere, since the British administration had declared they would no longer issue payments from the taxes and rates collected unless they received an assurance of loyalty from those local government bodies, many of whom had pledged allegiance to the Dáil Éireann.

"Why would they do that?" Sidney asked, sharing my bewilderment at the Bank of Ireland's decision to take on such a risk. His eyes narrowed. "Or is it down to pure intimidation? Considering one of the directors of the bank's Dublin board was assassinated two months ago."

Alec crossed one leg over the other, leaning further back against the bench. "I won't deny that might be part of it, but I'll remind ye the Bank of Ireland has been facilitatin' activities for some time. The overdraft. The establishment of the National Land Bank. One of the directors, Andrew Jameson, has taken a shine to Mick, and he recognizes the potential. They've the capital to hedge their bets in Dublin and elsewhere, and so have chosen to do so rather than risk the city fragmentin' into further turmoil."

Sidney considered this. "And now that they've done so, I imagine other banks will follow suit. Munster and Leinster Bank, and the like." Their confidence having been bolstered by the larger Bank of Ireland's.

"Precisely."

It was an important moment for the rebellion because it demonstrated that the major Irish financial institutions now believed in the lasting security of local governments like the Dublin Corporation. Local governments who had pledged allegiance to the Irish republican national government. This was a sharp blow to the British administration.

"Dublin Castle won't be happy about this," I stated.

Neither would Ardmore. He would be livid. And for all the pleasure that gave me, I knew he had a tendency to lash out whenever he was crossed or foiled. While neither Sidney nor I were responsible for this financial plot's failure, I couldn't help the pulse of dread that thrummed through me, wondering how Ardmore would react.

"Probably not," Alec replied to my comment about Dublin Castle. "But for the moment at least, they can carry on in blissful ignorance."

I took that to mean that the details of the loan had been kept private. And if the Castle didn't know, then perhaps Ardmore was also unaware. Though, I didn't wager for long.

A couple appeared then, strolling arm in arm down the path, so I turned in toward Sidney, all but ignoring Alec at the opposite end of the bench. Sidney reached up to adjust the fur-lined collar of my coat against the chill in the air and I offered him a small smile, for it was a very husbandly thing to do.

"I understand you've been workin' with Burrows," Alec remarked. "That you've earned his trust. That's good." He glanced in the direction the couple had ambled, pulling the brim of his flat cap lower over his eyes. "And I know you're aware of the session of the Dáil that was interrupted at Fleming's."

"About that," I began diplomatically. "Who all knew that's when and where they would be meeting?"

"As far as I know, only the members of the Dáil."

I frowned. "But the hotel. . . ?"

"Is owned by Seán O'Mahony, who's a Teachta Dála." The equivalent of a member of parliament for the Dáil. "He may have told his nephew, who's the manager, but it's doubtful he told anyone else prior to everyone's arrival." By then it would have been obvious who was utilizing their meeting rooms.

Alec held up his hand. "And before ye ask, no one in the IRA was involved in that theft. No one would be that big of an eejit."

"You're certain?" I questioned, earning myself a stern look. "Because we had our fair share of idiots in the Secret Service. Every organization, no matter how lofty, seems to have them."

His lips quirked in acknowledgment of this jest. "Maybe so. But not one *that* hopeless."

I supposed I would have to take his word for it.

"However, I do have some information for ye that might prove useful." He turned to face us more fully. "Turns out O has another man with a criminal record workin' for him. This one for theft."

Given the recent revelations I'd witnessed about Mr. Hardy, this didn't surprise me. I suspected a number of O's agents had shady origins if not actual criminal records. O, himself, had murdered someone and gotten away with it.

"Who?" Sidney prompted.

"A fellow named Frank Caulfield."

I turned to exchange a speaking look with my husband.

"Ye know him, then?"

"We're acquainted," I replied succinctly, wondering if I'd been right from the beginning to suspect O was behind the jewel thefts.

"Well, he's one to watch, then." There were questions in Alec's eyes, but he didn't ask them, trusting we knew what we were about. It was the way our relationship had worked in Belgium, each of us trusting the other to get our tasks done and share what was crucial so that neither of us was any more vulnerable to compromise than necessary. After all, during torture, you couldn't accidentally blurt out what you didn't know. "Any more word from London?"

"Nothing except confirmation that they're still looking into matters," I replied dejectedly. Both Kathleen and Max, as well as the late Lord Rockham's first wife, Calliope. They had all promised to scour what records they had.

Alec nodded, his eyes narrowed in the direction of the trees along the path. I followed his gaze, trying to see what he might be seeing, but only detected foliage.

"I may have a lead on a member of the crew who stole the cylinders from the *Zebrina* and brought them to Ireland," he informed us guardedly. And well he should! For those men had killed the crew of the *Zebrina* in order to take their cargo. Killed all but one of them, anyway, who had narrowly escaped with the harrowing tale.

"Where—" I began to ask, but he cut me off.

"I won't say more 'til I know for sure."

He pushed to his feet, and I noticed then the lad separating himself from the trees. The manner in which he loped forward told me he was an ally, likely one of the messenger lads the IRA utilized when needed. He couldn't have been more than ten, but his shadowed blue eyes suggested he'd already seen more than his fair share of violence. With a wary look at us, he slipped a piece of paper into Alec's outstretched hand and then took off at a trot, disappearing deeper into the square.

"What is it?" I asked, seeing the forbidding expression that settled over Alec's face.

"A roundup in the mountains. I must go. I'll send word when I know about the other," he called over his shoulder as he, too, took off at a run.

We later read in the newspapers that about forty IRA men had been arrested in the Dublin Mountains while training and testing explosives. One of them had been killed.

CHAPTER 19

It had been a couple of months since I'd set foot inside the Wicklow Hotel, but it looked much the same. As did Peter, the hotelier, who had become somewhat of a friend during the days when I'd posed as Dearbhla Bell while searching for Alec. I'd elected not to don my disguise, suspecting Peter already knew who I was. That he might have known all along. In any case, I was able to ask more pointed questions about my current prey, as myself rather than a lass in a particular type of trouble looking for her "cousin."

I slid into my once familiar seat at the end of the bar, and Peter had just looked up and noticed me when a tall fellow stepped forward to plop his elbow down, all but blocking my view. Recognizing the lanky build and long fingers wrapped around a pint, I tried not to stiffen, though the fact that we'd just been talking about him not an hour earlier made it more difficult.

"Mrs. Kent," Frank Caulfield declared as he turned to observe me lazily through his hooded eyes. I couldn't decide if this wasn't his first drink, or he was *attempting* to appear menacing. "I never imagined I would find you here." The slur of his words suggested the former.

"Good afternoon, Mr. Caulfield," I replied, deliberately not answering his implied question.

He glanced behind me. "No Mr. Kent?"

"He'll be along shortly," I lied. Sidney had taken Nimble in the Pierce-Arrow out to one of the abandoned quarries southwest of the city for a bit of target practice. Sidney had claimed it was mainly for the benefit of his valet, who hadn't fired a bullet since the war ended, but I suspected my husband wished to blow off some steam as well.

Caulfield continued to eye me as if to unnerve me, but I was confident I gave nothing away. Frankly, his behavior was annoying, so I decided to set him back on his heels.

"I saw you at the Shelbourne the other day."

"Did you?" He leered.

"I was wondering if the thief would return to the scene of his crime, so I was paying particular attention to the crowd gathered outside. And there you were."

His brow lowered.

"I understand you were also at the party the Harringtons hosted to celebrate their daughter's engagement. One of the guests saw you emerging from the servants' stair."

"What of it?" Mr. Caulfield growled. "I'd gone out for a smoke. The same as any number of guests."

This had been a shot in the dark that Caulfield might have been the man Fitzgibbon had seen, but Caulfield had confirmed it. Though he'd also made a valid point about others having gone out the same way. The band had claimed much the same thing. However, I had an ace up my sleeve.

"Yes, but do any of those other guests have criminal records?"

Caulfield slammed his glass down, towering over me. "You're toyin' with me, Mrs. Kent," he snarled in a low voice. "And I don't much like it."

"It was merely a question," I managed to retort though my insides quivered.

"Is there a problem here?" Peter's voice broke through the tension. "Another Drogheda, sir?"

"No," Caulfield barked before stomping away.

I closed my eyes, taking a deep breath to settle my nerves, before opening them again. "Thank you, Peter."

He scrutinized me with his dark eyes, much like he'd done in the past when he was trying to figure me out. It wasn't unfriendly. "He's a bad one," he finally said, gesturing with his head in the direction Caulfield had stalked off as he removed his glass and wiped down the bar.

"I've come to realize that."

He nodded once, still eyeing me. "The usual?"

"Yes, please." I trusted he meant my usual when I needed something stronger and not the cup of tea I had sometimes requested.

A few moments later he returned with a glass and poured me a wee dram of good Irish whiskey.

"You know who I am?" I said as he finished, deciding it was best to be direct.

"Yeah," he admitted. "Just as I know MacAlister isn't yer cousin. And that ye *aren't* from County Antrim." His mouth tipped upward at one corner, evoking an answering smile from me.

"Fair enough. It was the accent that gave me away, wasn't it."

"Yeah, well, 'twas middlin'." ·

Which I took to mean that it had been complete rubbish.

I laughed, but then quickly sobered, realizing I'd been rather lucky Alec had been vouching for me on the other side. Taking a sip of whiskey, I savored its warmth and smokiness as it filled my mouth and then burned down my throat to settle in my stomach. "Peter, I wonder if you've noticed any other bad men lurking about." I looked up to find him watching me evenly. "One in particular. A Captain Willoughby."

His chin tipped up as he hummed in recognition.

"Do you know the name?"

His eyebrows arched in disapproval. "A charmer, that one."

"When he wants to be," I conceded. "Will you keep an

eye on him for me?" I knew it was a gamble asking for such a favor, but considering the fact we'd both been deceiving each other, I hoped he wouldn't hold my earlier subterfuge against me.

He rubbed at a spot on the bar that had seemed to me to be perfectly spotless as he considered my request. Then he nodded in agreement, before arching his chin. "But how will I get word to ye?"

I lifted my drink, my lips twisting wryly. "I suspect you already know."

When I lowered my empty glass, he merely chuckled.

The following day, September 20th, passed rather quietly for me and Sidney, when little did we know that the world—or at least Ireland—was descending deeper into mayhem.

In the small village of Balbriggan, north of Dublin, the head constable was killed and a sergeant injured in an altercation with the IRA at the local pub. This was bad enough, but the reprisals by the RIC that followed were shocking. The village was sacked, looted, and burned. By the police—the Black and Tans—the very people who were supposed to be maintaining law and order throughout the land. Two members of the local IRA were also summarily shot and killed.

And Balbriggan wasn't the only village to suffer such a brutal reprisal. In the days that followed, many more were shot up and wrecked by Crown Forces. Places with names like Carrick-on-Shannon, Tuam, Ennistymon, Lahinch, Milltown Malbay, Drumshanbo, Rineen, Ballinamore, and even Galway City. The list kept growing.

Meanwhile, Dublin Castle persisted in their denials that there was any proof the Crown Forces were at fault, or in instances when the evidence was laid bare for all to see in photographs and newsreels, blamed the IRA, claiming it was impossible to expect the police not to be overcome by the sight of their dead comrades and lash out in retaliation.

While I had every empathy for these policemen who faced such danger day in and day out, and especially for those who were shot and sometimes killed in the course of their duties—at times suffering horrific wounds—that didn't blind me to the fact that this was a perfectly stupid and horrendous excuse! To suggest that our soldiers and policemen were so lacking in self-control that they must lash out and set fire to a village or kill a twelve-year-old boy or maniacally ransack a town with two hundred of their brothers-in-arms. It was beyond idiotic! Where was the stiff upper lip and control our country was wont to brag about? Where was the proficiency and order?

One ransacking might be understandable. Maybe two. But over and over and over? That wasn't natural. It was a sign of instability. Or confirmation of official contrivance.

With each passing day I grew ever more furious and disgusted. Particularly knowing how many times I'd heard men condemn women for being too emotional and therefore unqualified or unfit for such duties as intelligence work. And yet here they were excusing the men of their Crown Forces for being so emotional they must avenge their comrades by burning and killing indiscriminately.

I could tell Sidney was also struggling. His anger was nearly a tangible thing, hovering at the back of his thoughts, but restrained by the discipline the RIC were so lacking. On the rare times he allowed himself to remark on it, he had more than few choice words to say about the officers who either allowed or commanded their men to behave so viciously. They knew better. There was no doubt about it.

Matters weren't helped when members of the Castle administration persisted in making light of the incidents and having more concern about the damage these reprisals did to Britain's reputation throughout the world than the people affected. When Sturgis complained that the burning of Balbriggan was what had really spoiled everything, I presumed

he meant because the photographs and newsreels of the damage were so damning. "Still, worse things can happen than
the firing up of a sink like Balbriggan," he'd said, brushing
the matter aside with the added hope that now more Irishmen would demand the rebels stop so that their own homes
weren't burnt to the ground. This completely ignored the fact
that they knew perfectly well who posed the most danger to
them, and it wasn't the rebels.

I'd had to plead an indisposition soon after these remarks,
before Sidney drew Sturgis's or someone else's cork. In the
days that followed we'd declined a number of invitations,
needing a respite from this Castle mindset before we said
something we couldn't retract. After all, we couldn't snub
them entirely. Not when we still had to locate the phosgene
cylinders, and the members of the Castle administration
might possess information that could prove useful. Giving
one of them a bloody nose certainly wouldn't further that
cause.

Another critical incident also occurred on the twentieth,
though we didn't realize just how important at the time.
Members of the First Battalion of the Dublin Brigade of the
IRA attempted to ambush a British Army ration party outside Monk's Bakery. Their goal was to capture the army's
weapons, but the entire raid went sideways from the beginning, resulting in a firefight in the street. One British soldier
was killed and two later died of their wounds. Meanwhile,
eighteen-year-old medical student and IRA Section Commander Kevin Barry was captured after his gun jammed and
he dived under the army lorry for cover. He was taken to
prison to await trial by court martial under the Restoration
of Order in Ireland Act.

"I heard he'd just returned from holiday and was to sit
his first-year medical examinations that afternoon," Nancy
told me a few days later at the Pillar Picture House when the
newsreels flashed images across the screen, of the corner of

Upper Church Street and North King Street, where Monk's Bakery stood.

She sounded mournful for the lad, but I didn't have strong feelings either way about Kevin Barry. At least, nothing stronger than pity that he'd lived in a time when his youthful enthusiasm for the cause should see him brought to such ruin. But of course, we'd also just seen the images of Balbriggan and the hollow-eyed residents who had lost their homes and businesses, most of whom had likely never seen a film camera.

We sat in silence for a short time as the film credits ran, grappling with our own thoughts. It wasn't until Mary Pickford appeared on screen that Nancy finally leaned toward me.

"I'm afraid I've nothin' worthwhile to tell ye. Lord Ardmore hasn't met with O in over a week." She sighed. "And 'tis proved harder than I expected to get my eye on any reports that *were* generated. Which makes it harder to inveigle information out of that adjutant I told ye about. Can't just be askin' about it out of the blue."

I was glad to hear that Nancy was being cautious, even though her response wasn't what I'd hoped for. "I suppose the repercussions from all the recent reprisals have taken up much of everyone's time." Everyone within the intelligence department, that is.

She frowned. "And that shooting in the Exchange Hotel."

I watched her out of the corner of my eye, waiting to see if she would say more. But then, perhaps what she *had* said was enough.

Some nights past, a group of men who turned out to be British soldiers stormed into the hotel and straight to the room where a Sinn Féin county councillor from Kilmallock named John Lynch was staying. The newspapers had reported that Lynch had pulled a gun on the men and fired at them before being killed, but I'd been in Dublin long enough to recognize that these sorts of stories weren't always as clear-cut as they appeared. Not when Dublin Castle was issuing the official statements and when most of the newspapers were reticent to push against British censorship restrictions.

Though Nancy had done nothing more than mention it, the fact that she was troubled by it and had classified it as a "shooting" rather than a shoot-out or something similar suggested I was right to be skeptical of the Castle's report. Had the soldiers identified themselves? Had Lynch actually shot at them? Had he even been armed? I didn't ask Nancy, but I wondered all the same.

"The only thing that *might* prove useful is that O asked the adjute to do some research into current RIC procedures. Though that very well may have more to do with the reprisals than Ardmore." She shrugged. "I offered to help him, but he didn't take the bait. But I'll see what else I can find out." The man two rows in front turned to scowl at us, but Nancy simply scowled right back at him, retorting, "Eyes forward."

The man did as she bid, though none too happily.

I stifled a laugh but decided it would be best not to goad the man further. After all, if he could hear us murmuring, who else might?

On the way home, I stopped by the Bank of Ireland to see if there was any correspondence from C in London, only to be informed that Finnegan had already departed for the day. His secretary, whom I'd come to realize I could similarly trust, was also absent, so I continued on my way empty-handed. When Alec had told us about the Bank of Ireland bailing out the Dublin Corporation, I'd spared a moment to wonder if Finnegan had played a part in influencing Jameson and the board's decision. It seemed to me that he must have.

When I finally arrived home, the sun was already sinking toward the horizon, the days growing ever shorter as autumn deepened its hold on the city. So when I was greeted by Ginny, who helped me out of my coat while Nimble was upstairs with Sidney, I asked her to wait a moment.

"I know you told me that you live out because your mother needs you, but I wondered if you might reconsider my offer of a room here." When she opened her mouth to speak, I hurried to finish what I had to say. "The truth is, I'm concerned for your safety now that the sun is setting earlier. There's so much violence spilling into the streets, and with all these patrols and raids, well . . . I'm worried for you."

Ginny met my gaze evenly, though her hands were wringing the apron tied at her waist. "I thank ye for your concern, ma'am. But I just can't. My mammy truly does need me."

"Will you tell me why?" I asked gingerly, not wishing to pry where I shouldn't, but this seemed too important to let go.

Her brow lowered in uncertainty, and I could tell she was debating whether to tell me the truth.

Rather than see her fib, I switched tactics. "Is there something we could do?"

She shook her head. "Naw, ma'am."

I stifled my frustration. "Then what of an escort? Would you allow Nimble to ensure you arrive here and return home safely?"

Her eyes widened almost in alarm. "I can't ask that."

"You're not," I said calmly. "I'm offering. And I'm certain Nimble won't mind." Considering his overblown protective instincts and the growing affection he seemed to feel toward her.

"Please, ma'am. Don't do that," she surprised me by pleading. "I'm perfectly safe. Truly, I am. I know the streets I take, and everyone there knows me. But a man like Nimble . . . a lone *Englishman*"—she shook her head—"he won't be safe. No matter his size."

The notion of this shocked me. For while I'd known to be wary, I'd never felt particularly threatened while roaming or cycling through the streets of Dublin except when there was a firefight or an army patrol passing. But I knew that I was well trained in the ability to blend in when needed. It was only when I needed to speak that I was wary of exposing myself, for accents and dialects were not always so easy to mimic. However, Nimble stood out wherever he went. There was no hiding who or what he was.

"But what of the Crown Forces?" I asked, thinking of how Nimble had saved her from being harassed by a pair of Black and Tans once before. "I know I extracted a promise from them to leave you alone, but I'm afraid most of them won't bother to find out who you are."

"I know how to avoid them now," she vowed. "I'll not make the same mistake again."

I didn't know what exactly this meant, but I did know that I couldn't force Ginny to either live in or accept an escort. "If you're sure," I replied doubtfully.

"I am."

She stood patiently, waiting for me to dismiss her, but when I nodded, scurried down the steps as if she feared I might change my mind.

CHAPTER 20

A few nights later, we found ourselves unceremoniously summoned to Devlin's pub yet again. This time, I seriously considered disregarding the request, but then Alec had been pursuing a lead on one of the crew members of the ship that had stolen the phosgene from the *Zebrina* and transported it to Dublin. What if he had genuine intelligence related to the location of the phosgene? In the end, I decided I couldn't risk it. Though that didn't mean I wasn't going to give Alec—and whoever was with him—an earful.

But before I could even utter a syllable as we entered the same back parlor where we'd met with Alec and Collins during our last visit, Alec was already apologizing.

"I know I promised not to be so high-handed," he said, raising his hand to forestall any words. "But I had no choice. Not when we don't have much time."

I glanced at the other man occupying the room. This time it wasn't Michael Collins but Tom Cullen, who I'd recently spoken to at the Phoenix Park Races. "You found the crewman?"

"Yeah, and he might not stay put for long," Alec confirmed. His gaze shifted to where Sidney stood just behind my shoulder. "We're waitin' for a few reinforcements to arrive and then we'll set out."

Some sort of silent communication seemed to pass between the two men, and I peered behind me to find out if my husband's expression was any more transparent. Unfortunately, his was just as maddeningly inscrutable. I narrowed my eyes in suspicion, but both men ignored me.

"The Big Fellow isn't planning to join us?" Sidney taunted lightly.

"Naw, he's got enough to contend with without riskin' his neck on this."

"Not that he wouldn't enjoy a good scrap right about now," Tom remarked under his breath, his eyes sparkling with mischief.

Alec grunted, nodding his head. He seemed weary, his shoulders bowed and his head hanging low as he leaned forward, resting his elbows on his knees.

"Is it because of the reprisals?" I guessed, sitting down on the edge of the one chair that still had a back. Its legs wobbled slightly beneath me. "Or perhaps Mr. Lynch?"

Cullen sank deeper into the sofa. "Mick was right furious about that."

Alec scoffed. "British Intelligence got the wrong Lynch. John was but a solicitor deliverin' national loan money from his county. He certainly wasn't armed. That much was a bald-faced lie." His head hung low again. "But then that lot at the Castle isn't above lyin' to advance their aims. In fact, lyin' is the least of what they're capable of."

"I assume you mean O and Captain King and . . . Hoppy?" I murmured, recalling some of the names he'd previously mentioned.

Tom smirked as Alec answered, "Captain Jocelyn Hardy."

"We call him Hoppy because of his limp," Tom explained.

"He lost a leg during the war, but don't spare him any empathy," Alec cautioned. "He's still capable of more than enough brutality without it. 'Tis him and King who interrogate the prisoners in the 'knocking shop' below the Castle."

My mind rebelled at the idea of British Intelligence agents using third-degree methods on their prisoners. That was something the German secret police within the occupied territories resorted to, not us. But for the fact that this was Alec, a former agent himself, telling me. He wouldn't have accepted this without proof, even if he had switched sides. Truthfully, how could I argue against the possibility when Crown Forces were resorting to violence and arson against innocent civilians?

"Mark me, one of them had a hand in the raid on the Exchange Hotel that ended in Lynch's death." Alec turned to stare absently toward the wall. "And we'll know for sure soon enough."

I turned to Tom, curious if he would elaborate, but he remained silent, making me suspect it was an ongoing intelligence operation, likely involving one or more IRA agents inside the Castle. Perhaps even Nancy. So I didn't press, not wanting to put her at further risk.

When I didn't speak, Alec turned to look at me, perhaps thinking I was instead concerned for the men who just two years ago might have been my colleagues within British Intelligence. "Don't worry, Ver. No one will get it who doesn't deserve it."

This was a rather chilling way to put it, and a rather effective way to remind me that there were no clean hands in this business. Everyone had blood on them, in one form or another.

"And no one will get it while the hunger strikers are still lingering." Tom sounded almost disgruntled about this.

MacSwiney and the other hunger strikers were still alive and still making headlines across the globe, though the reprisals were eating up some of their print space. Regardless, both played well into the rebels' hands in their propaganda war against the British government. Consequently, there had been somewhat of a lull in IRA violence, at least within Dublin, because the republicans didn't want to jeopardize the surge in sympathy and support they were receiving worldwide by people seeing Squad assassinations of policemen and government officials splashed across the newspapers. Though that didn't deter the county IRA battalions from continuing their ambushes and raids. I'd wondered if Collins might be chafing a bit under this restraint, and Tom seemed to signal he was.

As if sensing this didn't entirely meet with our approval, Alec sighed, rubbing the back of his neck. "We're all just tryin' to convince the British to bring this to an amenable end as quickly as possible. Griffith even tried to meet with Anderson"—the undersecretary—"yesterday, though it came to naught."

This admission was a surprising one, and something that wasn't widely known. Tom even seemed surprised Alec had mentioned it.

"Is that why you seem dead on your feet?" Sidney criticized. He stood with his arms crossed and his feet planted wide, revealing more than perhaps he realized of his disapproval of everything that had just been said. Then again, perhaps he didn't care if they knew how he felt.

Alec glared at him. "Didn't get a wink of sleep last night because the Crown Forces decided to raid Rutland Square"— he nodded his head in the vague direction of the street outside—"goin' house by house."

I tensed in alarm.

"Even heard noises up on the roof but turned out to just be a coverin' party for the soldiers in the square."

Sidney scowled. "If that's the case, should we even be here?"

Alec waved this off. "They won't be back."

Perhaps he thought so, but I suddenly felt anxious about being there, despite it being hours until curfew. I even jumped when the door was thrust open behind me and a lantern-jawed man stuck his head in.

This must have been a signal of some sort, for Alec pushed to his feet. "Right, then. Ver, you'll be stayin' here with Cullen."

I shot up from my chair in protest. "I will not."

"No!" Alec snapped, startling me, for he'd never used such

a tone with me. "This is not up for debate. This is my operation, and what I say goes. The man we're huntin' is a mercenary. One who kills without a second thought. And we cannot risk you bein' there as a distraction."

"I'm not—" I tried to argue again.

"Do you even have a gun?"

"No," I confessed, taken aback. "But—"

"Then you're stayin'." Alec turned to Sidney, his eyes posing the same question.

"Yes."

Alec nodded. "Let's go."

"Sidney," I protested.

But he ignored my objections as well. "Stay here," he ordered, albeit more softly.

My hands clenched at my sides in frustration as they strode through the door. "Don't get killed!" was all I had time to snarl before it shut firmly behind them.

I huffed, wishing I had something to hurl, remembering too late that I wasn't alone.

Tom was making very little effort to hide his amusement. "Are ye sure you're not at least part Irish?" he asked as I paced back and forth in a tight circle.

"Why?"

"Irish lasses don't much like bein' told what to do either."

I paused to arch a sardonic brow at him. "I've got news for you. No woman does." I crossed my arms in front of me. "Correction. No *person* does. Not when it's done in such an arrogant, overbearing manner."

Cullen shrugged one shoulder, and I resumed my pacing.

Several moments passed as I stewed over being left behind, wondering where they'd gone. Wondering if Tom knew. The thought of Sidney being out there alone with Alec and his "reinforcements" wasn't precisely comforting, though I trusted Alec knew I'd have his guts for garters if he let anything happen to Sidney.

"You're investigatin' those jewel thefts, aren't ye?"

I pivoted to face Tom, able to tell from his expression that this wasn't an idle question.

"Ye know about the theft at Fleming's?"

I nodded, curious why he was asking. "Were you there?"

"Sure. In case there was . . . trouble."

I moved to take my seat, sensing he had something of substance to tell me. "Which there was."

"Different kind of trouble. But yeah." His fresh complexion and young age seemed at odds with such statements. He reached into his coat to remove a pack of cigarettes. "Do ye mind?"

I shook my head. Anything was preferable to the stench of onions and sweat which seemed to linger in the room. I considered asking if we could open the window, but then remembered there were stables nearby and the breeze might not be favorable.

I waited until he'd lit his fag and taken his first drag before questioning him. "Where were you positioned? In the meeting room with the Dáil?"

"The lobby."

I straightened. "Then you might have seen the thief."

"I might have." He grimaced. "But I was payin' more attention to the blonde."

"What blonde?" This was the first I'd heard of her.

"Seated near that big urn. 'Twas hard to miss her. I can tell ye, every man that walked in there noticed her. She seemed to be waitin' for someone."

"Can you describe her?"

"Beautiful."

I cast him a withering glare. "I gathered that much."

He grinned, and I knew he was toying with me. He was one of Collins's top intelligence agents, after all. He must be observant, or he wouldn't have lasted this long.

"Blond curls." He tilted his head, studying my hair. "Cut

about like yours. Short. No more than five-foot, probably less. Cupid's bow mouth."

I arched my eyebrows at this.

"She seemed a bit nervous. Almost like she didn't like the attention. Kept fidgetin' with the buttons on her gloves. I thought for sure she was going to twist one clean off."

A clear image of Doris Fitzgibbon under the gleam of the chandeliers in the Shelbourne Hotel ballroom came to my mind. She had been twisting the buttons on her gloves then, too. While this wasn't necessarily a unique characteristic, it was still a telling one, especially when coupled with Tom's description of the woman at Fleming's Hotel.

"Did you see where she went when the alarm about the theft was raised?"

Tom was watching me closely through the haze of his cigarette smoke. I couldn't tell if he'd already known the blond woman was important and so that's why he was telling me, or if he'd only just realized it. "I'm afraid not. I was too busy hustlin' the Dáil out the door when the manager informed us the police had been called."

I tapped my lip with my forefinger, curious what Doris had been doing there. I didn't think she was the thief. Not when she was sitting quite prominently in the lobby. But she might have been acting as a lookout of some sort or a distraction, most likely for her husband or her brother. I truly needed to have a discussion with her, and the sooner the better.

Having come to this conclusion, I opened my mouth to ask Tom another question when the door suddenly burst open again. A thin young man with sharp, quick movements stepped in and I realized I recognized him. He was Joe O'Reilly. He acted as a sort of assistant and confidential courier to Collins.

"We've a problem," Joe stated to Tom in his rolling Cork accent.

Tom stood to cross the room, stubbing out his cigarette in

a dish as he walked past a table. At first, it appeared as if they intended to confer so that I wouldn't hear, until I stepped forward to join them. The look I fastened Tom with clearly communicated that I wasn't going to be left out of anything if it related to my husband, or Alec for that matter. Especially if they were in trouble.

Except it wasn't they who were in danger.

Tom nodded for Joe to continue.

Joe cast me one more fleeting, anxious look before speaking. "A military patrol just entered the pub."

Alarm shot through me as I paused to listen. It was true, the noises coming from below were softer than usual, as if everyone had fallen silent but for a few.

Tom swore. "Is Mick here?"

"Not yet. But I expect him any minute."

Tom shooed him toward the door. "Well, see if ye can slip out and waylay him before he arrives."

Joe nodded and hurried back out the door, even as Tom turned to survey the room, running a hand down his face.

"I can't be found here," I said, panic beginning to bubble inside me, followed by fury. Alec had insisted I would be safe here. That the raiding party from the previous night wouldn't be back.

"I know," Tom replied shortly. "I'd rather not be caught myself."

I fell silent, recognizing the consequences for him would probably be far worse than for me. Though if the soldiers realized who I was or took me to the Castle, my and Sidney's lives would invariably be shot to hell even if C did vouch for us.

Coming to some sort of decision, Tom beckoned me toward the door. "Follow me. But keep quiet."

We crept on silent feet down the corridor to the stairs and down one flight to the floor below. There he paused just outside two darkened rooms. To the left was a dining room which must have been positioned directly over the pub, for we could hear voices and creaks from below. The room across from it was the kitchen, and if I looked closely, I could see that the windows within were already opened, the curtains billowing inward on a light breeze. This, I supposed, was to be our escape route.

Tom gestured with his head for me to enter the kitchen. "Mind the floorboard just inside the door," he whispered.

I stepped long, hoping to avoid it and inched my way across the room toward one of the windows while Tom remained in the doorway listening. My eyesight having adjusted better to the dark, I peered out the opening and across the flat roofs of outbuildings and sculleries at the rear of the building, eventually leading to the stable. Upon discovering we weren't, in fact, trapped, my heartbeat slowed as I prepared myself for the eventuality I might need to climb through the window.

The minutes stretched by, practically quivering in the air as we waited, hardly daring to twitch let alone lift a foot. A few false alarms had Tom raising his hand and me reaching toward the window, only for him to shake his head and lower his arm again as the patrol failed to mount the stairs. Eventually the volume of voices coming from below the dining room began to rise again, though not in agitation. Tom murmured for me to remain where I was and then moved off to check.

A moment later, I heard Mrs. Devlin's voice calling up to tell Tom the soldiers had left. At this, I returned to the corridor to join him as Mrs. Devlin explained that they'd searched everyone below and broken a glass, but they hadn't asked to look upstairs. This seemed a somewhat foolish oversight on their part, but I wasn't about to question our luck. Not when they might return, and Sidney and Alec were still out searching for that crewman.

CHAPTER 21

I'd fallen into a doze in one corner of the horsehair sofa in the parlor when some hours later Sidney jostled me awake. "Mrs. Devlin has offered us a bed," he murmured as I blinked up at him, trying to remember where I was. As soon as I did, I shot upright, turning toward the window and then lifting the watch affixed inside my coat.

"It's after curfew," Sidney explained before I could work that out for myself. He glanced back over his shoulder at Alec and Tom. "And we don't think we should risk it."

Risk crossing the city and being stopped by a military patrol. Dressed as we were, even our curfew passes might not prevent eyebrows from being raised. Though the specter of the close call earlier still rattled me. Which reminded me of why we were there in the first place.

"Did you find him?" I asked, my gaze darting between my husband and Alec.

"Yes," Sidney said. "And he agreed to tell us what he knew for a small . . . fee." His expression was wry. "But one more substantial than what I was carrying on me."

I supposed this wasn't unexpected. The sailor was a mercenary. And it sounded as if Sidney had recognized this before I had, if he'd been carrying even a small bribe with him. However, their taut expressions suggested there was less encouraging news to follow.

"So we agreed to meet again tomorrow evening, but as he was striding back through the crowd of dockworkers toward his boat, he was stabbed and pushed into the water."

Had I not been gently reared by my mother and less rigorously trained by British Intelligence, I might have let fly with an extremely foul curse. As it was, I was hard-pressed to repress it. Though I suspected the men would have appreciated the sentiment. Instead, I pressed my head into my hands for a few moments before groaning. "So we're still no closer to finding the phosgene. Still no closer to catching Ardmore."

None of them responded to this, not that they needed to. Not when it was the stark truth.

When Sidney and I finally returned to our town house in the wee hours of the morning once the curfew had lifted and we could blend into the crowds of people making their way to their various jobs, we discovered that Nimble had also passed a restless night.

"Oh, thank heavens!" he exclaimed as we snuck in through the rear entrance. "When ye didn't return, I feared the worst."

Sidney pressed a hand to his shoulder. "Apologies. Believe me, it wasn't by choice. But it was the safest course of action."

Nimble accepted this with a nod, simply seeming glad to see us.

I began to trudge up the stairs toward our bedchamber, desperate for a few hours' undisturbed sleep. Or rather less disturbed than I'd been at Devlin's, jumping at every stray sound, unsettled by the very notion of accepting shelter beneath a rebel's roof, with Michael Collins possibly sleeping in the next room. We hadn't seen him, but that didn't mean he wasn't there. Unless Joe O'Reilly had managed to intercept him and divert him elsewhere.

"A message came while you were out," the valet said, halting me.

I turned to take it from him, noting it was on Bank of

Ireland stationery, which meant it was from Finnegan most likely. It was concise, as usual, but it made me frown, for it requested my presence "as soon as ever possible," not the usual, "at your earliest convenience." Somehow, I didn't think this was an oversight.

A glimpse at my watch revealed there were still three hours before the bank opened, giving me time for at least a short rest and a bath before I took the tram to College Green.

Three and a quarter hours later I was being led to Finnegan's office inside the Bank of Ireland, struggling to stifle a yawn. Even the magnificence of the building couldn't rouse me entirely from my stupor, for I'd already been inside too many times before. The bank had taken over the former Parliament House where the parliament of Ireland had conducted business before the Acts of Union in 1800, and as one would expect, it was all stately columns, gleaming marble, and soaring ceilings. The chamber which had been the House of Commons had been divided into offices, of which Mr. Finnegan commanded one of the largest, with numerous windows positioned high on the wall to allow sunlight to filter into the space.

Tobias Finnegan, a tall and angular figure, stood behind his desk, cleaning his round glasses. At my appearance, he replaced them on his nose and came forward to greet me. "Mrs. Kent." His gaze strayed beyond me as if he'd expected someone else to join us, likely my husband. Sidney would have, but he'd been sleeping so soundly when I rose to ready myself that I'd decided there was no need to disturb both of our slumbers.

Finnegan smiled as if to soften his presumption. "Please, have a seat." He gestured toward the pair of Windsor armchairs set before his desk. "I'm sure you're wondering why I asked ye here," he declared as he sat on the other side of the desk, clasping his hands together on its broad surface. As always, it was neat and tidy, with a minimum of paperwork and supplies littering its surface, all precisely placed or lined up.

When I didn't respond, instead wondering why he was belaboring the point, he cleared his throat. "Right. I've just returned from London."

"I see," I replied, understanding now. He'd met with C in person then, and he had something to convey to me. Something I probably wasn't going to like.

It was true, my recent reports had been rather sporadic and sparse, but that was because there had been little to share in the way of progress. This had been bound to irritate the chief, but there'd been no alternative. I could have elaborated further on our failures, but that would not have gotten us any closer to answers.

"How is he?" I asked, fishing for some sense of where I stood.

"He's . . . cross," Finnegan settled on after some consideration.

"Because of our lack of momentum."

He hesitated to continue, seeming agitated by what he must say. "He wishes you to return to London. Immediately."

I blinked in surprise before stammering, "You must be jesting. But why?" I narrowed my eyes. "This isn't about him still thinking I'm in the family way, is it?" I'd thought I'd made it clear that was a bluff months ago. I lifted my hands away from my still flat waist. "Because obviously I'm not."

He cleared his throat uncomfortably. "No . . ."

"Then . . . surely not the reprisals." For all the increased danger in Ireland, as more and more reprisals were reported each day, stretching into every county, C had sent me into far more perilous circumstances during the war without batting an eyelash.

"No, but he was in earnest."

I stared at him in the dawning realization that he was indeed serious. "But that's impossible," I protested. "We haven't found the phosgene."

"Nevertheless, he wishes ye to return." He frowned. "He says it's an order."

My hands clamped around my clutch where it rested in my lap, my fury spiking and my lack of sleep making it more difficult than usual to control it. "Considering the fact I no longer officially work for C and the SIS, having been deemed redundant after the war, I don't see how he thinks he can *order* me to do anything."

"Official or not, I'm sure you're aware he can make trouble for ye."

I turned to the side, knowing he spoke the truth, and the compassion in his tone only made it worse. Even without official recognition, being here at C's request had afforded us at least some legitimacy and protection—if not in the immediacy, then at least hypothetically if we were to find ourselves in a spot of trouble. Without even that, we could be at the whim of O or anyone else who might turn on us. Our status, reputations, and wealth afforded us great leeway in most circumstances, but in Ireland, those things mattered less and less, especially if the wrong person took it into their head that you were in league with the republicans and could produce even the slimmest evidence of it.

"But what of the phosgene?" I pressed. Perhaps C had lost confidence in me, but surely he couldn't allow something like that to remain in Lord Ardmore's hands, not considering his own suspicions about the man. Not considering the dire consequences.

"He says . . ." Finnegan flushed. "He says he's begun to question whether it still exists as a credible threat."

I felt as if a stiletto had been plunged into my side. To hear that the man I so admired—during the war and beyond, who had been with me every step of this investigation, now no longer trusted my assessments of the situation, absolutely gutted me.

"But we know that it is," I pleaded with Finnegan.

230 Anna Lee Huber

"And for what it's worth, I tried to convince him of that," he assured me in a low voice. "But the trouble is that there are simply too many things we've discovered through the republicans that we can't explain we know, because we have no plausible way to have learned about them without giving ourselves away."

Because Alec was no longer acting as a double agent. When he had still been ostensibly a British agent who had infiltrated Collins's inner circle, he had been our source, but since he went "missing" there had been no source to replace him with. Not credibly. And giving away our own connection with the rebels would mean mistrust and incarceration.

I gazed unseeing at the pristine blotter set before Finnegan, trying to puzzle my way through this. "Surely he doesn't expect me on the next ferry home." My eyes lifted as a thought occurred to me. "What about the jewelry thefts?"

He nodded. "I reminded C of your involvement with that, how Undersecretary Anderson contacted him before he asked you to investigate, and he conceded that it would be best for you to see that through. But he reiterated that you should drop the matter of the phosgene."

I scowled, pushing to my feet. "We'll see about that."

"Mrs. Kent," he said as I turned to go. "There is one more thing."

I looked back to find him holding out a letter for me.

"From Miss Silvernickel. She asked privately that I hand deliver it to you."

This more than anything caused my stomach to drop. For if Kathleen was going to such lengths to send me confidential information about the situation, it was dire indeed.

I thanked him and slipped the note into my pocket, wishing I could read it immediately, but it would be in code. So instead, I hurried home and straight to the writing desk in our private sitting room.

Sidney woke sometime later to find me still seated there,

the letter dangling from my fingertips as I struggled with its revelations. He was forced to say my name several times before I heard him, and then I merely passed him the decoded missive in response.

I hope I am not wrong to trust Finnegan with this, but I must get word to you somehow.

Thomson was here to see C. He was in a righteous fury and did not curb his temper enough for me not to hear every word he said. He claimed that you were interfering with intelligence work. That you exposed an agent named Digby Hardy and that you've been attempting to use your wiles on some of his best officers to get information.

This is obviously taradiddle, for I know you better than that, and so does C. But his last charge is more difficult to dismiss.

He asserts that Captain Xavier is alive and well— that he's been spotted in Dublin—and that he's defected to Collins. That you must know about it, and because of it, you're likely working with them as well.

C knows as well as I do how close you were to Captain Xavier. It's why he sent you to Dublin to look for him when Xavier dropped out of contact. So this charge is more difficult to ignore.

Your last report on Xavier said your best intelligence about him was that he'd been killed and his body thrown in a bog. I don't know if this is the truth or not, and I don't need to know. After all, I was fond of him as well, and sometimes it's easier to turn a blind eye than to betray a friend. But whatever the truth, you've been exposed.

As far as I know, C did not give you up. In fact, he cast aspersions on Thomson's claims and reminded Thomson that he has no authority over C's operations.

*But C intends to recall you, and all things considered,
it might be for the best.*

"Obviously, the snake has been pouring venom into his
ears," Sidney surmised, his voice crackling with rage.

O had been my first guess as an informant as well. Or Ardmore. Either way, "snake" was an apt description.

"I suspect Bennett and Ames are the officers you're meant
to have practiced your wiles on."

"I did meet with them," I responded dully.

"With *me*, months ago," Sidney scoffed. "This Digby Hardy
fellow. He was the chap exposed a week ago by Griffith?"

"I was at the press conference."

"But you'd never even *heard* of the man until that day."

I could see him scrutinizing me out of the corner of my eye,
but couldn't summon the energy to meet his gaze.

"Why didn't you wake me to go with you?" He was speaking of this morning when I'd gone to see Finnegan and evidently received this note from Kathleen.

I shrugged one shoulder. "It seemed silly for us both not
to be sleeping."

He stepped directly into my line of sight, forcing me to
either look up into his face or continue to stare at the tri-
angle of skin revealed by the part in his dressing gown. "Even
though you're even more tired than I am. I'm used to sleeping
in less-than-ideal circumstances."

"And I'm not?" I challenged. He might have spent the war
sleeping in trench dugouts and hovels, but I'd also spent a fair
amount of time catching a few hours' rest wherever I could,
be it barn rafters, the hollow of a tree, or under a broken-
down cart at the side of the road to escape the rain.

Sidney didn't rise to the bait. "Did he recall you?" he asked
gently.

I turned away, unable to face him as I sneered. "I've been
ordered to return to London."

He digested this information for a moment, and I expected him to be relieved to have an excuse to escort me back to safety. One that wouldn't require him to be the ogre. Instead, he shocked me with a softly muttered, "The hell you will! Not when we must be getting close." He pulled me to my feet. "That mercenary knew something. He knew something and he was going to tell us, and someone—almost certainly one of Ardmore's men—killed him because of it." He scowled. "My only mistake was not having enough blunt on me. But if Alec can find another member of the crew, perhaps they'll be willing to make the same deal."

"Don't you think Ardmore will wonder the same thing?" Truth be told, I wouldn't be surprised if a rash of sailors suddenly ended up dead in the docklands.

"Then we just have to get to them first."

"Something easier said than done."

He grasped my upper arms, forcing me to look him in the eye. His face still sported dark stubble and creases from his pillow, and his hair sprouted about his head in wild abandon. "Verity, don't tell me you're ready to give up?"

"I don't want to, but—" I broke off, biting my lip as he waited for me to continue. "If C withdraws what little protection he just tentatively extended to us, I don't doubt that O would have us picked up in a heartbeat on whatever trumped-up charges he can come up with."

"Then, we just need to make sure he doesn't." He tilted his head. "I know that hearing that C wants to recall you can't be easy, but it sounds like, despite whatever seeds of doubt Thomson tried to spread, he's doing what he can to shield you. After all, until today you were under the impression he would do no such thing. That if we were caught, we were on our own."

I hadn't thought of it that way, but he was right. C's ordering Thomson not to interfere with us was all but an admission that we were here working on his behalf. "And he did give us permission to finish our investigation into the jewel thefts."

Sidney nodded. "So we make sure we're seen investigating that, and do better at concealing the other. Meanwhile, we avoid Ardmore and any other British intelligence officers."

"Including Bennett and Ames?" I knew Sidney had believed they were helpful assets in our search for the phosgene cylinders, but that had now been called into question.

He frowned. "Yes."

"What of Frank Caulfield?" He knew Caulfield had admitted to being the man Hal Fitzgibbon had seen entering the servants' entrance at the Harringtons', and how he'd all but threatened me when I asked him about it at the Wicklow. "I don't think we can rule him out as a suspect."

"We'll have to tread carefully with him," he conceded.

"I suppose we also shouldn't be seen to be changing our routines," I murmured, wondering if it had been a mistake to withdraw temporarily when Castle society's reactions to the growing number of reprisals had repelled us. Distracted by its disarray, I reached up to smooth back Sidney's thick curls.

He agreed. "It could be construed in the wrong way."

I heaved a sigh. "I suppose that means we'll be attending the chief secretary's dinner party tomorrow evening."

"And the Powerscourts' house party on Saturday."

I grimaced, hoping Sybil didn't invite anyone too tedious, or worse, Lord Ardmore. I knew they were acquainted.

Sidney pulled me close. "Cheer up. It's reputed to have wonderful gardens."

"That may be, but I would rather be here searching dank and musty warehouses for a shipment of phosgene," I groused.

His forehead dipped to touch mine as he murmured wearily. "Me, too."

CHAPTER 22

Viscount Powerscourt's large country estate was located in the beautiful County Wicklow countryside. Sidney and I had driven down from Dublin in the rain, but there had been a break in the clouds upon our arrival, and so we'd gathered for tea with the other guests on the wide terrace overlooking the lake and expansive gardens, the mountains flush with October color beyond. Compared with the surrounding landscape, the house's Palladian-style façade with domed towers struggled to compete.

"Oh, Sybil, it's simply lovely," I exclaimed. "How do you ever leave?"

She chuckled. "It's difficult to tear myself away, I admit."

It proved not to be an overly large house party, but I was glad to see the Fitzgibbons and Rufus Beresford among the guests, as I'd yet to catch Doris at home the times I'd attempted to call on her. One would almost think she was avoiding me. When I greeted her, she made no reference to missing my calls, though I could tell from the nervous look in her eyes that she was aware of them. Following her cue, I opted not to mention them myself, hoping this would earn her trust enough that she might seek me out privately. Otherwise, I would simply have to corner her.

Sybil shared some of her plans for our three days at Powerscourt. "We shall motor up into the deer park to the waterfall, if the weather allows," she concluded before asking if we had any requests.

Her husband, Mervyn, spoke up first. "Don't forget we need to finalize plans for the fete at the RDS grounds."

"Yes, of course," Sybil replied. This was to be the central event to raise funds for the Dublin hospitals, which were struggling. It was to be held at the Royal Dublin Society grounds in Ballsbridge in a week's time. "I invited Dr. McCarthy to join us here, thinking it might be useful to have a physician's input, but he had to decline."

I remembered meeting Dr. McCarthy at the charity event at the Shelbourne and finding him to be a likable fellow.

"Mark still hopes to join us tomorrow if he can get away," Lady Rachel Sturgis remarked after taking a drink of her tea. "But he said to tell you it seems unlikely."

"Keeping him busy, are they?" Lord Powerscourt queried good-naturedly.

"Yes, especially with the Greenwoods and Anderson away," she replied, referring to the chief secretary and his wife, and the undersecretary. She shook her head. "It's these ridiculous reprisals. Mark says the shooting is one thing, but all this burning just spoils it all."

I wasn't cognizant of exactly how many villages and creameries had been burned and destroyed or how many innocent civilians had been killed, but the number was appalling and continuing to grow. Just in the last few days, the villages of Trim, Mallow, and Listowel had been added to the list. To make the British bumbling of the situation even worse, the chief secretary had promised that these reprisals would be stopped, only to immediately be proved a liar.

"No trouble here yourself?" Mr. Chatham asked His Lordship, making reference to the country houses which had been attacked in some of the western counties.

"Not a bit," Mervyn confirmed, leaning back in his chair.

"Though, of course, the house is full of what you'd call 'raidable' things. But I don't expect to be targeted."

"At least the reprisals have overshadowed the news about these hunger strikers," Mr. Fitzgibbon said as he passed his wife a tiny cake from the tray. Though I couldn't understand how the reprisals were any better. "The entire lot of them is still hanging on."

"They must secretly be fed," one of the other guests suggested.

"What's this I hear about Mark being offered the viceregal secretaryship by Lord French?" Sybil asked Rachel, apparently no more interested in discussing conspiracy theories about the hunger strikers than I was.

She laughed. "Well, it's supposed to be a secret, but since the cat's out of the bag, I think he should take it. It would mean the children and I could come over to live with him since we'd be staying at the Viceregal Lodge rather than the Castle, which is already overcrowded."

"Yes, but French is on his last leg," Lord Powerscourt cautioned. "And an association with him might hurt your husband's future prospects."

"Yes, that's why he's hesitant to take it without considering all aspects, though he is quite fond of the dear."

I opted to withhold my own thoughts about the lord lieutenant and his abilities. Whether because of the topic of conversation or the long drive, I was feeling antsy and pushed to my feet, expressing a desire to stretch my legs. Sidney began to set down his tea, as if to offer to accompany me, but Mr. Beresford surprised us all by rising first.

"That sounds like a capital idea," he declared with a sardonic grin. "You don't mind if I tag along, do you?"

"Not at all." I found myself curious whether he had an ulterior motive. Something to do with his sister, who watched us with wide eyes. Perhaps if I couldn't corner Doris, I might be able to pry some information from her brother.

"Just be mindful of the weather," Sybil called after us as we set off down the path leading toward the lake. "It looks like more rain."

Gray clouds were massing in the distance, and the wind had picked up, tugging at the brim of my hat, but I didn't intend to go far. Mr. Beresford easily kept pace with me, his hands clasped amiably behind his back. I liked that he didn't rush to fill the silence as so many people did.

"Is this your first time at Powerscourt?" I asked, marveling at the landscape. It was unclear whether he shared my awe.

"I'd been here once before." He narrowed his eyes at something far in the distance. "Before the war."

"You served."

It was more a statement than a question, for the fact was obvious to me. It had marked him as it had so many others. But he nodded all the same.

I would have left it at that, but he seemed to feel the need to add with a sneer, "Hal didn't."

This fact had also been obvious, but I didn't say so, instead focusing on another aspect of his statement. "You're not very fond of your brother-in-law, are you?"

He hesitated as if wondering if it had been wise to reveal so much, but then seemed to mentally shrug, as if deciding he didn't care. "Not particularly."

"Why? He seems fairly unobjectionable."

He laughed rudely. "And if that isn't faint praise, I don't know what is."

"Perhaps," I conceded, realizing he had a point. "But he seems to dote on your sister." I paused at the edge of the terrace. "That must be preferable to the opposite."

Beresford's brow furrowed. "My sister married that dolt because my father told her to. And he only told her to because he possessed one redeeming quality."

I could guess where this was going. "Wealth."

"Bravo, Mrs. Kent." He turned his jaundiced gaze on me.

"Don't tell me you also wed Kent for such mercenary reasons."

I affixed him with a contemptuous glare, not about to dignify that comment with a response, then turned toward the stairs that would take me down to the next terrace.

"Far be it for me to judge." He chuckled. "Not when Kent evidently seems happy with the arrangement."

I waited for him once I'd reached the next level, hoping to catch him off guard. "Is your sister?"

Standing where we were now, the other guests couldn't see us, and Beresford took the opportunity to speak frankly. "Listen. I know you noticed Doris's nerves when you were questioning her about the Harringtons' shindig. I told her she was a fool to have her staff turn you away rather than just telling you the truth." He crossed his arms in irritation, though I couldn't tell whether it was at me or his sister. "She's having an affair, all right?" He scowled. "Hal doesn't know."

"I see." I wasn't a fool. This possibility had crossed my mind.

"The bloke was at the Harringtons'. But he wasn't the jewel thief," he snapped just as I was opening my mouth to ask that very question.

"How can you be so certain?"

"Because I am."

I arched my eyebrows at this reasoning. Doris seemed just the sort of woman who might be convinced to aid and abet a criminal in the name of love. "What's the bloke's name?"

Beresford arched a sardonic eyebrow. "Now, why on earth would I tell you that?"

"So I can confirm you're telling the truth."

His eyes narrowed, perhaps believing this to be an insult.

"I could always ask Doris for it. Or maybe Hal knows him."

"I see the cat has claws," he drawled. "No, Hal doesn't know him. The lover. He's . . . a *republican*." He practically spat the word. This explained some of his reticence. "Shameful, I know. But Doris never did have much sense."

"Where else do they meet?"

"Hotels. Usually places north of the river where she won't be recognized. Vaughan's, Fleming's, and the like."

I supposed everything he'd said made sense. It certainly aligned with what I'd observed about Doris. Though I still wished I had a name to investigate and corroborate this information. Short of actually threatening to reveal Doris's affair to her husband, I didn't know how to pressure Beresford for the information, and I hesitated to do that unless necessary. Perhaps Doris might prove easier to convince, if only I could catch her alone.

That was easier said than done when either her brother or her husband was always by her side. I might have found it suspicious if not for the fact that Doris was clearly intimidated by me and embarrassed by her secret.

In any case, my focus took an abrupt turn on the second evening of the house party. A few of the guests had elected to retire shortly after dinner while the rest of us divided into tables to play cards. However, we were only into our second hand when voices upstairs alerted us that something was amiss.

"My ruby pendant. It's gone!" Doris exclaimed when several of us had reached the upper corridor. "I left it inside my pillow. Rufus said a thief would never look there." She was trembling, and Sybil gently guided her back into her room, sitting her on the settee and pouring her a glass of water from the ewer.

Rufus scowled furiously. "What blasted thief looks in a pillowcase?" He rounded on Lord Powerscourt. "And what sort of place lets a thief break in while there are guests dining below?"

"Let's all remain calm," Sidney urged. "We should assess the situation before jumping to any conclusions." He glanced at everyone who had assembled. "Is anyone else missing anything?" Most of the guests scurried off to check as he turned to Mr. Fitzgibbon. "Are you or your wife missing anything else?"

Fitzgibbon seemed stunned and uncertain what to do, but he shook his head.

"Did you check?" Beresford sneered.

This jarred Fitzgibbon out of his stupor as he frowned. "Yes. Though . . ." He turned to look at his wife. "Did you hide any of your other jewelry?"

"No. It's in my jewelry box." She sniffled. "My maid has the key."

I crossed to the dressing table, opening the bottom drawer where I'd deduced it must be kept. "Do you mind?" I asked before extracting it from the drawer after Doris shook her head. As I feared, the lock gave way with minimum jostling. It was empty of all but a few baubles made of paste.

Doris burst into tears at this revelation, and Fitzgibbon and Beresford began shouting recriminations.

"Perhaps you should check your own jewels?" I told Sybil as Sidney attempted to calm the men.

"I imagine my maid is already doing so," she replied resignedly. "But perhaps you . . ."

I jumped at the excuse to escape the chamber but was halted from reaching my own by two more guests who were missing pieces of valuable jewelry—one a bracelet and the other a pair of earrings. Thankfully, no one else seemed to have been targeted, including Lord and Lady Powerscourt. By the time I made it to our room, I was relieved to find it undisturbed.

I couldn't account for the thief's timing or his decision to steal from just three of the rooms, except that they were all in the same corridor. Perhaps he'd been disrupted during his search and chosen to make his escape before he was caught. As for his knowing that the Powerscourts were hosting a house party, this would not have been difficult to discover. It had probably been mentioned in at least one society column or perhaps he'd simply overheard one of the guests mention it during the week prior.

Unless the thief was, in fact, a guest himself.

A window in one of the vacant bedchambers was found to be opened, suggesting this was how he'd gained access. There was no ladder below the window, but it didn't appear that it would have been too difficult to scale the natural stone-work. A road bordering the estate lay less than a mile to the southwest where the thief might have left a vehicle in order to make a quick escape.

All of these things seemed to point to an intruder, but I wasn't certain we should entirely dismiss the possibility he was a guest himself. It was true, the jewel thief had already proven himself to be brash and unpredictable. But this seemed almost too brazen for an outsider.

Unless, perhaps, he was baiting us.

I posed the question to Sidney later that night when we were able to retire to the sumptuous chamber we'd been assigned, overlooking the terrace. Thoroughly questioning the Powerscourts and all their guests and staff and searching the grounds had taken no small amount of time.

"It's possible," he conceded, shrugging out of his black dinner jacket. "Though a house party here would naturally seem like a prime target for such a thief."

"Yes, but to strike while we were all at dinner and anyone might have returned upstairs at any moment?" I queried in disbelief. "That goes beyond bold to outright reckless."

He tugged open his bow tie, meeting my gaze in the reflection of the mirror as I removed my earrings. "You said you only brought paste jewelry. Were you expecting him?"

"No. But I thought it better to be wary. At least until he's caught." I took off my rhinestone bracelet and then the necklace, nestling them in the tissue paper inside my jewelry case which would slide back into my valise.

Sidney's hands came to rest on my shoulders, and I looked up to find him watching me in the mirror. "You've a little line . . . here." He lifted his finger to trace it between my eyebrows. "What's troubling you?"

I found myself struggling to put it into words, but this was Sidney, so I knew I should try. "It's just . . . Beresford."

"Ah, yes. What did you two discuss during your stroll the other day?"

"Mostly his sister. He claims she's having an affair and that's why she's been behaving so nervously and avoiding my calls. Why she was at Fleming's Hotel. He claims the lover is a republican."

Sidney's eyebrows arched. "You just used the word 'claims' twice. Don't you believe him?"

"I should, shouldn't I? It certainly explains Doris's odd behavior. And who makes such assertions about one's sister if they're not true?" I frowned. "And yet . . ."

"You don't," he finished for me when I left the sentence dangling.

"Not entirely. Though I can't put my finger on the reason why." I drummed my fingers against the dressing table. "Maybe it was his frank admission that he doesn't like his brother-in-law."

"That much is obvious," he stated wryly as he lifted his hands to begin unbuttoning his crisp white shirt.

"Yes, but you should have heard the way he spoke about him. He says Doris married him because of his money."

"Well, Beresford's father did manage to lose nearly his entire fortune on gambling and bad investments while Rufus was fighting at the front. That might explain some of his resentment."

"I suppose so." My eyes remained trained on my husband's

reflection and the ever-widening gap of his shirt. The undershirt did very little to conceal his impressive physique. Part of me wondered if he was deliberately trying to distract me. If so, it was working, though I did have one stray thought. "Perhaps we should consider setting a trap."

"For the thief?" Having tugged the hems of his shirts from the waistband of his trousers, Sidney looked up to find me watching him. The glint in my eyes must have communicated where my thoughts had strayed. Which explained why he didn't brush back the dark lock of hair that had fallen over his brow. He knew how much I enjoyed the sight of him tousled. His lips quirked upward at one corner. "It's worth a thought."

"It would have to be skillfully done," I heard myself reply in a silky voice, reaching back to begin unfastening my gown.

He took the cue, taking over for me. His clever hands worked quickly, skimming down my spine as he urged me to stand. "So as not to *alert* them that it's a trap."

"Precisely."

"Hmmm." His warm breath feathered over the skin where my neck and shoulder met. "We'll have to give it some deliberation."

"Yes," I breathed, turning to drape my arms around his neck as my gown pooled on the floor. "Thorough deliberation."

"Hmm . . ." was all he managed before his mouth captured mine.

CHAPTER 23

Upon our return to Dublin the next day we were met by a relieved Nimble—who seemed to fret rather like a mother hen whenever we weren't in sight—and a flurry of correspondence. The first was a brief note written in Nancy's neat scrawl, requesting that I meet her the next day—this time in the churchyard of Christ Church Cathedral. This being practically on the Castle's doorstep, I wasn't surprised and dashed off a reply, anxious to learn what she'd discovered.

The second piece of correspondence was a letter addressed directly to me. I suspected it must be from Calliope and was proved correct. However, the late Lord Rockham's first wife had little to share on behalf of herself or her son—the new Lord Rockham. There were no records of either the marquessate or Rockham himself ever having owned property in Dublin or the entirety of Ireland. All of his holdings were either in England or Wales.

The only thing related to Dublin that Calliope had been able to find among his effects were a few entries among his secretary's list of contacts. She listed the three names for me, but I held little hope of them proving useful. Not when one of them was a baron who had since sold the property at the address listed, and the other two appeared to be actresses. I was well aware of Rockham's propensity for such women. After all, his second wife had been a dancer before he'd wed her. I fully expected these women, both listed with two directions—one to a theater and the other likely a personal address, one on Harcourt Place and the other Queen's Square—to be former mistresses.

I opened the third letter from Etta with almost a sense of dread. We needed a lead for the phosgene, and if Max couldn't provide us with one, I felt I very well might crack.

Etta's note warned me that Max was exhibiting the same signs of strain he'd shown before, but tried to bolster me with the knowledge that at least he wasn't getting worse. This was false comfort and did nothing to ease my worry for my friend. A fact Max seemed to be aware of, for he mentioned it in the missive Etta enclosed.

> *I know you're concerned for me, Ver. But I promise not to do anything rash. My sister recently scolded me about giving in to despair, and my niece's face when she overheard part of what was said was enough to set me straight. Between them and you, I shall pull through.*

I sniffled reading this, and Sidney wrapped his arm around me where we sat side by side on the Sheraton sofa with the letter between us.

> *But I also need you and Sidney to take care and make it home in one piece. So, no heroics! Just do what needs to be done and get out of there.*

"I suppose that's fair," Sidney allowed upon reading Max's admonishment.

We did both have a tendency to believe we were the only ones who could save the day. Though, in this instance, we very well might be right.

> *I am not aware of my father owning any property or holdings in Ireland, and I've not been able to find*

*any records of such. But I will continue to search. I am
still waiting to hear from my father's secretary, who
retired upon his death and now lives with his daughter
on Guernsey. Perhaps he will know of something that
I don't.*

*There is much discussion here about the reprisals,
both the denial that they are occurring and the notion
of making them official. As my contact told me,
"It seems to be agreed that there is no such thing as
reprisals, but they are having good effect." How the
government hopes to formally condone such acts
of violence and wanton destruction is beyond me.
Though in all but words, it is already true. Today
even the* Times *declared that our name is being sullied
throughout the world because of it and called the
government to task for trying to deny responsibility.
I can only think that soon Lloyd George will have no
choice.*

I'll report more when I can. Stay safe!

The letter was not all that I'd wished, but at least there
was still hope Lord Ryde's former secretary might know
something. As to the rest, about the reprisals, it was nothing
we didn't already know. Dublin Castle had recently issued a
statement acknowledging that the RIC had been involved in
reprisals in Tubbercurry, County Sligo. It was admission of
one singular incident, but considering all of the Castle's previous denials, it was significant, nonetheless.

With all the dry and sunny weather we'd enjoyed in September, it was easy to forget how damp Ireland could be.
October elected to remind us of this with a vengeance. It
lashed, it bucketed, it showered, it drizzled, it misted—but at
all times some sort of precipitation was falling from the sky.
One benefit of all this rain was that Nancy and I had the

Christ Church Cathedral churchyard all to ourselves as we strode along the grass with umbrellas clutched in our hands. They blocked much of the sight of the ancient cathedral, which had been established by the Vikings, of all people, in the eleventh century. The Normans had constructed the first stone building, though it had been significantly renovated and refurbished as recently as fifty years ago.

"I have news," she declared once she reached the cover of the boughs of the tree where she'd instructed me to meet her, away from the prying eyes of the street. She looked behind her, as we fell into step. "Ye asked me to find out why Ardmore has been meetin' with Colonel Winter."

"Yes," I prompted.

Her brow creased in confusion. "Well, 'tis odd, but apparently they're discussin' the RIC's mob control methods, the current protocols, and whether any changes should be made."

"Mob control?" I repeated in surprise.

"Yeah." She clearly shared my bewilderment.

"Do you have any idea why or what changes they're proposing?"

"No, but it seems an odd thing for His Lordship to be involved with."

It did, indeed. Then again, we'd speculated that Ardmore likely intended to deploy the phosgene on some sort of crowd. Perhaps he wanted to ensure it imposed the maximum amount of damage by making sure that whatever crowd control policies were in place did little to mitigate the impact. And wasn't that a horrifying thought!

Nancy glanced behind us again, her hands tight around her umbrella handle.

"What's wrong?" I asked. "Do you think you were followed?"

"Naw." She didn't sound certain. "'Tis only I saw Caulfield standin' outside the pub on the corner. But I don't think he recognized me or cared."

"Frank Caulfield?"

She turned to me in surprise. "Ye know him?"

"Yes."

We both recognized the risk of being seen together by one of O's right-hand men. Perhaps he would think nothing of it, but it was more probable he would.

"I'll leave by another route," I suggested.

She nodded. "There's a back alley. Skirts the side of the cathedral to Winetavern Street and down to Wood Quay."

I hurried away with a wave of thanks, following her directions, then hopped on a tram headed east. If Caulfield—or anyone else for that matter—had managed to tail me without my noticing, by then I'd lost him. But it didn't ease the growing sense I had that I was living on borrowed time.

"I've had a thought," Sidney announced the following afternoon as we motored over the River Dodder into Ballsbridge. He braked as the Pierce-Arrow came upon a tram and then passed it before accelerating again.

I clutched the fur-trimmed rolled collar of my aubergine wool coat closed tighter. Fortunately, the rain of the past six days had let up just in time for the fete that was to be held at the RDS Grounds to raise funds for the local hospitals, but a decided chill had entered the air. "What's that?"

"You're undoubtedly aware of some of the lachrymatory agents that were used during the war. Ethyl bromoacetate and xylyl bromide and the like."

I turned to him, uncertain of his intent. "Tear gas, yes?"

His hands tightened around the driving wheel. "I've heard that the United States has created grenades filled with the stuff. That they propose to use it for riot control."

Realization dawned that he must have been thinking about what Nancy had told me several days past. "And you think Ardmore might be influencing O to do the same?"

Sidney shrugged.

"But phosgene isn't a simple tear gas," I pointed out. It was deadly. Its victims died in horrific fashion.

"No, it isn't."

"Then . . ." I subsided in silence, uncertain how to connect my scattered thoughts.

Sidney was sympathetic. "It seems we're still missing a step."

I nodded, still grappling with the problem. Though I didn't have long to do so. Not now that we'd arrived at the Royal Dublin Society Grounds.

Sidney and I had volunteered to be ticket takers for the fete, the better to see who came and went. We doubted Ardmore would target such an event, but it being a crowded venue and the phosgene still not found, we were wary all the same.

I adjusted my tam hat and smiled broadly at those who passed through the gates, trying to forget my and Sidney's unsettling conversation. Within the grounds, stalls with festive flags and bunting were set up in a circle. Some featured games such as hoopla or guessing the weight of one local farmer's prized sow. Others sold raffle tickets for various prizes that had been donated, and others still offered food and drink—everything from jams and biscuits to cakes and cream teas to ales and stouts. A marching band played cheery music at one end of the field while the running races and pony rides were conducted at the other.

It was rather an awkward mixture of British and Irish traditions, but everyone arriving in their glad rags and Sunday best seemed happy to be there. It was an increasingly rare moment of enjoyment and shared comradery. If Ardmore had plans to sabotage it, I thought I just might take the pistol from the nearest policeman and shoot him.

Most of the members of the Dublin Castle administration stayed away, but many of our other friends and acquaintances were present, either assisting with the assorted booths and events or enjoying the blustery fall day. Lord and Lady

Powerscourt were in charge of overseeing the games and contests and awarding the prizes while the Quins, Chathams, Harringtons, and Fitzgibbons manned other stations. Even Rufus Beresford had been enlisted to help, gamely cheering on children playing hoopla.

One exception to the Castle's prudent boycott was Frank Caulfield, though most wouldn't have recognized him as a British Intelligence officer anyway. I, however, was suspicious of his presence, and was at pains to hide it as he passed through my queue. He said nothing to indicate he was aware of it, or in fact interested in me at all, merely doffing his hat and carrying on. But I kept one eye on him all the same until he moved out of my range of sight.

I was chatting with a pair of nurses from Richmond Hospital, one of the institutions which would benefit from the funds raised by the fete, when Dr. McCarthy appeared in my line.

"Mrs. Kent, lovely to see you," he exclaimed.

"And you as well," I replied. "Oh, but are you acquainted with Nurses Doherty and Quinn?"

His smile tightened as he turned to the women.

"Didn't you tell me you work at Richmond Hospital?" I asked by way of explanation, not wanting him to think I was attempting a bit of matchmaking or any such nonsense.

"Uh . . . no. Whitworth."

"Ah, then we're neighbors," Nurse Doherty replied, for Richmond, Whitworth, and Hardwicke Hospitals were some of the oldest hospitals in the city located together in a complex in North Brunswick Street adjacent to the former North Dublin Union.

He laughed nervously. "I-I'm new," he stammered.

"Well, welcome! We'll look for ye."

"Sure," he said with false cheer, waving weakly as they walked away.

I found myself scrutinizing him, wondering at his behavior. The easiest explanation might have been that he was shy around women, but I'd not noticed it during our previous interactions. At first, I was prepared to brush it off, but when he refused to meet my eye as I took his ticket and wished him a pleasant afternoon, my instincts told me I shouldn't.

Catching up to Nurses Doherty and Quinn once our shift had ended, I asked if they recognized any other hospital employees—be they doctors, nurses, or other staff members— so that I could thank them. They quickly pointed out a few people, and while Sidney and I strolled through the fete I made a point of speaking to them. Several worked for the House of Industry hospitals, as the three red-brick institutions on North Brunswick Street were known, but none of them had ever heard of a Dr. McCarthy.

"I know that expression," my husband leaned over to murmur in my ear as we stood in the crowd, clapping as the prizes were awarded at the end of the fete. "You smell a rat."

I arched a sardonic eyebrow. "I didn't know I had a particular expression for that, but yes." My gaze sought and found Dr. McCarthy—or whatever his name was—standing several rows ahead of us near the Fitzgibbons, Beresford, the Chathams, and a couple who went by the double-barreled name of Dillon-Plunkett, whom we'd just been introduced to. "Dr. McCarthy has been lying to us. And I can't help but note that he was present during or soon after at least two of the burglaries."

He was also acquainted with most, if not all, of the victims and had attended the charity gala at the Shelbourne, where we'd believed the thief was scrutinizing the jewelry on display, selecting his next targets.

"He does have dark hair and a medium-to-tall build, and he passes himself off as a gentleman," Sidney concurred, citing the only definitive descriptors we'd received of the thief, from the hotel employee who'd lent him his key.

"Sybil also invited him to her house party, but he couldn't attend."

He nodded, his eyes sliding back to where Dr. McCarthy stood. "Then perhaps it's time we start asking some more direct questions about him."

I agreed but, as if he sensed our intentions, he slipped away as the awards were wrapping up, disappearing into the dispersing crowd. Though we did manage to catch up with the Fitzgibbons and Mr. Beresford. "Do any of you know where Dr. McCarthy went?"

"He said he had something to attend to back in Dublin." Hal Fitzgibbon eyed me askance, sensing my frustration. "Hospital business, most likely."

"Tell me, how well do you know him?"

He seemed taken aback by the question but then answered honestly. "Not well at all, I suppose. We only just met him at the Harringtons' soiree."

"Did they introduce you?"

He exchanged a glance with his wife and Beresford. "I'm not sure I recall who introduced—" Hal began only for Doris to interrupt him.

"No one did. Remember?" She sniffed. "He nearly spilled punch on my taffeta gown. He apologized profusely and then we introduced ourselves."

"Yes, of course," Hal agreed.

I might have suspected Dr. McCarthy of being Doris's alleged lover except for the fact she was so calm and composed as she responded.

Beresford, on the other hand, was on guard, seeming to have caught a whiff of the same thing I had. "I suggest asking the Harringtons."

I nodded, intending to do just that. But first, I decided to wait until we returned to our town house so that I could double-check the guest list Mrs. Harrington had given me. There was no Dr. McCarthy on it.

I recalled now that when I'd been introduced to Dr. McCarthy at the Shelbourne, I'd thought the name had sounded familiar, but I'd never bothered to actually verify. There was a McCarthy on the list, but not Dr. Archie McCarthy.

Furious at myself, I telephoned the Great Brunswick Street Police Station and asked for Detective Inspector Burrows. "Mrs. Kent," he exclaimed when I was patched through. "How may I help you?"

"I have a potential suspect for you."

Once I'd relayed all the details, he promised to look into it, starting with contacting the Whitworth Hospital to try to track him down. "You believe he's our jewel thief."

"I believe he's not who he claims to be, and that very well might mean he's our thief," I hedged. "I'm not sure yet."

I imagined Burrows smoothing his finger over the edges of his waxed mustache as he considered this. "Either way, I'll find out."

When I rang off, I turned to find Sidney leaning against the wall, his hands in his pockets. "If McCarthy's smart, he'll take the first ferry out of Ireland tonight."

"Burrows is no fool. He'll have anticipated that and have men watching the boats at Kingstown." I drummed my fingers against the desk. "Though if he heads north or south to one of the other ports, it'll be harder."

"Either way, Burrows has a better chance of finding him than we do."

It was why I'd called him. But something was still bothering me, and Sidney could tell.

"If he gets away, he gets away. There's nothing more we could have done."

I nodded, though I didn't think that was what troubled me. No, that was harder to put my finger on.

CHAPTER 24

We were invited back to Powerscourt on Friday, for Lord French had returned to Dublin and was coming to dine, with the Sturgises and some other members of the Castle administration motoring up the following day. However, Sidney and I decided to take the risk of declining. Informative as the weekend might prove to be, there was too much to do in Dublin. Too much we could miss.

Wick had sent me one of his terse notes, asking me to meet him on Saturday at the little restaurant in Dawson Street he seemed to prefer. It was a lovely little establishment and they served the best gin rickeys in the city.

I found him seated at his usual table tucked away in the corner near the kitchen, which afforded him a measure of privacy. Papers were scattered across the surface, and half a dozen cigarette butts filled the pewter ashtray at Wick's elbow. The front of his hair stood on end as if he'd been running his hands through it in frustration.

"Looks like I'm interrupting," I declared as I shook the rain from my coat. It had resumed in earnest.

"Verity," he replied in some surprise, glancing distractedly at his watch. "What time is it? Ah! Apologies." He began gathering up his things as I sat across from him.

"Lost track of time?"

"Aye." In the midst of his paper shuffling, he leaned forward to buss my cheek in greeting. Then at the waiter's prompting, he told him to bring me a gin rickey, knowing me well.

Furrows scored his brow, and his shoulders all but bristled with tension.

"That bad, is it?" I said lightly, noting that many of the memos were news bulletins.

He heaved a sigh, dropping the stack next to his near empty glass of stout. "Well, let's see. Several men in Galway were dragged from their beds and shot by the Auxies. Two rail wagons of military supplies were fired at in Kingsbridge Station, undoubtedly by the IRA." He gestured to the stack of papers. "We've more policemen murdered. More reprisals. Derry City's gone to hell. And Lloyd George is givin' speeches in Wales, spoutin' off about how ye can't have a one-sided war in order to justify his Black and Tans brutalizin' civilians and burnin' down villages."

"But I thought it wasn't war." They'd been very careful to avoid using such a term. It was never a war, just a police conflict with a band of armed thugs.

He pointed at me in emphasis. "Exactly!" He sat back, crossing his arms. "'Tis only war when they wish it to be. When it serves their narrative."

I'd read the reports about the prime minister's speech the previous day. I'd also seen a copy of the latest issue of the *Weekly Summary*, the RIC's internal newspaper. The British stance could be boiled down to something along the lines of: Reprisals are bad, but they're the fault of the IRA killing policemen, so stop the murders and we'll stop the reprisals. A somewhat questionable assertion considering that not all reprisals followed a policeman's murder, and with discipline within the Crown Forces having already deteriorated to an alarming degree, it was doubtful it would snap back to appropriate standards so promptly.

Meanwhile, the Dáil's *Irish Bulletin*'s rebuttal was to

claim that the goal of most IRA attacks on soldiers was to acquire arms, and murder was sometimes the unhappy consequence. This, of course, excluded the assassinations committed by Collins's Squad, but the intelligence war was in a way its own thing. An effort to silence the enemy before they silenced you. Though the number of civilian casualties the *Bulletin* ascribed to the fault of Crown Forces was startling, particularly since it was nearly double that of the number of IRA men they'd killed.

It was all so wearying.

"Is there any *good* news?" I dared to ask.

Wick raised his hand, as if at a loss. "The Dáil Loan is purported to have raised fifty percent more than its target. I suppose that's considered good news if you're a republican."

Which I strongly suspected Wick was, though I knew better than to ask him.

The waiter returned with my gin rickey and a second glass of stout for Wick and then melted away again. We both took long drinks—a bit of liquid courage to help us carry on in the midst of all these frightening circumstances.

"Now, then. Your problem." He dug a paper from his coat, passing it to me. "These are all the names that I could find associated with your fellow, Ardmore. Companies and businesses he either owns or is heavily invested in, even a few suspected aliases. He's got his hands in a lot of pies, he does."

I skimmed down the list of names, recognizing many of them. "What's this one?"

"A munitions manufacturer."

I looked up in alarm.

"Odd thing is, they don't seem to do a great deal of manufacturin'." His eyebrows arched. "Might be worth lookin' into." Wick had included an address, making this easier.

"Yes," I murmured, wondering how Kathleen and Alec had missed this. But Wick had his own sources, and many of them weren't strictly legal.

"If ye flip the page over, I also noted any significant donations the chap has made in the last five years. Figured, if
ye want someone beholden to ye, givin' 'em loads of money
might do the trick."

"Oh, brilliant!" I gasped, uncertain whether anyone else
had thought of this angle. Almost immediately a name leaped
out at me. "This is just south of the Liffey, isn't it? Near the
Grand Canal Docks?" I asked, pointing to an entry.

"Aye."

Ardmore had given quite a healthy donation to the Sailors
Home. Something that ostensibly raised no red flags. After
all, he'd worked with Naval Intelligence in some sort of shad-
owy manner during the war. As such, donating to a charity
which supported old and injured sailors seemed fitting. But
when we'd searched a garage near there, I remembered pondering whether he might have recruited some of those soldiers
to assist him, either wittingly or not. After all, just because
they were no longer able to work in their normal capacities
didn't mean they were incapacitated. It would behoove us to
do a bit more digging there, as well.

"Thank you," I told Wick earnestly as I tucked the list
away.

He nodded. "I expect the first report when ye find it."

"You will," I promised.

We chatted a few more minutes about nothing as we enjoyed our drinks and Wick smoked another cigarette, but the
tension that had been hanging about him like a cloak never
truly dissipated. I supposed the strain was wearing on us all.
I'd looked in the mirror just that morning and wondered at
the woman with solemn eyes staring back at me. I'd become
acquainted with her during the war and especially after Sidney's alleged death, but now she seemed to settle into the
gentle grooves of my face, sharpening them.

It was one thing to be confronted with the evils of an enemy. It was quite another when that enemy was you. Or at

least, it used to be. Quite honestly, I didn't know where my allegiances lay anymore. And that terrified me!

"Be careful, Ver," Wick said as I began to gather my things to rise.

"I was about to say the same thing to you," I confessed with a marked glance at his jumbled stack of papers. I'd heard enough rumbles from those within Dublin Castle to know that the administration was not taking kindly to the newspapers that were flouting their censorship restrictions. There was nothing they could do about the foreign press. Nothing that wouldn't make matters far worse for themselves, in any case. But there was talk of cracking down on Irish papers like the *Freeman's Journal* and the *Irish Independent*, where Wick worked. I'd even heard they'd taken a disliking to the London-based *Daily News*, because their reporter Hugh Martin's dogged reporting was starting to cause trouble for them, though touching him would be trickier.

"I've faced worse," Wick responded blithely, though I wasn't so sure about that. During the war, he'd risked injury being so close to the front, but he hadn't had a personal target painted on his back by the intelligence service of his own country.

He leaned across the table, eying me intently. "But, you. I've heard rumors about this Ardmore, and I'm not entirely sure he has a conscience."

This was no less than I was already aware of, but it made my pulse quicken all the same.

"Be careful you don't end up in his sights."

Too late for that.

The rain stopped and the sun came out the following afternoon just in time for the Gaelic football match at Croke Park where we were to meet Alec. It was a charity match between Kildare and Dublin to raise funds for the munition workers strike fund. The refusal by railway and dock workers to load, unload, or transport military personnel or munitions had stretched into its fifth month and had proved to be a major headache for the British. However, it had also cost a great deal of those workers their jobs, and many of them had families to support.

It would not have been my preferred place to meet given the charged atmosphere, but after the incident at Devlin's pub, I decided it was superior to being trapped again by a raid. It hadn't helped that Alec was late, hustling up to join us in our seats fifteen minutes into the first half.

"Apologies," he pronounced brusquely as those around us protested a call by one of the referees. "Mick called an emergency meeting."

I turned to search his taut features, trying to deduce what it might have been about.

"The Brits seem intent on makin' an example of young Barry," he replied without taking his eyes from the match. "Roughed him up pretty good durin' his interrogation, too."

It took me a moment to recall the name. He must have been referring to Kevin Barry, the eighteen-year-old who'd been captured hiding under a lorry when his gun jammed during the firefight that had resulted from the IRA's botched raid for arms outside Monk's Bakery. Three soldiers had died from injuries received during the incident.

"But that's not what ye asked to meet me to discuss." He turned to meet my gaze. "You've uncovered somethin'."

"Maybe," I hedged before relaying what I'd learned from Wick.

"I know the area where this address is," Alec said, tapping the paper I'd given him with the munition manufacturer's direction on it. "'Tis near Collinstown Aerodrome." Which lay north of the city in a fairly rural area. "And it's certainly worth lookin' more closely at the Sailors Home. Word is one of the other members of that crew that stole the phosgene from the *Zebrina* may have a connection to it."

"When did you learn that?" Sidney asked with a frown.

"Two days ago. I sent a dockworker there to visit an old friend to discover what he could. He hasn't reported back yet." Alec caught the direction of my scrutiny as it passed over the breadth of the stadium yet again, searching for anything out of place. "Still think his target is a crowded event?"

"I'm more certain than ever." I explained what I'd discovered about Ardmore's interest in RIC mob control procedures.

This darkened Alec's features, and he, too, began to take more of an intent interest in our surroundings—in the cheering crowds and verdant pitch, and the gates and fences that surrounded it. "Then Croke Park might be the place."

"I'm not so sure." Sidney crossed his arms, tilting his head. "Seems to me he would choose something more directly related to the rebellion or the government."

"Like the Castle or one of the military barracks? But they're too heavily guarded," I countered.

"I agree. I'm thinking more of something closely related to Ardmore's queries."

"Like a protest or demonstration. A mob or a riot," I agreed, seeing the correlation.

Sidney nodded. "Previously, we thought it might have to do with the hunger strikers. It's been nearly sixty days now. They can't last much longer."

Alec's manner was solemn. "We've been expectin' word any day now."

"Will there be a demonstration if they die?"

We'd been hearing rumbles of one for months, that the rebels' reprisals for it would be swift and violent, but thus far none had come to fruition.

"For the funeral for MacSwiney, undoubtedly. *If* his remains are allowed to pass through Dublin on their way back to Cork." He seemed doubtful of this and was probably right to be. Dublin Castle would be anticipating just such a thing.

They might even try to insist that the former lord mayor of Cork be buried in England where he died, though doing so risked as much, if not *more* upheaval. "But fervor has lowered a bit."

I turned to him in surprise. "Because the hunger strikers will almost certainly die?"

This seemed counter to the Irish mentality about martyrdom. After all, it was MacSwiney himself who'd written, "It is not those who can inflict the most but those who can endure the most who will conquer." Such quotes from him had been reprinted time and again, including those that expressed his thankfulness in knowing that his death would further the cause of Irish freedom more than his release.

Alec's expression was pained. "No, because some have taken exception to the fact he's fasted longer than forty days, and so has blasphemously surpassed Our Savior's record."

"You're jesting?"

"I wish I were."

I didn't know how to respond to this.

"But when he dies," Alec continued, "as it seems he must, things may be different."

We returned to the matter of the munitions manufacturer, making plans to meet the following evening outside the village of Drumcondra to proceed to the site.

Unfortunately, most of those plans went awry.

First, Alec and the men he brought with him were late to the rendezvous point because the tram and rail lines were being closely watched, forcing them to go a different route. This meant we got a later start than we'd intended. Then we'd struggled to locate the exact address. After a great deal of driving to and fro in Sidney's rather conspicuous Pierce-Arrow, we finally found it. Its shattered windows and overgrown lot and overall aura of abandonment and neglect had not inspired confidence, and a closer search had turned up nothing more than a few broken bottles and crates. If munitions had ever been manufactured there, it had been done long before the start of the war.

Which begged the question: Why did Ardmore own a stake in this company? If it was no longer manufacturing munitions, why hadn't it been dissolved?

Standing at the middle of the site, turning circles as I tried to understand its purpose, I couldn't help but feel that Ardmore was two steps ahead of us yet again.

The drive back to Drumcondra was done in silence, each of us brooding on the night's failure. But as we neared the town, it became obvious that something unusual had happened. Lights blazed and a number of military vehicles could be seen up ahead.

Alec leaned over the front seat, peering through the windscreen anxiously. Suddenly he pressed his hand to Sidney's shoulder. "Stop the car. We'll get out here."

Sidney didn't question this order, braking hard so the men could begin to scramble out.

"Is that really wise?" I countered. "What if they see you? How will you get back to Dublin?"

Alec briefly clasped my hand. "Don't worry. We've friends about." With this, he was gone, disappearing into the night.

"Shut the door before we're seen," Sidney ordered and I snapped back to attention, realizing that we were far from free of danger. After all, it was now after curfew, and while we had passes to be out, that didn't mean those soldiers or policemen would listen to or believe us.

"And put this in your garter."

He pulled his Luger pistol from somewhere concealed inside his coat and passed it to me. I stared at him with wide eyes, not knowing he'd brought it with him. It was too heavy for my garter to hold up for long, but of the two of us, I was the least likely to be searched.

"Let me do the talking," he added as we drew closer to the hive of activity.

Considering the fact that whoever stopped us would want to talk to Sidney anyway, not me, I agreed. Though I did swiftly murmur, "Swords Castle isn't far north of here."

He didn't acknowledge this statement, but then his attention was directed toward the soldiers and men in the black and tan motley uniform of the RIC swarming over the intersection and a road to the right. Whatever had occurred had been no small operation.

A handful of them stood with their guns at the ready as Sidney brought the Pierce-Arrow to a stop and rolled down his window to speak to the officer who appeared to be in charge of this small unit. "Good evening. What seems to be the trouble, Officer?"

Sidney's polite, upper-crust British tones caught the fellow off guard, as did the sight of me in the passenger seat smiling nervously at him as he shone his torch in our faces and around the interior of the motorcar. "Kind of late for a drive, isn't it?" he remarked, his voice tight with suspicion and censure.

Sidney held up a hand to shield his eyes from the glare of the torch. "Yes. I'm afraid we lost track of time, and then I got turned around looking for this Swords Castle my wife insisted on seeing."

I tinged my smile with apology at my alleged silliness.

"But we've curfew passes, issued courtesy of His Excellency himself." Sidney began to reach for the interior pocket of his coat, but then halted, lest the officer think he was going for a pistol. "May I?"

"Slowly."

In the gleam of the torches they were aiming in our eyes, it was difficult to make out any of their features, but it was clear from the officer's tone that he was a hair's breadth from calling our story rubbish and having us hauled in. He accepted the passes from Sidney, scrutinizing them and us even more closely. Clearly, he was weighing the potential consequences of arresting us. Our excuse for being here was rather flimsy at best.

"I need you to step out of the car and open the boot," he finally settled on.

Sidney sighed heavily, but complied while I waited anxiously where I was, conscious of his Luger pistol tucked beneath my skirt. I did my best not to fidget, keeping my hands in my lap. I heard the boot open but wasn't concerned. There was nothing there to find. However, if they looked too closely into the rear seat, I did worry they might find a shoe print or two, as well as dirt from our recent traipsing about that abandoned site near the aerodrome.

"Is this really necessary?" I heard Sidney's curt protest.

Shifting slightly in my seat, I saw him lift his arms to grasp the back of his head while a soldier stepped forward to search him. My heart quickened in fear that I would be next. Once this was finished, Sidney stood conferring with the officer a moment longer. When the man handed Sidney back the curfew passes and allowed him to return to the Pierce-Arrow, I breathed a fraction easier. But it wasn't until the lights were out of sight in the rearview mirror that I breathed normally.

"Did he tell you what that was about?" I whispered.

"No. But I gather at least one soldier was killed."

Two, in fact, we learned the next day. One of them had been the brother of Major Gerald Smyth, who had been assassinated by the Squad following the notorious Listowel incident in which he'd told the local RIC to essentially shoot first and ask questions later. His brother had just arrived in Ireland, eager to avenge his death. He'd been allowed to lead the raid on a Professor Carolan's home, where two IRA men who were believed to have been involved in Smyth's assassination were staying. Both Seán Treacy and Dan Breen had gotten away, though authorities believed they'd been injured. One had even crashed through the conservatory roof. But Professor Carolan had not been so lucky. He'd been shot in the neck and wasn't expected to long survive despite being taken to the hospital.

However, we were soon to learn that wasn't the only bit of excitement in Drumcondra that evening. There had also been another jewel theft.

CHAPTER 25

"Nearly got himself nabbed by the Tans," Detective Inspector Burrows exclaimed the next day when we met him at Burgh Quay. He shook his head. "Imagine that! Gettin' away with your burglarin' only to run into a raid for two rebels."

"It was that close?" I asked.

"Just round the corner from that Professor Carolan's place—Fernside."

"I wonder if he heard the gunfire," Sidney mused.

"May be what saved him, for by then the people he'd robbed had raised the alarm. Changed course, even riskin' runnin' back by the house he'd just burgled. They saw him from the upper window."

I could imagine the thief's panic when he realized Crown Forces were massed so close by. With the two men the police had been searching for—Breen and Treacy—also on the run, the thief might easily have been mistaken for one of them. It was an amazing bit of bad luck, and yet he'd still managed to escape.

"You said the victims raised the alarm?" I asked, watching the traffic pass along the opposite quay, the scarred buildings and hollow spaces from the 1916 rebellion beyond.

"Aye," Burrows confirmed, adjusting his bowler hat. "Woke while the thief was riflin' through their things."

"Good heavens!" I pressed a hand to my chest. "That was

quite the risk." It sounded like the thief was growing even more daring since the Powerscourt burglaries. But then, if he was, in fact, the man who called himself Dr. McCarthy, he knew we were on to him.

"So they saw him?" Sidney queried, turning to face the inspector as he leaned one hip against the cement embankment separating us from the drop into the waters of the Liffey.

"Not the husband. The thief shined a torch in his eyes, so he couldn't see much."

I nodded, for this was something since the previous evening that we now had an intimate understanding of.

"But the wife managed to get a glimpse. Apparently, he was curt but pleasant. Even wished 'em a 'good evening.'"

I scoffed. "The cheek!"

"Told 'em their phone lines had been cut, but if they just handed over their jewelry and let him go on his way, no one would get hurt."

"Did he have a gun?" I asked in surprise.

"Aye." Burrows's tone matched the seriousness of this development. In none of the previous burglaries had there been any indication the thief was armed. But of course, this was the first time we'd actually heard of him being confronted by any of his targets. "Kept it leveled on the husband the entire time."

"Then, I assume the woman did as she was instructed?"

Burrows nodded. "Which is when she was able to get a look at him, though it was limited considerin' her eyes hadn't yet fully adjusted to the darkness after the glare of the torch." The thief had certainly known what he was doing. "Described him as havin' a medium build with broad shoulders and pleasin' features, but hard-jawed and hard-eyed."

I frowned.

"And the victims' names?" Sidney queried.

"'Tis one of those double-barreled types that are a mouthful. Mr. and Mrs. Albert Dillon-Plunkett."

My eyebrows shot skyward as my husband voiced the

same realization. "Isn't that the couple we met at the fete at the RDS Grounds?"

"Yes," I confirmed. "They were speaking with Dr. McCarthy, the Fitzgibbons, and others."

"Then the thief *is* this Dr. McCarthy," Burrows deduced.

"Who I've been able to find no trace of, by the way. At least, not in the records of any of the hospitals I've spoken to."

Sidney slid his hands into the pockets of his charcoal-gray worsted trousers, gazing off toward O'Connell Bridge where traffic continued at a normal clip. "I can't decide whether he thinks he's too clever to be caught or he decided he needed one more score before leaving Ireland. Either way, his use of the gun is alarming."

Burrows agreed. "It escalates the crime. Makes me worried he's not afraid to actually use it."

"What is it, Ver?" Sidney asked, noting my silence and troubled expression.

"It's only . . . hard-jawed and hard-eyed? That's not how I would describe McCarthy." I held up a hand. "And before you say it, I know he might have been playing us for fools all along, but . . ." I grimaced. "I still struggle to see it." After all, the man had practically frozen when I'd introduced him to the two nurses from Richmond Hospital. "Nor would I ever describe his shoulders as broad."

Sidney considered this. "Maybe they merely seemed that way to Mrs. Dillon-Plunkett in her fright."

"Maybe," I conceded doubtfully. "But the cool self-possession of the man who confronted the Dillon-Plunketts, and so calmly examined Mrs. Thatch's pearls while she was in the next room talking to her *maid*." I shook my head. "That doesn't really seem consistent with what we know about McCarthy either." I turned to look at my husband, wondering if he grasped what I was trying to convey. "He may have been lying to us all about being a physician, but he didn't do it confidently."

"He was twitchy and uneasy," Sidney agreed.

"Which we all ascribed to his young age when evidently it was more than that. But none of this inspires me to believe he's our Irish Raffles." I locked eyes with Burrows. "Though we should still find him and talk to him. See what he knows."

"But if he's not the thief, then who is?" Burrows wanted to know. His mustache ruffled in frustration.

I turned to Sidney. "There were others who were speaking with the Dillon-Plunketts at the fete. Others who were in place to scout or pull off those robberies."

His eyes glinted with awareness. "There's no proof."

"No. But I can think of one way we might be able to get it."

His chin came up and I knew he realized I was speaking of setting a trap for him. I'd mentioned it at Powerscourt partly in jest, but now I was in earnest. "Maybe," he hedged.

Burrows watched us closely, but did not interrupt.

"You said yourself that his use of a gun during this latest theft is alarming," I reminded Sidney. "Perhaps the past burglaries haven't been as much of a pressing concern." Because the victims were all wealthy. They all had insurance and could recoup their monetary losses, if not the sentimental value. "But if he continues to escalate, the next robbery could end in injury or death."

My husband tilted his head, clearly wanting to argue with me, but realizing he couldn't. "It would be better for all if he were caught, before he can do something that is irreversible." He crossed his arms over his chest. "Do you have a plan in mind?"

With a glance about us to make sure no one was close enough to listen, I turned to address both men. "Here's what I'm thinking . . ."

Given the fact our plan would take several days to put into motion, and my twenty-fourth birthday was the next day,

Sidney proposed to take me out on the town to celebrate. However, I'd confessed my desire to stay in.

"Does that make me old?" I'd asked him.

He chuckled, pulling me close. "No. It makes you human."

"I feel like you're always needing to remind me of that." It was true that it wasn't the first time he'd said it.

"Only because so much of the time you seem to be super-human."

I smiled at him before resting my head against his shoulder. "Remember last year at the Savoy with Max and Daphne and George and Crispin?"

"When you were robbed, and Max received that letter setting us off on this mad search for the proof his father allegedly left us of Ardmore's treachery?"

"Yes." I sighed rather forlornly. "That was fun."

He chuckled again, and then sighed himself. "Yes, I suppose it was."

It had certainly been simpler, though I would never have believed so at the time.

After several moments, Sidney urged, "Come. Let's ask Mrs. Boyle to prepare some of your favorites for dinner." He lowered his mouth to within a hair's breadth of mine, his deep blue eyes sparkling with intent. "And I shall set about ensuring this birthday is as fun as the last."

I was hardly going to argue with that, draping my arms around his neck as he sealed that vow with a searing kiss.

Consequently, we retired early that evening.

Only to be woken sometime in the middle of the night by a series of loud noises—screeching brakes, pounding, raised voices. We both sat bolt upright, blinking at one another in incomprehension. Sidney realized first what it must mean. Throwing on his dressing gown over his bare torso, he hurried to the window, lifting the edge of the drape so that he could see out as bangs and shouts rang out from the street below.

I swiftly pulled on nightclothes and donned a wrapper before joining him. Peering out, I could see that one of the houses across the street was being raided. The Crown Forces had broken down the door and now poured inside with fixed bayonets on their rifles. A lorry-mounted searchlight pointed at the façade, throwing everything into stark relief, while another government tender armed with a machine gun was aimed at the house. Two lorries and an armored motorcar were empty of men, all of whom either had charged inside in full war kit or were standing about in the street, smoking and harassing those who emerged from neighboring houses to ask what was going on. Upper Fitzwilliam Street wasn't as used to such occurrences as other parts of the city, because most of the residents were either unionists or kept private about their views.

When a woman's scream rent the air, a chill trembled down my spine and I felt Sidney's muscles tense against mine, wanting to go to her aid. But there was nothing we could do. Not when several dozen heavily armed men stood between us and her. Not when interfering in any way would simply draw the Crown Forces down on us, and we had secrets to hide. So many secrets.

"Sh-should we. . . ?" I began to say, uncertain what I was asking.

Sidney seemed to know. "No. It's too late to run. If we were the target, our door would already be broken down."

I swallowed, burrowing close to his side as the events continued to unfold across the street. Pops, crashes, and thumps continued to issue from within along with the occasional shout as the house was ransacked, and the search continued for arms and evidence and hidden rebels. I had to blink my eyes to remind myself I was in Dublin—ostensibly part of the British Empire—and not Liége or Lille. The German secret police had menaced the Belgians and French in territories they occupied in much the same manner while searching for spies and soldiers downed behind enemy lines or while requisitioning further supplies.

If the events two nights prior—passing through multiple military checkpoints as we made our way home after curfew—had been unnerving, this was even more so. And yet the citizens of Dublin lived with it night after night, as the tempo of the Crown Forces' raids had increased exponentially in the past few weeks. The British were frantic to capture the rebels—or at least the most notorious of them—in their pincer grip. Only, the rebels continued to elude them time and time again, and so the raids had become more an act of terror than an operation justified by sound intelligence. A reckless policy of quantity versus quality, which entirely disregarded the effect on both the populace and the soldiers who were forced to carry out such orders. It was no wonder so many of the Tommies were smoking. I suspected it was as much to settle their nerves and stomachs as out of boredom.

This was not how it should be done. This was not how it *had* to be done. There were other options, other ways.

Unable to watch any more but unable to return to bed until it was over, I turned my face into Sidney's shoulder and wept. Wept for us all.

The following days were filled with unhappy news for the republicans, as well as some unsettling discoveries for me and Sidney. Seán Treacy, one of the men who'd managed to escape from the raid in Drumcondra, was hunted down and killed in a shoot-out in Talbot Street, Dublin, as well as a British Intelligence officer and two innocent bystanders. Another IRA man was killed during an attack on a British Army armored motorcar parked outside the Munster and Leinster Bank. And the sixty-two-year-old father of three members of Dublin's First Battalion was shot, seemingly in cold blood, on his doorstep during a raid when his sons were discovered not to be home.

When Alec didn't respond to my initial query for us to regroup over the issue of the Sailors Home, I didn't worry. But when a second query sent to him via the Capel Street library went unanswered, I did. We hadn't seen or heard from him since he'd leapt from Sidney's Pierce-Arrow at the outskirts of Drumcondra. Could he have been captured? If so, he must have given them an alias, a well-worn tactic of the IRA. Though, it was doubtful Alec would go unnoticed for long if he was taken to the Castle, but perhaps I was wrong. He had spent most of the war and the years prior embedded with the German Army rather than in London or elsewhere, so maybe his appearance was unknown to the intelligence officers under O. In any case, he knew quite well how to take care of himself. I reminded myself of this, but I worried all the same.

Until I marked him one day striding down Marlborough Street with several other men I recognized as being part of Collins's Squad. The hard set to his jaw and the manner in which he now inhabited his persona as a republican rebel made me hold back from hailing him. They seemed intent on a task of some sort and, if for no other reason than self-preservation, I sensed it was better not to get in the way of it. But it raised a sharp twinge of doubt within me.

How loyal was Alec truly? Could he merely be using me and Sidney to get his hands on the phosgene for Collins and the rebels? After all, he'd never shared his reasons for becoming so deeply committed to their cause. I'd understood his crisis of conscience in working for the British against them. I understood because I shared it. But it did not necessarily follow that then one began shooting British agents and soldiers instead. There had to be more to it. The terror the Crown Forces were perpetuating across the island might convince the Irish—even unionists—that peace could only ever be achieved if the British left Ireland, but it did not turn them all into gunmen.

When I finally received a reply from Alec the next day—

shoved through the letter slot per usual by a lad who then scarpered off—I felt I couldn't be blamed for my skepticism. Alec must have seen me when I spotted him, and so felt it necessary to send some sort of response to my queries, unsatisfactory as it was. He reported he'd been kept busy with other matters—including simply staying alive—and would contact us soon with what he'd learned. I presumed the "staying alive" comment had been meant to elicit sympathy and perhaps guilt for pestering him, but I only felt growing annoyance and deeper suspicion.

When Peter from the Wicklow contacted me to let me know that Willoughby had departed the hotel with some of his belongings, though he'd not checked out of his room, I didn't know what to think. Peter speculated he might be going out of town for a few days, but that begged the larger questions: Where and why? And what did it mean for the phosgene? Could they be moving the cylinders? Were they intended for someplace outside of Dublin? Perhaps Cork, where Alec had said the funeral for MacSwiney would be held after he died.

It was all enough to keep me up at night, and I was already not sleeping well. I'd not seen Mr. Finnegan since he'd issued C's order to return to London, avoiding the possibility of receiving further upsetting messages. Instead, I had Nimble deliver my coded reports—written in the most conciliatory terms as possible—to other branches of the Bank of Ireland, where it would be forwarded to Finnegan and on to London. However, conciliation could only do so much when there was no progress whatsoever to report.

As the day of the lord lieutenant's dinner party dawned, I could only be glad, for at least the prospect of catching the jewel thief gave me something else to focus on. Even so, nerves fluttered in my stomach as the cold weight of the diamonds and emeralds in the Treborough necklace Sidney's uncle had gifted me upon our marriage settled around my neck. They'd been delivered the previous day by special courier from London where I'd left them. As a determined old bachelor, Uncle Oswald had no wife or daughters to offer the marquessate's jewels to, so since Sidney was his heir, he'd decided there was no reason I shouldn't enjoy them. In truth, wearing them alarmed more than gratified me, especially to-night, but if they didn't dazzle our thief and tempt him to throw caution to the wind, I suspected nothing would.

CHAPTER 26

The Viceregal Lodge was ablaze with lights when we arrived, and most of the guests appeared in good spirits. All but the lord lieutenant himself, it seemed. Lord French was grumbling to anyone who would listen about the Greenwoods' failure to inform him they would be missing his dinner party until just hours before. There was already a great deal of tension between the chief secretary and lord lieutenant, considering the former had all of the actual power while the latter was now merely a figurehead, much as he loathed it. As such, most commiserated with him and then tried to change the subject.

However, he had forbidden all discussion of politics and was not above reminding people of this in a biting voice like a slap to the wrist. Such a thing was rather a novelty given that politics seemed to be all anyone wanted to talk about lately, but Lord French's manner of constantly reminding everyone of his restriction was overdone and a trifle obtrusive. To be frank, it smacked of sulking. Though far be it for me to tell him so. After all, we had only just returned to his good graces.

Because of this ban of political topics, I heard whispers of the coal strike in England and a schoolteacher informant disappearing in County Galway, but not much more. In any case, my focus was more on selling the story we'd concocted than anything else.

"Verity, your necklace!" Helen Wyndham-Quin exclaimed. "It's simply divine." She turned reticent. "But aren't you worried you might become a target of this jewel thief? After all, if he dares to strike at Powerscourt in the middle of a house party, where wouldn't he risk going?"

Bless Helen for enabling us so beautifully, though she was entirely unaware of the plot afoot.

"Don't you know?" I replied impishly. "We've caught him! Or rather, the Dublin Metropolitan Police have caught him." I glanced over my shoulder at Sidney with a smile. "With our able assistance."

"Why, that's marvelous!" Mark Sturgis interjected. "I knew the fellow didn't stand a chance against the Kents. But who is he? Was he working for the IRA?"

"An opportunist." I allowed my gaze to glide over many of those assembled, including the Chathams, Fitzgibbons, and Mr. Beresford, who were all listening with bated breath while one struggled to conceal their anxious twitching. "And one that many of you know."

"Who?" Sybil demanded as I paused for dramatic effect.

"He went by the alias Dr. Archie McCarthy."

The gasps that followed were profoundly gratifying, as was the smirk of triumph one individual wasn't quite able to repress.

"I knew there was something off about the bloke," Mr. Beresford remarked.

"I didn't wish to say anything, but I did, too," Hal Fitzgibbon chimed in to agree, rolling his shoulders.

The look Beresford cast his brother-in-law was thoroughly annoyed. "Of course, you did," he muttered sarcastically before stalking off to the sideboard to refill his drink.

"Well, I'm glad he was apprehended, and I do hope everyone gets their jewels back," Helen proclaimed with a nod to the Chathams, the Fitzgibbons, and the Harringtons, who had recently joined our circle. "But I'm not sure I shall ever feel comfortable wearing my good jewels again." She shuddered, pressing her hand to the pearls draped around her neck, which she'd just revealed to be fake.

"My mother always said to put them in the icebox," Doris surprised everyone by chiming in to say. "That a thief would never think to look there."

Her brother turned to stare at her as if she'd gone a bit balmy, and even her husband looked a bit perplexed.

She tilted her head, seemingly oblivious to this. "Of course, that doesn't work if you're traveling. You can't exactly ask your hostess if you can store your pearls next to the butter and salted pork, but . . ." She shrugged one shoulder as if to say the principle still stands.

"An interesting thought," I replied diplomatically. "But I like to keep my jewels closer to hand." I leaned forward as if confiding a secret. "Or foot, as it were," I jested, displaying my elegant pale green strap pumps with a glittering rhinestone bow.

"Your shoes!" Mrs. Chatham blurted, clapping her hands in delight. "Oh, how brilliant!"

"That is quite clever," Sybil conceded. "I'm not sure I would have ever thought of it, but what thief would ever look in your shoes?"

"Certainly not mine," Sidney quipped, handily shifting the topic. "I'm afraid the smell alone might put them off."

Everyone laughed.

"Now, don't tell me yours are any better, Dicky," he teased. "Not with all the riding you do."

With this, the conversation flowed easily in a different direction. That is, until in the midst of dinner I had a chance to mention our intentions of going to the cinema the following evening as I discussed with Dicky the latest films we'd both seen. I didn't look to see who was paying attention, but I was quite certain the thief had caught this helpful bit of information.

"You were marvelous," Sidney murmured into my ear at the end of the evening as he settled my fur stole around my shoulders and took my arm to escort me from the lodge.

"You were quite impressive yourself," I quipped in return, in spite of the tension that had gripped me. "Now, we just have to wait to see if it was enough."

The following day the first hunger striker died. A Michael Fitzgerald who was incarcerated in Cork. It was a sobering reminder that these men had been suffering for months without food, all for the sake of their cause, and these were the consequences. We'd begun to talk about these men in terms of when they'd die, but now that it had happened, it was a shock to the system and a stark recognition of just what was at stake.

However, it wasn't the only death that day. An IRA man was killed by Crown Forces while fleeing a raid in Rutland Square. And the RIC detective sergeant from Tipperary who had been brought to Dublin in order to identify the body of Seán Treacy was murdered, almost certainly by members of the Squad. It seemed that now that the first hunger striker had fallen, Collins's earlier restraint had fallen with it, and all bets were off. Regardless, we had to remain focused on catching the jewel thief.

A focus which was almost entirely derailed by the arrival of a letter from Max. Nimble returned with it in the late afternoon, just about the time we should be preparing to depart, but I couldn't set it aside without reading it. Sidney gathered close to read over my shoulder.

The first part of the letter was filled with news from London and the general state of politics. Discussions about making the reprisals official continued within the Cabinet, though word was that Lloyd Geroge intended to wait until after the American presidential election before taking drastic steps on any issues related to Ireland. Particularly given the Ameri-

cans' diplomatic protests to a letter written by General Tudor
which had been leaked to the press by Sinn Féin's publicity
bureau. How the republicans had gotten their hands on the
letter was unknown, though I suspected it had to have come
from one of Collins's contacts inside the Castle, but in it Tudor made it clear that because they believed some weapons
were being smuggled into Ireland on American ships, all US
sailors were now suspect and should be treated and searched
accordingly.

I read through all of this impatiently, as well as his promise
to report back on the parliamentary debate over Balbriggan
and the other reprisals, which was to take place in the House
of Commons in the coming week. When at length he came
to the missive he'd received from his father's secretary, I was
almost ready to begin pulling my hair out in frustration. Even
then, he insisted on relaying how the fellow was getting on living with his daughter on the isle of Guernsey—all of which I
was sure would be fascinating at any other time, just not now!

As to my father's holdings in Ireland . . .

"Finally!" I actually growled aloud, and Sidney squeezed
my shoulder in empathy.

*. . . he was unaware of any properties bought
or sold or owned there. However, Father donated
considerable sums to the building and upkeep of some
of the public institutions there. Namely the National
Gallery, the restoration of Christ Church Cathedral,
and the maintenance of the Royal Navy Sailors Home.*

I jolted upon reading this, all but skimming the rest so that
I could return to the important bit. "Then the late Lord Ryde
also contributed money to the Sailors Home. Could that truly
be a coincidence?" I queried skeptically.

"Doubtful," Sidney agreed. "Ryde had nothing to do with the navy, or sailors, or Ireland for that matter. He was a patron of the arts, and just about any nobleman can be convinced to donate to the restoration of a cathedral. Posterity and converting the heathens and all that."

"Or in this case, the Roman Catholics," I muttered wryly. Because condescension and confiscation had ever worked.

His eyes glinted with the same cynicism. "Right. But I can think of no obvious reason why Lord Ryde would have supported a Sailors Home in Dublin of all places, except by Lord Ardmore's influence."

"We need to look more deeply into this Sailors Home." I looked at the ormolu clock on the mantel and then jumped to my feet. "But not now."

The film we were allegedly going to see started in just thirty minutes. While Sidney called to Nimble to bring the Pierce-Arrow around to the door, I swiftly burned Max's letter, as well as Etta's brief note that had enclosed it. Then, tempted as I was to make sure the Treborough necklace was still nestled inside one of my shoes, I resisted, knowing perfectly well it was still there. We donned our coats and exited the house, climbing into the rear of the motorcar while Nimble played chauffeur.

As we pulled away from the door, I felt my heart rise into my throat, praying we'd planned for every contingency. Ginny had been sent home early and Mrs. Boyle was away at her sister's for the day, none the wiser to our intentions. As long as she didn't return early, and I didn't expect she would, they should prove to be no hindrance.

Nimble drove east on Fitzwilliam Street before circling Merrion Square and returning down Pembroke Street, letting me and Sidney out at the opening to the mews. From there, we hurried down its expanse, around the corner, and into the overgrown garden of the house next door to ours.

The home was in the midst of a renovation, which had been halted when the family fled Dublin earlier that year. This had served our purposes, particularly since a large hole had been knocked in the wall between the two homes. We had concealed it by removing the back of a wardrobe and positioning it in front of the hole. That was how I'd concealed my comings and goings as Dearbhla Bell during our search for Alec months ago, though it had not been put to much use recently.

We made our way silently up the three flights of stairs, dodging construction supplies and avoiding squeaky boards until we reached the top floor. There, in the back bedchamber, we lifted aside the tapestry we'd affixed low on the wall and scrambled through the hole and into the wardrobe. Pushing open its doors, I climbed out the other side into the guest chamber of our house. Sidney soon joined me after ensuring the tapestry fell back into place and rearranging the coats and garments hanging in the wardrobe to conceal the hole. Then he closed the wardrobe doors with an all but inaudible click.

We moved toward the doorway, pausing to listen at the top of the stairs. We couldn't risk descending until we were certain the thief had entered our bedchamber or else he would see us before we had the opportunity to catch him red-handed. As to the rest, we would simply have to hope Nimble and Burrows were in position to finish the arrest.

Time slid by slowly, marked only by the ticking of the clock in the chamber behind us and the occasional audible exhalation. Neither of us moved except our heads, highly conscious of any noise the shuffle of our feet or even the whisper of clothing might make. There was no telling how long we would have to wait, but we'd estimated that the thief would hesitate just long enough to ensure we didn't return, but not so long that our chauffeur might come back to the house.

It had reached the point when I was about to give up on him, thinking we'd not laid our bait as cleverly as we'd thought or that he might have seen us return, when the soft shush of feet against the floor runner on the flight of stairs below alerted us to someone's presence. I began to lift my foot, but Sidney halted me with a hand to my wrist, urging me to wait just a little longer. Approximately twenty seconds passed, during which I struggled to remember my training and wrestled control of my rapid pulse. Then Sidney stayed me once again, insisting he go first. He'd pulled his Luger pistol from his waistband, and I recalled that the thief was probably also armed. I nodded in understanding.

The house was almost eerily quiet as we descended, knowing someone was there but unable to hear them. With gentle pressure on Sidney's back, I reminded him of the loud groan the last step often made, and we both avoided it, lightly landing on the floor. Our bedroom door was ajar, telling us someone was definitely there. While Sidney approached it directly, I opted to enter the sitting room and wait at the door adjoining the two rooms while he confronted the thief. I had no gun, but I did have an electric torch, the better to illuminate and potentially blind the man in the dark.

Sidney seemed to sense when I was in position, for he waited until then to speak. "Put your hands up, Beresford, nice and easy."

Rufus Beresford did no such thing, instead turning and directing his own torch toward the doorway where Sidney crouched just out of the angle of Beresford's torch beam.

"Be aware, I've got my gun trained on you, and I won't hesitate to use it."

"Maybe, but I've got mine trained on you as well, and I've the benefit of not having a light shined in my eyes," Beresford countered much too calmly for my liking.

"Yes, but you're not as good a shot as I am."

"Aren't I?" His head swiveled left and right. "Is it just you?

Or is your lovely wife hiding somewhere as well?" When Sidney didn't immediately answer, he chuckled to himself. "I suspect it's the latter. She's quite the bearcat, isn't she? Wouldn't miss something like this for the world. Oh Verity, come out, come out, wherever you are," he called out in singsong.

But I was no fool. I stayed where I was and didn't utter a peep.

"Now, now. Is that really fair?" he taunted.

"This isn't about fairness," Sidney replied for me. "But you already know that, don't you."

"I suppose you're referring to my father pissing away my inheritance while I was off serving King and country, knee-deep in filth and death. And meanwhile, chaps like *Hal Fitzgibbon*"—he practically snarled the name—"are seated by their warm firesides, excused from real service while they profiteer from us lot. You know how it was, Kent. You were at the Somme and Passchendaele, poor bastard. You know how it is, knowing you lived while others died."

I couldn't see Sidney, but I could feel the pain each of these remarks caused him like physical blows. I could sense the strain as he struggled to withhold the dark memories they evoked.

"And what of these Irish?" Beresford continued. "I know you empathize with them, too. So many of them marched off to war because we'd convinced them Home Rule would be theirs just as soon as it was over. But they were naught but machine-gun fodder, and once they began to question it, recognizing what all of our promises were worth, we cried 'foul!'" He barked a humorless laugh. "And, still, there's no Home Rule."

These comments were met with silence from Sidney, and I began to worry. For despite their truth, we were straying from the point. And I feared Beresford was also straying further to the left so that soon his torch's beam would blind Sidney entirely.

"Yet chaps like Hal get to live on, oblivious to what the war cost us, and what's more, prospering from it." He sneered. "Well, where's my prosperity? Where's my compensation?"

"That's why you stole the gems," Sidney stated, and I exhaled in relief to discover he wasn't entirely mesmerized by Beresford's rambling.

"I deserve something for my sacrifice, not to be beholden to a man like *Hal*."

"Or for your sister to be."

This momentarily silenced Beresford, and when he spoke his voice had turned as sharp as broken glass. "I don't know what you're talking about. Doris has nothing to do with this."

But clearly, she did. That was why she'd been so nervous. It wasn't because she was having an affair, but rather because she'd known about her brother's larceny. She'd known and likely aided him with it—scouting new targets or acting as a lookout or a potential alibi. However, that was a matter for the police to sort out, and pushing Beresford on it was only going to make him angrier and more unpredictable, as he was obviously protective of her.

Unfortunately, Sidney didn't seem to recognize this. "Then why was she at Fleming's Hotel?"

"I already explained that to your wife," Beresford ground out.

"Yes, a lover. But that doesn't really explain why she was seated in the lobby for so long."

I wanted to scream at him to shut up, but I couldn't do that without giving away my position and the element of surprise. My nerves were already strained with tension as I tried to decide when the right time to intervene would be, not wanting to leave it too late.

Then Beresford made the decision for me.

"That's not something you'll have to worry about much longer," he snarled as he stepped wider, trying to blind Sidney with his torch.

At that moment, I flicked mine on, blinding Beresford, who exclaimed in surprise at the same time he fired his gun. My heart slammed into my ribs as the bullet struck something hard. But had it struck Sidney first?

A second later, a second shot was fired, but this time it plainly hit Beresford, who recoiled. Not risking his having time to recover, Sidney barreled forward into the room, slamming Beresford to the ground and knocking his pistol from his hand. It skidded across the floor and underneath the bed. I moved closer to better illuminate Beresford and to block him from reaching for his gun. But there seemed to be no need, as the man lay still.

"Did you. . . ?" I began to ask, but then stopped myself, not wanting to say the words.

"No," Sidney replied, panting. "But I knocked him out cold."

I could see now that Sidney had made a clean shot through Beresford's shoulder. He would recover, but it would be done behind bars.

The sound of pounding feet was heard coming up the stairs as the cavalry arrived. Sidney and I both stepped back and allowed DI Burrows to take charge, explaining in a minimum of words what had happened. We were ushered into the sitting room while the DMP did their jobs, and Beresford was carried out on a stretcher to an ambulance in police custody. I could only imagine our neighbors' consternation when confronted with the sight of the police in their street again, albeit in very different circumstances.

Nimble fretted over the chunk the bullet had taken out of the doorframe, revealing how narrowly Sidney had escaped being shot himself. The valet wanted to blame himself for not entering sooner, but we assured him he couldn't have known. We had yet to give the signal, shining the torch through the window to alert them. The gunshots had done that, and rather a bit more.

"I'm afraid I'll have to take your pistol as well," Burrows told Sidney somewhat regretfully.

There was no longer any use in hiding it. When he'd been forced to shoot Beresford, his possession of the Luger had become undeniable. Still Sidney resisted.

"Ye can apply for a permit to get it back," Burrows coaxed.

Which would be denied. The British Army had begun confiscating all arms with permits weeks ago. But this wasn't Burrows's fault. Something Sidney realized even as he scowled, passing the weapon to the inspector. Beresford's Webley had also been seized.

"Oh, and we found your Dr. McCarthy," Burrows informed us as they were wrapping up.

"You did?" I replied.

"Holed away in a flat above a plumber's shop. Admitted to lyin' about bein' a physician." He nodded toward our bedchamber, where all the action had recently taken place. "But as ye correctly deduced, he wasn't a thief. Just a reporter. Apparently, he got assigned the society pages when their normal columnist quit, and he panicked."

He must have created an alias to try to weasel his way into events. I frowned. Then he was no doubt the reason some of the newspapers had been so well-informed about some aspects of the burglaries. I supposed I couldn't blame him. Sometimes you did what you must to survive.

My heart clenched at the thought, turning to Sidney as Nimble saw Burrows out. Judging from the furrows between his brows, he was still fretting the loss of his Luger.

"Cheer up, darling. We'll find you another."

He grunted in agreement, but I wasn't entirely sure he'd heard me.

CHAPTER 27

Now that the jewel thief had been caught, it was more imperative than ever that we located the phosgene cylinders and found hard evidence of Ardmore's treachery, or risk being ousted from Ireland. Not that C could truly oust us, but he could make our lives very difficult and altogether more dangerous if he chose. I wanted to believe he would never resort to such tactics, that he was merely appeasing Thomson and his cronies with his hard line toward me—or less charitably, covering his own tail—but I'd seen him apply pressure to other agents before. He certainly wasn't above it.

Unfortunately, our queries at the Sailors Home were met with either a stone wall of silence or a regretful declaration of ignorance. A cursory search of the buildings on Rogerson's Quay surrounding it—a linseed crusher, a postal telegraph office, and the Ferryman pub—yielded no better results. The truth was, we needed Alec's connections, but he remained gallingly out of communication, either too busy with other jobs or possibly too at risk of capture. Neither was a comforting thought. There had been a massive raid on one of Collins's various offices, so it was possible he was lying low because of that.

During the first part of the week, the news was dominated by the debates in the House of Commons over Balbriggan and the other reprisals. The chief secretary, Sir Hamar Greenwood, was even called to report on the state of Ireland, which he did with less than complete honesty. Stating, for instance, that there wasn't "a tittle of evidence" that the Crown Forces had destroyed any creameries when Hugh Martin from the *Daily News* and other reporters had been able to come up with ample proof. The motion put forth by the Labour Party to hold an impartial inquiry into the reprisals was defeated, but the Labour Party themselves had vowed to conduct their own investigation into the matter.

Meanwhile, Kevin Barry—or the Bakery Gun Boy, as some had taken to calling him—was formally charged with murder for his part in the Monk's Bakery ambush and tried before a court martial in Marlborough Barracks. The next day he was found guilty and sentenced to death to the astonishment of a public who were surprised to discover they could still be shocked.

There had never really been any doubt of this being the verdict, regardless of what anyone said. According to the Hague Conventions, Barry—a soldier in the Irish Republican Army—should have been treated as a prisoner of war, and therefore kept imprisoned until the conflict came to an end. But the British government refused to classify this as a war—except when it benefited them to do so. And so, Barry was categorized as a criminal, and therefore was tried and sentenced like one, albeit before a military court martial rather than a jury. He would undoubtedly be executed like one as well. The contradictions in this case were astounding.

I kept abreast of all of it through the newspapers and what sources I had, bracing for what I knew must soon be coming, and struggling with the haunting likelihood of failure. Willoughby was still gone from Dublin, possibly with the phosgene in his possession, either bound for Cork or somewhere else. Even if the phosgene was still in Dublin and intended for some terrible purpose here, we still couldn't find it. Consequently, with each passing day my shame doubled, and my dread grew. While all the while the cycle of ambushes and reprisals continued, and the raids went on.

Then I received another message from Peter at the Wicklow. Willoughby had returned. At first, all I could do was wonder what this meant. Did that mean his part was finished? That the phosgene had been delivered to its target? Or was he back in Dublin to complete the task?

While I wrestled with myself about what to do, another stroke of bad news fell. Terence MacSwiney, the lord mayor of Cork, had died while on hunger strike in the prison he'd been taken to in England. He'd lasted seventy-four days. Shortly after, another hunger striker, Joseph Murphy, also died.

I didn't know these men. I really had no stake in their life or death. But I felt their passings keenly all the same, like two sharp stabs to the chest.

Though, also, in a sense, it was a sort of release. We had been waiting for weeks on tenterhooks for word of this, and now it had finally happened. Whatever was to come next, could now do so.

Dublin Castle expected swift revenge from the Sinn Féin, but they didn't know what form it would take. There was bound to be great trepidation around the funerals, but then that seemed both too obvious a moment for an attack and also a foolish notion, for it would take away from the solemnity of the moment and the greatness of their martyrs' sacrifices.

There were simply too many questions, too many unknowns, and I found I could no longer sit and do nothing about it. Even if it was the wrong move, I decided one had to be made. Sidney had set out for Phoenix Park and the Private Secretary's Lodge earlier to try to inveigle what information he could from whomever he might be able to convince to go for a ride. But I decided I couldn't wait for him, instead arming myself with a jaunty hat and a swipe of rose lip salve and setting off to catch the tram at Lower Baggot Street.

When I arrived at the Wicklow Hotel, I knew there was every chance Willoughby wouldn't be in. But as fate would have it, Willoughby *was* there, seated at a corner table in the bar. I hesitated but for a moment before approaching Peter to order a whiskey and water. Willoughby's back was to us, but I still kept my communication with the hotelier to a minimum. Fortunately, there wasn't much to convey; Peter knew almost as little as I did.

Straightening my spine, I picked up my drink, receiving a wink from Peter, which I supposed was to communicate he had my back, and then turned to stride over to Willoughby's table. "Is this seat taken?" I asked, sitting down in the chair opposite him before he could reply.

He appeared relatively well rested for someone who had recently returned from parts unknown, but then again perhaps he'd only been in another area of Dublin and his departing with some of his luggage had been to throw us off.

"Verity," he said by way of greeting, using my given name without being invited to. I elected not to take exception to it since I needed him to talk. He lifted his glass of stout to take a drink, pausing to say before he did so, "I thought you were returning to London."

That this was meant to make me wonder where he was getting his information from was obvious, but I refused to be distracted. "You know I can't leave yet." I took a drink of my whiskey, enjoying the burn at the back of my throat. It was the jolt I needed.

His gaze dipped to my glass before returning to my face. "I'd had you pegged as a gin girl."

I shrugged one shoulder, feeling no need to tell him he'd been correct. "I suppose I'm full of surprises."

His lips quirked in amusement. "That you are."

"I surprised you in Baarle-Hertog."

He knew I was speaking of the moment I'd thrown a damning—at least from the British government's perspective—intelligence report I'd recovered into the raging fire of a burning cottage rather than hand it over to him and consequently Ardmore. "You did," he conceded.

I tilted my head in consideration. "I suppose you bore the brunt of Ardmore's displeasure for that." My tone was not without empathy.

"Yes, but . . ." An unexpected smile curled his lips. One that was rather spiteful in its glee. "In that instance, I'm not sure I minded all that much."

It was a smile I returned, sharing in his enjoyment of my foiling Ardmore even in that one thing. It suddenly gave me a glow of confidence that maybe I *could* do so again. And maybe I could convince Willoughby to help me.

Then his mirth swiftly died. "But defiance doesn't serve one for long. You know what happened to Smith."

It was meant as a warning, but I could hear the melancholy lurking behind the words.

"He was your friend," I deduced.

"Of a sort." It was a weak qualification. Smith had been his friend, and yet he'd killed him. At Ardmore's behest, yes, but he'd killed him all the same.

It was an unsettling thought, but for the awareness that he'd clearly still felt himself an officer following orders from his commander. Orders that he now regretted. The bitter stench of it fairly seeped from his pores. Perhaps this was something I could exploit.

"I was amazed Smith fell in love with Miss Baverel," I said, taking another sip of whiskey. "I didn't think he had it in him."

"Yes, well, every man is susceptible to that from one quarter or another," I was surprised to hear him admit. "But yes, outwardly, Smith would have seemed more impervious than others. I could tell you stories." His eyes glinted in enjoyment, calling a few to mind.

"I'm sure you could," I muttered dryly. Before the incidents in France, Belgium, and the Netherlands earlier that year, I would have described Smith as a lecher and a bounder. However, his devotion to Miss Baverel had seemed to be genuine.

"But that's because you weren't aware of his choice in reading material. He carried around a battered copy of *Fanny Hill*," he leaned forward to confide after taking a long drink.

I frowned in confusion. "But isn't that. . . ?" A lewd text. One which had largely been banned and exactly the type of book I would have thought Lieutenant Smith would prefer.

Willoughby understood what I meant and chuckled. "I used to tease him that he only read it for the sparky bits. But the latter section where Fanny meets Charles again and they confess their love and marry was particularly dog-eared."

It struck me then. This was exactly the sort of information we'd been looking for! George, my cryptographer friend, had said that the code Smith had used in his journal was most likely a book cipher, and that it would be virtually impossible to work out without knowing the actual book, since he'd exchanged whole words or parts of words from various pages of the text. Though it would make sense if he'd eventually come to favor a particular section. What if that book was his dog-eared copy of *Fanny Hill*?

It took every ounce of my fortitude not to alert Willoughby to this revelation or to immediately excuse myself and race home to inform Sidney. He wasn't there anyway, I reminded myself. Instead, I had to force myself to converse and banter, all the while searching the captain for any evidence he was aware of what he'd revealed. After all, Ardmore must be aware by now that we had Smith's journal in our possession, and I wouldn't have put it past him to instruct his henchman to attempt to mislead us. It could be a trick, but considering it was the best lead we'd received in some time, it could not be ignored. Not when it might reveal something about the location of the phosgene.

I tried to temper my excitement with the knowledge that any information contained in Smith's journal was likely to be desperately old, but my hope would not be dampened. I hurried home as quickly as I could through the streets of Dublin without raising too many eyebrows. When I practically burst through the door, I was ecstatic to find Sidney already there.

Relaying my discovery between as few breaths as possible, I was gratified by his equally enthusiastic response. "We have to send an urgent telegram to George," he said.

"Yes, but will he even be able to obtain a copy of *Fanny Hill*? Isn't it still banned?"

"Oh, I'm sure there are more than a few copies floating around Oxford, illegal or not." He shook his head. "No wonder Smith baited you about being clever enough to figure out his cipher, the rotter."

I'd not thought of that, but the implication now made me blush.

Sidney saw it and pulled me close to press a kiss to my forehead. "I'll go now myself to send the telegram."

I gripped his hand, halting him before he could go. "Be careful."

His smile was tender. "Always."

With that he was gone, leaving me to wait for George's response, and wishing I had a copy of Smith's journal and a copy of *Fanny Hill* to attempt the decryption myself, regardless of if it set my cheeks on fire.

Sidney and I both struggled to keep ourselves occupied the rest of that day and the next, hesitant to leave the house lest a response from George arrive while we were out. I'd been avoiding reading the newspapers for they only made me anxious. It was but more tales of ambushes, raids, and reprisals, in addition to summaries of the ongoing parliamentary debates over the issue of Ireland, usually tinted by the political persuasions and loyalties of whoever owned the paper. However, with nothing else to do, I found myself picking them up to read about the events in Ballinderry; Toureen; Moneygold, Sligo; and Boyle, as well as Dublin, where matters appeared to be heating up if the number of raids and shootings— random or otherwise—were any indication.

Hugh Martin's article for the *Daily News* describing his own mistreatment by an Auxie in Sackville Street just three nights prior, and some of the other incidents he'd witnessed, was particularly striking. He was an Englishman writing for the English press, and as such, his stories were harder for the Castle to dismiss as rank Irish propaganda. I felt a stirring of admiration for Martin, but also concern for his safety. I imagined the Auxies and other members of the Crown Forces would not take kindly to his reports. I hoped he was taking proper precautions.

Eventually, I could take no more news of the violence meted out by both sides and turned my thoughts back to our quandary. Though I didn't wish to face it, there was every possibility that *Fanny Hill* would not prove to be the correct book and Smith's cipher would remain unbroken. Or even if it was broken, it might not lead us to the phosgene—the intelligence contained within too old to be of use. We had to consider other alternatives.

Loath as I normally was to do so lest it fall into the wrong hands, I decided it was time to set thought to paper, to lay out everything we knew about the missing phosgene and Ardmore, as well as the people and locations wrapped up in the search. I even took out a map of Dublin, marking and scrutinizing it for any indication of something we'd missed. Sidney joined me in this objective, eventually becoming so wrapped up in it that we almost failed to note the knock on the front door.

We both stilled, looking at each other as we heard Nimble's lumbering footsteps answer the summons. His deep voice rumbled a response to whatever the person at the door had said, the conversation over in two statements. Then we hurried toward the entrance to the parlor, waiting for Nimble to climb the staircase to join us.

His progress faltered as he caught sight of us before he hastened up the remaining steps, holding out the telegram toward me. "'Tis for Mrs. Kent."

I snatched it from his fingers, tearing open the envelope and almost ripping the telegram strip inside. My heart leaped in my chest. "It's from George. He's done it! The code is broken."

I laughed in delight and relief as Sidney picked me up and twirled me around, nearly forgetting the gravity of the situation in all of our excitement. "He says he's working as fast as he can to decipher it all."

But Smith's journal was not short. Even if George took a sabbatical from his duties as a professor, it would take days, if not weeks, to decrypt it all. I feared we didn't have that kind of time. MacSwiney's funeral would be in a matter of days, and the British government wouldn't wait long to hang Kevin Barry either. Since those were our best guesses as to a crowded event where the phosgene might be deployed, we couldn't wait weeks to uncover the phosgene's location. George needed greater direction.

My jaw set, I returned to the parlor.

"What are you going to do?" Sidney asked, clearly aware I'd set my mind to something.

"Telephone George." I held up my hand as I sat before the desk where the candlestick telephone rested. "I know it's a risk, that we might be overheard, but I think it's one we must take."

He nodded firmly in agreement as Nimble looked on.

With a deep breath for courage, I picked up the earpiece and spoke into the mouthpiece to issue the directions for George's residence in Oxford, England.

It was some moments before we could be connected, but once I heard George's bright tone over the crackle of the wires my heart gave a surge of relief.

"Verity, is that you?"

"Yes, George."

"You must have received my telegram."

"Yes, George. And listen," I insisted, speaking over whatever he was about to say. "I know you'll work as quickly as you can, but there's one piece of material we need as soon as ever possible. Tomorrow, if we could."

"I'll do what I can. What is it?"

"The phosgene." I knew it was risky stating the word aloud, but my brain could substitute no applicable code word swiftly enough. "Whatever it can tell us. Particularly its location."

"I'll work backward then, and telegram what I find. I can send you the rest later."

"Thank you, George! You're a darb. And I owe you a first edition of *Great Expectations*."

"An end to this business and your safe return will be enough. Be careful, Ver."

"Always," I declared before ringing off, though we both knew this wasn't true. It was a familiar refrain between us. As a cryptologist in OB40, he had forever been protected in the Admiralty's old building, while I had ever been flirting with danger in the field, even before C had officially made me an operative rather than an office analyst and typist before that. Even demobilized, I was still doing it.

I turned to Sidney and Nimble, suspecting they'd understood the gist of the conversation even just hearing my end of it. I sighed. "And now, once again, we wait."

CHAPTER 28

Even if we had to wait, that didn't mean there wasn't still much to be done. I'd considered making our excuses to the hostess of the soiree we were supposed to attend that evening in Dublin Castle, not wanting to miss George's telegram. Now that it had come and any further information from him would likely be days away, there was really no impediment to our going except our own disinclination. But it was to be a large gathering, including numerous Castle officials who I hoped might be willing to discuss the arrangements for Mac-Swiney's funeral and whether the body was to pass through Dublin. Since this seemed to be one of the most probable targets for Ardmore, it would behoove us to uncover as much about it as we could.

With that in mind, we dressed quickly and set out for Dame Street. Having been included on the guest list and being recognizable in our glad rags, we had little trouble entering through the Palace Street gate, unlike my last visit to the Castle. One couldn't help but notice the extra military presence that evening, with additional guards stationed outside the gate as well as within, all spit-and-polished to a shine in their parade uniforms. I suspected most of the guests found this sight bolstering, but it caused me a moment of unease. Not only because of *why* their presence was necessary, but also because of who Sidney and I had contact with and the awareness that C had threatened he was a breath or two away from withdrawing his support of us.

As we were escorted through the Lower Castle Yard, my gaze couldn't help but stray toward the top of the Record Tower and the machine gun I knew was positioned atop it. For all their age, the walls of Dublin Castle were tremendously thick, tall, and imposing. It was neither easy to enter nor exit, and for some reason this thought preyed on my mind. Even though these were *my* people, *my* country in control, *our* boys at the gate, I felt rather like when I'd waded into one of the German-controlled government buildings in Brussels, feigning the Belgian people's patent blend of deference mixed with bravado toward their occupiers.

Though this by no means meant I was more comfortable outside the castle. Dublin was not my home nor were the Irish my people. It was rather like being a land unto myself. The sensation was alienating.

Struggling to stuff these unwelcome revelations back where they had come from, I clung to Sidney's arm and passed through Upper Castle Yard—or the Devil's Half-Acre, as the rebels called it—toward the State Apartments which comprised the entirety of the southern range. These were normally used by the lord lieutenant for state functions and entertaining, but over the past two years many of the rooms had been put to other uses. However, St. Patrick's Hall and the adjoining Portrait Gallery were still occasionally utilized for their original purposes.

The Portrait Gallery, as expected, was hung with paintings of past and current Irish viceroys, including Lord French. Meanwhile, St. Patrick's Hall was a long and rather ornate chamber, with large windows spanning one wall and mirrors on the opposite, and immense columns to separate them both. By far the most impressive feature, however, was the painted ceiling. Created by Italian artist Vincenzo Waldré, the work was split into three panels with chandeliers hanging from the ceiling between.

Wishing to appear at my most charming, I'd worn my emerald silk gown with tassels, but finding myself shivering in the drafty hall, kept my ermine stole draped around my shoulders. Something that did not go unnoticed.

"For all their impressiveness and beauty, these old halls aren't well heated," Undersecretary Anderson empathized when we approached to greet him.

"The poor typists set up in the Throne Room have to wear fingerless gloves and scarves to do their work," Sturgis agreed.

"I received a full report from Redmond"—head of the DMP's G Division—"about the arrest of Beresford for the jewel thefts," Anderson informed us. "And I'm grateful for all your efforts in apprehending him."

Sturgis shook his head. "I never would have thought it of Beresford. I knew he was rather jaded and cynical. Many men were turned that way by the war. But to become a second-story man?" He turned to survey the crowd milling about the chamber. "It defies belief."

I didn't bother trying to elucidate Beresford's motives. I got the impression that Sturgis didn't particularly want to hear them. He was struggling more to come to terms with the fact that he'd been fooled. Given that, I also decided it would be best not to mention my suspicions about Doris's involvement. The DMP hadn't charged her with any crime because there'd been little to no evidence against her, particularly since Beresford denied that she had anything to do with it. In some ways, this seemed fair, since I believed she'd been roped into it by her brother in the first place. It was only right that he protect her now with the help of her husband.

"Have they been able to recover any of the jewelry?" Sidney asked.

"Not so far." Anderson replied. "And Beresford's not talking."

"Probably hopes his sentence is light enough he'll still be able to enjoy the spoils once he gets out," Mr. Wylie, the legal counsel to the Castle, interjected with a scoff.

"Then they should give him a longer sentence," Sturgis countered, but Wylie merely gave him a long-suffering look rather than explaining how the legal system worked.

We were still standing near the door to the Portrait Gallery, and so able to see those passing by. Sturgis recognized someone and called out to them. "Winter, is that you? Good God, man, what are you wearing?" he exclaimed as the fellow, who did, indeed, turn out to be O in an atrocious getup, reversed course to speak with us.

Dressed in a trench coat, flannel trousers, and a bowler hat pulled down over a terrible wig, O was fairly glowing with self-congratulations. Even the ridiculous fake mustache affixed to his upper lip couldn't dim it. "Just came from quite a successful raid at the Munster and Leinster Bank. Managed to pinch some of Collins's war chest."

Considering the rumors I'd heard about O, I had to wonder just how much of it he'd pinched for himself.

"Surely ye took some Auxiliaries with ye to do that," Wylie said, appearing to echo my confusion as to why O would require a disguise for such an activity. Why he'd been part of the raid at all. That's what his intelligence officers were for. "There's proper procedure when money is—"

"Of course, of course," he said, all but brushing Wylie aside as if he were an annoying midge.

Presumably, the funds were part of the national loan that Collins as finance minister of Dáil Éireann was charged with raising. I found myself wondering just how much Dáil money O had been able to confiscate and whether it would cause a very great dent in the shadow government's efforts. My understanding was that the loan had been split up and deposited under various different trusted republicans' names in various different banks. So while O might have obtained a sizable chunk, he couldn't have gotten it all. Though subsequent raids on other banks might cause greater dents.

O's gaze abruptly shifted, meeting mine. It was odd looking at him without the contrivance of his monocle to distract from his beady little eyes. The monocle was an affectation he'd picked up from C, and I had to wonder if the decision to don a disguise was also. C was rather infamous for the delight he took in them.

"Mr. and Mrs. Kent," O said. "I understand you *finally* caught the jewel thief." He smirked. "Though I understand you were misguided enough to suspect Mr. Caulfield for a time."

"I wouldn't have said we considered him a suspect, per se," I hedged calmly. "But the fact that he happened to be at the scene of several of the thefts and refused to cooperate with us, despite knowing we'd been tasked with the investigation by the Castle, certainly raised our eyebrows."

Had I not glanced at Anderson, I might have missed the quirk of his lips that seemed to indicate he'd appreciated my subtly putting O in his place.

"Then you should have come to me."

I arched a single eyebrow at O, letting him and everyone else know that I knew perfectly well where that would have led. A stone wall.

He smirked before reaching up to peel the mustache from his face, changing topics again to his own glorification. "My sources tell me the shinners' tails are properly down. They know we're beating them. Which means there will be trouble."

"Yes, MacSwiney's funeral," Sturgis murmured, appearing none too happy to be discussing it, though it was precisely the subject Sidney and I needed information on.

"Is his body truly going to process through Dublin?" I asked.

"Sinn Féin is making plans as if it will," Anderson conceded. "But arrangements are still being discussed."

"What is there to discuss?" O objected. "If the body passes through Dublin there will be a riot." He sneered. "By all rights, he should be buried in England."

"Such an act would only draw wider international criticism, not to mention the ire of the Roman Catholic church, who have declared MacSwiney's death not to be a suicide. For the sake of political expedience, we have to allow him to be buried in Cork," Anderson explained.

Wylie concurred. "Sinn Féin will certainly make a big to-do, but they'll make an even *bigger* to-do if we don't allow it."

"And you can be sure they'd play up our cruelty and heartlessness at this further indignity," Sturgis contributed. "But at least Griffith has seen reason and urged the hunger strike to end." Lest they lose any more rebels to a tactic that the British would no longer kowtow to.

"Well, don't say I didn't warn you," O pronounced, before striding off, leaving me to wonder just what he'd meant by that. Could he be aware of the phosgene? Had Ardmore shared that with him? Was he party to the plan? This seemed doubtful, for surely O would understand the repercussions, but it wasn't outside the realm of possibility.

The trouble was, we didn't understand Ardmore's precise motives, only that he was playing both sides to some end. Did he intend to help the British win the conflict and crush the rebels? Or did he intend to assist the republicans in forcing the British to offer terms?

If we knew the answers to these questions, then at least we might have a better idea how he intended to deploy the phosgene. Did he plan to fire it into the ranks of police and military who would, no doubt, be on hand to monitor and control the crowds at a public event such as MacSwiney's funeral? Or did he intend to deploy the gas into the mass of Irish men, women, and children—an act of aggression so vile that the world must instantly turn on Britain with feverish condemnation. For no one would believe it *hadn't* been the Crown Forces who'd done so.

If I could just read Ardmore's mind!

And then, as if to taunt me, he appeared. I should have been expecting him to attend. Truthfully, if I'd taken a moment to consider, I would have. After all, he had many contacts among the Castle set *and* he was a British peer with property in Ireland. Of course, he would be invited. All the same, I stiffened when I heard him say my name.

I'd been winding my way through the crowd with a glass of champagne, attuning myself to other people's conversations, listening for any interesting tidbits of information or signs of a discussion I might be able to turn to my advantage. Instead, I was forced to turn and address the bane of my existence, lest my snub draw unwanted attention.

He approached, tilting his head as if in well-meaning concern. "You look tired, Mrs. Kent."

I was well aware that my sleeplessness had marked my features, but this remark had clearly been meant to bait me, not empathize.

"Perhaps you should heed Smith-Cumming's order to return home."

I took a languid sip of my champagne to conceal my reaction to his knowing this and give myself time to think. Though my act was nearly ruined when the bubbles tickled my palate, making me want to sneeze. I wrinkled my nose, feigning displeasure with the vintage. Truthfully, I *would* have rather had a gin rickey.

"My lord, how good to see you," I finally settled on, ignoring his use of C's name. "I wasn't sure you would be here tonight. It seemed you might have hared off to Cork."

He chuckled. "No, no. Though matters there have been exciting of late." This gave nothing away, but then I hadn't expected him to.

"Undoubtedly. But then they're exciting everywhere."

"I understand the former lord mayor's funeral is going to be quite the affair. They're expecting massive crowds."

He was definitely baiting me now.

"Yes, but then they're expecting massive crowds for the procession of his body as well."

"If it's allowed to come here." It seemed he was as well informed as I was. Probably more so.

"Hmmm," I hummed noncommittally. "Then for the protest of his body not being brought here."

Ardmore arched his chin, his cold gaze glittering like emeralds. He stood close enough now that I could smell the blend of Turkish tobacco he preferred and his cologne. Close enough that he could speak in a low drawl that others couldn't hear, and was all the more menacing for it.

"Far be it from me to question a lady's prerogative, but I do believe you shall wish you followed that order. It was a favor, and I don't often extend them." Not without expecting something in return, he meant. "But I should so hate to see this lovely face marred."

His hand lifted toward my cheek, but I recoiled, heedless of who was watching.

He smiled—a slow blossoming of vicious delight. "Take care, Mrs. Kent. I suspect we shall see each other again very soon." He glanced about us. "And in far less opulent circumstances."

With this, he strode away, hailing General Macready for all the world as if he hadn't just threatened me. It took everything in me not to stomp after him and demand loudly for all to hear what his intentions were. Only the realization that no one would believe me, that *I* would be thought the villain and a madwoman for attacking such a distinguished nobleman, stopped me from doing so.

That, and Sidney's appearance at my side. "Don't do it," he cautioned, telling me the intent had clearly been writ in my eyes. He guided me toward the edge of the room with a firm hand to the small of my back. There, he pivoted me so that I was facing away from most of the crowd and smirked down at me as if I'd just said something particularly witty. "Take a moment."

"To silently murder your bowtie?" I queried between gritted teeth.

"If necessary," he quipped, his lips still quirked.

The response was so preposterous and his expression so incongruous, I felt some of my tension loosening. "You are ridiculous."

"Undoubtedly. But I'm also occasionally useful." His hands landed on my waist heedless of who was watching. "I've gained us a letter of introduction to the superintendent of the Sailors Home."

"Truly?" Both times we'd attempted to speak to the man, we'd been turned away with the excuse he wasn't there.

He nodded. "We can pay him a visit tomorrow morning."

But events soon contrived against us.

Later that evening, Sidney rounded the corner of the narrow mews behind our town house only to have his headlights pick out a figure standing in the shadows at the end of the alley. He braked hard, causing my heart to lodge in my throat. Until Alec stepped forward to reveal himself, opening our carriage house door. Sidney pulled forward to park inside.

"What are you doing here?" I hissed as I climbed out to confront Alec. We all knew what trouble awaited us if Alec or any of Collins's men were connected to the house we were renting.

"I needed to be sure ye were home."

I frowned. "Why?"

"Because I've information for ye." He looked at Sidney as he rounded the motorcar to join us. In the dark interior of the carriage house, I could barely make out their features. "The superintendent at the Sailors Home is in Ardmore's pocket."

The same man we'd only just gotten a letter of introduction to?

"How do you know this?" Sidney demanded.

I heard the scowl in Alec's voice more than saw it. "I told ye I had a connection inside askin' about the crew that way-laid the *Zebrina*. He told me you've been there twice askin' for the super."

"Could your connection tell you anything else? Did he find that other crewman?"

"He died."

I stiffened.

"Two years ago. But my man is speakin' to the other residents, askin' what they've seen. But if *you* go sniffin' around there again, ye could get him into trouble, if not outright killed."

I didn't like this. I didn't like any of it. Alec had been acting strange and now he was telling us to stay away from our best lead. Something was off.

So I elected to stay silent about Smith's journal and how George had finally broken its cipher. At least, for now. At least, until we knew what it said. Until I felt more certain where Alec's loyalty lay, and that he and Collins didn't have plans of their own for that phosgene.

"But why did you need to make sure we were home to tell us this? You could have sent a missive."

"What?" he queried, all too obviously buying himself time to answer.

"In the past you've always sent a note asking us to meet you. You've never dared to actually risk coming here." I narrowed my eyes, trying to see him better in the darkness. "So why now?"

He shrugged. "I was in the neighborhood."

"Alec . . ." I warned him, letting him know I knew he was lying.

"It's true." He scoffed. "Not everything has to have a secret meaning, Ver."

Except this clearly did, and he was uncomfortable with it, no matter how he strove to hide it. Which made me anxious in turn.

"I've got to go before I'm seen." He began to back away. "But . . . just . . . don't go out again tonight."

"Why?" I demanded, following him.

"No reason. Just . . ."

"No!" I shouted. "Don't give me that bull!"

"Ver," Sidney cautioned, grabbing my arm.

I shook him off but lowered my voice. "Why, Alec? You're not . . ." I inhaled a ragged breath, uncertain how to phrase this, but knowing I must. "This isn't about the phosgene, is it?"

"No, I just—" he called over his shoulder, but then stumbled to a stop, pivoting to face me. "Are you actually asking me whether we have the phosgene and are going to deploy it?" He sounded angry now as he returned several steps to face me. It was an emotion I welcomed, though I was still wary of his ability to conceal his true thoughts behind a mask. Even the dim light cast by the streetlamp at the corner couldn't reveal the truth behind his eyes.

"I don't know, Alec," I bit out. "You tell me."

"I can't believe this! After everything! How can you ask that of me?"

"Because you're acting oddly. You've been almost silent these past few weeks, and now you show up here, ordering us to stay away from the Sailors Home, telling us not to leave our house." I threw my hand out in exasperation. "What am I supposed to think?"

"That you know me better than that!"

"But do I?"

He reared back as if I'd slapped him.

We stared at each other, our breaths condensing in the air between us as Sidney stood quietly at my back. It was several moments before I found my next words.

"There are times, Alec, when I think I know you. That you're the same man I dodged the German secret police with. But there are other times"—I inhaled raggedly—"when I'm afraid I don't know you at all. It was easy when I knew where you stood. When we were standing for the same thing. But now . . . now it's all so complicated."

"We still stand for the same thing, Ver," Alec argued, his hands clenched into fists at his sides. "Stopping Ardmore."

"And if Collins's wishes align with his?"

He appeared caught off guard by the question, but quickly recovered. "They don't." He seemed certain of this, but I wasn't. I supposed my silence conveyed this for he repeated himself more forcefully. "They don't!"

"And if we seize the phosgene, what then becomes of it? Does it get added to the arsenal of the IRA?"

"Better us, when we have none, than them," he retorted.

Except I wasn't sure that was for the best. Despite Alec's valid argument, I wasn't sure that the simple fact of the IRA possessing such a weapon didn't just raise the temperature of the water. Perhaps that was because I trusted the British government not to utilize such a horrible weapon on their citizens. Despite all the terrible things they'd done and continued to do to the Irish, I still believed they would never resort to such an unforgivable act.

Alec and many others no longer had this faith, and I couldn't say I blamed them. A part of me even feared they might be right. But that didn't mean I was ready to trust the rebels with the same horrible weapon and then worry about *two* sides making the wrong choice. This was a conundrum that I'd thought could wait until the phosgene was found, but now I wasn't so sure.

"The problem is, no matter our alliance against Ardmore,

we're not truly on the same side anymore." I shoved a hand through the tangled curls of my bob. "Not that I know precisely what side I *am* on, if any." I looked up at Alec. "But it's not the same as you."

Alec's expression remained shuttered, but there was a starkness to it I'd sensed only once before. It was a memory I didn't care to relive, but I called it to mind now. It came the morning after we'd slept together as he'd prepared to leave for the Hook to take the first boat back to England, while I'd been ordered to remain in Rotterdam a few days longer. When I'd told him it had been a mistake, that it couldn't happen again, that I was still in love with the husband I'd believed to be dead.

Then, Alec had recovered quickly and with a wink and a smile told me to give him a call if I changed my mind. I expected him to do something similar now.

But he didn't wink. He didn't smile. Instead, he closed his eyes and lowered his head briefly almost as if in prayer, before lifting his gaze to meet mine a moment longer. "The difference is, whatever side I am or am not on, I've always been on yours." Then he turned and walked away.

An aching hollow opened up inside me, one that told me I might have just made a terrible mistake. I'd clearly hurt Alec, and yet I was still too confused by a welter of emotions to form a response.

"Come," Sidney eventually urged, guiding me back through the carriage house.

He didn't speak as he closed the door behind us, so I didn't know if he agreed with what I'd done or not. There had always been a tension between him and Alec that should have made him glad to be rid of him, but I sensed that he was not. That, more than anything, left me feeling on shaky ground.

CHAPTER 29

In the end, as hard as it was, we elected to heed Alec's advice and not visit the Sailors Home, at least not until we'd heard from George. In any case, there was the more pressing concern of the discovery that a British Army officer had been living directly across the street from us, adjacent to the home that had been raided a fortnight earlier. At least two newspapers shared the supposition that he may have been a suspected intelligence officer, and that was why he'd been assassinated the evening before by members of the IRA.

Sidney and I were startled by both revelations. That an intelligence officer had lived so close to us and that he'd been assassinated. Neither of us had interacted with the man, but I couldn't help but wonder if he'd been placed there to keep an eye on us. Particularly since he'd arrived in Dublin less than a month after we had. I also couldn't help but wonder if his assassination went far to explain Alec's strange behavior the previous evening. If he'd known about the intended shooting—whether he was part of it or not—he might have been trying to make sure we stayed out of the melee, though the man was killed off Lincoln Place rather than closer to home.

If so, it only compounded the guilt I already felt. Alec was right. He had always been loyal to me, even if he was no longer loyal to the British Empire. And how had I repaid him? With mistrust and accusations.

But the death of an intelligence officer wasn't the only news. The newspapers had also announced that Kevin Barry—the Bakery Gun Boy—would be hung in four days' time, on All Saints' Day. I cringed upon reading this, for it was merely adding insult to injury to schedule it on such a solemn holy day, one of obligation for the Roman Catholic church. Protests over Barry's death sentence had already begun, and many were clamoring for a reprieve. They cited his youth, his status as a POW, and the dangerous effect his execution would have on the population. However, it seemed to me that the British government's resolve had been made clear. If they were willing to let men convicted of a far more minor offense die on a hunger strike, they were not going to reprieve a man convicted of murdering a British soldier, no matter how young he was.

I was certain Ardmore knew this as well, and I suspected he'd known Barry's fate long before the general public had been informed of it in the newspapers. I'd not mentioned it while questioning him, and he'd allowed me to believe the phosgene was bound for something to do with MacSwiney, but now I wasn't so sure.

Meanwhile, plans continued apace for MacSwiney's public funeral in Dublin before the body was transported to Cork for another funeral and burial. His body was due to arrive the next day, and the newspapers were filled with information about the procession. People were expected to begin gathering along the route in the early hours of the morning.

The tension was palpable, and I found myself pacing up and down the parlor, racked with dread and uncertainty. If only we knew where the phosgene was. If only we knew Ardmore's plan. If MacSwiney's procession was the intended target, we were running out of time. There had to be *something* we could do!

I was not good at waiting. I'd discovered that during the war. I had to keep occupied. But there was nothing to keep myself occupied with except poring over my notes and the map of Dublin, hoping, praying, *begging* for inspiration.

Sidney was more accustomed to it, having spent much of his war waiting. Waiting to go up the line. Waiting to go over the top. Waiting through the next bombardment. Waiting for dawn to come again, or not. As such, he was better at biding his time with a book or a solo game of cards. Though even he had resorted to pacing at times.

I wasn't sure what Ginny and Mrs. Boyle thought of us. It must have been evident something was afoot, but not being privy to all of our secrets, they couldn't know what. Consequently, they simply tried to stay out of the way.

I was to the point where I was about to suggest one of the harebrained schemes which had occurred to me—such as breaking into the Sailors Home—when the doorbell rang.

At the sound of it, I leaped up from the sofa I'd flopped down on in a sulk only moments before. Racing past a startled Nimble, I hurled open the door to gaze out at an equally startled delivery boy from the telegram office. "Are you—" He hadn't even gotten the words out before I'd snatched up the envelope he held out to me.

"Thank you!" I hurried away, hollering to Nimble to give the lad a coin for his trouble.

Hearing the commotion, Sidney hurtled down the stairs to stand at my elbow just inside the dining room as I ripped open the message.

"It's from George," I exclaimed.

FOUND SO FAR MORE TO COME.
WILL OWE DUB LIN 22 OCTOBER 1917 RY AN
FERRY MAN SAILOR REST ROCK HAM GIRL.

"Clearly words were at a premium for old Bentnick," Sidney said with a scowl.

"It may have been how Smith wrote them in his journal."

After all, when writing in code, you tended to keep words to a minimum. In any case, I was used to deciphering such telegraphic language. Officers and agents were supposed to use "stop" and other punctuation shorthand in order to make sure their messages to headquarters were crystal clear, but that hadn't always been done. "And remember, it's a book cipher. So Smith may have been forced to get creative in order to form some of the words he needed."

The first line was self-explanatory. This was what George had found so far in the journal that might be pertinent, and he would send more when he'd decoded it. So I skipped to the second line.

"I'm not sure what WILL OWE means. Perhaps 'Willow.' DUB LIN is clearly 'Dublin' and then the date, which would have been shortly after the *Zebrina* was found beached near Cherbourg. So perhaps 'Willow' is a ship name."

"Maybe the one that intercepted her, stole the phosgene cargo, and killed the *Zebrina*'s crew," Sidney suggested.

I nodded in agreement. "RY AN FERRY MAN." I mused over the words. "Are they meant to be separate or together? A full name? A name and occupation?"

"Could SAILOR REST refer to the Sailors Home?" Sidney suggested. "So perhaps it's someone to do with that."

"There's a Ferryman Inn just along the quay," Nimble spoke up to say. I hadn't realized he was still behind us.

"Of course!" I recalled seeing it on Rogerson's Quay a few doors down from the Sailors Home. "Ryan" could be the proprietor. "Then the phosgene cylinders must have been brought ashore and stored somewhere between those two buildings." I turned toward the stairs, trusting they would follow. Entering the parlor, I moved toward where the map was still laid out, late afternoon sunlight spilling across the page through the tall Georgian windows, and swiftly found the River Liffey and then Rogerson's Quay along its southern bank. There were several buildings between and behind the pub and the rest home, and I supposed any of them could be the one we sought.

Sidney tapped his finger against the map. "But what of ROCK HAM GIRL?" His gaze lifted to mine. "'Rockham's girl'?"

I nodded. Lord Rockham had been involved with Ardmore. At least, until Ardmore had him killed. I frowned. "But what does Smith mean by 'girl'? His daughter? His wife? But which one? The first or the second?" I couldn't think how Gertrude, Calliope, or Ada had anything to do with this.

"Maybe George included those words by mistake."

I considered this but then shook my head. "No. George is too gifted a codebreaker. If he included them, then Smith meant for them to go together."

But why? I allowed my eyes to trail over the vicinity of the map we'd narrowed in on, searching for inspiration that would make the words make sense.

Sidney tried again. "Maybe Smith meant that Ada knew about the phosgene's location. Maybe he wrote it before she died." Under suspicious circumstances in prison.

"Maybe," I reluctantly conceded. I gave the map one last cursory glance and was about to give up, when suddenly I remembered. "Calliope's letter!" I reached for the small stack of papers I'd kept, which didn't contain incriminating evidence requiring immediate burning, and rifled through it. "She mentioned two entries found among her late husband's list of contacts which appeared to belong to actresses, for they both listed a theater address and a second address, which I presumed was personal. I also presumed he'd made these two entries because the women at one time or another had each been his mistress."

"'Rockham's girl,'" Sidney asserted, following my line of reasoning.

"Exactly!" I found the letter, brandishing it and then passing it to Sidney. "And one of those mistresses happens, or at least happened, to live on Queen's Square." I pointed to the place in question, which stood a short distance south of the Sailors Home. "Now, look here." I leaned closer. "Her home is on the north side of the square and the rear of her garden abuts Hanover Street."

"Didn't we search a garage on the opposite side of the street a few weeks ago?"

"Yes." It was probably the closest we'd come to actually finding the phosgene. At least, if Smith's journal and all of our suppositions were correct. "But look here." I traced a path with my finger. "These alleys connect both the back of the Sailors Home and the Ferryman—"

"With Hanover Street," Sidney finished for me.

"And consequently, Rockham's mistress's garden."

Our eyes met and held, neither of us seeming able to dare to believe we just might have done it. We just might have figured out where the phosgene was being hidden.

"We have to be sure," Sidney whispered.

I inhaled a ragged breath, one filled with equal mixtures of elation and trepidation. "Then let's go look."

Before either of us could second-guess ourselves, I hurried to pull on a coat, gloves, and hat, while Sidney briefly issued instructions to Nimble about what he should do if we didn't return by curfew. Then we set off on foot, jumping on and off trams as they were available. We didn't bother with Queen's Square, but went directly to Hanover Street, strolling quietly side by side.

By the time we reached it, the sun had already set, allowing us to cling to the shadows between streetlamps as much as possible. We passed the garage we'd previously searched and soon came upon the carriage houses that I deduced to be at the rear of the homes on Queen's Square. As on our earlier visit, the street was quiet, with few lights shining in the windows. This at least made it easier to sneak up to each building unobserved.

We didn't waste time picking locks at first, instead peering into the darkened windows or trying the doors. The second carriage house we attempted was open, and we were able to tell that it was not the place we were looking for. Or at least, that the phosgene wasn't there anymore. However, the third garage was a different story.

Light blazed from the high window on the side, seeming to indicate someone was inside. This might have scared us off, but I'd become determined that we were not going to return home without having found the phosgene. I'd also swiftly calculated that this was the outbuilding most likely attached to the rear of the actress's home. We couldn't by-pass it.

"Boost me up," I told Sidney.

He appeared as if he might argue, but then relented with a stern warning. "But we leave at the first sign of trouble."

I agreed, cognizant that we couldn't prevent the phosgene from being used if we were dead.

He removed his hat so that I could climb on top of his shoulders, grateful I'd worn my blue serge split skirt fastened into trousers for this excursion. Then cautiously I peered through the grime that had collected on the window. The sight I saw made my heart surge into my throat.

About half a dozen men were inside shifting some sort of cylinders. I could only guess at first that they were the phos-gene, for the men were in the way of my getting a clear view of the twenty-inch-long canisters. When they finally moved, I was baffled at first to see a white cross in place of the distinc-tive white star marking I'd expected. At least, the cylinders in the barrel we'd managed to get our hands on at Littlemote House had sported that symbol, indicating they contained a mixture of phosgene with chlorine, in order to help the denser phosgene spread better. Phosgene had rarely been de-ployed on its own because of this reason.

A few of the men were lifting the white-cross cylinders and

loading them into the back of a small lorry. As they moved aside, it offered me a clearer view of the men behind them who were painting white crosses over cylinders which originally displayed the telltale white star. I nearly gasped aloud at this discovery. For the white cross was meant to indicate a lachrymatory agent, a tear gas.

That was what Lord Ardmore had been up to when he'd discussed the RIC's mob control tactics with O. Sidney had said some parts of the United States had started adopting the use of tear gas for riot control. Had that been Ardmore's proposal as well? Or more likely, had he tricked O into making the suggestion? After all, Ardmore never put his stamp on something that could officially be traced back to him when blame was assigned.

Whatever the case, his intentions seemed clear now. He planned to pass these off as tear gas cylinders rather than phosgene and watch them be deployed into a crowd in the name of mob control. How exactly this was meant to happen wasn't entirely clear, but that was obviously the aim.

If some unit of Crown Forces fired phosgene into the middle of a crowd of civilians, the casualties would be horrific! And it wouldn't matter if it had been intentional or they'd believed it to be tear gas. The very result of their doing so, and the slapdash appearance of the cylinders, would convict us in the eyes of the world.

As Sidney lowered me to the ground, I towed him into a small space between two buildings a short distance away to relay what I'd seen. Our shared sense of horror was stamped across his features.

"What do we do?" I asked him, struggling not to be overcome by a sense of desperation.

The two of us couldn't hope to overpower six men. Particularly when neither of us now had a weapon and there was volatile poisonous gas involved.

Sidney turned his head to survey the deserted street, swiping a hand down his face. It was evident he felt as conflicted as I was.

On the one hand there was Alec. If we could track him down, surely, he could round up some of Collins's men to help us confiscate the phosgene. But then it might turn into a firefight. One which could draw the Crown Forces down on us and potentially escalate the situation into something far more deadly. Plus there was the aftermath to be considered. What would be done with the phosgene? Would Alec and the rebels insist on taking it?

Our other option was to go to the British and convince them of what we'd uncovered. Of the two options, the Crown Forces had the greater manpower and undoubtedly were better prepared for such an operation. They were also better equipped to dispose of the phosgene in the appropriate manner. However, they might prove difficult to persuade of the seriousness of what we'd witnessed. Especially now that we knew that someone had been casting aspersions on me and Sidney. Aspersions that had reached all the way to C.

"I think we have to go to Bennett and Ames first." He held up his hand as if I was about to argue. "I know that you aren't fond of either of them. I'm not either. But if these cylinders are meant to find themselves in the hands of the military, masked as tear gas, then our best bet is to alert British Intelligence at Dublin Castle in order to stop them."

I inhaled past the tightness in my chest and nodded. "All right."

He stilled, seeming surprised by my easy agreement, but his argument was sound. That didn't mean I was certain we were doing the right thing, or that I didn't feel guilty for continuing to doubt Alec's trustworthiness—or rather the trustworthiness of the men he was surrounded by—but we couldn't waffle in our decision, and this course of action seemed the soundest.

"All right?" Sidney verified.

"Yes," I confirmed. "Where do you think we'll find them?"

He guided me back out into the street, and we hurried east. "I don't know," he confessed. "But our best bet is to speak with them directly. Trying to convince someone at the Castle to send runners to find them will take too long." He frowned to himself, plainly thinking back over his interactions with them. "Let's try Kidd's Back first. Then Rabbiatti's." He grimaced. "But let's hope they're at Kidd's Back."

Located in an alley of Grafton Street, Kidd's Back was a pub notoriously frequented by British intelligence officers, and their informants. I said "notoriously" because the enemy was perfectly aware of it. I'd even seen some of their ranks mixing with intelligence officers who seemed oblivious to the fact, or else they would never have let such highly placed IRA intelligence agents slip through their fingers.

As we neared our destination, I began to realize my presence might not prove an asset to Sidney while he attempted to persuade Captain Bennett and Lieutenant Ames of our earnestness. Bennett knew me from my time passing in and out of the Netherlands during the war. He knew some of what I'd risked and accomplished for my country, yet he still did not respect me, and his cohort Ames took his cues from him.

As such, I suggested to Sidney that perhaps he would be better served by approaching them himself while I waited in the taproom of the Wicklow nearby. It was not what I would have preferred, but in this instance, my wants were not what mattered. Not when intercepting that phosgene was of the utmost importance. Besides, Kidd's Back was a rough sort of place even in the daylight. I shuddered to think what it was like after dark.

Relying on my husband to induce Bennett and Ames to act, I squeezed his hand in reassurance and hurried into the street adjacent. Inside the Wicklow, I was relieved to see Peter presiding over the bar. Business was bustling at this hour, so it was a few moments before he could make his way over to me.

"Have you seen our friend?" I asked, trusting he would know what I meant. I'd found it somewhat curious that I'd not seen Willoughby inside the garage on Hanover Street supervising.

Peter shook his head.

I searched the room in puzzlement, wondering if I'd missed something. So focused was I on my own troubled ruminations that I nearly missed the grumblings of those around me.

"You know they were never goin' to let him come here. Probably planned this all along," one man groused.

"'Twas probably always bound for Cork to deprive us of our just respects," a second chap agreed. "But at least his family will still get to bury him proper."

I realized then that they were talking about MacSwiney. A special edition of the *Evening Mail* was laid on the bar, and I snatched it up. Apparently, at the last hour, the government had changed its mind and MacSwiney's body had been loaded onto a special boat at Holyhead, which would sail directly to Cork rather than delivering him to Dublin to make the remainder of the journey by rail.

The entire affair was confusing and left me struggling to grasp what it might mean in terms of the phosgene. Would crowds assemble or not? And would this alter Ardmore's plans? By the time Sidney came to collect me, I was no closer to an answer.

"Where are they?" I asked when he appeared alone, alarmed they might have refused to listen.

"On the way to the Castle as we speak. We're to meet them there."

I exhaled in relief, hurrying alongside him. For time was of the essence, and I couldn't help but fear the clock was loudly ticking down.

CHAPTER 30

Sadly, Bennett and Ames didn't seem to feel the same urgency we did. Had I been able to scream at them without being instantly derided as a woman in hysterics, I would have. Even so, I was tempted to march out of the Castle and straight to Alec and Collins. Only the realization that this would take just as much time, and possibly prove deadly to myself and the rebellion, kept me anchored in the chair where I sat waiting while Sidney conferred with Bennett and Ames, and the commanding officers of the Auxiliaries who were to join us.

Sidney was acquainted with several of the Auxies, in their distinctive tam-o'-shanter caps, in particular a Captain Maxwell. They at least appeared to be taking his word and reputation seriously. Despite all my years of experience as an intelligence agent, I had none in combat or planning raids, so I remained in the background, able to recognize when I would hinder and distract rather than help. Even so, every once in a while, I caught Bennett or Ames casting me guarded looks.

By the time matters were set into motion and Sidney and I had crowded into a Crossley tender with a dozen or more Auxies, more than two hours had passed. It was an odd experience to rumble down the street in such a convoy of armed vehicles after observing them from the other side for so long. I'd thought one would feel a sense of power and invincibility as Dubliners darted out of the way, either cowering or glaring as we rolled past, but it was quite the opposite. There was instead a perception of vulnerability, of smallness, and the inescapable realization that a large majority of the public feared and hated you.

It gave me new appreciation for the difficulties our Tommies faced, though it didn't excuse those who abused their position or lost control of their emotions. It merely gave me greater insight to the pressures they were under. Pressures that I hoped and prayed wouldn't inflict greater damage on these men when some of them had already been damaged by the strain of the war.

As had always been my experience with our boys in uniform, they treated me with respect. One of them even offered me a piece of chewing gum. Still, I struggled to relax, all my thoughts bent on that garage in Hanover Street. I'd been ordered to remain in the Crossley with the driver, which I did even as Sidney joined the others. He'd been given a pistol to use by one of the Auxies.

In the end, I was surprised by how quickly the carriage house was taken without firing a single shot. Until I heard angry shouting from within. I recognized one of the voices as Sidney's and the other as Bennett's. One of the Auxies waved me over, and I joined the men standing before the empty garage. A great deal of foul language was being uttered as Bennett accused Sidney of wasting their time and Sidney countered with equal ferocity that their dithering had allowed the phosgene to slip through their fingers.

Underneath my own flash of fury was a deep well of despair and weariness that I felt myself teetering at the edge of. But I knew what I'd seen. I glanced toward the window I'd peered through. They'd been here such a short time ago. In the corner, I found the proof I needed. Not that it was enough for Bennett and Ames.

"Here's the white paint they used." I gestured toward the heap of cans.

Lieutenant Ames scoffed. "Many garages have paint stored in them."

I bent to pick up a piece of oiled paper, splattered liberally with white pigment, holding it up in the light of the headlamps of one of the lorries, which had been directed into the outbuilding. "And the stencil of a cross they used."

This, surely, was harder to dismiss.

But Bennett merely shook his head and stalked away, muttering about duck decoys, with Ames following behind.

My gaze flew to Sidney's for this was the exact thing Alec had warned us would reveal that Bennett was on to us. But on to what exactly? We hadn't been lying, and tonight's operation certainly hadn't involved rebels.

I narrowed my eyes, new suspicions blooming inside me that they weren't just careless intelligence officers but actually lackeys of Ardmore. What else explained their lollygagging, their refusal to examine the evidence or even to stick around to question those in the buildings nearby?

I turned to discover Captain Maxwell had been observing me as I watched Bennett and Ames depart, but in discretion or agreement, he made no remark about it. Instead, he tipped his hat to me and ordered his men to return to their vehicles.

I stood aside as he exchanged a few words with Sidney, taking his pistol back from him, before shaking his hand. "It was a pleasure to meet you, Mrs. Kent," he said before glancing about the dank garage. "Despite the circumstances."

"Likewise," I replied politely as he took his leave. Sidney had declined his offer of an escort back to our home.

As they pulled away, I was left with more of a sensation of stupefaction than anything else. That we'd found and then lost the phosgene again, all in the space of a couple hours was stultifying. "What now?" I murmured, my voice barely loud enough to hear.

Sidney ceased his angry pacing to look at me. "Now . . .

we go home. The rest"—his shoulders abruptly deflated as he gave a weary sigh—"we'll figure out."

I nodded weakly, but then lifted my hand toward the rear of the garage as I had a thought. "Perhaps if we spoke to the actress . . ."

He shook his head, cutting me off. "She's not there. Some of Maxwell's men checked. The house is closed up. No one's been there for some time."

My shoulders drooped. "Right. Let's go."

We managed to make it home before curfew, and I went straight to bed without dinner. I couldn't stomach the idea of food. All I wanted to do was sleep.

But sleep proved elusive yet again and I found myself still awake, staring up at the canopy as the clock ticked over to three. Wrapping a blanket around me, I went to stand at the window, heedless of the chill of the floor, and gazed out at the silent street below and the full moon above. I was overcome with a staggering sense of failure and doom, one too great for even tears, and I found myself praying—begging really—that it wasn't too late, that we all be spared from such a tragedy. That somehow, I be granted the strength and wisdom to prevent it. Or if not me, then someone else.

I didn't know how long I'd been standing there, the same thoughts and recriminations circling around and around in my head, when Sidney's arms slid around me from behind. He stood with me there for a few moments before, without a word, he picked me up in his arms and carried me back to bed. It was then that I finally let the tears fall, burrowing into his shoulder as I sobbed. And it was there that I finally found respite in slumber, my cheeks still damp, but my body secure in his embrace.

The next morning when I woke, I braced myself for news of a gas attack or some other violence. When by noon it didn't come, I realized MacSwiney's funeral procession in Dublin had not been the target after all. That, or Ardmore had changed his plans once the former lord mayor of Cork's body was diverted straight to Cork. Either way, I could only be grateful we still had a chance to stop him.

A skim of the morning paper revealed a great deal of indignation over the British government's last-minute changes, as well as more shootings and more reprisals, and more British politicians saying the reprisals would stop once the shootings stopped. At this point, this was all par for the course, and sadly, expected. The pertinent thing was that none of this gave us any hint as to precisely what Ardmore would do next.

Our best guess was that the phosgene was intended for one of two events. The first option was that it had been taken to Cork to be used on the massive crowds that were expected for MacSwiney's funeral on Sunday. The Dáil had declared it to be a national day of mourning, and members of the press from all over the world were expected to attend. In this case, there was nothing we could do short of racing off to a strange city with no preparation and little to no idea where to look.

Which meant that I was rooting for the second possibility— if "rooting" was even the appropriate word. That the phosgene was intended for the crowds that were already beginning to gather outside Mountjoy Jail in prayer and protest of Kevin Barry's pending execution. It was all but certain the size of the mob would continue to grow right up to the moment when Barry was scheduled to hang on the morning of Monday November 1st—All Saints' Day. In this instance, we might be able to stop the attack, but we needed help.

There was no need for discussion. Sidney and I knew who we had to ask. Though after my accusations, there was every chance he might say no. Still, we set out for Devlin's pub on Rutland Square in the late afternoon, with our hats in our hands, so to speak. We had no idea if Alec would be there, but it was as good a place as any to begin our search.

Fortunately, Joe O'Reilly, Collins's assistant, was at the bar when I approached, asking Devlin if MacAlister was there.

"I know who ye are," Joe declared, making me wary, until he offered me a boyish smile. "MacAlister said if ye were ever to ask for him, I was to take ye to him straightaway." He looked over my shoulder at Sidney, twinkling with private amusement. "And ye, too."

With this, he hopped up from the stool and set off toward the door. Devlin shrugged when I looked to him in query, so I turned to follow O'Reilly. Sidney and I had to scramble to catch up as he scurried across Great Britain Street, dodging a tram and a trio of bicycles, to the eastern side of Rutland Square. About halfway along its length we came to Vaughan's Hotel, a building I was familiar with from my time trying to track down Alec. The four-story building of red brick served various functions for the rebels, including at times a safe house for Collins and other members of the IRA. However, the Crown Forces had recently become aware of this, for it had been raided numerous times, making it more of a risk to be there. Though, to be fair, almost everywhere was a risk.

We followed O'Reilly inside and passed the hotelier, who hailed him by name. Then we climbed the stairs to a room on the second floor at the front of the hotel overlooking the square. It appeared Alec had been alerted to our arrival, for he stood at the door, waiting for us. One glimpse over his shoulder into the room showed us he wasn't alone. Collins sat in a chair in a corner by the window, one leg crossed over the other, watching us and, no doubt, calculating.

I ignored him and focused on my friend, for that was what Alec had always been. His face was drawn, his eyes shadowed, telling me what a toll his role in this revolution was having on him. And I had only made it worse.

Guilt and remorse lanced through me, and I reached for his

hand. But when I opened my mouth to apologize, he shook his head minutely.

"None of that," he murmured, flooding me with the balm of his ready forgiveness. So much so that I actually felt tears burn at the back of my eyes.

The corners of his lips lifted in a strained smile and then quirked into something more deliberately mischievous as his gaze shifted to Sidney. "Not unless it comes with something more substantial. Say, a kiss of reconciliation?"

"Don't push your luck, Xavier," Sidney drawled in a low voice.

Hearing them bicker like old times made me smile.

Alec squeezed my hand where it still gripped his and then released it to lead me into the room. It appeared like any other hotel room but for a large dent in one wall and Collins still smirking at us by the window. Alec gestured for us to take a seat wherever we could find one while he perched on the edge of the clothespress.

"I take it this isn't a social call," he quipped as Sidney and I sank down on the edge of the blue counterpane draped over the bed.

I clasped my hands nervously in my lap. "We found the phosgene."

Both rebels straightened in surprise.

I grimaced. "And then lost it again."

I described what we'd seen, how the markings on the cylinders were being changed to those denoting a less toxic lachrymatory agent. That was the easy part, for I, then, had to explain how we'd gone to Bennett and Ames for assistance, only to return to discover the cylinders had been moved. Sidney or I might have remained behind to monitor the situation, but the results would have been the same, for we would have had no way to stop them or to follow them to discover where they were going.

Neither Alec nor Collins was pleased to hear we'd gone to

the British first, and I recognized the sad irony in our now being here to ask them for help, but another part of me was annoyed. For what did they expect?

"We thought with the phosgene and those men now in British custody, we would have a foothold in proving Ardmore's treachery," I replied in our defense. "An advantage for us all! Or would you rather have him free to wreak havoc and release phosgene on the unsuspecting population of Ireland?"

Collins's scowl was black, and I could perceive the restrained violence within him. I just didn't know if it was directed at me or Ardmore.

Alec obviously sensed his fury as well, for he stepped into the breach. "So why are ye here now? To warn us?"

I reared back slightly. "Because we need your help. We have to find it. To stop him. We can't let all those people be gassed. If the winds are favorable enough, hundreds could succumb."

"And how exactly are we goin' to find it? Again," Alec added unnecessarily, though I understood his testiness.

"By figuring out where it's headed." I leaned forward. "Think! We know it must be bound for a crowd event. Otherwise, why encourage changes to the mob control policy? Why change the markings on the cylinders?" I searched their faces, determined to make them see. "Now that MacSwiney's body has been diverted from Dublin straight to Cork, it seems to me there can be only two potential targets."

"The funeral in Cork," Collins deduced, recognizing what I had.

I nodded. "Though there are a number of factors that make me think that's the less probable option, chief among them being that the cylinders have to be transported there."

"Then what's the second option?" Alec asked.

I turned to Collins. "How many demonstrators do you think will gather outside Mountjoy Jail for Barry?"

Collins considered the question. "We've not specifically

asked anyone to gather, but they will." His brow furrowed. "To pray for the poor lad, if nothin' else." The way he said this last bit made me wonder if he had something up his sleeve. "Especially since the day before has been decreed a day of national mourning for MacSwiney and the other hunger strikers. Most will stay home because of it, and I imagine quite a number of them will end up outside Mountjoy then or the followin' mornin' before All Saints' Day mass." He nodded his head more firmly. "They'll be there, perhaps in the thousands. There'll be no more lonely scaffolds in our time."

Alec studied this man he'd chosen to throw his lot in with when he'd betrayed his oaths to the Crown, seeming to derive from and understand far more of what Collins had said than I ever could. Though I suspected the most important points translated.

"Then, that's most likely their target," Sidney stated. "The military will already have plans in place and be expecting protestors. I've seen the photographs from the demonstrations for the hunger strikers back in April. They'll have a routine, and Ardmore's disguised cylinders will simply be added to their arsenal as a new deterrent. He'll only need to provoke them into using them."

"So he'll have men planted among the crowd," Alec speculated.

Collins agreed. "Throw a punch or two, and that'll start a row."

With feelings already running high, all of the pent-up grief and anger from the deaths and reprisals and nightly raids—it would be like setting a match to a powder keg.

"Then we station men along the routes to Mountjoy to keep an eye out for these cylinders," Alec proposed. "Intercept them."

"Unless they've already been delivered," Sidney warned, throwing cold water over our plans.

I groaned, covering my face. "God, please, no." I lowered my hands, spreading them outward. "For now, let's assume they haven't." Because if they had, I didn't know what we were going to do. Storming the well-armed troops who would be stationed outside the jail to get to the Livens Projectors—for they would undoubtedly use many, all firing synchronously—would be suicide. For heaven's sake, they'd even used a tank as a deterrent back in April.

"With any luck, we can seize it from them before it's delivered," Alec finished.

Which would then mean the rebels would have their hands on a stockpile of deadly phosgene, but we would just have to address that issue if it came to pass. After all, Sidney and I had done what we could to utilize the proper military channels to have the cylinders confiscated by the British. It was Bennett and Ames's fault we had to resort to this. The memory of their accusations against us the night before burned raw within me.

"You came to us," Alec retorted, misunderstanding the source of the irritation tightening my muscles. "What else would you have us do?"

"I know. I'm not upset at you," I responded shortly, feeling Sidney's hand press gently against my back.

Alec stared at me a moment before comprehending. "Then, why are ye upset at yourself? Ye figured out more of this than any of us. Ye can't have expected to anticipate all of it." His voice dipped when he next spoke, and I knew he was referring to an error I'd believed I'd made years earlier, which had compromised his position in the German Army. "The trouble is ye still think of yourself as all-knowin', Ver, when you're not."

"But I *did* know in this instance. I knew better than to trust Bennett and Ames, and when push came to shove, I did so anyway."

"It's hard not to trust the systems that are in place. 'Tis what we were trained to do." Alec was being too kind, and it smarted. "And Bennett was with ye in Holland. Ye should've been able to trust him."

"Except I never did there either," I muttered.

Alec's mouth quirked. "Ye always have had good instincts." His gaze shifted to Sidney, bobbing his head toward him. "Except when it comes to this one."

Sidney arched a single sardonic eyebrow in response.

Alec preened. "I'm clearly the better choice."

This moment of levity broke the tension. That is, until Collins spoke.

"Well, if ye ask me, your mistake is in trustin' any of the men under the Holy Terror's sway." He crossed his arms over his chest, addressing Alec. "See that the men are put in place, and alert Lynch." The man in charge of one of the IRA's munition factories we'd met with at the bookshop on Dorset Street. "He'll know better how to handle the situation than any of us."

A sudden pang of doubt filled me. "And if we're wrong? If it's bound for Cork instead?"

Collins nodded, conceding my concerns. "I'll contact the men there. Be sure they're on the lookout for it as well."

I supposed that was the best we could hope for. Better than nothing, in any case, which was where we currently stood.

With this decided, Collins stood and left the room. I watched him go, conscious of a slumping of his posture, a gravity to his steps that I hadn't sensed in our previous encounters.

"It weighs on him," Alec pronounced softly, deducing my thoughts. "These deaths. He knows they're part and parcel of the struggle, but he hates them anyway. He'll not sleep a wink Sunday night."

That was part of the reason he inspired such loyalty from his men, I reasoned. Because he genuinely cared about their fate, and consciously or not, empathized with their struggle. He carried it in his body.

Sidney and I rose to leave, knowing Alec had much to do, and the sooner Collins's men were in place, watching the route to the jail, the better.

However, Alec had one more unsettling revelation to impart. "Have ye considered that Ardmore might have known ye would eventually find where he'd hidden the phosgene?"

"What do you mean?"

"Just that, he knows how clever ye are. So, what if he wanted ye to find it . . ."

"Only so he could snatch it away again? But that's . . ." I couldn't finish the sentence, for all of the qualifiers—dastardly, audacious, Machiavellian—described Ardmore to a tee. I shook my head, for it was preposterous. "But how would he have known his men could still get away? No one spotted us. And he must have known we would fetch—" I broke off again, not liking the picture that was forming, even though it was one I'd already considered.

"Bloody hell," Sidney growled, sharing my thought. "Bennett and Ames were in on it."

Considering the delay they'd caused, there would have been ample time to warn Ardmore's men so they could move the cylinders before we arrived. Which made the accusations they'd flung at us even more vile.

"Just something to consider," Alec finished, though it was no longer necessary.

I didn't bother to respond. What trust I'd held in those two men had already been obliterated. This was merely pouring salt on the wound. But forewarned was still forearmed.

CHAPTER 31

I was seated in the parlor, thinking back over every conversation I'd ever had with Lord Ardmore or Willoughby or Smith, or any of their other known associates, most of whom were now dead, and scrutinizing them for anything useful when there was a knock at the front door. This was unexpected, and for a moment I sat listening as Ginny answered it. Nimble and Sidney were in the carriage house, doing some maintenance on the Pierce-Arrow and making a few adjustments. When the door closed after a brief exchange of words, I decided it must be some sort of message, and Ginny's appearance in the parlor soon confirmed it.

I took the telegram and then dismissed her with my thanks. It must be from George, I decided, though I'd not been expecting word from him again so quickly. Maybe he'd uncovered something important.

Crossing to the desk, I slit open the envelope to pull out the slip to discover a series of numbers. It was a code, but not one devised by George. It was from Kathleen Silvernickel. She'd utilized the same cipher we'd worked out between us since the early days of the war. I picked up a pencil to swiftly decode it, soon realizing it was a telephone exchange. One of the secure lines which rang directly to C's office, or rather, as his secretary, Kathleen's.

My pulse was hammering in my ears, for I knew that if she

was risking not only such a telegram but also an actual telephone conversation that the situation must be dire, indeed. Picking up the phone, I gave the switchboard operator the direction before I could change my mind.

In a matter of minutes, I heard Kathleen's voice over the crackling wires. "Verity?"

"Yes. I got your message."

"I haven't long to speak, but I had to warn you." She spoke rapidly in a hushed voice. "Thomson stormed in here earlier today, ranting and raving about your interference with his agents and wasting their resources."

"Because we *found* the phosgene. And then lost it again, quite possibly due to the duplicity of those agents, if not their incompetence," I snapped.

This gave Kathleen pause. "I'll pass that along to C, but listen, Ver. He said he can't shield you much longer. That you *must* return to London."

I felt a surge of bile in my throat and a rush of panic, but I suppressed them both, determined to do what needed to be done. "Give me two days. I'll either have the phosgene by then or . . . there'll be a lot more serious consequences to consider."

She didn't immediately respond, but I could tell she'd grasped the implication. "Two days," she repeated. "And Verity . . . watch your back."

The trees in St. Stephen's Green were in full color late the following morning when I met Sybil there. The pavement was still slightly damp from the night's rain, but the skies were clearing.

When she'd telephoned to ask me to meet her there, I'd initially hesitated, not wanting to be far from home lest a note arrive from Alec or news from Cork reach us. So far, there'd been no word of catastrophe at MacSwiney's funeral, and I could only pray it remained that way. However, Sybil had managed to convince me with her candor.

"I intended to invite you to lunch," she'd said. "But Mervyn tells me that practically the entire country plans to close down for this day of mourning for Mr. MacSwiney, so I thought we'd better not try it. However, I do need to speak to you. Quite urgently, in fact."

So I found myself strolling through the square at her side while MacSwiney was buried and the last scramble was made by various factions to gain Kevin Barry a reprieve.

The press on neither side minced words—one side denouncing the execution as "blind vengeance" while the other derided reckless young men like Barry as being "the main cause of the present disturbances in Ireland." It seemed to me more of a case of the British having backed themselves into a corner, knowing that if they didn't make an example of Barry and exercise the full extent of the law, that they might lose all control over the soldiers and policemen whom they'd, at the least, allowed and, at the most, encouraged to shoot, burn, and rampage in reprisal. For the execution certainly wasn't doing anything to discourage the rebels, but rather inspiring them with Barry's valor, just as MacSwiney's endurance had taken on the mantle of heroism.

The account of Barry's ill treatment by guards in the North Dublin Union where he was interrogated definitely wouldn't help matters. Though it was only printed in the Dáil's *Irish Bulletin*, it would certainly make its way into other newspapers in the coming days. As would Griffith's "Message to the Civilized Nations of the World"—a somewhat overblown title—which sought to compare the alleged fair treatment of British military prisoners by the IRA to the rough handling received by the IRA from the British. It was all part and parcel of the propaganda war being waged alongside the military and diplomatic one. The same as we had done during the Great War.

Sybil and I exchanged a bit of small talk, but as we neared the pond, she suddenly fell silent. From the pleating in her brow, I could tell she was troubled by something, and that it was likely the reason she'd asked me to meet her. I might have prodded her then, but I decided it would be better to allow her to broach the subject. That perhaps she might reveal more. So instead I focused on the ducks gliding over the water's surface and the pair of children tossing bits of bread to them over the side of the bridge with their governess looking on.

"You once told me something that has stuck with me."

I turned to her in query.

"That Lord Ardmore's words and actions are always quite deliberate."

The skin at the back of my neck tingled and I didn't think it was because of the breeze playing with the ends of my bobbed hair tucked beneath my roll-brimmed hat.

She frowned at our feet. "He recently tried to intimate to me that you aren't exactly who you seem." She lifted her gaze to meet mine. It was sharp and penetrating, but for all that, not unkind. "Well, I could have told him that, if he'd cared to listen. Anyone with a modicum of imagination can see that there's more to you than fluff and fashion," she quipped dryly, in what I supposed I should take as a compliment. "But I gathered what he was really trying to imply." Her demeanor turned serious again. "That you're not like me and therefore you can't be trusted."

I might have expressed outrage and made denials, but the steadiness of Sybil's stare told me they would be pointless. She'd already made up her mind about me by inviting me here, by telling me this.

"I thought you should know. Because it's unlikely I'm the only person he's spoken to."

I was certain she wasn't, but I elected not to strain the point. "Thank you," I said instead, infusing those two words with gratitude that she'd had enough fortitude and respect for me not to allow herself to be poisoned by his words, and that she'd told me.

She nodded, directing our steps toward a gap in the trees where we had a better overlook of the pond. The ground below us was littered with damp leaves, their colors vibrant against the gray sky and deeper gray water.

"There is one more thing," she added in a lighter voice. "That fellow I saw you dancing with at the benefit at the Shelbourne. 'Willoughby' was I believe what you said his name was. I've recalled where I saw him."

I'd forgotten she'd told me as much and struggled to temper my reaction to a simple, "Oh?"

"Some weeks ago, I was returning to Dublin from the botanic gardens when I saw him striding over the bridge that crosses the canal near the orphanage. I presume he was coming from Glasnevin Station, as it's not far from there, but what an odd place for such a decorated military officer to be," she remarked in consternation. "Though I'm sure he must have had *some* reason for being there."

She was right. And I had a strong suspicion of what.

For Mountjoy Jail wasn't far from there, and if Ardmore had intended to make the switch all along, he would have wanted a site close to the prison in which to store the cylinders. A place from which his men ran less of a risk delivering them. A place we needed to find.

We spent the remainder of the day and the wee hours of All Saints' Day—except the hours of curfew between midnight and three o'clock—searching the area surrounding Glasnevin Station for a garage or carriage house or warehouse which might conceal that old lorry and its cargo of phosgene. It was by no means a simple task for Alec, the few men he pulled from surveillance, and us. It was dark for much of it, and it seemed we were constantly dodging military patrols. Appar-

ently, an attempt to break Barry out of prison was expected—
something Collins and his men had proved adept at in the
past—and the authorities were taking no chances.

There was also the added complication that, the day prior,
while MacSwiney was buried without incident and the na-
tion was supposed to be in mourning, the IRA brigades in
other parts of the country seemed to have been more bent
on revenge, killing or wounding no less than ten members of
the RIC. All of which were followed swiftly by reprisals and
retaliation, some so severe that they would later be termed
sieges. That the Crown Forces expected a similar incident
here was obvious.

All of this compounded our difficulty, for even if . . .
when . . . we found the phosgene, our ambush of the lorry
might call the Black and Tans down on us with alarming
speed. All we could do was press onward, but as the sky began to gradually lighten and the first rays of dawn peeked over
the horizon, the hour drawing ever closer to eight o'clock, we
knew we had run out of options. It was to be an ambush
along the roadside or nothing.

We crept back to our positions along the junction of Phibs-
borough and North Circular Road known as Doyle's Corner,
at least able to concentrate the men at this approach to the
prison, though a smattering had been left at a few other junc-
tions on the chance we were wrong. We were close enough
to the prison that we could hear and see the crowd gathered
outside praying the Rosary and singing hymns. There were
thousands of them. So many that they clogged the streets and
blocked traffic, all monitored by soldiers formed into ranks
along the ground and positioned atop their armored cars and,
yes, the tank that the Castle seemed to tot out whenever there
was an incident like this, purely for the intimidation factor.

"Everyone seems calm," I murmured charily from our position near Blacquiere Bridge, which spanned the Broadstone
Branch of the Royal Canal.

"Yes, but they won't remain that way for long if our suspicions are correct," Sidney replied, checking the ammunition yet again in the pistol Alec had loaned him.

Alec glanced at his wristwatch, and I could tell what he was thinking, for I was thinking it as well. If Ardmore's plan was to deliver the cylinders this morning, it would have to be soon. Or else it would be too late to be of any use.

An unsettling feeling washed over me. One more pronounced than the anxiety which had twisted my insides for days. Cautiously, I ventured farther out into the street, staring east toward the crowds gathered on North Circular Road before the prison, and then west toward Doyle's Corner where I could see a few of the rebels peeking their heads out to watch me.

"Ver?" Sidney asked me in confusion.

"Something's not right," I stated with a certainty I had no tangible justification for. I continued to look up and down the road, undecided about what to do, while my husband and Alec joined me.

Alec was the first to recognize what my instincts were telling me. "You think the phosgene has already been delivered."

"Yes," I choked out, grappling with the horror of such a reality.

Without giving myself time to think, I began to walk toward the prison, my steps lengthening with each stride. Sidney quickly fell in step with me, and Alec soon caught up after issuing some sort of instructions to his men, no doubt.

"What do you intend to do?" Sidney asked me.

"Find it. Stop it." I turned to look at him. "We don't have any other choice."

I saw in his features what I knew must be reflected in mine. Uncertainty. Terror. But also resolve. We were not going to let innocent people die because of the machinations of one mad man. Ardmore could not win. Not when the consequences were this high.

I turned briefly to Alec, seeing the same determination reflected in his eyes, and knew that in this, at least, I was not alone.

The trouble was, there was a crowd between us and the armored vehicles where any cylinders would be kept. Those at the back were stretched out sparsely, but the deeper we waded, the tighter they would be packed together, making it difficult to move quickly if at all.

"Where would they set up the Livens Projectors?" I asked Sidney.

"Near the gate to the prison, I suspect," he replied, confirming my fears. I looked upward, toward the roofs of the DMP police station and the other buildings strung along North Circular Road outside the prison. "Is there another way around?"

"Not without getting shot at by snipers," Alec scoffed.

I nodded, spotting one.

"Give me a moment." Alec retreated the way we'd come, leaving Sidney and me to turn in circles, trying to find a solution.

The soldiers who were lined up along the perimeter of the crowd nearest to us were paying us no attention, though I'd feared our rapid approach might have alerted them. Any great disturbance on our part could draw them down on us, or worse, set off the use of the phosgene cylinders masked as tear gas, so we had to exercise caution. When Alec returned a few moments later, he was not alone.

"Clear a path, boys," he instructed the four men he'd brought with him. "But do it quietly and delicately. We don't need the body snatchers takin' potshots at us."

I set off, following in their wake, with Sidney before me and Alec behind. We made swift progress at first, but the nearer we drew to the narrow turn which led up to the gates of Mountjoy, the harder it became to move, and the less accommodating people became, some growing angry at us for disturbing their prayers for Barry. All the while, I kept my eyes on what troops I could see, and swept the crowd for any signs of brewing trouble.

It was during one of these sweeps that I spotted Willoughby. He was standing at the edge of the crowd along the pavement, in his uniform, with the soldiers at his back. Alarm spiked through me. For if Willoughby was here, then the disguised cylinders had been delivered. There was no longer any question. I wanted to scream at Alec's men to move faster, but I knew that would do no good and would possibly set off a panic.

Then Willoughby's gaze shifted, and I knew he was looking at us. For a moment, I even felt certain our eyes met. I waited in dread for him to point us out to the soldiers behind him, but he didn't move. Not except for his chin, which shifted to a point slightly past me. I swiveled my head, curious what had averted his attention and spied the sight we'd been looking for. The Livens Projectors—several of them lined up on the bed of a lorry. Whether Willoughby had alerted me to them purposely or his glance had been an unconscious reaction to the sight of me—knowing what we sought—I didn't know. All that mattered in that moment was getting to the projectors.

I alerted Sidney and Alec, and Alec diverted his men toward the new objective. It was positioned in a long line of armored cars at the junction to the lane leading to the prison's gates, at a spot where the cylinders could be fired in multiple directions as needed. Strategically, it made sense, but I was simply glad we didn't have to wade through two thousand more bodies to reach it. However, there was a phalanx of soldiers with helmets and fixed bayonets standing between us and the lorry bed.

As we reached them, Alec and his men faded into the background, allowing Sidney and me to move to the front. "I'm Sidney Kent. I demand to speak to your commanding officer," he barked at the men before him, using the tone he'd once utilized as commanding officer of his brigade at the Western Front.

For a moment, it seemed this would work, the men before him recognizing the voice of authority even as Sidney repeated himself. But then one of the soldiers narrowed his eyes. "Sure, ye are. Sidney Kent. Here in Dublin." He laughed derisively. "And who's that behind ye?"

His suspicion meant it was likely he'd recognized one or more of the rebels who had been with us, but Sidney ignored this, beginning to sound like a broken record, even as Alec and his men melted further back into the crowd. "I'm Sidney Kent, and I demand to speak to your commanding officer."

"What's the meaning of this?" someone queried behind the phalanx of Tommies in full kit.

I couldn't help but stare at the boxes which would contain their gas masks. They dangled around their necks. I tried to recall if they normally wore them while on duty here in Ireland. Or had they been specifically instructed to include them today?

"Are you the commanding officer?" Sidney asked the man who'd approached. "I demand to speak to the commanding officer on a matter of urgency."

"You can demand all you want," the subaltern retorted, continuing to argue with him.

This was getting us nowhere except to make the soldiers and demonstrators around us agitated. A hymn was being sung by the rest of the crowd, its strains floating upward and over the prison walls, where I was sure it was meant to be a comfort to Kevin Barry, who was awaiting the hangman's rope. But the fear flooding through my veins turned the sweet notes to something far more sinister and haunting. The words almost taunted me for my inability to stop what I knew was about to happen to all of these unsuspecting people. Then some sort of disturbance seemed to pass through the crowd. It was barely a ripple at first, not even disrupting the singing, but it began to grow, and I knew, without hesitation, that this was the disturbance meant to set off a row.

We were out of time.

Alec and the other rebels now stood several rows back, their eyes fixed on the developing commotion ahead of us. There was nothing they could do without being shot on the spot for interfering. Sidney continued to argue with the subaltern, nearly shouting in his desperation to make him understand, but it was clear the lieutenant had no intention of giving in and was, in fact, on the verge of detaining him. Beyond them, I could now see the commanding officer giving instructions to the men nearest the lorry bed and the Livens Projectors, his eyes on the surging crowd. I could see several of the doctored cylinders, waiting to be deployed.

It was up to me.

With a tremulous breath, I took advantage of the small hole that had been created in the line as the subaltern had pushed through it to cross words with Sidney. With a twist and a bend, I shot through the gap, racing toward the commanding officer, my hands raised. I was terrified someone would shoot and ask questions later. They'd certainly done that often enough of late. So I made it as clear as possible that I was unarmed.

"Stop!" I screamed. "Stop, stop, stop!"

The commanding officer and the men turned to me in astonishment.

"That's not tear gas! It's white star! It's phosgene! They painted over the symbols."

Their temporary shock over, one of the soldiers grasped me roughly, forcing my hands behind my back as the subaltern who'd been quarreling with Sidney appeared, attempting to explain. I ignored them all, keeping my gaze locked with the commanding officer's, knowing he was my only hope.

As I watched, his gaze began to harden and his mustache quivered.

"Please," I pleaded. "I'm telling you the truth. You'll kill hundreds of these people. And . . . and destroy our reputation around the globe."

"Young lady, that's simply not possible."

"But it is!"

He nodded to the private restraining me as he turned away, muttering to himself. "Delusional."

The soldier began to drag me away. "Come with me nicely, miss," he ordered through gritted teeth. "Or I'll have to use force."

Nicely?!

My fury at their dismissal, at Bennett and Ames's duplicity, at Ardmore's despicable games and the knowledge that he was going to get away with murder—mass murder—yet again, boiled over inside me. Pushing off with my feet, I allowed the private's momentum as he tugged against me to work against him, even though it tore the ligaments in my shoulder, threatening to dislocate them. He stumbled backward, caught off balance as I landed and twisted away from him, driving a knee into his groin.

I raced toward the lorry and past the officer, leaping up onto the bed. Grasping one of the cylinders, I saw that Ardmore's men had done as shoddy a paint job as I'd suspected. I pulled the scraper I'd had the forethought to bring from my pocket, knowing it would likely come down to this to convince them. Then I dragged it across the metal surface, cringing at the metallic sound.

"Good God, woman!" the officer barked as rough hands grabbed me again. "You are mad."

The cylinder and scraper tumbled into the lorry bed with a

bang. I was tugged backward, but not quickly enough to stop me from seeing what had been revealed.

"Look!" I shrieked. "Look!"

The side of the cylinder that had rolled to face us clearly showed the letters "pho" peeking through the slapdash white cross as well as the point of a star. The second coat of paint had not been given long enough to entirely dry, nor was it thick enough to completely conceal what it was supposed to. The cans I'd noticed left in the garage had appeared more like the consistency of whitewash. This might have been laziness on Ardmore's men's part, or deliberate, hoping to cast blame on the rebels or vengeful members of the Crown Forces once the error was detected after the fact. That is, if the cylinders weren't entirely destroyed upon deployment.

The commanding officer and other men had stilled at the sight, but now the officer was galvanized into action. "Scrape the rest of that off," he ordered. "Scrape it off. And check the others. Carefully!"

I stood panting beside the lorry, my arms still tightly restrained, watching them. When the truth was no longer deniable, the officer rounded on me, scrutinizing me from head to toe. He made a motion to the man behind me, who released me. "How did you know this? Who are you?"

"Verity Kent," I replied, rubbing my aching wrists. "As for how, that's classified." I knew I risked being seized again for such cheek, but after the treatment I'd just received when I was also saving his hide, I wasn't in the mood to explain myself. "Speak to Captain Bennett and Lieutenant Ames with Special Branch and Captain Maxwell with F Company. You'll find them all based out of the Castle."

"That's her husband," one of the men on his right murmured, nodding in Sidney's direction where he was still being restrained by several soldiers. "Captain Sidney Kent."

The commanding officer might not have recognized my name, but he certainly recognized Sidney's. "Let him pass."

He peered over his shoulder at the men on the lorry bed. "And see that all the projectiles are quarantined."

Sidney charged forward like a rabid bull, but he pulled up at the last moment, his military training too deeply ingrained in him from four years of war. Though his words were sharp and vehement, they were not insubordinate. For my part, I suddenly felt woozy. The night with no sleep, much of it spent on my feet, was catching up with me now that the danger had passed.

At least for us.

A bell suddenly tolled from Mountjoy's tower, indicating the hour of eight o'clock. I straightened, realizing that at that very moment Kevin Barry's body was taking the hangman's short drop behind the prison walls. The crowd hushed and then many of them began to sob, while others continued to pray. The Tommies watched it all in silence. Even Sidney and the commanding officer fell mute.

The disturbance, it seemed, had been quelled, either on its own or with the assistance of other soldiers or perhaps the mourners themselves. All was still as the Bakery Gun Boy breathed his last.

CHAPTER 32

There was an urgency to Sidney's movements as we hurried home through the bustling streets of Dublin. An urgency I knew I should share, but my limbs were too tired, my mind had gone sluggish, and I felt nauseous from lack of food. This last problem Sidney remedied by diverting into a shop for some boxty. Ingesting the potato pancake settled my stomach and revived me. Unfortunately, it also set my thoughts to spinning.

We had risked much in order to prevent the use of that phosgene, the least of which had been confronting that artillery officer. And for all the elation I felt at having finally foiled Ardmore, I was equally frightened as to what that might mean for us. I'd been warned many times that he was not to be crossed, that I'd previously been shielded from the full extent of his wrath because he enjoyed this macabre game of chess we'd been playing. Now that I'd captured his queen and exposed him to risk, I was wary of how he would react. A blow was coming. I just didn't know from where.

Given Ardmore's part in convincing O and the RIC to change their mob control protocols and whatever role he'd played in supplying the cylinders, he rightly should have fallen under heavy suspicion. The damage to his reputation and greater scrutiny of his loyalties and activities should be forthcoming. Investigations that C would be able to contrib-

ute what evidence we had already compiled to. But I knew
Ardmore well enough to know that he had a contingency
plan. Someone else would take the blame, with him receiving at most a slap on the wrist. No, he was too powerful to
topple without definitive proof, which he made certain never
existed.

But my fears over Ardmore's next move were not what
troubled me most. Rather it was the fact that Sidney and I
had been seen in the company of known rebels. This was the
sort of mistake O and Thomson would pounce on if it was
reported. The type of thing they wouldn't hesitate to capitalize on, particularly since C had already been told to order me
back to London.

Accordingly, neither Sidney nor I needed to state the obvious. We needed to get out of Dublin. Today, if possible.

When we reached our rented home, we immediately began issuing orders. Ginny and Mrs. Boyle were told to begin
packing our things while Nimble was sent off with the messages for three telegrams I swiftly dashed off. The first to C,
informing him the phosgene had been located, the plot foiled,
and that I would debrief him fully in person the next day. The
second to Max, informing him of the same. And the third to
George, asking him to hold off sending any more decryptions
from Smith's journal.

I also had an obligation to Wick for his part in helping us.
So I sat down to write what details I could share, intending
to have Nimble deliver my note to the offices of the *Irish Independent* when he returned. The ferry to Holyhead from
Kingstown would not leave until that evening, but Sidney felt
we should be gone from Upper Fitzwilliam Street sooner. We
were counting on affairs at Mountjoy Jail taking some time
to unravel before questions of our loyalty were raised.

I had only just risen from the writing desk in the parlor
when I was alerted to a disturbance at the front of the house.
A chill swept down my spine as a familiar pounding began,

20

but this time on our door. Ginny and Mrs. Boyle were on the floor above me and Sidney was in the carriage house, preparing his Pierce-Arrow. This meant I was closest to the door, but by the time I'd even made it to the drawing room to peer out at who was below, it came crashing in.

I heard Ginny shriek, and my heart started, as much from the sight in the street below as the loud bang. A lorry and two Crossley tenders were positioned crossways in the middle of the road, soldiers filing out to line the perimeter much as they'd done on the night of the raid. I could already hear men rushing into the house below.

I might have made a run for it, up two flights of stairs to the guest chamber and the hole concealed behind the wardrobe. But the chances of my even making it to the staircase now without being spotted were minimal, and there was also Ginny and Mrs. Boyle to think of. I couldn't leave them behind to confront those men alone, to take the blame for my escape and whatever else they decided to charge them with. For their sake, I knew there was nothing for it but to stand and face the music.

Moving into the corridor, I was immediately met by a trio of Auxiliaries in their distinctive tam-o'-shanter caps, weapons drawn. "Against the wall!" one of them ordered me.

I complied, but apparently not quickly enough, for he shoved me against it.

"Hands where I can see them!"

This I also complied with, pressing them flat on either side of me.

"Now, see here . . ." I began to protest, injecting aristocratic umbrage into my tone.

"Are you Mrs. Verity Kent?" he demanded, cutting me off.

"Yes. What is the meaning—?"

"We've got her!" the Auxie yelled down the stairs.

I inhaled a ragged breath, until that moment daring to believe that perhaps this was a mistake. That they weren't there for me. That hope flickered and died, along with the hope that perhaps these men's commanding officer was Sidney's friend Captain Maxwell. The officer who appeared in my peripheral vision where I was pressed against the wall was both shorter and older.

"I demand to be told the meaning of this!" I blustered angrily, hating the tremor I heard in my voice. "Barging into a person's home. Do you know who I am? Do you know who my husband is?"

"Aye, we ken who ye are," the officer retorted in a harsh Scottish brogue. "And we're here to give ye a lift to the Castle where they've some questions for ye."

"I don't need a lift. My husband can take me himself, thank you very much. All they needed to do was send a note requesting my presence. I would have complied."

"They're packing," someone informed the officer, undoubtedly referring to Ginny and Mrs. Boyle's actions upstairs. I hoped they hadn't hurt them.

The officer must have given an order to the man whose rifle was pointed at my back, for once again my arms were forced behind me and I was turned to face the Scotsman. His face rather resembled a bulldog. "Makin' a run for it, Mrs. Kent?"

"Of course not. We've been recalled to London, leaving on the evening ferry. Which we shall miss if you don't cease with this nonsense."

The corners of his eyes narrowed. "I think that's goin' to be the least o' your concerns."

With that he jerked his head to the right, and I was unceremoniously propelled toward the stairs. I might have resisted, but this time I had no doubt they would retaliate with a rifle butt to the face, knocking me out. Instead, I summoned as much dignity as I could muster and marched down the steps to the level below.

Sidney and Nimble had been corralled into the dining room, where they were being restrained even as Sidney demanded to know where they were taking me. I offered him as reassuring a smile as I could muster, but he clearly knew I was terrified. How could I not be? I gave Nimble a fleeting glance, wanting to tell him to look after Sidney. I trusted he already knew. Then I thought of the letter I'd written for Wick upstairs on the writing desk waiting for Nimble to deliver it. Internally, I cursed. It and the notes and maps I'd carelessly left scattered across the table in the parlor would no doubt be used against me and Sidney if they took him into custody as well.

In the street outside there were people gathered at both ends, watching from behind the lines of Auxies serving as barricades. I didn't turn to look at them. I couldn't. I was too worried that the trepidation I knew I would see stamped upon some of their faces would make me lose my grip on my own failing bravado. As it was, tears were already threatening, my eyes being gritty from lack of sleep.

I was brought to a halt before one of the Crossley tenders and waited for the door to be opened for me. Then I was placed in the rear seat between two guards and surrounded by four more hanging off the sides of the armored motorcar. The Scottish officer joined us a few moments later, slamming the door and ordering us away.

The Auxies slowly parted the crowd for us, the lorry and other Crossley remaining behind to finish business. My heart stuttered as I prayed it didn't involve violence to Sidney or any of our staff. It was this thought that made my gaze lift, catching sight of two figures in the midst of the crowd, doing little to conceal themselves. The first had his hand clamped on the other man's arm, restraining him. Though I was sure Michael Collins was thinking mostly of his own interests by doing this, his brow furrowed in consternation, I was grateful anyway. For nothing good could come of Alec confronting the men arresting me. Not now. Perhaps not ever.

Even so, it took every ounce of training and self-possession not to become unmoored as the Crossley picked up speed, carrying me away from everyone and everything that was safe, toward the unforgiving stone walls of Dublin Castle.

ACKNOWLEDGMENTS

Some of the scenes from this book have been living inside my head for years, driving me to distraction when I probably should have been paying closer attention to my current reality. Being highly aware of this, I have to thank my husband for indulging this musing, as well as my ramblings about history and book plots, and my demands for a sparring partner so that I can choreograph how my characters might get themselves out of a sticky situation. To his credit, he's no longer fazed by such queries as, "Pretend you have a knife . . ."

Many thanks also to my daughters, who tolerate me wallpapering the hallways with my plotting maps and eating a Plowman's lunch for dinner for the fourth time in a week while I'm on deadline. But in all seriousness, my family's love and support, their hugs and kisses, and their being proud of me mean the world. Because they are my world.

Heaps of gratitude to my tremendous publishing team! To my agent extraordinaire, Kevan Lyon, for her wisdom and guidance. To my editor, Wendy McCurdy, for her keen eye and enthusiasm. And to the other publishing team members, including, but not limited to, Sarah Selim, Carly Sommerstein, Jane Nutter, Madeleine Brown, Ann Pryor, Alexandra Nicolajsen, Andi Paris, Kristin McLaughlin, Kait Johnson, Amanda Kreklau, and copy editor Tory Groshong.

I also want to thank all of my family and friends for the

myriads of ways they love and support me. Especially my parents, siblings, in-laws, cousins, aunts and uncles, and friends from church and Mom's Group.

A big thank-you also goes to my readers. It's because of you, because you keep reading my stories, that I get to keep writing them. Thank you.

And finally, thanks and praise to God, from whom all blessings flow, and who inspires in me the words and direction when I don't know if I can find them.

Don't miss the next Verity Kent mystery
from nationally bestselling author Anna Lee Huber,

The Bravest Hour,

on sale everywhere books are sold
in the fall of 2026.

Read on for a sneak peek . . .

CHAPTER 1

November 1, 1920
Dublin, Ireland

If I'd thought the sight of Dublin Castle was mildly alarming on my previous visits, I quickly discovered that entering it as a prisoner was infinitely more terrifying. Its stark, imposing stone edifice draped with barbed wire and topped with meshwork meant to deflect bombs, and canvas screens supposed to hinder snipers, may have seemed intimidating before, but now I could barely summon the saliva to swallow as I eyed the cast-iron gates reinforced by steel plates before me. They were flanked, as usual, by guards and policemen with guns at the ready, all of whom stared at me with rampant curiosity where I sat stiff-backed in the rear of the open-topped British Army's Crossley tender, a woman surrounded by no less than eight soldiers in full kit.

I knew it was too much to hope that one of the guards hadn't recognized me, either from my previous unescorted visits to the Castle, or because my image had been plastered across the pages of newspapers countless times over the past few years, be it posing in my glad rags for the society columns or because of my exploits with my war-hero husband, foiling murderers and treasonous plots. I wondered how long it would be before someone leaked to the press that I was now the one being held on suspicion of treason.

I forced myself to take deep, calming breaths even as my heart pounded wildly in my chest as the Crossley was cleared to continue through the Palace Street gate. It was the first time I'd entered via the main archway rather than the small side door, and I decided I would have been quite content never to have had the experience. Especially when the Crossley rolled to a halt only a short distance inside and a rifle butt was thrust unceremoniously into my side by one of the Auxiliaries seated next to me. "Move!"